INDEXING

By Seanan McGuire

Indexing

October Daye
Rosemary and Rue
A Local Habitation
An Artificial Night
Late Eclipses
One Salt Sea
Ashes of Honor
Chimes at Midnight

Incryptid
Discount Armageddon
Midnight Blue-Light Special
Half-Off Ragnarok (forthcoming 2014)

Velveteen
Velveteen vs. The Junior Super Patriots
Velveteen vs. The Multiverse

As Mira Grant

Newsflesh
Feed
Deadline
Blackout

Parasitology
Parasite

INDEXING

———

SEANAN
MCGUIRE

Text copyright © 2013 Seanan McGuire
Originally published as a Kindle Serial, May 2013

Published by 47North, Seattle

www.apub.com

Amazon, the Amazon logo, and 47North are trademarks of Amazon.com, Inc., or its affiliates.

ISBN-13: 9781477809600
ISBN-10: 1477809600

3 1907 00321 9812

Cover design by The Book Designers

Library of Congress Control Number: 2013940103

Printed in the United States of America

This book is dedicated to my fairy tale girls:
Catherynne Valente, Michelle Dockrey, and Amy Mebberson.
Good things can come from once upon a time.

Attractive Narcolepsy

Memetic incursion in progress: estimated tale type 709 ("Snow White")
Status: ACTIVE

Alicia didn't feel well.

If she was being honest, she hadn't been feeling well for a while now. The world was spinning, and everything seemed hazy and unreal, like she was seeing it through the filter of a dream. Maybe she was. Dreaming, that is; maybe she was dreaming, and when she woke up, everything would be normal again, rather than wrapped in cotton and filled with strange signs and symbols that she couldn't quite understand. Maybe she was dreaming . . .

In a daze, she called a cab and left the house, the door standing open and ignored behind her. The dog would get out. In that moment, she didn't have the capacity to care. Alicia didn't feel well, and when you don't feel well, there's only one place to go: the hospital.

Alicia was going to the hospital, and when she got there, they would figure out what was wrong with her. They would figure out how to fix her, and everything would be normal again. She just knew it.

#

My day began with half a dozen bluebirds beating themselves to death against my window, leaving little bloody commas on the glass to mark their passing. The sound eventually woke me, although not before half a dozen more of them had committed suicide trying to reach my bedside. I sat up with a gasp, clutching the sheets against my chest as I glared at the window. The damn things had been able to get past the bird-safety net *again*, and I still couldn't figure out how they were doing it.

A final bluebird hit the glass, making a squishy *thump* sound. Feathers flew in all directions, and the tiny birdie body fell to join the others. I glared at the bloody pane for a few more seconds before turning my glare on the clock. It was 5:22 a.m.—more than half an hour before my alarm was set to go off, which was entirely unreasonable of the universe.

"Once upon a fuck you people," I muttered, shoving the covers off me and onto the floor. If I wasn't going to get any more sleep, I was going to get ready for work. At least in the office, there would be other people to receive my hate.

Wildflowers had sprouted from the hallway carpet again, this time in a clashing assortment of blues and oranges. I didn't recognize any of the varieties, and so I forced myself to step around them rather than stepping *on* them, the way that I wanted to. Research and Development would be able to figure out what they were, where they originated, and what tale-type variants they were likely to be connected to. The wildflowers were usually random as far as we could tell, but there had occasionally been enough to give us a lead. Rampion flowers meant a three-ten was getting started somewhere, while the strange blue-white blooms we had dubbed "dew flowers" meant that a three-oh-five was under way. It wasn't an exact science, but very little about what we did was anything like exact.

Turning the water in my shower all the way to cold produced a freezing spray that chased away the last unwelcome remnants of the previous night's dreams and left me shivering, but feeling like I might have a better day than the one indicated by the heap of dead bluebirds outside my window. Really, if all that went weird today was a few dead birds and some out-of-place flowers, I was doing pretty well.

I work for the ATI Management Bureau. Our motto is "*in aeternum felicitas vindactio*." Translated roughly, that means "defending happily ever after." We're not out to guarantee that all the good little fairy-tale boys and girls get to ride off in their pumpkin coaches and on their silver steeds. They've been doing that just fine since the dawn of mankind. They don't need any help from a government-funded agency so obscure that most people don't even suspect that we exist. No, our job is harder than that. Fairy tales want to have happy endings, and that's fine—for fairy tales—but they do a lot of damage to the people around them in the process, the ones whose only crime was standing in the path of an onrushing story. We call those "memetic incursions," and it's our job to stop them before they can properly get started. When we fail . . .

When we fail, most people don't hear about that, either. But they do hear about the deaths.

There's no dress code in my office, not even for the field teams, since many of us have reasons to avoid the more common suits and ties. I still liked to keep things formal. I pulled a plain black suit out of my closet, selecting it from a rack that held ten more, all of them virtually identical. Pairing it with a white button-down shirt and a black tie left me looking like an extra from the set of *Men in Black*, but that didn't bother me much. Clichés are relatives of the fairy tale, and tropes aren't bad; they go with the territory.

My gun and badge were on the nightstand next to my SPF 200 sunscreen. I scowled at the bottle. I hate the smell of the stuff—it smells like a shitty childhood spent locked in the classroom during recess because the school couldn't take responsibility if I got burned, but also like trying to find the right balance between flesh-toned foundation and sun protection. None of that changed the fact that if I went out without lathering up, I was quickly going to change my complexion from Snow White to Rose Red. "Lobster" is not a good look for me.

My phone rang as I was finishing the application of sunscreen to the back of my neck. I glanced at the display. Agent Winters. "Answer," I said curtly, continuing to rub sunscreen into my skin.

The phone beeped, and Sloane's voice demanded, "Where are you?"

"In my bedroom," I said, reaching for a tissue to wipe the last of the clinging goo from my fingers. "I'm getting ready for work. Where are you?"

"Uh, what? Are you stupid, or just stupid? Or maybe you're stupid, I haven't decided. Have you checked your texts this morning?"

I paused guiltily. I hadn't taken my phone into the bathroom while I showered, and I could easily have missed the chime that signaled an incoming text. "Let's say I didn't, to save time. What's going on?"

"We have a possible seven-oh-nine kicking off downtown, and management thought that *maybe* you'd be interested in, I don't know, *showing the fuck up*." Sloane's voice dropped to a snarl on the last few words. "Piotr sent everyone the address ten minutes ago. Most of the team is already en route."

Full incursions are rare. We usually get one or two a month, at most. Naturally, this one would kick off before I'd had breakfast. "I'll be there in five minutes," I said.

"You don't even know where—"

"Good-bye, Sloane." I grabbed the phone and hit the button to hang up on her with the same motion, pulling up my texts as I bolted for the door. Even obscure branches of law enforcement can break the speed limit when there's a good reason, and a Snow White starting to manifest downtown? Yeah, I'd call that a damn good reason.

# # #

There are a couple of things you'll need to know about fairy tales before we can get properly started. Call it agent orientation or information overload, whatever makes you feel more like you'll be able to sleep tonight. It doesn't really matter to me.

Here's the first thing you need to know: all the fairy tales are true. Oh, the specific events that the Brothers Grimm chronicled and Disney animated may only have happened once, in some kingdom so old that we've forgotten whether it ever really existed, but the essential elements of the stories are true, and those elements are what keep repeating over and over again. We can't stop them, and we can't get rid of them.

I'm sure they serve some purpose—very little happens without a reason—but it's hard to focus on that when you're facing a major beanstalk incident in Detroit, or a gingerbread condo development in San Francisco. People mostly dismiss the manifestations, writing them off as publicity stunts or crazy pranks. It's better that way. Not many people have the kind of ironclad sanity that can survive suddenly discovering that if you're born a seven-oh-nine, you're inevitably going to wind up poisoned and left for dead . . . or that rescue isn't guaranteed, since once you go inanimate, the story's focus switches to the Prince. Poor sap.

We use the Aarne-Thompson Index to map the manifestations as much as we can, cross-referencing fairy tales from all over the world. Not every seven-oh-nine has skin as white as snow and a thing for short men, even if Snow White is the best-known example of the breed. Not every five-eleven is actually going to snap and start trying to kill her stepdaughter or stepsisters, although the urge will probably rear its ugly head a time or twenty. Like any rating system, the ATI has its flaws, but it mostly gets the job done, and it's better than running around in the dark all the damn time.

Some folks say using the ATI dehumanizes our subjects, making it easier to treat them like fictional creatures to be dealt with and disposed of. Then again, most of them have never put in any real hours in the field. They've never seen what it takes to break girls like Agent Winters out of the stories they've gotten tangled up in before the narrative consumes them. Me, I got lucky; I got my sensitivity to stories by being adjunct to one, rather than being an active part. My mother was one of the most dangerous ATI types—a four-ten, Sleeping Beauty. She was in a deep coma when my twin brother and I were born, the misbegotten children of the doctor who was supposed to be treating her injuries and wound up taking advantage of her instead.

She slept through our birth, just like the stories said she should. We didn't pull the poisoned needle from her finger when we tried to nurse; we pulled her life-support cable. Mom died before the ATI cleanup crew could figure out where the narrative energy was coming from, leaving us orphans. Under normal circumstances, the narrative would have slammed us both straight into the nearest story that would fit. The cleanup crew didn't let that happen though, despite the fact that I was already halfway into the Snow White mold, and my brother was just as close to becoming a Rose Red. In a very real sense, I owe them my life, or at least my lack of singing woodland creatures.

Most of the subjects we deal with are innocents: people who wound up in the wrong place at the wrong time and got warped to fit into the most convenient slots on the ATI. Others are born to live out their stories, no matter how much damage that does to the world around them. It's not a choice for them. It's a compulsion, something that drives them all the way to their graves.

That's the second, and most important, thing you need to know about fairy tales: once a story starts, it won't stop on its own. There's too much narrative weight behind a moving story, and it wants to happen too badly. It won't stop, unless somebody stops it.

# # #

Whoever had initially scrambled the field team was following the proper protocol: I started driving blindly toward the address Piotr had sent to my phone, only to come up against a cordon nearly half a mile out from my destination. It was disguised as a standard police blockade, but the logos on the cars were wrong, and the uniforms were straight out of our departmental costume shop. Anyone who knew what the local police were supposed to look like would have caught the deception in an instant. Fortunately for us, it was early enough in the day that most people just wanted to find a clear route to Starbucks, and weren't going to mess around trying to figure out why that officer's badge had the wrong motto on it.

I pulled up to the cordon and rolled down my window, producing my badge from inside my jacket. A fresh-faced man in an ill-fitting policeman's uniform moved toward the car, probably intending to ask me to move along. I thrust my badge at him.

"Special Agent Henrietta Marchen, ATI Management Bureau," I said sharply. "Tell your people to get the hell out of my way. We've got a code seven-oh-nine, and that means I've got places to be."

The young man blanched. "I'm sorry, ma'am," he said. "We were told to stop all cars coming this way, and we thought all agents were already inside the impact zone."

"Mmm-hmm. And while you're apologizing, you're not moving anything out of my way." I put my badge back inside my jacket. "Apology accepted, sentiment appreciated, now *move*."

He nearly tripped over his own feet getting away from my car and running to enlist several more of the "officers" in helping him move the barrier out of my way. I rolled my window back up to discourage further conversation, sitting and drumming my fingers against the steering wheel until my path was clear. I gunned the engine once, as a warning, before hitting the gas and rocketing past the cordon like it had personally offended me—which, in a certain way, it had. I detest lateness. When you're late in a fairy tale, people wind up dead. And not true-love's-kiss, glass-coffin-nap-time dead. Really *dead*, the kind of dead you don't recover from. I am notoriously unforgiving of lateness, and being late myself wasn't improving my mood.

The control van was parked at the absolute edge of the probable impact zone. I pulled up next to it. The door banged open barely three seconds later, and five feet eleven inches of furious Goth girl threw herself out of the vehicle, already shouting at me. At least, her mouth was moving; thanks to the bulletproof, charm-proof, soundproof glass in my car windows, I couldn't hear a damn thing. I smiled, spreading my hands and shaking my head. It was a shitty thing to do, but considering the morning I'd been having, winding Sloane up a little was perfectly understandable.

She stopped shouting and showed me the middle fingers of both her hands, an obscene gesture that was only enhanced by the poison-apple green nail polish that she was wearing. It clashed nicely with her hair, which was currently black, tipped with an unnaturally bright shade of red. Nothing about her could be called "subtle" by any conventional means, and that was how she liked it. The more visible she was, the less she felt at risk of sinking back into her own story.

"Getting a little saucy today, I see," I said, finally taking pity on Sloane and opening my car door so that she could shout at me properly. "What's the situation?"

"Andy's working with the grunts to clear out as many of the local businesses as possible before shit gets ugly," said Sloane. "And you're late."

"Yes, but if we're still clearing coffee shops, I'm not late enough that you've been waiting for me at all." I took another look around the area. In addition to our control van, I could see four more vehicles that were almost certainly ours, going by their paint jobs and lack of identifying features. "Who called it in?"

"Monitoring station," said Sloane. She shoved her hands into her pockets, slouching backward until her shoulders were resting against the side of the van. The resulting backbend made my own spine ache in sympathy, but she continued as if she weren't trying to emulate a contortionist, saying, "They started getting signs of a memetic incursion around two o'clock this morning, called it in, didn't get the signal to wake us because there was nothing confirmed. The signs got stronger, the alerts kept coming; on alert ten they woke me, I came into the office and sifted the data, and we started mobilization about twenty minutes later."

I nodded. "And you're sure it's a seven-oh-nine?"

"She has all the symptoms. Pale skin, dark hair, affinity for small animals—she works in a shelter that takes in exotics, and half the pictures we were able to pull off of her Facebook profile show her with birds, rats, or weird-ass lizards hanging out on her shoulders."

The image of the bluebirds committing suicide via my windowpane flashed across my mind, there and gone in an instant. I managed not to shudder, turning the need for motion into a nod instead. "Have we identified her family members?"

"Yeah. No siblings, father remarried when she was nine years old, stepmother owns a beauty parlor and tanning salon. She's pretty much perfect for the profile, which is why we're here."

"Mmm-hmm." I considered Sloane. She was our best AT-profiler; she could spot a story forming while the rest of us were still looking at it and wondering whether it was even in the main Index. But she was also, to put it bluntly, lazy. She liked knowing where the stories were going to be so that she could get the hell out of their way. She didn't like knowing the details behind the narrative. Details made the victims too real, and reality wasn't Sloane's cup of tea. "And we're *positive* about her tale type?"

Irritation flashed briefly in her eyes, there and gone in an instant. "Jeffrey confirmed my research, and he said we haven't had a seven-oh-nine here in years. We're due."

"If that's all we're going by, we're due for a lot of things." Some stories are more common than others. Seven-oh-nines are thankfully rare, in part because they take a lot of support from the narrative. Dwarves aren't cheap. Other stories require smaller casts and happen more frequently. Sadly for us, some of the more common stories are also some of the most dangerous.

Sloane's expression darkened, eyes narrowing beneath the red and black fringe of her hair. "Well, maybe if you'd shown up when we were first scrambling this team, you'd have been able to have more input on what kind of story we're after. You didn't show up for the briefing, so the official designation is seven-oh-nine."

I bit back a retort. Another promptly rose in my throat, and I bit that back as well. Sloane didn't deserve any of the things I wanted to say to her, no matter how obnoxious she was being, because she was right; I should have been there when the team was coming together. I should have been a part of this conversation.

"Where's Andy?" I asked.

"Behind you," said a mild, amiable voice. It was the kind of voice that made me want to confess my sins and admit that everything in my life was my own fault. That's the type of quality you want in a public relations point man.

I turned. "What's our civilian situation?"

"I've cleared out as many as I could, but this isn't an area that can be completely secured," said Andy, as if this were a perfectly normal way for us to begin a conversation. Tall, thick-waisted, and solid, he looked like he could easily have bench-pressed me with one arm tied behind his back. It was all appearances: in reality, I could have taken him in either a fair or an unfair fight, and Sloane could mop the floor with us both. What Andy brought to the table was people skills. There were very few minds he couldn't change, if necessary, and most of those belonged to people who were already caught in the gravitational pull of the oncoming story.

Put in a lineup, we certainly made an interesting picture. All three of us were dark-haired, although Andy and I were both natural, while Sloane's intermittent brushes with black came out of a bottle. Andy had skin almost as dark as his hair. Sloane was pale but still clearly Caucasian. I had less melanin than your average sheet of paper, and could easily have been mistaken for albino if not for my blue eyes and too-red lips— although more than a few people probably assumed that my hair was as dyed as Sloane's, and that my lip color came courtesy of CoverGirl. We definitely didn't look like any form of law enforcement. That, too, was a sort of truth in advertising, because the law that we were enforcing wasn't the law of men or countries. It was the law of the narrative, and it was our job to prevent the story from going the way it always had before—impossible as that could sometimes seem.

# # #

We set the junior agents and the grunts to holding the perimeter while we walked two blocks deeper into our isolation zone, trying to get eyes on our target. We found her getting out of a cab that had somehow managed to get past the cordon—not as much of a surprise as I wanted it to be, sad to say. Most of the police didn't have any narrative resistance to speak of, and our junior agents weren't much better. If the story wanted her to make it this far, she'd make it. The obstacles we were throwing in her way just gave her tale one more thing to overcome.

There are times when I wonder if the entire ATI Management Bureau isn't a form of narrative inertia, something gathered by a story so big that it has no number and doesn't appear in the Index. We'd be a great challenge for some unknown cast of heroes and villains. And then I push that thought aside and try to keep going, because if I let myself start down that primrose path of doubts and disillusionment, I'm never coming back.

Our target paid her cabbie before turning to stagger unsteadily down the sidewalk. She was beautiful in the classical seven-oh-nine way, with sleek black hair and snowy skin that probably burned horribly in the summer. She looked dazed, like she was no longer quite aware of what she was doing. One of her feet was bare. She probably wasn't aware of that, either.

Andy pulled out his phone, keying in a quick series of geographical tags that would hopefully enable us to predict her destination before she could actually get there. Finally, he said, "She's heading for the Alta Vista Medical Center."

I swore under my breath. "Of course she is. Where else would she be going?" Alta Vista was the largest hospital in the city. Even if we'd been able to close off eighty percent of the traffic coming into our probable impact zone, we couldn't close or evacuate the hospital. Not enough people believe in fairy tales anymore.

"Shoot her," said Sloane.

"We're not shooting her," said Andy.

Sloane shrugged. "Your funeral."

"Let's pretend to be professionals . . . and pick up the pace," I snapped. Sloane and Andy exchanged a glance, briefly united against a common enemy—me. They knew that I wanted them to be mad at me rather than each other, and they accepted it as the way the world was meant to be. Besides, we all knew that our job would be easier this way.

We followed the target all the way down the road to Alta Vista, hanging back almost half a block to keep her from noticing us. Our caution was born more of habit than necessity; she was deep into her narrative haze, moving more under the story's volition than her own. We could have stripped down and danced naked in front of her and she would just have kept on walking.

"If we're not going to stop her from getting where she's going, why are we even bothering?" Sloane walked with her hands crammed as far into the pockets of her denim jacket as they would go, her shoulders in a permanent defensive hunch. "She'll play out whether we're here or not. We could go out, get breakfast, and come back before the EMTs finish hooking her to the life support."

"Because it's the polite thing to do," said Andy. He was always a lot more at ease with this part of the job than Sloane was, probably because the only thing Andy ever escaped was a respectable profession that he could tell his family about. Sloane missed being a Wicked Stepsister by inches, and she's always been uncomfortable around the ATI cases that tread near the edges of her own story. I can't blame her for that. I also can't approve any of her requests for transfer. Jeff's fully actualized in his story, and I'm in a holding pattern, but Sloane was actually averted. That gives her a special sensitivity to the spectrum. She's the only one who can spot the memetic incursions before they get fully under way.

"She's a seven-oh-nine," snarled Sloane, shooting a poisonous glare in Andy's direction. Metaphorically poisonous: she never matured to the arsenic-and-apples stage of things. Thank God. Once a Wicked Stepsister goes that far, there's no bringing her back to reason. "You can't do anything for them, short of putting a bullet in their heads. Even then, the dumb bitches will probably just get permanently brain-damaged on the way to happy ever after."

Andy raised an eyebrow. "Gosh, Sloane, tell us how you really feel."

The target approached the doors of the Alta Vista Hospital. Even at our half-block remove, we saw them slide open, allowing her to make her way inside. If the story went the way the archivists predicted, her own Wicked Stepmother would be waiting inside, ready to hand her a box of poisoned apple juice or a plastic cup of tainted applesauce. That would let the story start in earnest. That's the way it goes for the seven-oh-nines.

All the Snow Whites are essentially the same, when you dig all the way down to the bottom of their narratives.

Sloane shifted her weight anxiously from one foot to the other as we waited, looking increasingly uncomfortable as the minutes trickled by and the weight of the impending story grew heavier. Then she stiffened, her eyes widening in their rings of sheltering kohl. "There isn't a five-eleven anywhere inside that hospital," she said, and bolted for the doors.

Swearing, Andy and I followed her.

Sloane had been a marathon runner in high school, and she'd continued to run since then, choosing it over more social forms of exercise. She was piling on the speed now, running hell-bent toward the hospital doors with her head slightly down, like she was going to ram her way straight through any obstacles. Andy had settled into a holding pattern about eight feet behind her, letting her be the one to trigger any traps that might be waiting. It wasn't as heartless as it seemed. As the one who had come the closest to being sucked into a story of her own without going all the way, Sloane is not only the most sensitive—she's also the most resistant. She could survive where we couldn't.

"Sloane!" I bellowed. "If it's not a seven-oh-nine, what is it?"

She didn't have time to answer, but she didn't need to. She came skidding to a stop so abruptly that Andy almost slammed into her from behind, both of them only inches from the sensor that would trigger the automatic door. Those inches saved them. I could see the people in the lobby through the glass as they started falling over gently in their tracks, all of them apparently sinking into sleep at the same moment.

I let momentum carry me forward until I came to an easy stop next to Sloane and Andy. "Great," I sighed. "A four-ten."

I hate Sleeping Beauties.

# # #

The cleanup crew cordoned off the entire block surrounding the hospital, buying off the inevitable media and local police with stories about a natural gas leak. "Radon gas," said Andy to a dewy-eyed reporter who looked like she had six brain cells to knock together, all of them devoted to keeping her from falling off her stiletto heels. She was nodding gravely in time with his words, making me faintly seasick. Andy can be damn convincing when he wants to be. "It's invisible, it's scentless, and . . ." he stepped forward, moving in for the kill, "it's deadly."

The reporter took an unconscious step back, dewy eyes widening even further. She looked like a startled deer. "Where did it come from?"

"Natural caverns, ma'am. The city's riddled with them," said Andy. I groaned to myself, making a mental note to tell our media division to plant some old city records about natural caverns. Undaunted, Andy continued, "Don't worry. As long as we can keep this area clear of civilians, we'll have this all cleaned up in a matter of hours."

The reporter nodded, thrusting her microphone into his face as she recovered her composure enough to start asking inane questions about the supposed gas leak. I turned my attention from Andy to Jeff, our group archivist and speaker to the impossible, which was virtually everything we interacted with on a daily basis.

"It's not *really* radon gas, is it?" I asked. Stranger things have happened once a four-ten shows up on the scene. As long as people fall down and don't get up again, it falls within the borders of the story. The narrative doesn't care how little sense it makes.

"No," said Jeff. I let my shoulders start relaxing. "It's a new strain of sleeping sickness that's somehow managed to hybridize itself with the H1N1 flu."

I stopped relaxing. "You're saying we have an airborne Sleeping Beauty?"

Jeff nodded. "Her influence is confined to the hospital right now, probably because the vents were closed when she went fully infectious, but eventually it's going to start spreading."

"How bad could this get?"

"Bad enough." His expression was grim. "There's no vaccine, since it's a new disease. Antibiotics won't work on a virus. It seems to spread through the air. One little crack and we could have a citywide outbreak. City turns to state, and hell, we could lose the whole seaboard. This thing *wants* to spread, Henry. It wants to get bad enough—"

"—to attract a Prince," I finished grimly. "Some opportunistic son of a bitch out to nail a Princess for the sake of a payoff. I hate Princes. The goddamn things are worse than rats." I froze, considering the implications of that statement.

"I don't like them much either, Henry, but I don't see how else we're going to stop this story before a lot of people get hurt." Jeff gave me a sidelong look. "I don't like that look on your face. What are you thinking?"

"Get me Sloane," I said, my own gaze swinging toward the hospital. "I have a job for her."

# # #

"You're insane," announced Sloane, folding her arms across her chest and distorting her skull-and-crossbones T-shirt graphic into something that was less pirate and more Picasso. "I've always known that you were going to go over the edge one day, but this is worse than I thought it was going to be. I just figured you'd start talking to bunnies and singing into wishing wells."

"Be as nasty as you want, Sloane; that won't change what I'm asking you to do." I met her eyes as calmly as I could, trying to ignore her digs at my borderline seven-oh-nine status. I had all the hallmarks—a dead mother, a redheaded twin, and a deadbeat father who tried to claim custody over the protests of his flaxen-fair trophy wife—but I dodged that bullet years ago, and I've been dodging it ever since, bluebirds and unwanted wildflowers aside. Sloane knows that, just like she knows that I'll never respond in kind. It wouldn't be fair.

"What makes you think this is even going to work?"

"It's going to work because we're dealing with a pathogenic Sleeping Beauty this time. The story's trying to buck us off its trail and keep us from disrupting the narrative. That's fine, because if it's a disease, it falls under the AT Index for 'vermin,' and if the problem is vermin, we can resolve the story with another story."

"So you want Sloane to find you a two-eighty?" Andy shook his head. "I know you don't like the four-tens, but don't you think this is reaching a little?"

"It's reaching, sure, but Henrietta's got the right idea," said Jeff abruptly. We all turned to look at him. Our resident archivist had his copy of the Index open, propped on one arm, his finger anchored midway down the two-eighty column. He always had a paper Index in the van: the story could change computer readouts if it got enough momentum, but there's nothing that changes a printed copy of the Aarne-Thompson Index. "There's a reported variation here where the two-eighty killed the village that refused to pay him by piping the Black

Death into their houses while they slept. Pipers can control disease. The narrative supports it."

"Then it's settled," I said, firmly. "We're going to give it a try. Sloane, you're our fairy-tale detector. Go do your job. Find me a Pied Piper."

"I fucking hate you sometimes," she snarled, and turned to stalk away.

Andy waited until she was out of earshot before he asked, "Do you honestly think this is going to work?"

"I have no fucking clue," I replied. "But that's not the important question here, is it?"

"What is?" he asked, eyeing me suspiciously.

"Can you think of anything better?"

Andy was silent.

I nodded. "I thought not," I said. "Come on. Let's get back to the van. The coffee should be ready by now."

# # #

The containment team estimated that the hospital would be able to hold our Sleeping Beauty—identified by the research crew back at headquarters as Alicia Connors, age seventeen, daughter of a fairly prominent local family that had also been reported as inexplicably asleep—for approximately six hours before the contagion started to spread. They were close. The people nearest the hospital began slumping gently over approximately five-and-a-half hours after our four-ten went inside, marking the first cases outside the hospital walls.

"If Sloane's not back soon, we're going to need to look at pulling our men back," said Jeff, watching as Andy continued his attempts at crowd control. "We can't afford to have an entire team fall asleep for a hundred years. The strain on personnel would be unbelievable."

"She'll be here," I said. "God, I hate Sleeping Beauties." Why that story, out of all the possible stories, should have the sort of staying power it does is beyond me. Centuries of helpless girls, half of them rotting away years before their Prince could come. It makes me sick.

"I know," said Jeff. "Look, Henry—"

Whatever platitude he'd been preparing about hating the story, not the subject, was cut off as Sloane came storming back up the street, managing to stomp at a pace most people can't manage when running. She was hauling a frail-looking slip of a teenage girl along by one arm. The girl was clutching a concert flute in one hand, and she looked distinctly alarmed. I couldn't blame her. Sloane is distinctly alarming.

"Here," announced Sloane, shoving the girl in our direction. "Demi Santos. She's a music major at the community college. I followed the pigeons. You explain what's happening to her. I'm going to go twist the heads off some kittens." She spun on her heel and went stalking off again.

The brusquely identified Ms. Santos shot us an alarmed look. Jeff, trying to be helpful, said encouragingly, "Don't worry. Sloane very rarely twists the head off anything."

Demi Santos, now officially convinced that she'd been abducted by crazy people, burst into tears.

"Jeff, handle her," I snapped. "Sloane!" I stalked after my runaway team member, who didn't stop, slow down, or turn to look at me. "*Sloane!*"

"Fuck you, princess," she said, holding up a hand and once again showing me her middle finger. "I did what you asked. Now go save the day like a good little hero while I slink off like a good little *villain.*" Her last word dripped with venom. I found myself wanting to retreat as my inner Snow White stirred, alarmed by the presence of danger.

Forget that. "You want me to write you up?" I demanded.

She stopped walking. I didn't.

"I could do that, you know," I said, pulling up even with her. "All I have to do is send in one little report that says you're not as redeemed as we all want to believe you are, and you're going back to rehab for another six months. I don't want to file that report. Do you want to make me?"

"I hate you," she said, without turning to look at me.

"Sometimes I hate me too," I said. "But I can't care about that right now, and neither can you. I need to know what's up with that girl. With—what did you say her name was?"

"Demi Santos," said Sloane, voice dropping to a mumble. "She's a music major. Theory and composition. There were pigeons lined up on the windowsill of the practice room. Mice and cats in the grass, all listening to her. She's our girl, Henry. She's been primed to go for years, but nothing's ever managed to push her over the edge, because she has her music, and she has her family, and she's never felt the *need* that makes a Piper. She's never reached for the power." She finally turned to look at me. Her mascara had run down her cheeks like liquid tar. I didn't need to ask how long she'd been crying. "She never wanted to be a story, and we're going to force her."

"We have to. If we don't—"

"There's always another way."

"What do you want us to do? Should we kill Alicia? Because that's one way to end the story—assuming we could get close enough to pull it off, that is, which I seriously doubt. Should we find a Prince? Waking one of *them* would do just as much damage as waking our Piper. Maybe more—if we have a Prince and a Beauty both, the odds are damn good that we're going to get an Evil Sorceress. You're the closest candidate. Do you want to risk that?"

Sloane looked away. "No," she mumbled.

"You think *I* want to do this to her? Sloane, you *know* me. You know better." The idea of someone deciding that *my* story needed to be completed, that *my* fairy tale needed to be awakened . . . it was enough to turn my stomach. And yet I knew full well that if someone ever managed to get a Magic Mirror to work, I was likely to find someone from the head office standing on my doorstep with an apple and an apologetic expression.

"You sent me after her."

"Yeah, because what I want doesn't always mesh with what I need in order to do my job. But I promise you: we're not going to hurt this girl for nothing. This thing . . . it has the potential to infect the whole city, maybe the whole state. We're saving a lot of lives."

Sloane was silent.

I sighed. "Do you need a little bit?"

"Yeah."

"I'll be back at the van. Come join us when you're ready." With that said, I turned and walked away from her, giving her the space that she needed to come to terms with what she'd just done. Giving Demi to us was tantamount to betraying her, in Sloane's mind: she had just condemned the girl to life on the ATI spectrum.

Now we just had to make sure that it was worth it.

# # #

Andy was still trying to calm Demi down when I returned. She was holding an open can of Diet Pepsi, taking small sips and hiccupping occasionally as he reassured her over and over again that we weren't going to let Sloane anywhere near her. I stayed well out of the way, waiting for her to stop crying and dry her tears. I am not one of nature's more reassuring people, and even if this city contained another Pied Piper—which was statistically unlikely; the story is popular, but it's not *that* popular, and there aren't that many variations—we didn't have time to send Sloane out to find them. The contagion was continuing to spread while we all stood around getting in touch with our feelings. If Demi wasn't up for the job, the entire city was at risk of an extended, unplanned nap time.

Andy straightened, waving to me. "Henry, I think you can come over now," he called, giving Demi an encouraging smile. "We're mostly calmed down."

"Thank you, Andy." I walked over to them, offering Demi my hand. "I'm Special Agent Henrietta Marchen. I assume that my friend Andrew has given you a basic rundown of the situation?" She sniffled, nodding. She didn't take my hand. After a second of awkward silence, I withdrew it. "Well, that's good; it saves time. Has he told you what we need you to do?"

"No, ma'am," she said. Her voice was barely above a whisper. Honestly, I was just relieved to hear her speak. If she'd turned out to be a Little Mermaid, I think I would have screamed.

"Okay, Demi, here's the situation: we have a Sleeping Beauty in that building." I pointed to the hospital. "Her particular story takes the form of an airborne infection. I need you to play your flute and lure in rats from as far away as you can manage. Once you have them here, I need you to send them into the hospital, pipe the sickness into them, and then pipe them into the sewers to drown. Think you can do that for us?"

Demi stared at me. Finally, in the tone of someone who was just starting to catch up with the rest of the class, she said, "You people are insane."

"Probably," I agreed, without malice. "We fight fairy tales for a living. We're the definition of 'people who go among mad people.' But whether we're insane or not, my proposal is a simple one. I think you'll like it."

"What's that?" asked Demi, with natural, understandable wariness.

I smiled. I know how creepy I am when I smile. Whoever came up with "skin as white as snow, lips as red as blood" and thought people would find it attractive really wasn't thinking things through. "Pipe the rats into the hospital, and we'll let you leave."

# # #

"Agent Marchen!"

The shout wasn't a surprise. If anything, the surprise was that it had taken so long to come. I swallowed my irritation and pasted my best expression of bland obedience across my face as I turned to face the officious-looking little man who was storming in my direction, dark clouds and thunder virtually visible above his head. Deputy Director Brewer was thin as a whip, with dirty blond hair that had probably been thinning years before he pissed off the wrong person and got himself reassigned to the ATI Management Bureau. Probably. I mean, we were pretty aggravating before you got to know us—and more aggravating after you got to know us—but I didn't think we had the power to make a man's hair fall out.

According to Sloane, the deputy director not only wasn't on the ATI scale, he was so far from being a fairy tale that he practically came out the other side to become an anchor to the "real" world. I found that reassuring, somehow. It meant that he was one man who'd never stand up and announce that he'd discovered his inner Prince Charming. His inner bureaucrat, maybe, but in his case, "inner" was right up on the surface.

And oh, did he look *pissed*.

"Yes, Deputy Director?" I asked.

"What's this I'm hearing about a civilian?"

I resisted the urge to glance back to the van where Demi was going over sheet music options with Jeff, who was absolutely delighted to have an excuse to download half the great composers of Europe on work's time. They were focusing on pieces composed during the Black Death, since they were more likely to match up with the timeline on our Pied Piper variant. "I'm afraid you'll have to be more specific," I said. "There are a lot of civilians involved in this action."

"Yes, but as most of them are currently unconscious, I think you know damn well which one I mean. Where's the girl?"

I raised both eyebrows, emphasizing the fact that the whites of my eyes were almost the same shade as the white of my skin. "Do you mean Demi Santos, by any chance?"

My expression had the desired effect. The deputy director stopped in his tracks, actually rocking onto his heels for a moment before he recovered and pressed on, snapping, "Yes, I mean Demi Santos. I have several eyewitnesses who claim that a woman who sounds suspiciously like Agent Winters entered

Miss Santos's music class without invitation and physically removed her from the premises. The police were called."

"Uh-huh. Did you call them off? Because we really don't have the time or manpower to deal with the police right now. I know this is piling shit on top of shit, but seriously, if you make me try to talk to some beat cop who doesn't want to be here, I'm going to scream. And if I scream, the bluebirds will find me."

Deputy Director Brewer blinked at me as if he had no idea what I was talking about, and even less idea of how to handle it. Again, he recovered quickly, shaking his head as he said, "I don't know what you think you're doing, Agent, but you can't simply—"

"Demi Santos is a half-awakened two-eighty, as you would know if you had stopped by the control van to read my mission log before coming out here to confront me," I said calmly. "In case you can't remember the ATI off the top of your head right now, that means she's a Pied Piper. A Pied Piper at music school with no control and no handler is a threat to public safety. She was going to go live any day, and when that happened, a lot of people were going to get hurt."

He went even paler, if such a thing was possible. "Are you saying we have two concurrent memetic incursions?"

The temptation to say yes and see him run was almost irresistible. I resisted. "No, I'm saying Demi Santos is on the ATI spectrum, and is thus my responsibility, not yours. She's aiding us with this investigation."

"Aiding you *how*?"

"Jeff can explain better than I can, sir," I said. "I assure you, it will all be laid out very clearly in his notes, as well as in my own. For the moment, may I please recommend that you leave the scene? You'll be safer behind the cordon."

His eyes narrowed. "Safer how?"

Deputy Director Brewer had risen to his current position by being a by-the-book kind of man. The trouble was, his book didn't have any happy endings, and it certainly didn't have evil witches, wicked stepsisters, and talking mice. Sometimes getting him to understand the reality of what fieldwork entailed was more trouble than I had the patience for. This was one of those times.

"That hospital is ground zero for a sickness the likes of which we haven't seen in centuries," I snapped, jabbing a finger toward the looming shape of the Alta Vista Hospital. "There is a teenage girl asleep in there who's going to kill us all if my team doesn't prevent it—and when I say 'all,' I mean *everyone in this city*. That means coming up with an out-of-the-box solution. Enter Demi Santos. Now, I can't say for sure what's going to happen to you if you're still standing here when she breaks out her flute, but I can say that you're probably not going to like it. The rest of us have been touched by these stories. We have some resistance. *You do not*. Now, with all due respect, *sir*, I suggest that you get behind that cordon, before you get a hell of a lot closer to ever after than you ever wanted to be."

There was a moment of silence. It stretched out long enough that I started to worry I had gone too far. Then the deputy director nodded tightly, said, "I look forward to your report," and turned to walk back toward the cordon.

I stayed where I was, watching him go. When I was sure that he wasn't going to turn and come charging back, I sighed and made my own turn, heading for the van. It was time to put my money where my mouth was and stop another story before it got big enough to eat us all.

# # #

Demi Santos—who was nineteen, only two years older than our Sleeping Beauty—lifted her flute to her lips, blowing an experimental note. According to the records Jeff had produced, she was a natural musician. She didn't have her first lesson until she was sixteen. Six months later, she was already good enough to play with any symphony orchestra in the world, and was going to college mainly to get the paperwork to prove it. That kind of musical gift is one of the characteristic hallmarks of the Pied Pipers—no matter how poor their beginnings, they can always play their chosen instruments better than they have any right to.

"I still think you people are out of your goddamn minds," she muttered.

"And you're still not wrong," said Andy amiably. He was wearing headphones as a precaution against her song. They were tuned to a white noise station that should keep the effects of her story to a minimum. We hoped. Like I said, fairy tales are not an exact science.

Demi shook her head, closed her eyes, and began to play.

It was a light, frothy classical piece—something that sounded like it should be accompanied by harps and followed by polite applause. Instead, it was accompanied by the manholes on the sides of the road beginning to rock in their sockets, and the sound of Sloane's shrill, indignant scream.

And the rats came.

The manhole covers were shoved aside as a flood of gray and brown bodies boiled up from the sewers, surging seamlessly into the streams of rats pouring similarly out of the alleys on every side. Sloane's scream was repeated, just before a pack of squirrels came stampeding from the direction of the park, joining their cousins in the assault on the hospital. Even a few of the local pigeons got into the act, making up the aerial branch of the vermin assault force. The blended mass of squirrels, rats, and pigeons slammed into the hospital's automatic doors, overwhelming the sensors and stampeding, scampering, and soaring their way inside.

Demi's playing had stopped somewhere in the middle of the onslaught, her flute dangling forgotten in her hands as she stared at the hospital doors. It didn't matter whether she played or not; at this point, she'd given the instructions to her army of vermin, and they were going to do what she told them to do.

"I always knew pigeons were just rats with wings," commented Andy. Sloane—stomping up with scratches on her cheeks and forehead, probably from standing in the path of the squirrels—just glared at him.

"Did I do that?" asked Demi, sounding stunned.

The van door slammed open and Jeff emerged, grinning so broadly that I could practically count his fillings. "You did it!" he said, jumping down to the street and running over to take her by the elbow. "Come on. I've figured out the best musical selection for you to use when you're piping the virus into the rats, and from there, it's a pretty standard descending trill to get them to commit mass suicide. You're doing great so far. I'll get you another soda, and we can go over the sheet music—" Still talking, he led the unresisting two-eighty away.

I stayed where I was, watching the hospital doors. Rats and pigeons occasionally flashed by in the lobby, briefly visible through the glass. Andy touched my shoulder.

"They'll wake her up," he said. "No Prince. No kiss. Just a disease scare and a major reduction in local pest control business for a while."

"I know."

"She'll probably never even know what happened."

"I know."

Sloane interjected sourly, "But we're going to have to figure out what the hell to do with a live Piper. She's started her story now. Either we defuse her or we bury her in a shallow grave somewhere off the interstate."

"I know which one you're voting for, and the answer is no," I said, and turned away from the modern-day castle where a silly little girl who'd pricked her finger on something she shouldn't have been touching was sleeping through the day that she'd been born for. "Besides, there's a third option."

"What's that?"

"We hire her." I smiled a little, without amusement. "Who doesn't dream about fairy tales coming true?"

Sloane eyed me with something close to respect. "Sometimes I think they got our Index numbers reversed," she said.

"Sometimes, so do I," I replied, and turned to follow Jeff's route to the control center, where our little two-eighty would be preparing for the performance of a lifetime. There's one thing the Brothers Grimm got very, very wrong: There's no such thing as "ever after." That would require that the story ever end.

Musical Patchwork

Memetic incursion in progress: tale type 280 ("Pied Piper")
Status: ACTIVE

Demi Santos was becoming increasingly sure that she was being pranked. It was the only explanation for what was going on around her. First, that weird Goth girl had pulled her out of class, and then the skinny man with the glasses had pushed the flute and sheet music into her hand, and after that . . .

Well, after that, things got a little blurry. She remembered playing her flute. She remembered the rats—it would have been impossible for her to forget the rats, fat and brown and *everywhere*, looking up at her with beady little eyes that were somehow worshipful, like they knew that she was meant to be venerated above all others. She remembered a woman with skin as white as snow, lips as red as blood, and hair as black as the feathers of a raven's wing. She remembered being bundled into a black van, and a strange taste in her soda, almost buried under the more familiar chemicals. Everything had gone away after that, and now she was here, in a bare little room, with one hand handcuffed to the table. There was a mirror on the wall across from her. Years of watching crime dramas with her

Gram-Gram told her that the mirror was probably one of those fancy ones that were clear on one side and reflective on the other. Someone was probably watching her.

If I had my flute, I'd show them, she thought viciously, and froze, trying to figure out where the thought had come from. Show them what? How to play "Hot Cross Buns" one-handed? A flute wasn't a good blunt instrument, and it was an even worse lock pick.

But she didn't have her flute, and she didn't have any way to get herself out of the situation she had somehow gotten herself into. The feeling that this was all some huge, cruel practical joke wasn't receding. If anything, it was getting worse the longer she sat alone, waiting to see what was going to happen next. Anyone would have been welcome by that point. Even the weird Goth girl.

The door opened. Demi twisted in her seat, trying to see. A thin, balding man in a plain black suit was walking across the room toward her. He had a folder in his hands, and when he met her eyes, he smiled without any warmth.

"Ah, Miss Santos," he said. "Now what are we going to do with you?"

# # #

ATI Management Bureau Headquarters

It's customary for the field team to take a break after a confirmed memetic incursion into baseline reality—in layman's terms, we're supposed to get some time off after we stop a fairy tale from rewriting a major metropolitan area into an evil, R-rated version of Disney World. *"New and improved! Now*

with extra incest and murder!" Normally, time off isn't that hard
to arrange. There are several field teams in every office, and we
don't tend to get more than one or two memetic incursions
in a given week. We should have been packing our gear and
heading home for naps, beers—whatever helped us to cope. It
is not, however, customary for a field team to go after one fairy
tale and stop to intentionally awaken another, no matter how
good the reasons seemed to be.

Reports from the hospital said that Alicia Connors, our
erstwhile Sleeping Beauty, was already awake, unaware of the
bullet she'd just dodged. She wouldn't need a Prince to save
her. She wouldn't sleep through her own rape and pregnancy,
or any of the other horrible fates that await the four-tens. She
would be referred to in our files only as "ATI subject 308 (confirmed 410)," and she would be able to put her story behind her
with no effort at all, because it hadn't been given the time to
become truly hers. And my reward for saving her, for granting
her a second chance at happy ever after?

Paperwork. Oceans and seas and fjords of paperwork.
Virtual kingdoms of paperwork, spread out across my desk like
the vanguard of an invading army, all needing to be defeated if
I wanted to avoid an internal review of my actions. I scowled
at the sheaves, which did nothing to fill out or file any of the
waiting forms. Most agencies the size of the ATI Management
Bureau have gone paperless by now, as much out of mercy as
out of any desire to protect the environment. That wasn't an
option for us, no matter how much we might want it to be.
There are a lot of things in the Index that can only be documented the old-fashioned way, with paper and specially
prepared typewriter ribbons. Even those don't work as well as
doing it by hand; there's a whole team of admins whose only

job is ink and quills, every day, until retirement comes to save them.

Sometimes I have nightmares about being reassigned to the steno pool. The very fact that we *have* a steno pool should say something about how outdated and archaic life in our office really is. But it has to be done. Enter a report into a computer, where no eyes can see where it goes, and sometimes it will change. Those changes are never good, especially not if someone reads that modified story and takes it for the original. That's how variants are born. The first time a seven-oh-nine got done in by a poisoned ring instead of a poisoned apple, it was because the story had been allowed to deviate.

I put my head down in my hands, massaging my temples with the tips of my fingers and desperately wishing for some sort of semi-horrible disaster to strike the office. Nothing major. Just something to destroy the paperwork before it actually devoured my soul.

"*Henry!*"

The shout was shrill and angry, and cut through the ambient noise of the office like a buzz saw through an enchanted hedge. I winced and kept massaging my temples with my fingertips. When I'd wished for a mildly catastrophic event, I'd been thinking something a little less terrifying than—

"Henrietta Marchen, what the *fuck* is going on?"

That was the kind of targeted demand that meant I needed to pay attention or pay the consequences. I raised my head to watch Sloane Winters—ATI Management Bureau Agent, failed Wicked Stepsister, and never-ending pain in my ass—come storming down the narrow aisle between desks, nearly knocking over several precarious towers of paperwork in the process. She was wearing a *Devil's Carnival* T-shirt and ripped jeans, and her red-tipped black hair was tied into stubby ponytails. She would have looked like any other generic Hot Topic Goth Girl if not for the sheer murderous rage in her eyes.

"I don't know, Sloane," I said. "It's a pretty big world. There are potentially a lot of things going on right now. Do you want to narrow down the field a little bit, or should I start making wild guesses and see how long it takes for you to get pissed off and just tell me?"

Sloane's eyes narrowed, her rage pulling back until it was merely a looming threat, rather than an immediate danger. "Have you read the after-action report on our four-ten yet?"

"No, Sloane, I haven't, because I was busy doing site cleanup at the hospital, and helping Andy deal with the witnesses, and debriefing the doctors, and taking statements, and oh, about a dozen other things you don't have to deal with." We no longer allowed Sloane to interface with the public, and hadn't since an on-air interview when she tried to get a little too candid about a beanstalk incident. We'd been able to downplay her apparently deranged ravings as the result of a little too much coffee, but that plus her temper meant that she was not considered a public face of the agency.

"So you didn't see the staffing updates."

I resisted the urge to fling a stack of paperwork at her head. "No, I didn't, since in order to see the staffing update, I would have needed to read the after-action report. As I did not read the after-action report, you can safely assume that I haven't seen anything that it contained."

Sloane's lips drew back in what would have been a smile coming from anyone else. From her, it was more like a dominance display. "They took your suggestion. They're hiring that Pied Piper that I found for you."

"Good. Demi Santos has a lot of potential." Potential to do good, working with us; potential to do a whole lot of damage, left to her own devices. As a fully activated individual on the ATI spectrum, she was limited only by the shape of her story. The poor girl.

"They're assigning her to our team."

My mouth dropped slightly open as I stared at Sloane, who smirked. With an effort that felt entirely out of proportion to the size of the movement, I forced my mouth closed and swallowed before I said, "You can't be serious."

"Would I joke about something this annoying?"

"We're a field team. We're *the* field team. They can't give us a rookie who hasn't even known about the Index for twenty-four hours."

"And yet they are." Sloane folded her arms. "So come on, irritating boss lady. What are you going to do about it?"

# # #

Deputy Director Brewer's office door was closed, and his blinds were drawn, a sure sign that our fearless leader wanted to be left alone. Too bad for him that I've never really given a crap what anyone in management wanted. I hammered against the doorframe, and when that didn't get an immediate response, I hammered against it a second time, even harder. The skin of my fist turned red from the pressure. I ignored it, pulling back my hand to try again.

The door swung open to reveal Deputy Director Nathaniel Brewer in all his frowning, rat-faced glory. He was the sort of man who could make even a bespoke suit seem poorly made just by putting it on, with dirty blond hair that seemed to fall out faster than any hair replacement treatment on the market could grow it back. His frown deepened when he realized who had been banging on his door.

"Special Agent Marchen," he said. "With the racket you were making out there, I assumed that you had to be Agent Winters. Can I help you with something?"

"You can tell me why you're assigning a rookie to the field team without putting her through the normal training program," I said, barely remembering to add a grudging "sir" at the end of my statement.

His eyebrows rose in feigned surprise. "Really, Agent? Aren't you the one who recommended that we hire Demi Santos?"

"Yes, I am, but—"

"And aren't you the one who authorized the activation of her memetic alignment during a field operation, potentially endangering dozens, if not hundreds, of civilian lives? I just want to be sure that we're both approaching this problem from the same starting point."

I stood up a little straighter, raising my chin as I replied, "I did those things, *sir*, but they were necessary at the time. They do not justify placing an untrained teenager on a field team. She will be in danger. She will endanger those around her."

"She's not an untrained teenager anymore, Agent Marchen," said Deputy Director Brewer. He didn't visibly change positions, but something in his posture shifted, becoming cold and hard. He looked at me with hooded eyes, and I was suddenly reminded of something that it was all too easy to forget in our day-to-day work: Brewer didn't get his job by calling in political favors or striving for the level of his own incompetence. He earned it the hard way, with dedication and with talent . . . until he pissed off the wrong person and wound up getting shuttled to the basement with the freaks who kept fairy tales from eating the rational world.

It was the sort of thing that could make anyone lose their temper. Hell, I *am* one of the freaks—have been since I was born—and sometimes it was enough to make *me* lose my temper. I couldn't imagine what it was doing to a career civil servant like Nathaniel Brewer.

"She's nineteen," I said, trying to rally.

Deputy Director Brewer just kept looking at me. "She's a story. She's nineteen, and she's a story. She was an untrained teenager, and then you sent your little associate to drag her out of the music room and into the role she'd somehow been avoiding for her entire life. What is she now? She's a threat to the very fabric of reality. She's a danger to everyone around her, including herself and her family and any friends who she may have had before you decided it was okay to turn her life upside down. But most of all, Agent Marchen—most of all—she's your problem now. Please try to keep her alive long enough to justify the paperwork." With that, he stepped back into his office and closed the door in my face.

I stayed frozen where I was for several seconds, staring at his nameplate and waiting for him to come back out and tell me that he was kidding. It didn't happen. Finally, I turned around and started walking slowly back toward the stairs that would lead me down to the bullpen.

It was time to explain to my team that we were getting a new member. Whether we were happy about it or not.

# # #

"You shouldn't have embarrassed him when he came to ask about Demi in the first place," said Andy, shaking his head. He was leaning against the edge of his desk, arms crossed, trying to look like he wasn't upset about the situation. He was doing a pretty decent job of it; if I hadn't known him as well as I did, I might have even believed the lie. Unfortunately for his attempt at rendering himself unreadable, he couldn't control the small muscle in his cheek that jumped whenever he was stressed. And oh, he was stressed.

"I'm sorry," I said. "I did what needed to be done in the moment. I'm not so good about considering the long-term consequences sometimes."

"That's what leads your type to eat the poisoned apples, isn't it?" sneered Sloane. She kept her eyes glued on her own computer screen, where she was surfing eBay on company time. "A lack of understanding that what you do today has an impact on what you're going to be able to do tomorrow."

"Can we at least try to look like a united front?" I asked. "And where's Jeff?"

Jeff was the fourth member of our jolly little band of the damned. He was primarily our archivist, although he was also responsible for things like helping Demi find the sheet music that had allowed her to pipe the rats of the city up from the sewers and into the streets. Sort of a jack-of-all-trades, master of none, and happy about the fact. Like most of the rest of us, he had joined the Bureau because he hadn't had a choice. He was a fully activated five-oh-three, part of a tale best encapsulated by the Shoemaker and the Elves. He did okay at resisting his urge to clean the office when the rest of us weren't looking, and he definitely made the best shoes I'd ever had the luxury of wearing. It was like walking on a cloud.

"He's with the new girl, getting her kitted out so that maybe she won't die off quite as fast." Sloane didn't look up from her computer. "We should start a betting pool."

"Betting pools don't count if you murder the person yourself," I reminded her, earning myself a look at her middle finger as she held it up for my inspection. "You know, I *am* technically your superior. You should really stop flipping me off."

"Then you should stop saying stupid shit that makes me want to," said Sloane. She clicked the "Buy It Now" button on a spiked leather collar. "Basically, you should shut the fuck up forever. Just pretend you're in a glass coffin and it'll come naturally."

"Could you lay off for five minutes?" I sat down at my own desk, causing one stack of paperwork to cascade gently over into another, creating an undifferentiated sweep of white across what was supposed to be my writing area. I fought back the urge to put my head down and use it as a pillow. "We're getting a new field team member. She's a Pied Piper. That has to be useful. Right now, Jeff's the only one of us who's fully activated, and he doesn't do much during incursions."

Sending someone whose passions were cleaning and shoe-making into an active fairy tale would very rarely make things better, and could frequently make things worse. We had to keep him far away from the five-ten-A manifestations, or every Cinderella who came along would wind up drafting him into the role normally played by songbirds and talking mice. And he wouldn't be able to fight them. Being tied to a story gives a person certain strengths—see also my affinity for woodland creatures and tendency to make wildflowers grow in the carpet. It also makes you vulnerable. Jeff could no more refuse to clean up a mess than Sloane could be trusted with apples and arsenic. We can fight our natures, but no one has yet figured out how to change them.

We'd never worked with an activated Piper before. Demi's strengths we knew; if something could be classed as vermin, she could control it. Given the most classic story attributed to her tale type, that said something unpleasant about how children were viewed in Europe during the Dark Ages. What we didn't know was where her weaknesses would be.

"Maybe she can pipe my damn bluebirds away," I added.

"I don't think anything can pipe your bluebirds away," said Andy.

I raised my head and looked at him flatly. "Really. That's your useful contribution to this discussion. That I am to be permanently plagued by happy songbirds."

Andy shrugged. "I never claimed to be useful."

I balled up a piece of paper and flung it at him. Andy laughed and batted it aside.

Unlike the rest of us—Sloane with her averted story, Jeff with his active story, and me in the middle—Andy was nowhere on the ATI spectrum. He was perfectly normal, with no more connection to the memetic undercurrent of reality than any other man on the street . . . except that once, before I graduated to full field agent, a four-ten manifested in a small beachside community, and no one noticed. She put the whole town to sleep, and this is the real world, which tends to be pretty straightforward about things like "humans need to eat" and "if you sleep for three weeks without any medical treatment of any kind, you will die." Andy's twin brother, Eric, had been living in that little town. By the time the four-ten herself died, breaking the spell cast by her presence, no one lived there anymore.

Most people would have written that off as a tragedy, the sort of thing that couldn't be explained. At the time, Andy had been going to college to study investigative journalism. He started following reports of a mysterious government agency that had been involved in the cleanup. He turned over rocks and knocked on doors until he stumbled into the middle of the biggest cover-up in the world: fairy tales were real, and Sleeping Beauty had been responsible for his brother's death.

Again, that's where most people would have walked away, or possibly run screaming. Andy asked for a job. When I showed up for my first day as field team leader, he was already there waiting for me to tell him what to do. I honestly couldn't imagine working a live field situation without him, even if we always had to remember that he wasn't on the spectrum, making him vulnerable to a lot of dangers that the rest of us could ignore. On the flip side, he didn't have to worry about glass coffins or the temptation of poisoned apples, so things balanced out, in their own way.

A throat was cleared behind me. I twisted in my seat. Jeff was standing in the aisle leading to our little slice of the bullpen. Demi Santos was behind him, still clutching her flute the way a small child might clutch a teddy bear. She looked faintly dazed and absolutely terrified, her dark eyes darting from side to side as she tried to take in every possible detail.

"Special Agent Marchen, Agent Winters, Agent Robinson, may I introduce Probationary Agent Demi Santos?" Jeff turned, trying to urge Demi to step forward with a small wave of his hand. She didn't budge. He held his position for a few more seconds before turning back to me, and saying, "Her personnel file is being prepared, and will be on your desk inside of the hour."

"Because more paperwork is exactly what my desk needs right now," I said, and stood. Demi visibly cringed. Oh, yeah, this was going to be a *great* working relationship. "Agent Santos, welcome to the field team. I assume Agent Davis has explained what it is that we do here?"

"This is a joke," she replied. "This is a horrible joke, and you're horrible people for going along with it. Who put you up to this? Was it Andres? Because I'm going to kick his ass when I get home. Do you hear me, Andres?" She raised her voice at the end of the sentence, eyes darting wildly as she searched for a security camera. "This is a shitty joke, and it's not funny, and you need to call it off *right now*."

"Agent Santos was very clear about her unwillingness to sign any sort of release form that might allow us to air this footage, as she's more than reasonably convinced that we're currently appearing on a 'prank' reality show," said Jeff. He sounded tired. I peered at him. I'd never seen him look frazzled before, and I wasn't sure I liked it.

"Did she sign everything else?" asked Andy, arrowing in on the potential liability issues like the investigative journalist he never got the chance to be.

"After reading everything six times and stating aloud that nothing on the paper cleared us to use her image on film, yes." Jeff shook his head. "So she's a fully signed and accredited government agent now. We just can't take her picture."

"Uh-huh." I stepped in front of Demi. She stopped scanning the room with a small squeak before she took a big step backward. I smiled thinly. "You seem to be laboring under a misapprehension about our agency. Since it's your agency too now, I think we should get that cleared up as quickly as possible. What part is confusing you?"

"What part—everything! You! Him! Her!" She stabbed a finger at Sloane, in case I couldn't figure out who "her" was supposed to refer to. "All of this! Fairy tales are *not* real, I *can't* control rats by playing the right song on my flute, and you are *not* a real government agency! My father would have been complaining for my entire life if there was a branch of government dedicated to stopping things that don't exist!"

"Oh, we're not a branch of the government, we're just an agency, and there are at least three agencies dedicated to dealing with things that most people don't believe exist. It's a natural result of living in a world with aspirations of rationality." I continued to smile. It was better than screaming at her, but not by much. "How much did Jeff tell you about what brought each of us to the agency?"

"He said most of that was your business," she said. "I figure it was a casting agency who brought you."

"You know, as stupid-ass delusions go, this one is pretty good," said Sloane. "It's consistent, it's logical, and it's fucking moronic. Gold star."

"Don't say 'moronic,'" said Jeff. "It's ableist language, and you know I won't stand for that."

"Fuck you," replied Sloane genially.

"Much less offensive," said Jeff.

"Ignore her," I said to Demi, as I pointed at Sloane. "That's what the rest of us do most of the time, and as you can see, it's worked out pretty well for us. Now give me a second. If you're assuming that we were hired by a casting agency, how are you accounting for my coloring?" I narrowly escaped being cast to play Snow White in the story of my own life. My story was still in waiting, lurking and looking for a chance to pounce. Until it either swallowed me whole or was somehow beaten back completely, I was blessed with suck in the form of the traditional Snow White coloring: skin as white as snow, lips as red as blood, and hair as black as coal.

In the cartoons and the storybooks, they make it look almost cute. Of course, when artists and animators design a Snow White, they essentially give their incarnation of my story a spray tan and some neutral lip liner. A true seven-oh-nine was nowhere near as marketable as those animated darlings. We're too pale, and our lips are too red, and we look like something out of a horror movie that didn't have the decency to stay on the screen.

"Pancake makeup and theatrical lipstick," replied Demi, without missing a beat. "You'd look more realistic if you'd bothered to blend the color at all, you know."

"Oh, believe me, I know." My teen years had been an endless parade of foundation creams and blending powders, all geared toward the simple goal of making me look less like the vanguard of an impending alien invasion. Some of them had even worked for a little while, as long as I remembered not to touch my face. I held out my hand. "Andy, can you give me that box of tissues?"

Andy, bless him, knew what I was about to do. "Here you go," he said, pressing the box into my hand.

"Thank you, Andy." I didn't take my eyes off Demi as I pulled a tissue from the box and held it up for her to examine. "Note that this is an ordinary tissue. Does it look like an ordinary tissue to you?"

"I suppose," she said, somewhat grudgingly.

"Good." I wiped the tissue hard across my lips, and then held it up again. "No lipstick. No nothing, because I'm not. Wearing. Any. Makeup."

"Lip stain," she said, without missing a beat.

"Fine, then. Lip stain is a thing; I'll grant you that, but there's no such thing as skin stain, not unless you want to get into paint. Regardless, if you've got makeup that thick on your face, nothing's going to get through it, am I right?"

"Yes," she said. This time she sounded almost suspicious, like she was sure I had a trick up my sleeve, but wasn't sure what that trick could possibly be.

"Just so we're agreed." I turned. "Sloane, I need you to slap me, if you would be so kind."

"You know what? I take it back." Sloane bounced to her feet, moving with the speed that she reserved for violence and free food as she closed in on me. "The new girl *rocks*." Then she pulled back and slapped me hard across the face. The sound was incredibly loud. It was nothing compared to the pain that immediately followed. Sloane might take a half-assed approach to a lot of things, but when it came to hitting people, she was fully committed, no questions asked.

Gritting my teeth to keep myself from swearing—or worse, whimpering—I turned to show my rapidly reddening cheek to Demi, who was staring at the two of us like we had just lost our minds. "If I was wearing pancake makeup, would there be a handprint on my skin?"

"Look, Ma, no special effects," added Sloane, holding up her palm for inspection. I gave it a sidelong glance. Her skin was a little reddened, but it was fading fast, replaced by a normal Caucasian pink.

Demi's only answer was the sound of the back of her head rebounding off the floor with a hollow *bonk* sound, like someone had dropped a coconut. She didn't move after that. The four of us stared at her for a moment.

"I just want it noted for the record that I was not responsible for killing the new girl," said Sloane to break the silence. "Can someone please put that in writing right now, before there's some sort of inquest?"

"She's not dead," I said, crouching down to check Demi's pulse. It was strong and steady. "She just fainted, which probably proves that she's the smartest person here."

"Isn't it customary to check someone's pulse *before* you declare that they're alive?" asked Andy.

"I'm pretty good at telling dead girls from sleeping ones, thanks." I straightened. "Andy, take her down to the break room and put up the 'Do Not Disturb' sign. Maybe when she wakes up she'll feel more like facing reality."

Andy snorted as he bent to scoop Demi's motionless form off the office floor. "I don't know what you've been smoking, Henry, but there's no reality in this building for her to face. She's barely even started down the rabbit hole."

"Then the faster she wakes up, the sooner she can start coping. Go. And when you get back, get started on your paperwork." I dropped back into my chair. "The world's not going to save itself from the collected works of the Brothers Grimm."

# # #

Having Jeff back at his desk was a definite relief: he could generally be trusted to do his own paperwork in record time, and then get bored and start helping everyone else with their share. Most forms didn't care who filled them out, as long as it was done correctly, and I shortly found myself in the enviable position of playing rubber stamp while Jeff shoved page after page in front of me to be signed. Sloane ignored us both, choosing to return to eBay's modern-day Goblin Market in search of treasures.

Andy stalked back up the aisle and glared when he saw my empty desk. He didn't need to see the look on Jeff's face to know what had happened. "Dammit, Henry, *again*?" he asked.

I smiled at him broadly as I shrugged. "It's a symbiotic relationship. Jeff enjoys doing paperwork; I enjoy not doing paperwork. Everybody wins."

"Everybody but me," grumbled Andy, and dropped down into his seat. "Why do I have to do my own stupid reports?"

"Because I'm the boss and you're not," I said, scrawling my signature on the last report. "Sloane, is there anything coming up on the radar?"

"Nope," she said, not taking her eyes off the screen. "Clean as a whistle."

"Uh-huh." I turned to my own computer and called up the monitoring program, even though I knew that it would confirm Sloane's statement. She was uncanny when it came to predicting oncoming intrusions. It had something to do with her having been averted. Jeff was fully manifested, and now subconsciously accepted fairy tales as a normal part of the background radiation of life. Normal people were blind to them. His eyes were open too wide. And as long as I was holding my story in abeyance, I couldn't be open enough to feel another story coming. Sloane was unique.

Our four-ten was listed under the "recent" column on the ATI incursion tracker, as was Demi's own two-eighty. The four-ten was labeled "neutralized." Demi was labeled "fully active." I felt a little twinge of guilt at that. She'd been living a normal life until we came along, and no matter where her life went from here, normal was never going to be put back on the table.

Of course, she was living a normal life in the middle of a minefield, one where any careless word or casual encounter had the potential to trigger her story into sudden motion. At least this way, she'd been activated under controlled conditions, giving her the potential to find a way that she could live with it. Jeff had already managed to find that balance. It was possible. And I was a total hypocrite, because I was sitting at my desk, safe in my own frozen narrative, and thinking about how waking up to learn that you were secretly a fairy tale wasn't actually that bad.

"She's going to need weapons training," said Andy. "She probably has no clue how to handle a firearm."

"About that," said Jeff. "I think it would be a good idea if she *didn't* carry a firearm. She can get by just fine with her flute, and between that and maybe a harmonica or some other form of small backup instrument, I think she'll be able to deal with any situation she's likely to encounter."

Sloane snorted. "Sure. If she gets mugged, she can just flute them to death."

"Once she's a little more confident in her powers, yes, she probably can," said Jeff.

We were all quiet for a moment, contemplating that. There had been no active two-eighties in the service prior to Demi. We didn't really know how she would play out—so to speak— not in any practical sense.

"She's going to be that powerful?" asked Andy finally.

"She's going to be that *versatile*," said Jeff. "In a situation like this, flexibility is more important than raw strength."

"Oh, this just keeps getting better," muttered Sloane. "What's the good news?"

"If we take away her instruments, she'll be essentially powerless—"

"That's good," agreed Sloane.

"—until she finds something else that she can use to make music—and as a Piper, she can make music from virtually anything," Jeff finished. "Whether or not we're happy about having her assigned to our field team, she needs to stay within the agency. She's too dangerous to be left unsupervised."

"Then why did you let Henry suggest activating her?" demanded Andy. He actually sounded agitated for the first time. I guess being reminded that fairy tales can be dangerous was freaking him out.

"Because it was this or let a Sleeping Beauty impact half the city," said Jeff. "That, and I honestly figured the stress of piping the fever into the rats would kill her, and we wouldn't have to deal with this part of things. I guess she's stronger than I expected."

There was a momentary silence while we all stared at Jeff. Finally, Sloane said, "Dude, that's cold. I was almost a Wicked Stepsister, and I'm *still* impressed by how cold that is. Are you sure you're not from my tale type?"

Jeff sniffed, looking defensive as he said, "It was the practical solution, and it was tidy. I like things that are tidy."

"And that, right there, is why not everyone who works here can be on the spectrum." I sighed as I pushed my chair away from my desk. "I'm going to go check on our sleeping newbie. Hopefully she's having really pleasant dreams, and won't start whistling in her sleep."

"I don't think she could whistle us to death," said Jeff.

"Well at least that's something," I said flatly, and walked away.

#

Being a government agency, however secret and unusually staffed, means we've been supplied with a decent base of operations by good old Uncle Sam. Being an agency that no one wants to claim either ownership of or responsibility for means that our "decent base" started life as a research lab dedicated to biological warfare . . . before a big-ass city decided to expand its borders to include the lab's location. Not wanting to turn into the Umbrella Corporation from the *Resident Evil* movies, the US government promptly decommissioned the lab, bombed the whole thing with enough bleach to kill any creepy crawlies that might be lurking there, and moved the ATI Management Bureau in. Because fairy tales are apparently better for property values than aerosolized Ebola.

To get from our part of the bullpen to the break room where Demi was sleeping, I had to go up a flight of stairs, walk through something that used to be an air lock, and enter the space-age glass and chrome domain of the Dispatch Unit. Four dispatchers were currently at their desks, headsets in place and eyes glued to their screens. I tried to look unobtrusive as I followed the path through the center of the room. Dispatch is a hard, unforgiving job that doesn't come with the supposed "glamour" of fieldwork. Just hour upon hour staring at a screen, waiting for something to pop, and knowing all the while that if you miss anything, people are going to die.

I was almost to the door when a voice behind me said, "Henry? If you've got a second?"

"Sure thing," I said, keeping the urge to roll my eyes at bay as I turned around. Experience has taught me that you should never refuse a reasonable request from a dispatcher. Not unless you want to spend the next six months chasing phantoms and "likely incursions" rather than actual incidents.

Birdie Hubbard, who was generally responsible for my team's assignments, was standing up at her desk and leaning over her computer, blinking at me owlishly through her thick-lensed glasses. "We were wrong?" Her voice was plaintive, almost wounded—the tone of a child asking whether or not Santa Claus was real.

"You were right about the incursion," I said, walking back toward her. The other three dispatchers were listening. They were trying to pretend that they weren't, but human nature wins out over almost everything else in this world. "There was definitely a story trying to break through, and if you hadn't sent us, it would have succeeded."

"But it wasn't a seven-oh-nine." Birdie looked utterly ashamed of herself. "I'm so sorry. We didn't prepare you properly."

"Hey. Sloane confirmed your ID when she got to the scene. She said the girl was a seven-oh-nine, and we followed the protocol accordingly. I saw our subject with my own eyes, and she had all the hallmarks. We could have been cousins." Not sisters, not quite; you don't get coloring as extreme as mine unless one or both parents were also fairy tale–afflicted. Our latest Sleeping Beauty had been spared that particular indignity.

Rather than looking reassured by what I was saying, Birdie's look of shame and confusion deepened. "So you also thought that she was a seven-oh-nine?"

"Up until people started passing out in the hospital lobby, yes, I did." I frowned. "Birdie? What's wrong? This was a hard call, and you had to pick a type to activate the system. The one you picked wasn't quite right, but it was damn close."

"You don't understand." She looked to the other dispatchers. "We need to tell her."

"We're not ready," said another dispatcher, a slim Asian man whose name I didn't know. "We need more data."

"We have four incursions," countered Birdie. "How much data do you think we need?"

"I'm standing right here, and I can hear every word you're saying," I said. "How likely do you think it is that I'm going to walk away without one of you explaining what the hell it is that you're talking about?"

Birdie turned back to me. "We've had four incursions recently that presented as one tale type and turned out to belong to another part of the Index. In every case, the original type was less dangerous than the actual type." I paused. If it had been possible for me to go pale, I think that I would have. "You're saying that the stories are intentionally camouflaging themselves?"

Birdie nodded. "We think so."

"Do you have any evidence to support this?" Evidence would be good. Evidence could be refuted.

A lack of evidence would be even better.

"There's not much, but we're monitoring every incursion, and what we're finding isn't encouraging," said Birdie. "It's getting to where we can't reliably guess what you *might* find out there, much less tell you what you *will*."

"Okay, so this is all terrifying," I said, clapping my hands together. "Birdie, I want all your findings on my desk at your earliest convenience. Jeff and I can go over them together and see if there's anything that we can confirm from a field perspective that you haven't already documented. Maybe we're lucky, and this will just turn out to be a period of memetic instability or something."

"Do those exist?" asked the other dispatcher dubiously.

I shot him a quick glare. "Think about where you work before you ask me whether something is real. If it means the Index hasn't somehow started hiding itself from us, then yes, we're going to hope that memetic instability exists."

"I'll have it all on your desk inside the hour," Birdie assured me.

"Thank you." I sighed. "Now if you don't mind, I need to go check on our newest recruit."

"You mean the Pied Piper? Is she really going to come and work here?" Birdie perked up, her earlier distress forgotten in the face of something interesting that she could focus on. "I've never met an actual Piper before. What's she like?"

"She's confused as all hell," I said, unable to keep the disapproval from my tone. No one who isn't on the ATI spectrum can really understand what it's like to live your life knowing that you're halfway between unique individual and structured story. Half of who we are was decided years before we were even born, shaped by the narratives that we were intended to embody. Hell, I'm living proof of that: both of my parents were brown-eyed brunettes. So how did they have a blue-eyed, black-haired baby girl? Easy: the story made them do it. "She's only been a two-eighty for a few hours, and she has no idea what's going on."

Birdie looked instantly contrite. "Oh, the poor thing. I guess it's too bad that her story couldn't have been averted. She wouldn't have to deal with us then."

"No, but we'd be dealing with a four-ten in the middle of downtown, so I'm going to call this one a fair trade."

"Isn't it a little strange that we've had so many Sleeping Beauties in the last few decades?" Birdie's hand twitched, like she was fighting the urge to reach for her mouse. "Demographically speaking, it's not that popular of a story, and—" She gasped, hand twitching again before she used it to cover the perfect O shape of her mouth. "I'm so sorry, Henrietta! I forgot!"

"Yeah, well. I don't like to make a big thing about it." I smiled stiffly. "Now if you'll excuse me, I have a recruit to see to." I turned quickly and walked on before Birdie could start apologizing. If I let her reach the mindless platitudes stage, I'd be here all night long.

It's funny, but most people forget that my mother was a Sleeping Beauty. They have better things to worry about, like whether Sloane has poisoned the coffee, or whether they're going to find me sleeping in a big glass box one day. Working in a building where half the people are living fairy tales and the other half are memetically vulnerable makes for some interesting times, and I'm so clearly a Snow White that people don't associate the Sleeping Beauty story with me in any way, unless they've read my file.

We all have our tragedies. That's part of what brings us all to work for the ATI Management Bureau—and that brought me full circle back to Demi, whose story, like mine, had been kick-started by proximity to a four-ten. In my case, the Sleeping Beauty gave birth to me. In her case, the Sleeping Beauty forced us to activate her story in order to save lives. I guess in a way, a Sleeping Beauty gave birth to both of us. I just didn't think the common ground would mean much to Demi at the moment.

I just hoped that once she came to better understand what we did here, she'd be able to forgive us.

# # #

The break-room door was closed when I finally arrived. I paused outside, and decided that discretion was the better part of valor. Rapping my knuckles gently against the wood, I called, "Miss Santos, are you awake? It's Agent Marchen."

"That's the word for 'fairy tale' in German, isn't it?" asked a voice behind me. I whirled and found myself facing Demi Santos, who was standing in the hallway with a paper cup of bad government coffee in her hand. "I mean 'marchen.' Doesn't that literally mean 'fairy tale'? How do you people expect me to believe that this isn't a big prank when you're literally *named* 'Agent Fairy Tale'?"

"My parents were drawn into a story like the one that we asked you to help us prevent today," I said. Normally, I tried to avoid discussing my past with the new recruits. But this one was my fault. If she wanted to ask a few questions, I didn't see any good way to refuse to answer them. "My mother turned out to be a four-ten—that's what we call Sleeping Beauties. She was very much like the story we asked you to help us with, because she was the *same* story. She was unconscious the whole time she was pregnant with my brother and me. We accidentally pulled her life support cables out when we were born. She died before anyone could get to us."

Demi gasped. "Oh my God."

I shrugged a little. It was a painful story, but it was painful in part because of reactions like hers. I'd never known my mother. She wasn't even a dim memory; she was just another tragedy in the long list of tragedies the fairy tales had left behind. "It was a long time ago. Anyway, as my brother and I were effectively orphans, we were taken in by the ATI Management Bureau. We were raised by one of the department heads, who was delighted to have children of his own, and we were given the last name 'Marchen' because we didn't belong to any family but our own. So yes, my name is 'Agent Fairy Tale,' but I came by it honestly, and I assure you, this is not a prank."

Demi sighed. "Yeah. I'm starting to get that impression."

"I know this is a lot to take in."

"You do, do you?" Her laugh was sudden, and distressingly brittle. "You just told me you were *raised* here. This has *always* been your world. There was never a point where you thought that stories were just stories. You always knew. Now you're telling me that *I'm* a story, and you expect me to be okay with it, just like that. Like this doesn't change everything. Like this doesn't turn my life upside down."

"Yes, exactly," I said, choosing to ignore her sarcasm. Sometimes it was easier that way. "You were always a story. If we hadn't triggered you when we did, people would have died, and one day you would have triggered on your own. Now you get to learn how to control the narrative, rather than letting the narrative control you."

Demi's face wrinkled in thought. After a moment, she asked, "What about my education? I have classes."

"We're a government agency. We may not be one of the big flashy ones, but we can get you a degree in anything you want, from any college in the country, without the mountain of student debt that would normally go along with it."

"Can I go home?"

That was a trickier question. I hesitated. I must have hesitated a little too long because Demi's expression darkened, and she took a step toward me.

"I have a family. They're going to wonder where I am."

Not if she stayed away from them for long enough, they wouldn't. People who are *outside* the spectrum tend to forget about people who are *inside* if they don't see them for a little while, no matter how beloved those people may have originally been. It's just one more way that the narrative protects itself. "I am not personally opposed to you going home to your family," I said, choosing my words with care, "but we need to check with Jeff first."

"What? Why?"

"Because I'm a Snow White, and that meant my birth mother had to die," I snapped.

Demi froze.

"Sloane? She was meant to be a Wicked Stepsister. Her story's frozen right now—and you'll learn about the stages a narrative goes through; you're active, I'm in abeyance, Sloane's frozen. Accept that for right now; the distinctions don't matter. What matters is that Sloane was meant to be a Wicked Stepsister, and on the day she began showing signs of her story, her biological father was killed in a fire. Do you begin to understand? We need to check with Jeff so that he can make sure that you going home won't cause the memetic incursion that you represent to start targeting your family."

Demi's eyes had gone wide and were glossy with unshed tears. Finally, in a small voice, she asked, "Can we do that now? Right now?"

"Yes, we can," I said. "Come with me."

# # #

The two-eighty narrative turned out to be completely devoid of family members in all of the iterations that we had on file.

The Piper arrived in town as a stranger, did his or her business, and then left, usually taking something precious along in lieu of the original payment. After rattling off that special little fact, Jeff smiled broadly and said, "That's why you'll be the first one in the department to receive your check every pay period, Miss Santos. We don't want your story to decide that we're trying to short you something that's rightfully yours!"

"Because having magic flute girl go all *Scanners* on us with an arpeggio would be a stupid-ass way to die," contributed Sloane, without taking her eyes off her computer screen.

I wadded up a Post-it note and threw it at her. "How many pairs of shoes do you need? Turn around and pretend you care about good team relations."

"Uh, point the first, I *don't* care about good team relations," said Sloane, spinning around in her chair so that I could see her face when she flipped me off. "Point the second, I stopped shopping for shoes an hour ago. I'm buying bulk lots of hair dye now."

"I don't understand any of this," said Demi blankly.

"Don't worry," said Andy. "Neither does anyone else."

Jeff cleared his throat. "If the rest of you are done goofing around, I'd like to call your attention to some of the finer points of the Pied Piper clade of stories . . ." And then he was off and running again, listing a dozen possible variations on a theme that we were all about to become intimately familiar with. I watched Demi out of the corner of my eye while he talked. This was going to impact her most of all, after all.

I'll never understand what it's like to find out that you're on the ATI spectrum. I was raised knowing what I could potentially become. So was my brother, Gerry. Neither of us had a single day where we thought of ourselves as "normal" or believed that fairy tales were anything other than a fate to be avoided. Demi was just finding out about that world now. It was becoming real for her, and there was nothing that I, or anyone else, could do.

I should have felt guiltier than I did. Her story might never have triggered. But in the end, all I felt was grateful that we'd been able to avert a Sleeping Beauty, and that no one had needed to die.

Jeff was still talking. I shook off the clinging shreds of my thoughts, and forced myself to listen. If Demi's story ever took a turn for the dark, I might need to know what he had said in the beginning, when we still thought she had a chance.

# # #

Between the paperwork, dealing with Demi's gear, and everything else, I didn't make it back to my car until ten minutes to midnight. The time was enough to make me wince. Midnight is a bad hour for anyone on the ATI spectrum. We don't like it. Too many stories set their watches by it, so to speak.

The wince got worse when I pulled out my keys and Sloane stepped out of the shadows of the carport. Her bangs were hanging over her eyes, and her lips were set firmly into a frown.

"Can I get a ride home?" she asked.

I didn't ask how she'd been able to get to work in the first place. I didn't suggest that she call for a taxi. I just nodded, and said, "Get in."

She didn't say anything for the first six blocks of our drive. Then she said, quietly, "The Pied Piper is a cipher. He's not good. He's not bad. He's just a man who does a job and gets mad when people try to rook him."

"I know."

"Snow White's good. The Wicked Stepsisters are bad. Pied Piper . . . that could go either way."

"So we'll watch her. We'll make sure she picks the right path." I shrugged. "This isn't our first fairy tale, Sloane. It'll be okay."

"Maybe. But one day, it won't be. What's going to happen then?"

I didn't have an answer for her. So I turned on the radio, and we rode in silence toward midnight, and the distant landmark the stories only ever know as "home."

Honey Do

Memetic incursion in progress: tale type 171 ("Goldilocks and the Three Bears")
Status: UNRESOLVED/POSTPONED

Jennifer Lockwood didn't so much "open the door" as "collapse against it while scrabbling vaguely at the doorknob" until gravity took pity on her and allowed her to stumble into the front hall of her small rental home. Working three shifts in a row at the diner was a good way to pay the bills, but a bad way to take care of her physical needs. Sleep, for example. Sleep had been discarded as a luxury at some point in the previous day and a half, and she wasn't sure she'd ever be getting it back. She was equally unsure that she would be able to make it to the bed before passing out.

Her cat, a gray tabby with the uninspired name of Puss, came and twined around her ankles as she walked, making it even harder to traverse the hall into the darkened living room and onward to her bedroom. Jennifer struggled to keep her eyes open. If she let them close, she knew that she was going to wake up on the floor again, with a crick in her neck and the alarm in her bedroom ringing too loud to let her sleep and too late for her to get to work on time.

"Look out, Puss," she mumbled, after the third time she kicked the cat. Puss purred and plastered against her leg again. Jennifer dropped her purse and kept on walking.

There was an art to removing clothing while remaining in motion. Teenagers mastered it effortlessly, creating endless trails of fabric leading to their lairs. Adults tended to lose the skill, but Jennifer had worked hard to retain it. Between her job at the diner and her classes at the university, she needed to cut corners wherever possible, and that included the three minutes it would have taken her to remove her clothing in the usual way. So her pants and underwear wound up on the living room floor, while her apron and shirt were discarded in the hall. The bra was the hardest part—undoing those little hooks without slowing down never got easier—but practice made perfect, and she dropped it just as she stepped into her bedroom.

The window shade was open again. "Stupid cat," she mumbled, and half-walked, half-stumbled across the room to pull it down. The last thing she wanted was for the sun to rise and wake her up before she was ready.

Amazingly—considering her condition—she actually noticed something large and brown just outside the window, blocking her view of the backyard. Jennifer paused, squinting as she tried to figure out what it was. She was still squinting when the bear turned around, pressing its round black nose against the glass.

Jennifer had time for one good scream before she passed out, which was something like sleep, at least.

The bear stayed outside her window for a good long time before it rose and walked away, and when she woke up to the sound of two alarm clocks ringing stridently, it was easy to convince herself that the whole thing had been a dream. It was simpler that way.

At least until the next night, when the bear came back . . . and brought a friend.

# # #

ATI Management Bureau Headquarters

"Good morning," I grumbled as I walked into the bullpen, a bag of donuts in one hand and a tray of coffee cups in the other. If I didn't sound all that enthusiastic, well, maybe the breakfast offering would make up for things. "How is everyone today?"

"I dropped out of college," said Demi glumly, not lifting her head out of her hands. She had her fingers laced so tightly through her bark-brown hair that I wasn't sure she *could* lift her hands. Not without getting a pair of scissors. "The registrar's office sent the confirmation that I am no longer enrolled in any classes. I am a failure."

"Mike and I had a fight last night about how much of my job I'm not allowed to discuss with him," said Andy, although he at least reached over and took one of the coffee cups. "He still wants to adopt, and he's worried that writing 'redacted' on our papers will slow the process down."

"Did you try pointing out that you work for a government agency, which will probably make it *easier* for you to adopt?"

Andy leveled a cool look on me. "Please don't take this the wrong way, Henry—you know I love you and Gerry both—but if I let the folks who run this place help me find a baby, I'm going to get a kid who's already halfway sucked into a story, and I can't do that. Not after what happened to my brother."

"No offense taken," I said quietly.

Jeff was nowhere to be seen. I put a coffee cup and a donut down on his desk, where he could find them later, assuming no one stole them in the meantime. Our office may be responsible for preventing fairy-tale incursions on the so-called real world, but we're still paid like government employees, and unguarded food has a tendency to go missing.

The last member of our little team didn't even wait for me to get to her. She literally climbed over Andy's desk, knocking over his pencil holder in the process, and grabbed for the bag. I jerked it back, out of her reach.

"Give them to me," snapped Sloane, and grabbed again.

"No," I replied. "You either wait for me to offer, or you ask."

"I *am* asking," she said, making a third grab. This one nearly knocked over the picture of Andy and his husband. He picked it up and hugged it to his chest, frowning at Sloane. Even Demi lifted her head, attention caught by the shenanigans unfolding in front of her.

"Are you allergic to the word 'please'?" I asked, finally allowing Sloane to snatch the bag of donuts from my hand.

She crab-walked triumphantly back into her seat, where she folded herself like a particularly content praying mantis and began rummaging through the bag. "Yes," she said, not looking up. "It's a legitimate health complication that comes with my position on the ATI spectrum, and I don't feel very good about you rubbing it in my face like this. Maybe I should be reporting you to Human Resources for discrimination, huh?"

"Shut up and eat your donuts," I said, and turned to Demi, who was looking at me with a blankly questioning expression.

"Sloane is full of shit. She's not allergic to the word 'please,' which is good for her, since if she were, we would all stand in a circle around her making polite requests until she went into anaphylactic shock. She just enjoys being horrible to the rest of us, and we let her, because we honestly can't think of a way to make her stop."

"I've thought of a few, but we never get them past the folks in HR," added Andy in a low rumble.

"I've told you before, Andrew, dousing her with a bucket of water won't make her dissolve, no matter how much she chooses to act like the Wicked Witch of the Worst." Jeff appeared between two desks, smoothly winding his way around the obstacles in his path as he walked over to sit in his chair. He had a large book open in one arm, and never looked up from its pages, not even as he settled, picked up his coffee, and took a long drink. "Thank you, Henry. You always get the exact right amount of sugar."

"I try," I said, claiming my own coffee cup before someone could get ideas about swiping it. "Where were you?"

"Dispatch." He finally looked up from the book, gray eyes concerned behind the wire frames of his glasses. "Birdie left a note on my desk asking me to come and see her as soon as I came in. Since I was running early—"

"When are you *not* running early?" muttered Sloane. "Kiss-ass."

Jeff ignored her as he cleared his throat and tried again: "Since I was running early, I thought I would go down and find out if she had any pressing news before the rest of you got here. That way, we could hit the ground running, if necessary."

I nodded. "Good thinking." As our primary dispatcher, I didn't know what hours Birdie Hubbard actually kept, since it seemed like she was in the office any time that we needed her to be; for all that I knew, she slept on a cot somewhere in the Dispatch Unit. She took her job very seriously. All the dispatchers did, and that was a damn good thing, because at the end of the day, they were the first line of defense between the everyday world and the looming memetic incursions of the Aarne-Thompson Index spectrum. My team and I? We were the last line of defense, no matter how unprepared we might sometimes seem. As the world had not yet been sucked into an unending once upon a time, I figured we were doing pretty well.

"Do you remember Jennifer Lockwood?" Jeff asked.

I hesitated, trying to recall exactly why I knew that name. Andy did the same. Demi, who had been with us for less than a week, just looked blank. It was becoming her default expression.

Sloane didn't share our mutual confusion. "Tall, skinny, blonde hair—out of a bottle, but it was natural when she was a kid, so she still fits the primary narrative cues—and she's an averted Goldilocks," she said, rattling off the information like it was written on a piece of paper in front of her. "She's a weird one, isn't she?"

Jeff nodded. "She's been averted three times. Once at age six, again at age twelve, and a third time at age fifteen. She's twenty-seven now, working full time as she tries to put herself through college."

A light went off in my head. "That's why I recognize her name," I said. "She's one of the case studies I had to review when I took over the field team. Our lords and ladies in waiting."

"What?" asked Demi.

"That's what we call the ones who were almost stories, and somehow managed to pull back at the last minute, either because we intervened or because they changed their personal narratives enough to keep from going over the edge," said Andy. "Henry's a lady in waiting."

"Yes, thank you for the reminder," I said sourly. "Okay, so we all know who Jennifer Lockwood is. Why is this relevant?"

"Because Dispatch intercepted a call she made this morning, shortly after four o'clock, in which she said, quote, 'it was a bear, it was right outside my window, it was a real bear.' She assured Birdie—whom she thought worked for the police—that she wasn't crazy. I have the transcript: she repeated that part eight times. 'I'm not crazy, it was a bear, I'm not crazy.' Birdie promised her that she'd send some officers out to look for signs of the bear."

"Officers meaning us, right?" asked Demi.

Sloane rolled her eyes. "And this is the prodigy that the field team couldn't live without. Wow. The world is super safe now."

"Sloane, be quiet," I snapped. "Everyone else, grab your gear. We have a bear to find."

# # #

Jennifer Lockwood lived in a run-down neighborhood that looked like it had been teetering on the edge of "slum" for years, only to be kept from toppling over by the combined efforts of the residents, none of whom were willing to let it fall. Younger children played in the narrow strips of weed-choked grass that served as front lawns, while the older children had set up a game of soccer in the middle of the street. "Car!" shouted the lookout as we came around the corner, and all the players pulled back to the sidewalk, watching solemnly as we drove past.

"Nice place," said Sloane, with her customary sneer.

Demi, who was riding in the backseat, raised her head so that the reflection of her large brown eyes was staring directly at us in the rearview mirror. "Yes, it is," she said. "I wish I'd grown up somewhere this nice."

For once, Sloane didn't have a smart comeback. I pulled over and parked in front of Jennifer Lockwood's house, leaving room for Jeff to fit the van in behind me. He and Andy would stay in the vehicle, out of sight, unless something came up that required either an archivist or public relations. Considering that I was about to walk up to an averted Goldilocks's door with a trainee and Sloane—who was practically an invasion of privacy on two legs—I was pretty sure we were going to need Andy.

"Now, Demi, remember: your job is to stand quietly and observe," I said, as we closed our car doors. "I'm going to do all the talking, and Sloane is going to do all the Sloane-ing, while you learn how to do this without me."

"Remember, kids, you're only one poisoned apple away from advancement in your chosen career," said Sloane. There was something automatic about the barb, like she was saying it because she knew that it was expected of her. She seemed distracted, her eyes darting from side to side in small, erratic bursts. I stopped, putting my arm out so that it blocked her passage. Sloane hates to be touched. She stopped immediately.

"What are you getting?" I asked. "Are we walking into something that's going to get us all killed?"

"Yes," said Sloane. "No. I don't know." She shook her head, the distracted expression spreading until she looked utterly baffled. "There's a one-seven-one nearby. And there's . . . there's also *not* a one-seven-one nearby. I don't know what the f—"

She was cut off by the front door swinging open and Jennifer Lockwood appearing in the doorway. "Are you from the police, or are you here to offer me a copy of the *Watchtower*?" she asked. "Because I'm either going to need to see some badges or I'm going to have to ask you to leave."

"We're from the Bureau of Urban Wildlife, ma'am," I said, dropping my arm and dipping my hand into my jacket, where I withdrew the badge that Jeff had prepared for me. Fake departments and bureaus were one of his simple joys in life. It was better than having him spend all his time making shoes that no one wanted to wear. "The police don't have jurisdiction over bears, I'm afraid."

"And you do?" asked Jennifer. She took my badge, studying it carefully as she tried to reassure herself that it was real. It wasn't, of course, but she'd never be able to figure that out on her own.

"Inasmuch as anyone can have jurisdiction over bears, yes," I said, taking my badge from her hand. "I'm Agent Marchen. These are my associates, Agent Winters and Agent Santos."

Jennifer turned a wary eye on Demi and Sloane. Demi looked cautiously back. Sloane kept looking around like she expected us to be attacked at any moment. It was starting to make me nervous about remaining out in the open.

Still, this was an opportunity to see what we might be up against if Jennifer was in the process of going fully active. Using her study of my team and me as cover, I studied her right back. She looked basically like Sloane's description, but with an added dimension of quiet exhaustion that I wouldn't have guessed. She looked like the sort of woman who had long since given up wishing for a fairy-tale ending, and was just hoping to make it through the week without collapsing. Too bad for her that the fairy tale hadn't given up so easily. She wasn't armed, and she didn't look particularly dangerous.

I've been bitten by that assumption before.

"You look legit," she said finally.

"It's the shoes, ma'am," I said.

I was only halfway kidding. As a civilian-interface field operation, this required a bit more subtlety than our usual Island of Misfit Toys approach. I habitually wore black suits and sunglasses to work anyway, trying to overwrite my natural Snow White tendencies with the more modern fairy tale of the Men in Black. Sloane and Demi were more iconoclastic, and had required a stop by the Wardrobe Department, located across from Dispatch, before they were ready to go. The results, however, spoke for themselves. My teammates looked like they shared my tailor—probably because they did, everything in Wardrobe having been stitched by either Jeff or one of his fellow five-oh-threes.

Both Demi and Sloane had chosen to forego the sunglasses, Demi because they left her essentially blind and Sloane because she wanted to be able to see the scene more clearly. Whatever she was seeing, she didn't like it; her agitation was becoming difficult to ignore. I cleared my throat.

"Agent Winters? Is there a problem?"

"We shouldn't be standing out here in the open," she said. There was a note of real fear in her voice. That worried me. Sloane rarely shows fear. "This is a bad place to be when the bears come."

The word "bears" brought about an immediate change in Jennifer. She visibly flinched, looking from side to side as she demanded, "Where?"

"Miss Lockwood, may we continue this inside?" The situation was in danger of getting away from me, and I needed to prevent that from happening. Jeff and Andy could watch the street and notify us if any bears decided to appear.

"You *did* call us, ma'am," said Demi softly.

Jennifer flinched again before nodding and stepping backward, into the relative safety of her own home. "Yes, of course. I'm sorry, I don't know what I was thinking, making you stand outside like this . . ."

Sloane cast me an anxious look as we followed Jennifer inside. Territorial urges went with the story.

One way or another, the bears were going to get in.

# # #

Jennifer was unhappy about leaving me in the living room while she took Sloane and Demi on a tour, but I insisted, and she was beat down enough not to argue beyond a few weak protests. I waited until the sound of their voices was muffled by the kitchen wall before pulling out my phone and calling Andy.

"What's going on?" he asked.

"No signs of breaking and entering, but Sloane is tense. Just standing in the yard got her pretty agitated, and she said that the bears were coming. Do you see any bears?"

"No bears," said Andy. "Could she be talking about metaphorical bears?"

"Okay, well, do you see any large gay men—apart from yourself—or motorcycle gangs?"

Andy snorted laughter before replying, "No, but I'll keep an eye out. Jeff is going over possible variations now. He'll let you know as soon as he finds something."

A horrible thought was occurring to me, swimming slowly out of my knowledge of the narrative and what the ATI spectrum was capable of doing to people who didn't get out of its way quickly enough. "Please do. There are three of us here."

There was a pause while Andy processed my meaning. Then he swore. "Shit, Henry, do you really think—"

"I really do," I said. "Demi's new—she's a baby agent; Sloane was nearly pulled into a classical female story by the ATI spectrum; and I have a male name. It's not perfect casting, but since when has an ongoing memetic incursion cared about being perfect? We're ripe to become her Three Bears, if we're not careful."

"I'll be right in," said Andy. The phone went dead.

That hadn't been my intention, but it would serve as well as anything, since having four members of my team in the house would keep us from falling neatly into the holes that were open in Jennifer's narrative.

By the time Jennifer returned with Demi and Sloane, Andy was standing in the living room next to me. She stopped, paling, her eyes widening in a way I was all too familiar with. She thought that she'd been lied to, that our badges were fake, and that we were here to rob her, or worse.

There was a moment when things could have turned ugly, but that sort of moment is why we have Andy. He smiled, stepping forward, and offered her his hand. "Agent Robinson," he said. "I apologize for my tardiness, but I was asking some of the neighbor kids if they'd seen anything unusual, and I lost track of the rest of my team. I'd lose my own head if it wasn't screwed on tight." He knocked the knuckles of his other hand lightly against the smooth brown dome of his skull, as if to illustrate his point.

Jennifer didn't take the offered hand. Instead, voice shaking slightly, she said, "I'd like to see your badge, please."

"Of course, ma'am." Andy reached into his jacket and produced his badge, which looked, naturally, exactly like mine, save for the name and photograph. He handed it to Jennifer. "Would you also like the number for our supervisor?"

"Yes," said Jennifer immediately.

"No problem, ma'am." Andy produced a business card.

Jennifer snatched it out of his hand, pulling her phone out of her pocket and taking a large step backward as she dialed. Andy moved to stand beside me, and Sloane and Demi moved to flank us, the four of us presenting as unthreatening a line as we could while we waited for the inevitable scene to play out.

"Yes—wait, really? That's really the name of the agency?" A pause, before Jennifer said, sounding alarmed, "No, ma'am, I didn't mean to imply that you were lying to me, I was just surprised. I've never heard of you before, and—" There was another pause. "Yes, ma'am, they're here. No, they haven't done anything wrong. I just wanted to verify their credentials before I let them inside."

Sloane rolled her eyes. I gave a minute shake of my head. If Jennifer wanted to pretend to be more cautious than she was, that was her business.

"Yes, ma'am. Thank you, ma'am." Jennifer lowered her phone, looking stunned. "You're really from the Bureau of Urban Wildlife," she said, holding Andy's badge out for him to take.

He also took back the business card. At that particular moment, she was too confused to notice. By the time she realized that she didn't have it anymore, we would hopefully be long gone.

"I assure you, we are here only to guarantee your safety and the safety of the people around you," I said. "The Bureau takes reports of urban bears very seriously." Especially when they came from women who were flagged as borderline fairy-tale nexus points.

"All right," said Jennifer, seeming to deflate and tense at the same time. She no longer had to devote energy to being scared of us, and could go back to worrying about the real danger: the bears. "Come with me. I'll show you where I saw them."

# # #

Jennifer's bedroom matched the rest of the house in all the ways that counted: small, shabby, but clearly making an effort to stay as clean and well maintained as possible. There was a gray-striped tabby cat on the bed, curled in the classic half-comma position preferred by felines everywhere. It woke up when we entered the room, lifting its head and turning interested green eyes in my direction. I winced. Experience told me what was going to happen next—and sure enough, the cat stood, jumped off the bed, and raced to start twining around my ankles.

"Wow," said Jennifer, sounding impressed. "Puss doesn't like anybody but me. I guess if my cat approves of you, you must be okay."

Sloane rolled her eyes so hard that I was afraid she was going to sprain something, but she kept her mouth shut, thankfully. Animals are not the barometer of humanity that some people make them out to be—not unless those animals have started talking, and then they present a whole new set of problems.

"Anyway, this is where I saw the bears," said Jennifer, walking to the room's single window and gesturing toward the glass. "The first night, I thought it was just a dream, you know? I've had weirder dreams, and how often do you get bears in the city?"

"You'd be surprised," said Andy, somehow managing to sound reassuring and warning at the same time—we were the people who dealt with bears, and so we would see them a lot, according to his tone, but people like Jennifer shouldn't have to worry about unscheduled ursine incursions. "How many times have the bears been back?"

"And when did it become 'bears,' plural?" asked Sloane. "You only mentioned one bear before. I thought this was a single bear situation."

"It was the first night, when I thought it was a dream," said Jennifer. "The second night was when the second bear came. I would have thought I was still dreaming, but . . ." Helplessly, she gestured to the window.

Careful not to trip over Puss in the process, I walked to the window and looked through. Jennifer's backyard was as shabby-looking as everything else in the neighborhood: more mud than grass, with an unpainted fence made of splintering boards separating her from the next yard over.

"I pay extra for the view," said Jennifer defensively, as if she could anticipate our thoughts.

"It's nice," I said. I meant it, in my way. This was what she had, and she was making the best of it. Far be it from me to judge someone for taking the hand that life dealt to them. And it *was* a nice strip of yard, in all its sparse weediness; it was something growing in the middle of a city, and that was beautiful.

It was probably a little more reassuring before something clawed great gouges into the windowsill and ripped up the dirt underneath the window itself, but that was virtually beside the point.

Sloane pushed her way in next to me, nose quivering as she looked down at the gouges in the wood. "Something's wrong," she said, voice pitched low in an effort to keep Jennifer from hearing her. It was surprisingly thoughtful, for Sloane. Then again, maybe she was worried about the fact that we were clearly standing in bear country. "The bears shouldn't be trying to break into *her* house. She should be the one who's trying to break into *theirs*."

"Variation?" I suggested.

"It's possible, but this is a pretty damn big variation," said Sloane.

"Excuse me," said Jennifer. "I don't mean to be rude, but what are the two of you talking about? I'm the one with bears in her backyard. I think I should be the one getting answers."

"Yes, ma'am, and you will be getting the answers that you're looking for," I said, turning to face her. "I'm afraid, however, that it isn't entirely safe for you to be here right now. Would you be willing to come back to the station with us? Just for some routine questions, I promise. No one's in trouble here. There's no law against having bears force their way into your backyard."

"What about Puss?" she asked, suspicion hooding her eyes again. "If it's not safe for me to be here, how can it be safe for him?"

The idea of sharing a car with her overly amorous cat, which was now rolling on its back and trying to entice me to rub its belly, made me feel faintly ill. I managed to keep my neutral expression fixed firmly in place as I shook my head and said, "We can't have animals at the station, but I assure you, your cat will be perfectly fine. Bears don't eat cats."

Demi gave me a bemused look. I was probably wrong about bears and cats. It wasn't like keeping up on bear facts was a normal part of my job. And anyway, it didn't really matter: once Jennifer was out of the apartment, the bears would follow. There was no danger here without her.

"I'm really not sure—"

"Ma'am, what we do can be somewhat alarming, if you're not expecting it," said Andy soothingly. "We just want to ask you a few questions—nothing serious, just getting an idea of your daily routine, anything that might have attracted the bears to this specific location, rather than one of the other yards in this area. Once that's done, we can set you up with some bear defenses, although hopefully you won't need them by then—" Still talking, he slipped an arm around Jennifer's shoulders and led her out of the room.

"That's got to be a narrative we just don't know about yet," said Sloane, shaking her head as she watched Jennifer and Andy leave. "How the hell does he talk people into going along with him like that? It must be magic."

"That, or he actually knows how to talk to people without sounding like he's about to pull their hair out," I said. "Demi. I need you."

The newest member of our team actually jumped a bit, looking at me guiltily, like she'd been hoping to be forgotten. Too bad for her. There was a reason she'd been recruited. "Yes, Agent Marchen?"

"Did you bring your flute?"

Demi's guilty expression deepened. "Yes. Was I not supposed to? I was going to leave it behind, but when I tried, I felt sort of sick to my stomach, so I brought it with me. I'll never do it again, I promise."

"You should be promising the exact opposite," I said. "You're a Pied Piper. That flute is the best weapon you have. Sloane, you're heading back to the station with Andy and the subject. I need you to keep an eye on her. Watch for further memetic flares, and for the love of the Index, call me if any bears show up."

"Got it," said Sloane, and left the room.

Demi's eyes widened as she watched Sloane go. Swinging her gaze back around to me, she said, "She didn't fight with you. She didn't even flip you off or call you a melanin-deficient bitch."

"You know, they're still slurs when you're just repeating them," I said mildly. Demi promptly flushed a deep red, verging on purple. "Sloane isn't the easiest person to work with. That doesn't actually make her unprofessional. Her job is to figure out where the narratives are going, pinpoint the memetic incursions, and help us stop them. She's very good at what she does."

Demi didn't say anything. She didn't have to. Her dubiousness was written broadly across her face for anyone to see.

"Anyway, this is going to be your first official field action. Don't worry about how many regulations we're breaking. I'll help you do the paperwork when we finish."

Demi's eyes widened. "Paperwork?"

# # #

Even with Andy nudging her steadily along, it took almost ten minutes to get Jennifer into a coat and a pair of shoes and hustle her out the door to the car. I waited until I heard the front door slam, and then moved to the living room to watch them drive away. The van was still parked at the curb. Jeff being Jeff, he might not even have noticed that half of the group had left.

"All right," I said, turning to Demi. "That's your cue."

"You really think this is going to work?"

I smiled thinly. "Never underestimate the power of a good story."

We returned to the bedroom, where the bears had already been seen—and more importantly, where the neighbors were less likely to report strange goings-on to Jennifer when she returned. A Latina girl in a black suit playing the flute was definitely strange by the standards of almost any neighborhood.

The window was surprisingly difficult to open. That was probably a good sign; Jennifer hadn't been unconsciously raising it for the bears while she was asleep. Demi produced her flute from inside her jacket, took a deep breath, and began to play.

It was difficult to describe her music: it was like every good thing in the world all run into a single melody, simple but deceptively complex. The taste of good coffee, so deep and complex that it was almost a crime to describe it by a single name. The sound of rain falling on the pavement, the smell of petrichor and moistened loam. The color of a single raven's feather in the sunlight, rainbows caught in ebony—

I was so absorbed in Demi's song that I didn't even hear the front door open. Jeff came pelting inside, moving as fast as his legs would carry him, with a pair of noise-blocking headphones in his hands. I gave him a dizzied smile, and didn't move away as he clamped the headphones down over my ears.

Demi's song cut off abruptly, replaced by a yearning emptiness. I tried to lift my hands and take the headphones off, but Jeff was too fast for me. He grabbed my wrists, forcing me to stay where I was while his lips formed the word "No." I blinked. He continued to hold my hands, and bit by bit the urge to take the headphones off slipped away, taking the emptiness with it. I blinked again, and stopped trying to raise my hands. That was when he finally let me go.

He turned toward Demi, who was still playing her flute, and said something I couldn't hear. She stopped, lowering the instrument from her lips and staring at him blankly. Jeff flashed her a thumbs-up and removed the earplugs from his own ears before turning back to me.

I took that as a hint and removed the headphones. "What the hell . . . ?"

"I figured you'd try to use Demi to attract the bears—that *was* your goal, wasn't it?" He paused long enough for me to nod before continuing, "What I *didn't* figure was you being dumb enough to do it without ear protection. She's a Pied Piper, Henry, not a birdcall."

"She was playing to attract bears," I protested.

"You're a narrative in abeyance. It doesn't matter what she's playing to attract. And besides that, you didn't get the sheet music for bears." He turned back to Demi. "How are you feeling? Any dizziness, numbness, nausea . . . ?"

"I just played the song that wanted to be played," she said, eyes wide and a little frightened. "I didn't mean to do anything wrong. I'm really sorry. It was an accident."

"Oh, honey." Jeff put his arm around her shoulders, shooting me an aggravated look. "You didn't do anything wrong. Henry's the one who fucked up, not you."

I folded my arms and glared at him, all too aware that my coloring was betraying me once again and displaying the hot blush I could feel rushing into my cheeks. He was right: using Demi as a birdcall was a good idea, but I'd gone about it badly. I should have done more research before jumping straight to the easy solution.

"Although to be fair, your presence is probably influencing the rest of us to think 'oh, hey, call the Piper' at every opportunity, so we'll need to be on guard against that," continued Jeff. "Did we get bears?"

I took a quick look out the window at the backyard, which now held every dog, cat, pigeon, and crow in the neighborhood. But that was all. "No bears," I confirmed. "Is it because we didn't use a bear-specific song?"

"If the bears were close enough to hear Demi playing, they should have come," said Jeff. "And believe me, if they were within a mile of here, they were close enough to hear her playing."

". . . oh, that's great," I said, envisioning all the Lost Dog and Missing Cat posters that would be cropping up in the surrounding neighborhoods. "Is there a song that Demi can play to pipe all of these animals back where they came from?"

"Yes, and I brought it with me," said Jeff, holding up a piece of sheet music.

My face relaxed into a smile. "You're so good to me."

"Remember that when it's time for reviews," he said, and moved to stand next to Demi. "Okay, let's just go over this a few times before you play it—some of the stops can be tricky . . ."

I tuned him out as Demi started nodding. Music isn't my thing, and I wasn't going to understand most of what he said. Puss was twining around my ankles again. I scooped up the cat and deposited it on the bed, moving away from the window in the process. If the massed wildlife outside caught sight of me, there would be a stampede as they tried to claim their places at my side. I may not be a fully manifested Snow White, but there's a point at which that ceases to matter.

Eventually, Jeff signaled for me to put my headphones back on, and Demi raised her flute to her lips, beginning to play a melody that I couldn't hear. I didn't hear the animals leaving the yard either. The headphones blocked out everything . . . including the sound of my phone ringing.

In retrospect, I should probably have put it on vibrate.

# # #

We were walking back to the van, having locked Jennifer's door behind us, when Jeff's phone started to ring. He dug it out of his pocket, answering as we walked. "Hello?"

"Did I do all right?" asked Demi, shooting me an anxious glance.

I nodded. "For your first time in the field, you did incredibly. Most of the mistakes were mine. We'll review them when we get back to the office and finish dealing with our Goldilocks."

"I'm surprised you still make mistakes," she said. Her tone was hesitant, like she expected a reprimand for even saying something.

"The only people who don't make mistakes are the dead ones," I said, and paused, frowning. "Where's Jeff?" We both stopped walking and turned to look behind us. He was standing in the middle of the walkway, the phone still pressed against his ear. All the blood had drained from his face, until he was almost as pale as I was. It wasn't a good look for him.

"Jeff?" I said.

He raised a finger, signaling for me to be quiet. I stopped talking. Demi, standing beside me with a puzzled expression on her face, did the same. Seconds ticked by, until finally Jeff said, "Yes, I see. Yes, we're on our way." He lowered his phone and started power-walking toward the van.

"Jeff?"

He didn't stop. As he blew past us, he called, "There's trouble at the office! We have to move!"

"What kind of trouble?" I demanded, turning around and running after him with Demi at my heels like a large, confused puppy in sensible shoes.

"Bears!"

Well. That explained a few things, even as it created a whole new category of problems. "I'll drive," I said.

# # #

By putting on the siren and breaking every traffic law I came into contact with, I estimated that we would arrive at headquarters in approximately thirty minutes. As I drove, Jeff sat in the back of the van with the Index open on his lap and shouted his findings toward the front: "I have a few variations recorded where Goldilocks didn't initially break into the home of the three bears—they came in *her* home and took it over. Then, when she tried to chase them out, the normal 'larcenous little girl' narrative started to unfold. We're probably looking at one of these home-invasion scenarios."

"But she doesn't live where we work!" protested Demi.

"That's irrelevant," I said, taking a sharp turn without slowing down. It felt like one of the van's wheels lifted off the ground. That probably meant that I should take my foot off the gas, at least a little. I didn't. "The narrative doesn't give a crap about whether it makes sense. The narrative just wants to *happen*. The memetic incursion that's starting around Jennifer Lockwood calls for bears. Apparently, since our office is now where Jennifer is located, that makes it her home, and that's good enough to qualify for bears."

"But that doesn't even make any *sense!*"

In the rearview mirror, I saw Jeff lean over the seat to put a hand on her shoulder. "It does make sense, I promise you, but it's hard to understand at first. You'll get there. What matters right now is that Henry is going to kill us all trying to get back to the office before those bears eat Andy and Jennifer and everyone else in the building."

"What about Sloane?" asked Demi, almost reluctantly.

I snorted. "Do you really think a *bear* can take her out? They should be worried about being locked in with her. They're not used to a story that comes with an actual villain." There was a stop sign up ahead. I tore through it without slowing down, leaving blaring horns in our wake. "Jeff, do you have your gun?"

"Yes, but—"

"Good. Find some bear-fighting music for Demi, something that calms them down without distracting the rest of us. We'll be in the parking lot in five minutes."

"Bear-fighting music—on it," said Jeff, and disappeared from the mirror as he retreated to resume his perusal of the Index.

"I don't like this," said Demi.

"Welcome to the club," I said, and sped up.

# # #

From the outside, it wasn't obvious that the building that housed the ATI Management Bureau belonged to the government. It was unmarked, and there were an unusually high number of security cameras, but those were the only sign that most people would have that anything was unusual about the place. Everything else about it screamed generic office building, probably belonging to some start-up that hadn't bothered to invest in exterior signage yet. That was the way we liked it.

There were no bears in the parking lot when we came roaring through the gate, and there were no people standing outside on the sidewalk. That could be a good sign—they hadn't evacuated the building—or it could be a bad one—they hadn't had *time* to evacuate the building. I parked our van at the curb closest to the entrance, ignoring the fact that it technically wasn't a parking space, and cautiously opened the door.

"Coast looks clear," I said, swinging my legs out of the car. When nothing came roaring out of the bushes to attack me, I got the rest of the way out, drawing my gun in the same motion. Still there were no bears. "Okay, you two, we're moving for the building."

"Do we have to?" asked Jeff.

"*Now*," I snarled.

Demi and Jeff got out of the van.

We made our way down the sidewalk to the front door, only to find it locked from inside. The windows were shuttered. It hadn't been obvious from the parking lot with the midday sun glinting off the glass, but up close, it was clear that we wouldn't be getting any visual clues as to what was happening inside.

"There's a back entrance," murmured Jeff.

"Does it lock down when the alarm is pulled?" I asked.

"It's supposed to, but the circuit doesn't always connect," he said. "I've been asking Maintenance to fix it for months."

"Well then, let's hope they didn't finally decide to start doing their jobs," I said. "Lead the way."

Jeff took us in a counterclockwise circuit around the building, finally ducking behind a scrubby-looking tree and into a narrow alcove. There was a clicking sound, followed by the soft creak of hinges. "We're in," he said.

"Demi, get your flute up," I said. "Let's go."

# # #

Jeff's back entrance let us into a hall that didn't seem to be used for much of anything; it was spotlessly clean, but had that dead-aired quality that only comes from isolation and abandonment. The lights were dim, and I took point as we made our way toward the main building. The hall was straight, and the bullpen and interview rooms were all in front of us. That was convenient. I'm not sure I could have handled a labyrinth under these conditions.

This little unsealed door revealed a massive flaw in our security system—I was going to have Maintenance's ass for this. Once lockdown began, once a narrative was loose and live in the building, the agency was supposed to become impregnable. Well, we hadn't worked all that hard, and we were inside.

Worrying about security was a matter for another time. Right now, we had bears to deal with.

We were almost to the interior door when sounds began filtering through the thick, blast-reinforced steel. Alarms: someone had triggered the internal lockdown system, and it was making sure everyone knew about it. And screams. They were softer than the amplified alarms, but they were somewhat harder to ignore.

Jeff tapped me on the shoulder. I turned, and he offered me a pair of earmuffs.

"Demi's almost certainly going to need to play," he said. "There's nothing we'll need to hear in there that we won't be able to pick up through visual cues."

"I'm not so sure about that," I said, but took the earmuffs, making sure that they were firmly in place before I looked back to my teammates, nodding once, and hauling the door open.

We stepped through into chaos. Red light bathed everything, and screams came intermittently from behind closed doors, loud enough to be audible even through my earmuffs. No one moved in the wreckage of the bullpen. I motioned Jeff and Demi forward, and we picked our way into the open, heading for the hall that would lead us to the interview rooms. That was the most likely place for Sloane and Andy to have taken our unwitting Goldilocks, which would make it the epicenter of the bear attacks.

We were halfway there when a bear lunged out of the space between two filing cabinets, teeth bared and claws reaching for my throat. I had time for one dizzied moment of introspection—*How the hell did a bear even fit in there?*—before the business of keeping myself and my teammates alive took priority. I fired three bullets into the bear's face. It dissipated like smoke, wisping away into nothing but a burning smell and the memory of terror.

"Ghost bears," I snarled. "Oh, that's just perfect."

I turned. Demi was staring with wide, frightened eyes at the place where the phantom bear had been. Her flute was in her shaking hands.

"Play something!" I shouted.

She shook her head and mouthed something that looked like "But Jeff didn't—"

"Just play!"

Demi nodded, raised her flute, and began to play.

More bears emerged from the shadows and the thin spaces between the walls and the furnishings. They came in every size and type imaginable—even koalas, which aren't actually bears. They lumbered and they raced and they were coming right for us.

Jeff and I took up positions to either side of Demi, shooting at the phantom bears as they came toward us. Only one bullet seemed to be required to dissipate the smaller ones; the big ones, the grizzlies and the Kodiaks, took two or three. I paused twice to reload. Jeff fired more slowly, and he covered for me whenever I was unable to shoot. The whole time, we continued down the hall, making our way step after step toward the interview room.

We were almost there when the door slammed open and Sloane crashed out into the hall, a fireplace poker in her hand. The incongruous nature of her weapon aside, it was effective; she slashed it through the three nearest bears, opening a path for the three of us. "Come on!" she snarled, lips moving in an exaggerated fashion as she tried to make herself understood despite our earmuffs.

She didn't have to tell us twice. We rushed past her into the interview room, Demi piping all the while. Sloane slammed the door behind us. Andy and Jennifer were there: Andy with his gun drawn and his eyes on the door; Jennifer facedown on the table and apparently unconscious.

"Report," I said, pulling my earmuffs down and letting them dangle around my neck. "What the hell happened?"

"She said she needed a nap, and as soon as she closed her eyes, bears," said Sloane. She shot a glare at Jennifer. "We've been trying to wake her up. Bitch sleeps like the dead. And stop that!" She transferred her glare to Demi. "We don't need more bears, okay? We have plenty of fucking bears. There is *no* room at the inn."

Demi lowered her pipe, looking guilty.

"Okay," I said. "So she's finishing her story at this point. She's gotten so far along that she's going to complete. Jeff?"

"Most variations, the bears wake Goldilocks up and she runs away, never to trouble them again," he said. I started to relax. He continued: "In others, the bears rip her to pieces as a warning to anyone else who might try breaking into their home."

"Fuck," I muttered. "Andy? Sloane? Did the bears actually hurt anyone when they showed up?"

"At least three people dead, possibly more by now," said Andy. "We locked ourselves in here, since this is the epicenter."

"And we didn't shoot her because ghost bears don't necessarily fuck off when you kill their Goldilocks," added Sloane. "We could just wind up haunted."

"Ghosts are real?" demanded Demi.

There was a moment of silence, save for the distant sirens, as we all turned and looked at Demi. Finally, Jeff said, "Magic is real. Ghosts come with the package. It's just that the narrative is usually more subtle than this. It doesn't want to be seen, because it doesn't want to be stopped. Ghost bears aren't something you can overlook under normal circumstances."

"What do we do?" asked Andy. "We could throw her out of the building, but that won't stop the bears. It'll just move them into an unprepared populace."

There are rarely easy answers when there are fairy tales involved. Still . . . "The bears came into her yard, but they never entered her home," I said. "They're sticking to the story, at least to a certain degree. How is it supposed to end?"

"They wake her up, they scare the pants off of her, and she promises never to break into a stranger's house again," said Jeff. "Or, as I mentioned before, she gets eaten."

"Okay," I said. "This is what we're going to do . . ."

# # #

Demi, Sloane, and I had nearly been tagged as Jennifer's bears, before we shunted the narrative and caused a ghost bear invasion. So now it was the three of us who stood in front of her, separated only by the table. "Now, Sloane," I said.

"Who's that sleeping in my bed?" Sloane boomed, and emptied the pitcher of water in her hand over Jennifer's head. Jennifer sat up with a gasp, eyes wide, wet hair slicked back and sticking to her neck and cheeks.

"Wh-what—"

"We'll ask the questions here," Sloane snarled. "Who told you to make that prank call to 911? Don't you understand that this is no laughing matter?"

"Couldn't it at least have been funnier?" asked Demi stiffly, like she was having trouble remembering her lines.

"Bears," I scoffed. "As if."

Jennifer looked at each of us in turn, starting to shake. "I didn't . . . I mean, I was . . ."

"We've searched your neighborhood, Miss Lockwood," Demi said. "There are no bears there. Did you call us because you had a bad dream? There are laws against this sort of thing."

"We should lock her up," said Sloane. "Make an example."

"We should let her go," I said. "Show mercy."

"What's going to stop her from doing the exact same thing the next time she has a nightmare?" Demi demanded. "No, punishment is the only answer."

Somehow, Demi's tone made the words sound just right. "I won't do it again, I swear!" Jennifer leaned across the table, grabbing for my hands. "Please, believe me. I didn't mean to do anything wrong. Please!"

The three of us looked at her solemnly, but inside, I think that we were all smiling.

# # #

Andy drove Jennifer home. The bears were gone; they had disappeared as soon as Jennifer apologized. Maintenance was already working on the back door, and EMTs were swarming in the halls, helping those who had been wounded by the ghost bears and collecting the bodies of the fallen. I, and the rest of my team, wound up sitting in the interview room, waiting to be debriefed.

"You realize that poor woman will have psychological issues and a fear of authority after this," said Jeff.

"Narrative never plays nicely with any of us," I said.

"Still . . ."

"We did what we had to do. What we'll always do. We stopped the story before it could get to ever after." I shook my head. "Better a few ruined lives than an entire ruined world."

Silence fell between us. For once, none of us had anything left to say.

Blended Family

Memetic incursion in progress: tale type 315 ("The Treacherous Sister")
Status: UNRESOLVED/AVERTED

Everything was too loud and everything hurt.

Sloane Winters peeled her eyelids open through a combination of Herculean effort and pure spite. Something had to be making that horrible clanging, roaring noise that was ripping through her head and setting her teeth on edge. She was going to find it, and she was going to kill it. Once it was good and dead, she might even bury it in the backyard, just so that she could have the privilege of dancing on its grave. Then, and only then, would she be able to go blissfully back to sleep, no longer harassed by uninvited shrieks from beyond.

The noise stopped as soon as her eyes were open.

"What the . . ." Sloane caught herself before the curse could pass her lips. Instead, she sat up and ran her fingers through her tangled, bleach-fried hair. She hit a knot and winced as new pain was added to the existing pain left behind by the infernal clanging. When she had been sitting long enough to be sure that her head wasn't going to fall off and roll around the room, she straightened, looking around with narrowed eyes.

Everything seemed to be normal. The birdcage in the corner was still covered, which eliminated one possible source of the din. Lovecraft was not a quiet bird, but like all parrots, he truly believed that it was nighttime when he couldn't see the light—or at least he pretended to believe that, and Sloane, who was anxious to coexist with *something* she didn't want to kill, allowed him to think that he was fooling her.

The walls were covered in a thick layer of posters, flyers, and bumper stickers. It looked more like a sixteen-year-old's bedroom than the domicile of a grown woman, but what did that matter? Not even Sloane herself was quite sure how old she was. Too many years had been lost in the struggle to evade her story. Those years were never coming back, and if she felt safer in her nest of teenage rebellion and outdated angst, then no one was going to convince her that she should do anything differently.

She was cautiously stretching one leg toward the floor, preparing to slide out of the bed, when the shrieking roar began again. Sloane clapped her hands over her ears and screamed, the sound swallowed by the greater scream of whatever was invading her privacy. She thought she heard Lovecraft squawking under the noise, but couldn't be sure; she couldn't move under the weight of that painful din.

As the unseen sirens clamored on, Sloane Winters collapsed back onto her bed, clamping her hands down until her nails scratched her scalp hard enough to draw blood, and waited for the noise to stop.

# # #

ATI Management Bureau Headquarters

"Where's Sloane?"

I stopped in the process of putting my bag down on my desk chair, frowning at Andy. "What do you mean, 'where's Sloane?' Is this a trick question? And have we cancelled 'good morning' for the foreseeable future? I was never overly fond of it to begin with, but it's a ritual thing, and I do appreciate a good ritual."

Andy crossed his arms and glared at me. Being more than a foot taller than I was, with shoulders like a linebacker and the sort of craggy, determined face that was designed for either male modeling or law enforcement, he did so excellently. Andy was such a champion glarer that Jeff had been known to spend entire afternoons trying to goad him into a good glare. Most of the time, it worked. Andy was a friendly man who believed in doing his job, and doing it well. But that didn't grant him infinite patience—and thank Grimm for that. If he'd been smart, athletic, good-looking, *and* a saint, I would probably have been forced to shove him into the path of an oncoming story just on general principle.

"I mean, where is Agent Sloane Winters, who was supposed to be here an hour ago?" he said. "Her computer hasn't been turned on. She isn't in the office."

My frown deepened. I finished putting my bag down, removed my sunglasses, and asked, "Did she have today off? Maybe this is one of her weird Sloane-specific holidays, like Australia Day, or National Cotton Candy Day."

Sloane's part in the narrative had been averted sometime before I'd joined the Bureau, and she had been living a normal, if angry and maladjusted, life ever since then. Part of her conception of "normal" included a flat refusal to live by any social convention that even smacked of story. Sloane worked on Christmas and stayed home on April Fools' Day, which she celebrated—last I checked—by carving faces into cantaloupes and inviting the local kids to smash them with hammers.

The door opened. Andy and I both turned, only to pause and frown again when we saw that the figure slipping into the bullpen was Demi Santos, and not Sloane. Demi blinked at us as she approached her desk. "Why are you both staring at me?" she asked, her trepidation visible in her face. "Did I forget about a meeting?" She blanched, her complexion taking on a distinct waxy undertone. "Is there an incursion?"

"Dispatch hasn't alerted us to anything, and no, there wasn't a meeting," I said, shaking my head. "We just hoped that you'd be Sloane, that's all."

"You hoped I'd be . . . Sloane." Demi raised an eyebrow. "Under what circumstances, ever, in this universe, would you hope that *anyone* was Sloane?"

"Our lovely young Miss Winters is probably relieved to wake up every morning and find that she remains Sloane, rather than becoming the nameless antagonist in some larger narrative," said Jeff, stepping out from behind a filing cabinet. I managed not to jump. It was a near thing. Not even years of dealing with our resident archivist's tendency to appear out of nowhere had rendered me completely immune to the surprise of it.

Demi laughed. "I guess that's true," she admitted. "I'm pretty happy to wake up in the morning and still be me."

"There you are. A good morning to you, Agent Santos, and to you, Agent Robinson, and to you, Agent Marchen." Jeff accompanied each greeting with a nod to the appropriate person. When he got to me, I smiled. He smiled back. Jeff was one of the few people I knew who wasn't disturbed by the contrast of too-red lips with too-white skin. A true Snow White looks more like a horror movie than a fairy tale come true, but Jeff always treated me like I was myself, nothing more or less than that. It was nice. In my own way, I was just as happy to wake up as Henry every morning as Sloane and Demi were to wake up as themselves, our respective stories aside.

"Morning, Jeff," I said. "We were just wondering if Sloane had the day off. We were a little surprised not to find her here waiting when we all got to the office."

"She left at her usual hour last night, and she hasn't been in yet today," said Jeff, a crease appearing between his eyebrows as he pursed his lips in concentration. "The duty roster posted in the break room has her on active for the entire week. I'm sure I would have noticed if she had a day off in the middle."

"I believe you," I said. As a five-oh-three, Jeff was a born archivist whose attention to detail bordered on the obsessive—if he said that something was so, then it was so, no argument needed. I wasn't certain, but I was reasonably sure he lived in the office, sleeping in one of the supply closets that were supposedly not in use. He left sometimes, but he always came back, and he was always in when we needed him.

It didn't bother me. Whatever it takes to get through the day and survive your story, that's what you've got to do.

"Should we call her at home?" asked Demi. "Could something have happened to her?"

"Things don't happen to Sloane," said Andy. "Sloane happens to things."

"Please don't start making Chuck Norris jokes," I said, turning to face Andy. "Still, we should check. I'll go up to Dispatch, see if Birdie can raise her. Sloane won't be happy about it, but she's less likely to get violent if the call comes from someone whose job is knowing where we all are."

Andy looked relieved. "Would you, Henry? I don't like to admit it, but I'm worried about her."

"I don't like to admit it either, but thanks to you guys, now I'm worried too. I'm on my way." I paused long enough to unclip my badge from my purse strap and clip it to my lapel, and offered the rest of my team members a little wave as I turned and started back toward the stairs.

Even when I'm not out in the field, it sometimes seems like a field commander's work is never done.

# # #

Memetic incursion in progress: tale type 315 ("The Treacherous Sister")
Status: UNRESOLVED/UNDETERMINED

The noise had stopped long enough for Sloane to empty the top drawer of her dresser out onto the floor, pawing through the tangle of torn fishnets, worn-out bras, and mismatched socks until she found the pair of earmuffs she'd been issued when they had that Snow Queen incident to clean up in Ann Arbor. She clamped them down over her ears, letting out a sigh of relief when even the small ambient noises of the room stopped. They might not hold against a full-on aural assault, but they would at least let her keep her wits long enough to get dressed and get out.

"Someone's going to die," she announced to the room, as she staggered back to her feet. Her knees were still shaking, and her head spun with every motion. Hands out to help her hold her balance, she made her way to Lovecraft's cage and pulled off the sheet that covered it.

Lovecraft, looking as affronted as it was possible for a Black Palm Cockatoo to look—which was remarkably affronted, thanks to the years they'd spent together—opened his beak, emitting what was doubtless a deafening screech.

"Sorry, dude, but you don't want to be in here right now," said Sloane, opening the cage door and sticking out her arm. "Come on. I'm moving you to the aviary cage."

Lovecraft screeched again before resentfully stepping onto her arm. Sloane smiled.

"For once, you fail in your 'make me go deaf' campaign," she said. "I'm wearing earmuffs. Neener-neener."

Lovecraft responded by sidling up her arm to her shoulder, where he began nibbling on her hair in a grooming motion that was as soothing as it was familiar. Sloane moved away from the cage, grabbing the clothes she'd laid out the night before— thank God for Internet housekeeping advice sites, or she'd be pawing through her closet while she waited for the sirens to resume.

"Momma's going to commit a murder today," she said conversationally, tucking her bundled clothing up under her arm as she started for the door. "That's right. I'm going to find whoever woke me up, and I'm going to rip out their heart and show it to them before they have a chance to finish dropping dead. Won't that be nice, sweetie? Won't that be nice and bloody?"

Unheard, Lovecraft screeched.

# # #

ATI Management Bureau Headquarters

Most of the building that housed the ATI Management Bureau was old wood and older design, like a stage set transported from the 1970s—which was, not coincidentally, when the building had been originally constructed. The Dispatch Unit was a science-fiction dream, all chrome, glass, and unnecessarily streamlined plastic fittings. I always felt like I was leaving a hard-boiled crime drama and stepping into something with starships and empires when I had to visit the dispatchers in their home territory. Still, "we may have misplaced our Wicked Stepsister, do you think you could give her a ring for us" wasn't the sort of question I felt comfortable asking over the phone.

Three of the dispatch desks were occupied when I arrived. Two of the dispatchers were hard at work, coordinating their own field teams as they investigated possible incursions by the narrative responsible for fairy tales and folklore the world over. Human belief focused the narrative, and in our modern age of mass-produced DVDs and endless television reruns, incursions were becoming more and more common.

The third dispatcher, a small, round-faced woman with fluffy blonde hair and thick-lensed glasses, was leaning back in her chair and staring thoughtfully up at the exposed steel beams of the ceiling. I walked over to her desk, crossed my arms, and waited.

People wind up in Dispatch after they've been touched somehow by the Aarne-Thompson Index spectrum, but have failed to show the reflexes and capabilities for fieldwork. Most people expected Jeff to go into Dispatch, given both his nature and his narrative. He surprised them all when he wound up in the field. Birdie Hubbard surprised no one when she chose a nice, safe desk job.

After standing patiently and waiting to be noticed for more than a minute, I cleared my throat. Birdie jumped in her chair, knocking over a coffee cup full of pencils and nearly sending herself on a quick trip to the floor. I started to step forward to help her, and paused as she grabbed the edge of the desk.

"Not going to fall?" I asked carefully.

"A-Agent Marchen!" she said, half gasping for air. "You startled me!"

"I got that when you tried to teach yourself how to fly," I said, taking a careful step back, into my original position. "Are you okay now?"

"I am, yes. How long have you been standing there?"

"Not long." I shook my head. "Have you heard anything from Sloane this morning? She hasn't checked in for work, and we're concerned about her."

Birdie blinked guileless blue eyes behind the magnifying lenses of her glasses, and asked, "Did you try calling her at home?"

"This is Sloane we're talking about. We decided that Dispatch would be less likely to invoke her undying wrath."

That earned me a chirpy giggle. "I guess that's true," Birdie admitted. "How is she doing with her story? I know she's been in abeyance for a long, long time now."

The fact was, none of us knew exactly when Sloane's exposure to the narrative had occurred. She predated every other member of the team, and given the spectrum's ability to influence people's genetic makeup—witness my coloring—there was no reason not to believe that it could keep someone frozen at a particular age if it really wanted to. "She's Sloane," I said, with a shrug. "She does her Sloane things, and we try not to encourage her to kill us. She's mostly stopped threatening to jam Demi's flute down her throat, so I guess she's been having a good couple of weeks. Can you call her house now?"

"Sure." Birdie swung back toward her computer, only to pause, blinking. "But there's no need, really."

I frowned. "Why not?"

"Because she just used her badge at the front door. I— Agent Marchen?"

I didn't stop to find out what else Birdie was going to say. I just kept walking toward the exit. When I was halfway there, I broke into a run. I didn't know why, and I didn't question it. I just knew that I needed to get to Sloane, fast.

# # #

Memetic incursion in progress: tale type 315 ("The Treacherous Sister")
Status: UNDETERMINED/UNDETERMINED

Settling Lovecraft in the aviary cage had been easy. He didn't like getting off Sloane's shoulder, but he was easily bribed with a thick slice of mango, which he accepted with all the gravity of a king being given his crown. Once he was safely locked inside the larger cage, Sloane stripped off her nightshirt, dropping it carelessly on the living room floor, and pulled the rest of her clothing roughly on, ignoring the wide picture window to her left. She was giving the backyard a show. Let anyone who might be standing out there look. She'd get them back for staring at her soon enough. She'd—

Sloane shook her head, almost hard enough to dislodge her earmuffs. "Don't think that way," she muttered, taking comfort mostly in the way her lips shaped the old, familiar words. It didn't matter whether she could hear them or not. They were out there in the world, and that was what really mattered, at least according to the therapists employed by the ATI Management Bureau. They were quacks, every single one of them, but they'd prevented her from going on a murderous rampage thus far, and that made them quacks that she was willing to listen to.

For now.

Her coworkers would have been surprised by the size and airiness of her house. Henry had seen the gatehouse a few times, when Sloane didn't feel like riding the bus home after work, but Henry had never been inside, and she'd certainly never realized that Sloane lived in the big house on the other side of the overgrown lawn. It was safer that way. Better to keep your cards hidden until it was time to put them on the table; better to know that your haven was actually a haven, and not just one more way station on the way to an inevitable fairy-tale demise.

Sloane was aware that this was just one more example of "thinking like an antagonist," something she had been regularly coached against by the Bureau quacks. In this one instance, she didn't care. Princesses had towers, right? Keeping your sanctuary safe didn't *have* to be a wicked thing to do. It could just be pragmatic.

"And if the good guys can't be pragmatic, I wanna be there when they burn Henry at the stake," she said, yanking her boots on. Only silence greeted her. Slowly, cautiously, she reached up and tugged the earmuffs away from her ears. Maybe it—whatever it was—was finally over, and she could—

The sound was practically a physical assault this time, hitting so hard and so fast that it drove her to her knees. It seemed to bounce back and forth inside her skull, magnifying in that confined space until it was enough to make her stomach turn over. The earmuffs had fallen to the floor a few feet away. Sloane collapsed forward, stretching one shaking hand toward them.

She had almost caught hold of the band when the pain became too much, and she blacked out completely.

# # #

ATI Management Bureau Headquarters

I managed to catch up to Sloane in the main hallway, while she was still trying to get her key card back into the tiny, coffin-shaped box that she continued to pretend was a purse. One small mercy: her desire not to have any of us looking at her stuff meant the little coffin was a black one, rather than a clear one that she could taunt me with on a daily basis.

"Sloane! Wait up!"

She stopped walking, her chunky boots making a clomping sound on the cheap floorboards. "I'm not in the mood today, Henrietta," she said.

There was something wrong with her voice. She had never been the most vivacious of people, but there was normally a sort of energy to her words, a thick chain of braided resentment and hope lurking just under the surface. Today, she sounded . . . flat, like all that energy had been yanked right out of her. "Agent Winters?" I said, cautiously.

"I told you, I'm not in the mood." She turned to face me, scowling. "My fucking fire alarm broke this morning. It's been blaring for the last hour. Does that count as me checking in with the boss, or do you need me to fill out some forms in triplicate?"

"Oh, hell, Sloane, I'm sorry," I said quickly, using the socially acceptable sympathy to cover my shock. Sloane—who was normally the most invested in her personal appearance, even if her particular fashion choices weren't ones that I would have made—looked like hell. Her short plaid skirt was wrinkled, and there was a run in the knee of one black tight, showing the pale, sun-deprived skin underneath. She was wearing a rumpled red hoodie over a black T-shirt with a glittery apple appliqued on the front. It was tugged up at the hem, and she didn't have the matching, glaringly offensive red apple jewelry that she always wore with that shirt.

Her hair was an uncombed snarl—and what's worse, she didn't have any makeup on. Her muddy hazel eyes were devoid of their customary rings of protective kohl and shadow, and her lips were only a few shades darker than the skin around them.

She followed my gaze, naked lip curving upward in a reassuringly familiar sneer. "I'm *so* sorry if I'm offending your sensibilities right now. Some of us didn't get narratives that came complete with a permanent makeover, okay? I'll put my face on when I get to my desk."

"Get some coffee first," I advised. Technically, she wasn't supposed to spend work time doing things like fussing with her cosmetics. Under the circumstances, there was no way that I was going to report her. "You look like you could use it."

There was an almost palpable beat and then, much to my surprise, Sloane's mouth relaxed into something that could almost have been mistaken for the shadow of a smile. "I'll do that," she said.

"Okay," I said.

"Okay," she echoed, and turned to continue on her way.

I remained where I was for a few more seconds, trying to process the situation, before turning on my heel and making a beeline back toward Dispatch.

The ATI Management Bureau is such a small government agency that we have virtually no budget for anything that doesn't involve saving lives, which includes facilities. Instead of having a specially designed headquarters suited to our needs, we were crammed into a labyrinthine old medical building, which was frequently aggravating . . . until one of us needed a shortcut.

Sloane would go to the break-room kitchen for coffee, because the break-room kitchen always had better stuff than the individual kitchenettes scattered around the building. By cutting through Dispatch, I could beat her back to the bullpen and warn the others that she'd had a particularly hard morning. Sloane didn't like it when we talked about her behind her back, but under the circumstances, I was willing to risk a little displeasure. Anything to keep her from biting Demi's head off over nothing.

Birdie looked up as I came blowing past. "We've got a three-ten forming downtown," she said. "I was just about to call it in to your team. Are you ready for fieldwork?"

A three-ten was a Rapunzel. I have no idea how they keep happening, given the incredible specificity of the narrative that they have to work with, but still, they crop up a lot more frequently than I like. I had to make the call.

"Call it in to Andy," I said, only slowing down a little as I spoke to her. "He'll start scrambling the supplies, and we'll be ready to roll in ten."

"Got it," said Birdie, turning her attention back to her computer.

Sloane would understand. Maybe she'd even appreciate the chance to get straight to work. After all, idle hands are the devil's playthings, and given the way she'd looked at me when she first turned around in the hall, Sloane needed something to keep her hands from going idle.

# # #

Memetic incursion in progress: tale type 315 ("The Treacherous Sister")
Status: UNDETERMINED

Everything was too loud and everything hurt. Again.

This time, when Sloane managed to peel her eyelids open, she was greeted with a distant thread of familiarity buried underneath the alarm bells that were ringing in her head: Lovecraft was screeching and rattling the bars of his cage, apparently in a panic.

"Stupid . . . bird . . ." she muttered, grabbing the earmuffs and shoving them down over her ears. All sound immediately stopped. She staggered to her feet, practically lurching across the room as she made her way back to the birdcage. "Hush, big guy. Hush."

The black-winged parrot continued to flap and flail, beak opening again and again in protests that she couldn't hear anymore. The sound had to be upsetting him as much as it was upsetting her, maybe more, even. He couldn't shut it out the way she could. He was smart, for a bird, but even the smartest bird couldn't understand something like this.

"Lovecraft, sweetie, hush," she said, hoping that he could hear her under the din. He kept flapping. Sloane grimaced. If she wanted to calm him down, she needed to hear what kind of noises he was making. Unlike many parrots, Lovecraft had never bothered learning more than a few words, preferring to express himself through a variety of unholy screeches and ghostly whistles. Cautiously, she reached up and tugged one earmuff aside. The sound of a parrot in the middle of a full-blown fit promptly assaulted her already bruised eardrums. Lovecraft was unhappy, and he was going to make damn sure she knew it.

There was no unholy roar filling the room, no horrible noise without a source. The only horrible noise she could hear was coming from her parrot.

"Hey," she snapped. "Be *quiet*."

With one final indignant whistle, Lovecraft stopped. He turned his head to the side, looking at her with one eye, and raised his crest to half-mast in what she had learned to interpret as the equivalent of a teenager folding his arms and sulking. Except for a certain ruffled look around the edges, he seemed perfectly normal.

A horrible thought was starting to creep around the edges of her mind, slowed down by the headache but still finding its inexorable way toward the forefront of her thoughts. "You didn't even hear the noise, did you, buddy?" she asked. "You were just upset because I fell down. I control the mango slices. I'm not supposed to fall down."

Lovecraft whistled long and low. It was such a *normal* sound that it brought tears to her eyes. Of course he hadn't heard anything strange. He was just a parrot, and she was . . .

She was . . .

Sloane barely remembered to grab her purse off the table next to the front door as she ran out of the house. She needed to get to the office. She needed to get away from Lovecraft, and from her things, and from her neighbors, who were perfectly nice people, even if she generally professed to hate their guts.

She needed to get away from all the things that she might hurt. She needed to be around people who would be able to stop her.

# # #

ATI Management Bureau Headquarters

The word from Dispatch beat me back to the bullpen; ah, the wonders of modern technology. Jeff and Andy were already packing the field kit for a three-ten when I came thumping down the stairs and announced, "Sloane's in the building. She's getting coffee now, and then I'm going to ask her if she wants to come with us."

Jeff straightened, giving me a perplexed look. "What do you mean, ask her if she wants to come? She's at work, this is a field excursion, she should be prepared to do her job. If she can't do her job, she should have used a sick day."

Sloane hadn't used a sick day since I'd joined the Bureau, and I didn't think she'd used them before I joined. I shook the comment off, saying, "She's had a rough morning is all. We should probably take it easy on her."

"How rough?" asked Jeff, as he slid a book into his bag. The laws of physics said that the book shouldn't have been able to fit in there. It disappeared without so much as rippling the fabric.

"Rough enough that I'm telling you we need to go easy," I said firmly. "Jeff, do you have sheet music for Demi, or are we going to wing this one?"

Demi looked alarmed by the thought of "winging it." Luckily for her, Jeff nodded and said, "I've got something that should help us out."

"Good." I didn't ask what kind of music you used on a girl with hair extensions and mommy issues; he didn't volunteer the information. Of such silences are good working relationships made.

There was a slam behind me. We all turned to see Sloane come stomping into the room with the largest coffee cup in our kitchen clutched firmly in her hands: a novelty mug someone had brought back from Disneyland with Grumpy—as in the dwarf—blazoned on the side. The scowl on her face dared us to so much as crack a smile. I bit the inside of my cheek to prevent myself from doing precisely that. Normally, nothing about dwarves will make me laugh. Seeing Sloane with that cup was enough to make me want to start.

"Why do we even have that cup?" asked Andy. "Isn't it a little on the nose?"

"I will kill you all and feast upon your hearts," snarled Sloane, and stomped past us to her desk. She paused halfway there, eyeing the field bags. "Are we going somewhere?"

"There's a three-ten starting up; we're going to stop it," I said. "I was going to ask if you felt up to coming along."

"It's my damn job, isn't it?" She gulped back half of her coffee in a single long gulp before slamming the mug down on her desk so hard that for a moment, I was afraid she'd broken it. Amazingly, the cup kept it together—which wasn't something I was sure I could say about Sloane. She didn't explode on us though, simply growling, "I can put my eyeliner on in the car. Let's go fuck up a fairy tale."

# # #

Memetic incursion in progress: tale type 315 ("The Treacherous Sister")
Status: UNDETERMINED

The sound didn't come back as Sloane was staggering down the pathway to the street, or if it did, her earmuffs blessedly prevented her from hearing it. She made her way past the gatehouse, and from there to the bus stop, where she slouched onto the bench, knees together, feet splayed, and bent forward until her forehead rested on the cottony material of her tights. She had no idea what was going on, but she hated it.

She hated everything.

The thought was like an eel moving through the silt that clouded her mind, flashing by so fast that it barely registered. But it left clouds of angry, puzzled loathing in its wake, churning up resentments so old that she'd believed them safely dead and buried. How dare the universe do something like this to her, when it had already done so many other horrible things? The people she worked with thought she was a bitch—they had no idea. They had no idea how hard it was to be her, caught in the claws of a story that told her to be wicked, that told her to be cruel. She tried to turn those impulses into affectations, choosing rudeness over actual evil, but it was *hard*, it was so hard, and they never gave her an inch of credit.

Well, why should they? Their stories were all sunny ones, full of saviors and sorcery. Not like hers, which was blood and betrayal, all the way down to its bones. They still believed in happy endings. None of them knew how hard she struggled every day not to slit their throats.

Sloane was so deep in her own misery that she barely heard the hydraulic growl of the bus pulling up to the curb in front of her. A few seconds later, a hand touched her shoulder. "Miss Winters? Are you all right?"

Kill him kill him for touching you how dare he how dare he, doesn't he know who you are?

But he *did* know who she was—he'd called her by name. Sloane forced her head up and met the eyes of the bus driver who'd been picking her up at least three times a week for the last eight years. He never commented on how she seemed to stay frozen in the same protracted adolescence; she never yelled at him or threatened to call his superiors and have him fired over some imaginary infraction. She didn't know his first name, but she supposed that he was a friend, inasmuch as she could have friends.

Swallowing the rage that threatened to overwhelm her, Sloane lifted her head and offered him a wan smile. "I ate something I shouldn't have last night, and got food poisoning for my sins," she said. "I'm fine. Thanks for stopping for me."

The bus driver's eyes flicked to her ears. Sloane raised one hand to touch the earmuffs, which were sitting slightly askew. She must have knocked them out of place when she put her head down, and that was how she'd been able to hear the bus arriving and the driver saying her name.

"I was cold," she said, a brief flare of anger only half-buried under the words. *How dare he question her?* The fact that he hadn't said a thing didn't seem to make a difference.

Whatever he saw in her eyes, he didn't care for it much. Looking nervous now, the driver took a step backward before he asked, "Are you going to ride with us today, Miss Winters? I need to get back to my route."

It was harder this time to swallow her anger; it took an effort that was almost physical. Finally though, she managed to push it all the way down and forced herself to nod. "I am," she said. "Thank you." She didn't say anything else as she followed him to the bus. She didn't trust the words that might come out of her mouth. Instead, she slunk to her seat and tried to pretend that the other passengers weren't looking at her the way that mice look at a snake that has suddenly slithered into their den.

She would get to the office, where her colleagues were, and her headache would go away, and everything would be fine. Everything had to be fine.

She still reached up and moved her earmuffs back into place. Just in case.

# # #

Memetic incursion in progress: tale type 310 ("Rapunzel")
Status: IN PROGRESS

The latest Rapunzel to haunt our fair city was the adopted daughter of the woman who owned the local organic grocery. If we really dug into her past, we'd probably discover that her birth parents had lived nearby when she was born, and that they'd either owed money to the woman who adopted her, or had been somehow guilty of shoplifting. That was how it worked with the Rapunzels, little girls becoming the payment for a few stolen heads of lettuce. It was a ludicrous way of measuring value. The narrative didn't care.

This girl was named Holly. She had a medical condition that kept her from leaving her room very often, and had decided when she was eleven that she would grow her hair out until she won the world record. The neighbors had been calling her "Rapunzel" for years, turning it into some sort of local joke.

"Why don't we hear about these 'local jokes' before somebody's about to get hurt?" I demanded, casting a glare at Jeff. He put his hands up.

"Hey, don't shoot the messenger," he said. "I'm just the guy who went and talked to people when you said we needed to know what was going on."

"What *is* going on?" asked Demi. "We're just standing out here staring at this poor girl's window. Shouldn't we be talking to her, or . . . something? I don't understand what good we think we're going to do out here."

"The easiest way to avert a Rapunzel is to cut her hair off, but that leaves you open to be recast as the wicked witch if the narrative can get a good grip on you," said Andy. "That's why we don't just hand Sloane a pair of scissors when something like this comes up."

"There are a lot of issues with the three-tens," I said. "First off, a lot of the time, the poor kids who wind up cast as 'princes' get thrown out of second-story windows and permanently maimed. There have been reports of Rapunzels who sunk so deep into their stories that they actually could cure blindness with their tears, but we haven't had one of those in years, and it's not company policy to let unmonitored memetic incursions progress to that level."

"What Henry means is that we can't leave this poor girl trapped in the story even if something *does* happen to her boyfriend," said Andy. "She'd have to be homeless for at least a year, and give birth while she was out on the street. Even if we thought that was a humane way to treat a sheltered teenager, she wouldn't survive it. She has kidney trouble. That's why her mother has kept her isolated like this—she needs regular dialysis just to stay alive."

"Why the hell did the narrative target her, then?" I put my hands on my hips, glaring up at her window. "She should have been too fragile to make a good victim."

"Oh, right, because the narrative cares so damn much about all the lives it ruins," snarled Sloane. She was looking more like herself now that she had her face on, but there was still a waxy undercast to her skin, making her look sick and drawn. "Did it give a fuck when it turned you into the lost Queen of the Emo Kids? Because it sure didn't give a fuck when it decided to hammer into me."

"Much as I hate to admit it, Sloane has a point," said Andy. "The narrative may just have seen her as a weak spot. It doesn't have to finish every story it starts. It just needs to find a way to widen the cracks in the world."

"That's what we're here to prevent," I said, trying to pull the discussion back on course. "Does anybody have a suggestion?"

"Yeah," said Sloane. "Me." Before I could stop her, she shoved her way between Demi and Jeff and went storming toward the closed, locked door of the grocery. The rest of us stood frozen for a moment—long enough for Sloane to begin hammering her fist against the door.

"What the *hell* is she doing?" I ran after her.

Not fast enough. The door opened, revealing Holly's mother. She was a tall, broad-shouldered woman who had obviously been crying. "We're closed," she said.

"Your daughter needs you to be a rational damn human being," replied Sloane. "Pull your head out of your ass and stop making empty threats. So she's pregnant. So what? Sick people have babies all the damn time. *Steel Magnolias* stopped being relevant years ago. You sit down and you talk to her about what she wants to do, and then you talk to the boyfriend, and you find a way to get all three of you through this."

"I—what?" Holly's mother stared at Sloane. I did much the same. I couldn't even find the words to ask her what she was trying to pull.

Sloane continued to glare. "If you don't make this right, then you're going to lose her forever. Do you get that, or do I need to draw a diagram to hammer it through your thick-ass skull? You'll become the wicked witch in her private fairy tale, and even if she lives, she'll never love you again. You're so close right now. You're so close that I can *smell* it. Is that what you want?"

Holly's mother was silent.

Sloane took a step forward, eyes blazing. "*Is it?*" she screamed.

"No!" Holly's mother put up her hands as if to ward Sloane off, shaking her head at the same time. "No, of course not! She's my daughter and I love her, no matter what!"

"Good. Then you go and tell her that, and tell her you're thrilled as shit by the chance to be a grandmother, even if you wish she'd made things clear a little sooner." Sloane took a step back. "And for God's sake, don't cut her hair yourself. Let her keep it long if that's what she wants, or take her to a goddamn Super Cuts and get it whacked off by a professional. That's the least that she deserves. Got it?"

Holly's mother nodded mutely.

"Good. Now close the damn door and go talk to your daughter."

There was a pause. Holly's mother glanced in my direction, possibly seeking some sort of sanity check for the scene that was unspooling in front of her. She must not have found any sanity in my puzzled face, because she shut the door. The sound of a dead bolt clicking home punctuated the whole thing.

Sloane stayed where she was for several seconds before turning to face me and saying, with no satisfaction whatsoever, "Averted. The story just snapped around us. Our little Rapunzel isn't going to get a happy ever fuck you after all. Now can we go back to the office? I've got a headache." With that, she stormed past me again, her hands balled into fists at her sides.

I turned to watch her go, wide-eyed and bewildered. I was still standing there when Jeff and Andy walked over to join me, Demi trailing along behind them like a confused puppy.

"What just happened?" asked Jeff.

"Sloane just yelled at the story until it went away," I said blankly.

"Is that possible?" asked Andy.

"I didn't think it was, but Sloane says the narrative has been disrupted, and she's never been wrong before." I glanced past the rest of my team to the car, where Sloane was climbing into the backseat. "I'm worried about her."

"I am, too," said Jeff. "She doesn't normally interact directly with the narrative if she can help it. Interacting directly with the narrative is what caused me to go fully active."

I turned and stared at him, a chill racing across my skin. "Are you saying this could force Sloane into an active state?"

"I don't . . . I don't think so?" He shook his head. He looked as perplexed as I felt. "She was averted before I joined the Bureau. If a bad day was enough to bring her story back to life, she'd have switched sides years ago."

No matter how ill-tempered and unpleasant Sloane got, she was stable. If she wasn't stable, she wouldn't have been allowed to do fieldwork, since a villainous narrative coming suddenly to life while we were dealing with another story would have been bad for everyone in its path. I gathered this certainty close, stood a little straighter, and nodded.

"So we're done here; the Rapunzel has been averted, and we don't need to worry about a sudden desert springing up outside the city. Sloane's methods may have been unusual, but we've used unusual methods before." I glanced at Demi, who represented the most unusual method possible. "Let's get back to the office and file our reports."

"What report?" asked Andy, sounding frustrated. "We didn't *do* anything."

"We watched Sloane do something. In this particular instance, that's going to have to be good enough." There was a bang as Sloane slammed the car door. When I turned, I could see her in the backseat of the car, head bowed, hair hanging so that it concealed her face. That chill ran across my skin again.

Something was very wrong, and I had no idea what it was . . . and that meant there was no way that I could fix it. All I could do was stand by and wait for everything to explode.

# # #

Memetic incursion in progress: tale type 315 ("The Treacherous Sister")
Status: UNDETERMINED

Sloane got to the office, and everything was not fine.

The bus dropped her at the end of the block, just like it always did, and the jolt from the heavy vehicle rolling to a stop threatened to slide her butt out of the easy-clean plastic seat, just like it always did. This time, for whatever reason, it felt like a personal affront. Sloane lunged from her seat, a curse forming on her lips, and pulled back when she saw the startled faces of the passengers around her.

"No," she said. Her voice came out louder than she'd intended; the earmuffs prevented her from gauging her volume. The faces around her grew more startled. "No, this isn't right."

The driver turned, his mouth moving in a question that she couldn't hear.

The urge to slit his throat was overwhelming. Sloane grabbed her purse, stammering, "This is my stop thank you good-bye," and ran for the door, almost slamming her shoulder against it as it slid open. Then she was outside, she was blessedly *outside* and away from anyone she could hurt by mistake. She dropped to her knees on the sidewalk, tearing her stockings, and twisted around to watch the bus pull away from the curb and drive off.

"This isn't right," she whispered.

The earmuffs had been knocked askew again when she hit the sidewalk. She reached up to feel them, and then, when the sound from earlier did not return, she slid them off and stuffed them roughly into the pocket of her hoodie. They formed a visible bulge, but she was confident that no one would ask. Most of the people she dealt with on a daily basis simply didn't want to know.

Her headache made walking the half-block to the office more difficult than she could have dreamed. She staggered along the sidewalk like a drunk, putting out her hands to catch herself whenever the pain became too much to deal with. And bit by bit, she was getting a handle on it. The pain was no less severe, but it was becoming almost normal, one more part of the world that deserved to be a target for her hatred and scorn. The more she hurt, the more she hated, and the more she hated, the less it seemed to matter that she hurt.

By the time she reached the door, her headache barely registered with her conscious mind. She pulled her ID card out of her bag and swiped it against the scanner, snarling at the little light until it beeped and turned from red to green, unlocking the office door. She yanked it open, harder than she needed to, and stepped inside.

What's happening to me? The thought was small and almost inaudible over the roar of blood in her ears. *Why is this happening?*

She was still fumbling with her key, trying to get it back into her purse, when a voice behind her shouted, "Sloane! Wait up!" Henry. Just the sound of that frigid Snow White knock-off's syrupy soprano was enough to set Sloane's teeth on edge.

"I'm not in the mood today, Henrietta," she said as she stopped walking, hoping that the other woman would hear the warning in her voice. She wasn't sure how long she'd be able to keep her temper.

She wasn't sure how long she'd keep wanting to.

"Agent Winters?"

The bitch sounded nervous. Good. "I told you, I'm not in the mood." Sloane turned, scowling. "My fucking fire alarm broke this morning. It's been blaring for the last hour. Does that count as me checking in with the boss, or do you need me to fill out some forms in triplicate?" It was a good lie. It would do.

Sympathy suffused the bitch's red-on-white features, making her look even more like a caricature than she normally did. "Oh, hell, Sloane, I'm sorry," she said. Her eyes raked across Sloane's body, weighing, measuring, *judging*.

How dare she judge me? This time, the thought was very loud. "I'm *so* sorry if I'm offending your sensibilities right now. Some of us didn't get narratives that came complete with a permanent makeover, okay? I'll put my face on when I get to my desk."

"Get some coffee first," said the bitch. "You look like you could use it."

And just like that, Sloane's headache burst, and everything became finally clear. "I'll do that," she said.

"Okay," said Agent Marchen.

"Okay," Sloane echoed, and turned away. It was all so clear now.

All she had to do was kill the bitch, and all her troubles would end forever.

# # #

ATI Management Bureau Headquarters

It didn't take long to write up our reports, since they mostly consisted of variations on "Rapunzel confirmed downtown, field team dispatched to resolve the incursion; incursion resolved when Agent Winters shouted at it until it agreed to go away. Resolution mechanism not recommended for future incursions." Demi's was even shorter: "Barely made it out of the car."

Sloane herself vanished into the kitchen for about twenty minutes, returning with a bottle of painkillers from the first-aid kit, a sour expression, and a fresh mug of coffee. She sat down at her desk, and for a brief moment, I was afraid that she was going to get to work on her own after-action report. Sloane never did her paperwork without being reminded over the course of at least three days. If she started documenting our day without prompting, it would be time to call one of the departmental therapists for an emergency appointment.

To my sublime relief, Sloane just opened a web browser, went to eBay, and started browsing listings for stompy boots. Just another normal day at the office.

"Are you going to do your after-action report?" I asked, just to be sure.

Sloane responded by raising her left hand and flipping me off, without turning away from her computer.

"Just checking." I picked up my own empty coffee mug. "Jeff, you want to come with me to scavenge for donuts in the kitchen? I didn't get breakfast before we got dispatched."

"Happily," he said, picking up on the ulterior motive in my words. He'd know if there was something wrong with Sloane—and maybe more importantly, he'd be able to find out if there was any way for us to fix it.

"Bring me back an apple fritter," said Andy laconically, sinking deeper into his desk chair.

"If I find one," I agreed. "Demi?"

"No, thank you," she said, looking confused. "I'm on a diet."

Sloane snorted audibly. "You don't need to be on a diet. You're already going to blow away in a stiff wind."

"My body is my business, Agent Winters," said Demi. Her tone was cold. That was a bit of a surprise. Our newest team member rarely stood up to Sloane, preferring to make herself as small a target as possible. We all tensed, waiting for the explosion that would follow.

And then, against all odds, Sloane smiled. "That's true. What you do or do not put into your body is none of my concern. My apologies, Agent Santos." She turned back to her computer, leaving the rest of us gaping.

I grabbed Jeff's shoulder. "Kitchen," I said. "Now."

# # #

We didn't talk until we were far enough away from the bullpen that I was confident of not being overheard. "What's wrong with her?" I asked.

Jeff frowned. "That's rather blunt, don't you think?"

"She's been acting strange since she came in, and not in a good way," I said. "Is she all right? Should we be looking for an ensnarled narrative?"

"I don't think so," said Jeff. "She shouldn't be able to get caught in a secondary story as long as she's in abeyance—not the way that you or I could. She's probably just having a bad day. It happens to the best of us. I've even seen it happen to you."

"Most of us don't have the potential to do as much damage as she could."

Jeff sighed. "Henry. You know as well as I do that any one of us could do a great deal of damage if we set our minds to it. Demi is the human equivalent of a nuclear bomb. I could cripple the power grid for this entire coast. You could—"

"Rally the squirrels of the world to my defense," I finished sourly. "So you're sure she's all right? This is normal?"

"There is no normal in our line of work, my dear Henry," said Jeff. "Sloane is normal for Sloane. That's as much as we can ask for."

I cast an uneasy glance down the hall toward the bullpen. "I hope you're right," I said.

Jeff put a hand on my arm. "Believe me, so do I."

# # #

Memetic incursion in progress: tale type 315 ("The Treacherous Sister")
Status: ACTIVE

The others were busy with their computers, with their ordinary little problems in their ordinary little lives. Sloane glanced between them, making sure that neither was looking her way. Henrietta and Jeff were gone. This was her best chance.

Quickly, she typed a new search into her browser. The first link was for a chemistry supply company. She added items to her cart with the quick, easy clicks of a practiced Internet shopper, and barely even noticed the tears that were running down her cheeks. They offered overnight shipping on sodium cyanide. That was a nice bonus.

Her headache was completely gone by the time she clicked the checkout button.

Cruel Sister

Memetic incursion in progress: tale type 510A ("Cinderella")
Status: CONCLUDING

Jenna bent over the stove, trying to ignore the aching in her feet and the burning in her eyes from the sweat that trickled down her forehead. If she could just get dinner on the table before her stepmother started yelling at her again, she'd consider this day a win. Maybe her standards for "victory" were lower than they could have been, but she had to take her happy endings where she could. They sure weren't thick on the ground anymore.

When she'd been younger, right after her mother . . .

No. This wasn't the time for dwelling, not if she wanted to get dinner on the table.

When she'd been younger, her father had sent her to see a therapist who specialized in grief counseling for preteens. Jenna had been resistant at first, until she realized that having a therapist gave her the one thing that was more valuable than gold or diamonds: someone who *listened*. Ms. Brooke was paid to pay attention to the emotionally damaged children who clogged her waiting room, and yet somehow, whenever Jenna had been alone with her, she felt like the doctor was only interested in what *she* had to say. It helped her believe that things were going to be okay. Somehow, someday, things were going to be okay.

It was Ms. Brooke who'd taught her to treasure the little things, what she called the "street pennies" of daily life. "Find a penny, pick it up, and all day long you'll have good luck," was one of Ms. Brooke's favorite sayings. "It doesn't have to be literal," she had said. "Every good thing you find, no matter how small, is a penny for you to put in your pocket. Gather them close, and treasure them. Someday you'll have a future where you feel rich enough, emotionally, to spend them freely."

Jenna couldn't really imagine that future on a daily basis—it was too tiring—but she could allow herself to think about it sometimes, in moments like these, where she had a simple chore to finish and just enough space to breathe.

She was so focused on stirring the pan of beef and onions sizzling in front of her that she didn't hear the kitchen door swing open or the sound of footsteps on the floor. "Jenna?" said a voice from behind her. "Mama wanted me to come and see how dinner was coming."

"Elise!" Jenna jumped and turned at the same time, clutching the spatula to her chest. Her elbow hit the edge of the pan, sending it, and its contents, crashing to the floor. Hot grease splattered her ankles and calves. Jenna didn't cry out. It was hard, but learning to swallow her pain had been necessary if she wanted to survive.

Her stepsister's eyes went very wide, making her look almost comical for a moment. "Oh, God, Jenna, I'm so sorry! I didn't mean for you to—are you all right?" Elise dropped into a crouch before Jenna could recover her senses enough to respond, and started scraping the ruined meat back into the pan. "Your poor legs . . ."

"Elise, please." Jenna knelt awkwardly on the grease-covered floor, trying to push her stepsister away without actually touching her. "You have to get out of here or we're both going to get into trouble. You can't . . . you can't be in here."

Elise stopped scraping and sat back, looking sadly at Jenna. "We've really treated you horribly, haven't we? Me, Mama, Camille . . . how can you stand us?"

"You're my family," said Jenna simply. "I don't have anyone else in the world."

That answer seemed to make up Elise's mind for her, somehow. She nodded once as she stood, holding her hands out for Jenna to take. "Go to your room, wipe that crap off your legs, and put some clean clothes on before Mama sees you and yells at you for looking like a common ragamuffin."

Jenna took her stepsister's hands automatically, allowing herself to be tugged from the floor, and asked, "Are you trying to get me into trouble? I need to finish fixing dinner."

"Don't worry about it. I can start a new pan of beef and have it ready to go by the time you get back. Then I'll just tell Mama I wanted to snatch some cheese slices before we ate, and she'll be so busy yelling at me for spoiling my appetite that she won't notice that you've changed your clothes. Camille and I do that sort of thing all the time." Elise spoke with calm, easy certainty, like she had no doubt that her plan would work.

"But . . ." Jenna frowned, searching her stepsister's face for signs of treachery. "Why are you being so nice to me? You hate me." That wasn't strictly true. Out of the three of them—Elise, Camille, and the eponymous "Mama"—Elise had always been the nicest, like she somehow understood how much Jenna had suffered since the loss of her biological family. And maybe she did understand, on some level. Elise was also the older of Jenna's two stepsisters. Maybe she remembered her own father, and how she'd felt after he died.

"I don't hate you," said Elise gently. "I just don't like looking at you. You remind me too much of what could have happened to me."

The honesty of Elise's words was staggering. Jenna stared at her for a moment more before she decided to take the risk. "Thank you," she said. "I'll be right back." She turned and ran out of the room before her stepsister could change her mind. The sound of her bedroom door slamming came a few seconds later.

Elise stayed where she was, counting slowly downward from ten. When Jenna didn't return, she smiled. It was a dark, wickedly pleased expression, and if Jenna had seen it, all doubts about her stepsister's motivations would have fallen away on the spot. "Yes, dear sister," Elise purred, as she sashayed her way across the room to the fridge. She was vamping it up for an audience of dust bunnies and spilled onions, but that didn't matter. Some of the greatest scenes in cinema history had been focused on a single actress, emoting her heart out for the camera's unquestioning eye.

The second pack of ground beef was on the second shelf of the fridge. It was clearly a sign: the rat poison had been on the second shelf of the hallway closet.

Humming to herself, Elise turned and walked back to the stove. It was time to start fixing dinner.

# # #

Four years later . . .

We arrived at the Marlowe residence ten minutes after Piotr called us with the details. Unfortunately, that put us half an hour behind the local police. They had been called by a neighbor reporting a strange smell coming from the house—one that was bad enough to have crept over the fence into the next yard over. Pretty scary stuff, although not that surprising if you've ever been in the vicinity of a dead body. The bacteria that break down human tissue after death are some pretty powerful things. The smell of decay hit us as soon as we stepped out of the van.

Demi, who had never been near a dead body before, went pale and clapped a hand over her nose. "What *is* that?" Her voice was muffled by her hand, but that wasn't enough to conceal the way it quavered and wobbled at the end of her question.

"According to the police report, it's the Marlowe family," said Jeff, sliding out of the van. His copy of the Index was open on his arm, and his eyes were fixed on the page, considering and rejecting possibilities faster than I could even read. "Mother, two daughters, all found in the living room by the officers who answered the initial call. According to what they've filed so far, the Marlowes have been dead for at least a week. No one reported any of them missing."

"What Agent Davis isn't telling you is that we don't officially have any of this information yet, since he acquired it through illegal means," said Andy gruffly. He walked around the van to stand beside me. "How do you want to play this, Henry? They haven't called us in."

"They never call us in," I said, with a shrug. The front door was standing open to allow the police easy access as they came and went. No one was looking our way yet, but they would be soon. When a big black van that clearly belonged to the government pulls up in front of your crime scene and starts spilling out feds, you notice. "We're going to play this straight."

Andy looked dubious. "Are you sure about that?"

"I'm the senior agent," I said, and removed my badge from the pocket where it normally sat unused, replaced in the field by a dozen fakes that would play better with the public than the reality of the department I worked for. "Come on. Let's go say hello to the people we're replacing."

# # #

The officer in charge of the crime scene was named Troy, and we'd worked with him before. That was something of a relief. People don't always appreciate our butting in on their crime scenes, especially when we start talking about the staying power of fairy tales and how much the Brothers Grimm got right. Officer Nicholas Troy was one of those men who had either had an early encounter with the narrative and then blessedly managed to forget about it—more common than most people like to think—or he was just extremely open-minded, especially when it came to people who were willing to take complicated cases off the shoulders of his perpetually overworked and understaffed department.

Even with all that, he still frowned when he saw us coming across the lawn, following a junior officer who was less familiar with who we were and what our presence meant. "This is another of your special serial cases, Marchen?" he demanded, turning toward us. "I didn't see anything that would indicate that it was one of yours, or I wouldn't have let my men go inside in the first place."

His words were less rude than they seemed on the surface. Troy had been around long enough to know that sometimes the narrative can be contagious, grabbing onto whatever hosts it can find and not letting go. "Sometimes they can be subtle," I said. "You remember Agents Robinson and Davis?"

"Hello," said Jeff.

"Hey," said Andy.

"And this is Agent Santos." I indicated Demi, who still looked like she was about to toss her cookies at the earliest available opportunity. "She's our trainee, so please forgive her if she throws up on your shoes."

Officer Troy took a healthy step backward. "Where's your bitchy psycho girl?"

"You mean Agent Winters?" He nodded. I shook my head. "She's not feeling well. We left her at the office to monitor the situation from a safe distance."

"I had no idea she could get sick," said Officer Troy. "I would've thought she'd scare any virus that got too close to her."

"That's entirely possible," said Jeff, finally looking up from his copy of the Index. He sounded completely serious, which made me wonder whether or not he was joking. It was some-times hard to tell with Jeff. "May we see the bodies, please?"

Officer Troy looked uncomfortable. "I'm not sure that's the best idea."

"This is our crime scene now," I said. "If you have someone escort us inside, you can take your people and leave."

Maybe it was the thought of getting away from the stench, which was permeating everything it touched with a layer of decay that would take weeks to scrape off. Maybe it was just an understanding of the chain of command. Whatever the reason, Officer Troy sighed and said, "All right. I'll take you in myself."

I smiled thinly. "Thank you."

# # #

Demi did better than I had expected her to: she made it all the way into the living room, into the meat of the stink—pun intended—before she turned and ran for the yard. The sound of retching followed shortly after. Andy walked back to the door and stuck his head out for a moment before turning and walking back to the rest of us.

"She's tossing her cookies in the bushes," he said. "Nothing's been compromised."

"Except the hedge," added Jeff helpfully. Maybe he *could* joke.

"Good for us, if not for the hedge," I said. In situations like this, I was actually grateful for my dead-white skin tone. You can't go pale when you have no color in your cheeks. "Officer Troy, if you would walk us through the scene?"

"This is it," he said, gesturing to the horror show that occupied the living room. "We were starting an examination of the kitchen when you all showed up. If you'd been ten minutes later, we might have more that we could tell you. As things stand, this is your problem now." He sounded half-smug and half-relieved. This becoming our problem meant that he could walk away from it without feeling like he was leaving his job undone.

"Ah," I said. "Well, then, you can consider the handover complete."

"Thank you," he said. "Please notify the department if you find anything that might indicate that this case is somehow relevant to the real world." And just like that, he was gone, turning and rushing out the door without a word of farewell. I couldn't blame him. If I'd been given the chance to run away from the narrative—let alone three gruesomely decayed bodies—I would have taken it a thousand times over.

But that chance was never made available to me, and here and now, I had things I needed to do. Pushing away the faint resentment that Officer Troy's flight left in its wake, I turned my attention to the crime scene in front of me.

"Names, Jeff?"

"Christina Marlowe, age thirty-nine. She's a widow twice over, with two daughters by her first husband. She married Michael Marlowe five years ago; he already had a daughter, one . . ." Jeff turned a page in his copy of the Index. "Heather Marlowe. Christina formally adopted Heather three years ago. Michael was killed in a car accident six months later, and Christina became sole guardian of all three girls."

"So a new mother arrives on the scene with two little girls and manages to be left holding the whole package when she loses her husband." I snorted, and promptly regretted it as the action required me to take another lungful of the room's putrid air. "This is a familiar story."

"Explains the bodies, too," said Andy, stepping further away from the door. "Been a while since we've had a homicidal Cinderella. But it happens."

"Unfortunately, yes." Being Cinderella in the most traditional sense means taking endless servings of shit with a smile on your face and a song on your lips. It means believing that the world is an intrinsically good place, and that you are an intrinsically good person, while spending every day in squalor and suffering. Some Cinderellas rise above it and become the inspirational platitudes who get immortalized in fairy tales. They're triumphs of the narrative, people who are more story than self. Those are the rare ones. More commit suicide, slitting their wrists in bathtubs full of water—because even in death, your average Cinderella is dedicated to keeping things neat—or drinking nightcaps made from hemlock and bleach.

And some, a rare few, decide that they've had enough. It's easy for a girl who works in the kitchen to get her hands on a carving knife, and there are a surprising number of common household poisons that won't change the flavor of food. A Cinderella who decides to take the story into her own hands can do an awful lot of damage.

An awful lot of damage had certainly been done here.

There were three bodies, all female, one older than the others, if clothing and size could be believed. The older woman was sitting in an armchair with a good angle on the television, a TV tray on her lap with a plate of moldy, half-eaten food. This Cinderella hadn't bothered cleaning up after herself. The two smaller figures were together on the couch, with standing wooden trays in front of them. All three women had been dead for quite some time, and while it had taken the human neighbors a while to catch on, the neighborhood flies had been much quicker on the draw. The faces of all three bodies boiled with maggots, their fat white bodies glistening in the light.

"If our Cinderella did this, she's got a good head start on us by now," said Jeff. "She could be anywhere."

"If our Cinderella did this, we're finished," I said. "I won't say that these women would have deserved to die under normal circumstances, but if they pushed a five-ten-A into going homicidal, they probably did something unforgivable. She's already paid for this crime in advance."

Footsteps behind me announced the return of our youngest team member. I turned to see Demi standing in the doorway, wiping her mouth with the back of her hand. "I'm sorry," she said, before any of us could say anything. "All the houses on this block look alike. I didn't realize I knew these people until I saw the living room, and then I realized that if the Marlowes were dead, that meant Heather and Emily were dead, and that's just not fair. Not after everything else they've been through."

I frowned. "What do you mean, that meant *Heather* was dead? Heather's the one who fits the five-ten-A profile. She's our Cinderella. Wicked stepmother, two wicked stepsisters . . ."

"But she doesn't have two stepsisters anymore," said Demi.

Jeff put his hand up. "Hang on. Demi, what do you mean, 'after everything else they've been through'? Are you talking about Michael Marlowe's death?"

"No. I mean, yes, but not exactly." Demi stole a glance at the couch, blanched, and looked away again. "Heather *used* to have two stepsisters, until Jamie disappeared two years ago. It was all over the school. That was my senior year—she was a year behind me, and we were in band together. They never did find her."

"Wait." I looked at the bodies again. One adult, two teens. "Jamie would have to have been one of Christina's biological daughters. Jeff, are there any variations with just *one* Wicked Stepsister?"

"A few," he said slowly, "but they all have other conditions. This setup is pure Western Cinderella, which is the strongest form of the narrative in the modern American psyche. I don't think you could pull off a strict five-ten-A with only one Wicked Stepsister."

"Jamie and Emily weren't wicked to Heather," protested Demi. "They actually seemed to like her okay. Heather liked clothes and boys, which meant she had something in common with Jamie, and Emily liked being left alone to read. I think she was grateful to have someone to distract her sister once in a while."

I turned to look at the scene in front of me one more time, trying to push away my preconceptions, all the little tropes and touches that came with being absolutely sure of the fairy tale trying to unfold around me. Three bodies: a woman and her two daughters. All were dressed in equally nice clothing—not too fancy, but not shabby, either—none of the rags and tatters that we expected from a Cinderella. The plates of food were too maggot-eaten and decayed for me to tell what they had originally contained, but they all looked equally full. No one was getting shorted or denied her fair portion.

"Demi, you said you'd been here before," I said. "Where are the bedrooms?"

"Down the hall," Demi said. "Why?"

"Just a thought. Andy, you and Demi stay here, start photographing the scene. Jeff, you're with me." I gestured for the wiry archivist to follow as I started in the direction Demi had indicated.

My team has been working with me for long enough that no one questioned my instructions. Jeff fell in, and together we walked out of the living room, into the part of the house that had been touched only by dust, and not yet by decay. Behind us, the whir of Andy's camera started up. He'd photograph everything, even the things that never deserved to be recorded on film, because you never knew what a photograph might reveal that the eye would miss. His pictures would help as we began the hard task of figuring out what actually happened.

I hate cases like these, where we wind up taking over for the police instead of making it so that the police never have to get involved at all. The narrative was definitely at work here—I could smell it, under the reek of rotting human flesh—but I couldn't see the shape of it. Not clearly, not yet.

But I would. Jeff beside me, I walked on.

# # #

It was a good-sized house: big enough that all three girls had been able to have their own rooms, rather than being forced to share. But being big enough didn't always mean anything—I've been in mansions where the Cinderellas were forced into repurposed pantries or the back of laundry rooms.

There was none of that here. Heather's room was just as large as Emily and Jamie's rooms, and was decorated with the same mixture of nostalgia and rebellion. They were all teenagers, and they had their own ideas about appropriate décor, but I couldn't look at Heather's room and honestly say that she had been in any way neglected. If anything, she'd been a little bit spoiled. They all had.

Jamie's room was like something out of a model home. Everything was put away. The clothes were folded and the bed was made . . . and there was a thin layer of dust over the whole place, like it had been closed off and left as a memorial to a girl who was never coming home. I stood there looking at it for a long while, thoughtful and a little sad. Whatever happened to Jamie, she lost her home and family, and they lost her. That was as much as a tragedy as what was being documented in the living room right now.

A hand touched my elbow. I turned to see Jeff standing there, frowning. "I think I may have found something," he said.

"Okay," I said. I closed Jamie's bedroom door behind me as I turned to follow him. Let her shrine endure for just a little longer. The cleaners and the estate sales and the realtors would tear it down soon enough. That's what happens to all our private family churches, eventually. The real world can't let them stay.

Jeff led me to the door at the end of the hall: the master bedroom. Christina had apparently never redecorated after Michael's death. There were still little touches that clearly indicated the involvement of another person. They were small—a lamp here, a bedside table there—and that was what made me believe that she had never truly moved on from her husband's loss. Unlike most women who got pulled into the Cinderella stories of their stepdaughters, she had truly loved him. The narrative should never have been able to find a foothold here.

"Smell that?" Jeff asked.

I sniffed the air. This far from the living room, the smell of decay was virtually absent, and I was able to pick up a faint, lingering sweetness. "Perfume?" I guessed.

"Mmm-hmm." Jeff walked to the dresser, where he picked up a bottle. "She seems to have been devoted to a specific brand—Blue Wishes. It has a very distinctive scent. Neither of the girls would have been likely to wear this. It's too old for them. They would have thought of it as 'mom perfume,' and steered clear."

"All right," I said. "So a woman's bedroom smells like her perfume. Is that so unusual? I think most women's bedrooms probably smell like their perfume."

"Does yours?" asked Jeff.

I raised an eyebrow. "No," I said. "My bedroom smells like apples and snow. Thanks for asking." He had the decency to redden. "Now what is it that you wanted to show me in here?"

"Come on." He gestured for me to follow him again, this time to the closet on the far side of the room. It was big—bigger than the bedrooms I've seen some Cinderellas forced into—with shutter-style doors that allowed the clothes inside to "breathe" even when closed politely away from the public eye. The shutter on the left was standing open. Jeff moved to stand beside it, gesturing for me to take a look inside.

A small nest of bedding and pillows had been created on the floor of the closet, incorporating clothes pulled down from the nearest hangers. The smell of Christina's Blue Wishes perfume pervaded the air, rendered strong and cloying by the confined space. I pulled my head out of the closet, giving Jeff a curious look.

He shook his head. "She's been sleeping in there for at least a week; maybe longer, if she hasn't been dousing herself in that perfume. She might have been. There are dirt stains on the pillows, and there's blood smeared on the sheets. I don't think she was being allowed to shower."

I looked at him for a moment, rolling this new information over in my head as I tried to make sense of it. "So our prospective Cinderella is one of the bodies, and our likely Wicked Stepmother was being held prisoner in her own home. Okay . . . why?"

"I don't know," said Jeff, looking disturbed. "But I think we need to get Sloane over here. Something's missing, and she has a perspective that none us can actually share."

I nodded slowly. "All right," I said. "I'll call the office."

# # #

The cleanup team arrived about twenty minutes later and boiled out of their van with unhappy expressions on their faces that had nothing to do with the murder scene they were about to start sanitizing. The explanation for their unhappiness climbed out of the back of the van after them and sauntered across the lawn, somehow managing to look like she was clomping down a runway when she was actually walking on muddy grass while wearing platform heels. Her mouth was set in a line of firm disapproval. Sloane's eyes narrowed as she considered the front of the house.

The rest of us were waiting on the porch, as much to get away from the smell as to meet her. Jeff straightened, saying, "Ah, Sloane—"

"Can it, cobbler," she snarled, and clomped right on past him, into the death-scented living room.

Slowly—and in my case at least, afraid of the explosion that was almost sure to follow—the four of us leaned around and looked through the open door. Sloane was standing in the center of the living room, her arms hanging loosely at her sides, considering the scene. She was moving her head in small, bird-like jerks, taking in one thing after another. Finally, she turned and clomped toward the largest of the three bodies, stopping in front of what had once been Christina Marlowe. Bending close, she took a deep breath.

Demi gagged beside me, clapping a hand over her mouth and turning away. I put a hand on her back, hopefully providing a little comfort, but I didn't try to get her to turn back around. I had a pretty decent idea of what was about to happen, and it wasn't anything that Demi needed to see.

Sloane picked up the dead woman's spoon, lying on the tray next to her curled, maggot-covered fingers, and shoved it through the crust of mold that had formed on her plate, scooping up a healthy portion of whatever Christina had been eating right before she died. Sloane raised the spoon, studying its contents, which continued to pulse a little as the maggots she had collected along with her target writhed in dismay. Then she brought it closer to her face, sniffing once again.

Dropping the spoon back onto the plate, Sloane turned and clomped back to the doorway. "These people were poisoned," she said. "That's the good news."

"How is that good news?" demanded Andy. "I don't know if you noticed, but three people are dead in there."

Sloane waved her hand dismissively. "People die every day. Somebody died while you were thinking of that pithy comeback. Dying is amateur hour."

"If that's the good news, what's the bad news?" I asked, trying to keep us on track—or at least keep us from turning on each other. Sloane was in a clompy mood, and that meant her temper, never the most reliable of things, was on a hair trigger.

"The killer used cyanide mixed with applesauce. You can't really tell unless you break through the gunk that's growing on the plates, but all that's *in* there is applesauce." Sloane shook her head. "This was a fairy-tale murder. Are we looking at a five-ten-A?"

"We would be, except that our potential Cinderella is one of the bodies in there. Unless this was a murder-suicide, she didn't do it. And there's more." I took my hand off Demi's back, folding my arms in front of my chest. "The stepmother was sleeping in her closet. For at least a week, according to Jeff; maybe longer."

"That's messed up," said Andy.

Sloane didn't say anything. She just looked at me, a calculating expression in her kohl-rimmed eyes. Finally, after the silence had stretched out for long enough to become uncomfortable, she said two words: "Show me."

# # #

Everyone piled into Christina's bedroom this time: Andy because he wanted to see the closet, Demi because she didn't want to be left alone with the bodies. We hung back, letting Sloane explore the room in her own way.

She went to the closet first, and just stood there for several minutes, looking down on the tangled nest of bedding. Finally, she crouched and flipped over the pillow, studying the floor beneath it. "Two weeks," she said. "Maybe three. No longer than that. She'd have been shifting around in the closet if she'd tried to go longer, and that would have fucked up the carpet in here."

None of us asked her how she knew. In cases like this one, Sloane was our subject matter expert on tales involving wicked relatives. We'd allow the cleaning team to do a full forensic analysis of the place as soon as we cleared out, but we knew their findings would confirm Sloane's deductions. She was as lost as the rest of us when we were chasing a Little Mermaid or a Match Girl, but put us in a house with a Cinderella or a Snow White and the world was hers to unravel.

The narrative never does any of us any favors, even though it can sometimes seem that way in the short run. But I sometimes feel like Sloane got even fewer favors than the rest of us. She sees darkness everywhere she goes. She's not capable of looking away.

Sloane crossed to the bed, stopping next to it and cocking her head as she considered the fold of the covers, the position of the pillows. She pulled down the duvet, peering at the mattress for a moment before she turned around and said, "We've got a problem."

"The dire pronouncements are getting old," said Andy.

"What's the problem?" I asked.

"Someone was sleeping in our Wicked Stepmother's bed—someone who wasn't the stepmother, and wasn't either of her daughters." Sloane gestured toward the bed, continuing, "Someone with red hair. Christina was a blonde, one of the daughters was brunette, and the other was blonde like her mother." She narrowed her eyes at Andy and added, "There are pictures in the hall if you don't believe me."

"It's not that I don't believe you, Sloane," he said defensively. "This just seems like a pretty big jump to make."

"Not that big of a jump," said Jeff. He sounded . . . frightened. I turned to look at him, frowning.

"Jeff? You know something that you'd like to share with the rest of the team?"

"We were never sure that it was really a matter of the narrative expressing itself, and not just some random human behavior. That's why it never made it outside of the Archives."

"Except for when you consulted with me," said Sloane. "You tell them or I will."

"Jeff?" I repeated.

Our resident archivist sighed, turning to fully face me, and said, "We had a confirmed five-ten-A in Manhattan about four years ago. The local field team was dispatched to deal with it, and they got there when the story should have been fully manifested. What they found was . . . was a horror show."

"Many fairy tales are," I said. "We're standing in a dead woman's bedroom. What did the field team find, Agent Davis?"

Using Jeff's title seemed to help him center himself. He took a deep breath, straightened, and said, "The stepmother was dead, as was the prospective Cinderella and one of the two stepsisters. The other stepsister, Elise Walton, was gone. The incident was recorded as a five-ten-A gone wrong, turned murder-suicide, like some of them do, and it got filed as part of the overall five-ten-A record."

"Only about a year later, we got another narrative pop with the same attributes, or at least really similar ones," said Sloane, picking up the story. "There was a potential five-ten-A in Houston that was flagged as resolved when one of the stepsisters was killed in a car accident. That didn't stop the survivors from being poisoned at their dining room table, with cyanide mixed in applesauce."

"There have been two more killings that fit this profile since then," said Jeff. "They were both in different cities; they both involved unmanifested five-ten-A narratives."

"And let me guess," I said. "The Bureau—and the Bureau cleanup crew—got involved on every one of those calls, didn't we?"

Jeff nodded. "It's standard procedure. We don't want a repeat of what happened in seventy-two."

"Um," said Demi. "What happened in seventy-two?"

"There was a rash of killings connected to a memetic incursion gone wrong—a Snow White who didn't manifest the way that she was supposed to," I said. "The media got hold of it before it could be properly handled. Dubbed them 'the fairy-tale murders.' We lost half our funding over that incident, and the Snow White in question wound up getting arrested for her crimes."

"Isn't that what's supposed to happen when you kill people?" asked Demi.

She sounded so lost that I felt briefly guilty for dragging her into all of this. I pushed the feeling aside. This was neither the time nor the place, and Demi's story had been sealed long before I forced her into activation. "She killed eight more people while she was in prison, before we could get someone into her cell and take care of her. It was a mess, in every sense of the word, and it must never happen again."

The Snow White's name had been Adrianna. She'd looked enough like me that we could have been sisters, because all Snow Whites are sisters, somewhere deep inside the story. They made me recite her history while I was in school, drumming the failure that she represented deep into the marrow of my bones. Never again. Other stories could turn sour, but not mine: never again.

"So our cleanup crews hit every single one of those crime scenes and they stripped them down to fibers and forgetfulness," said Sloane. "The regular police knew something had happened, but they never got the details, and they never told the FBI to be on the lookout for a serial murderer with a fondness for families and poisoned apples."

"Great," I said. "Just great. If it's not a Cinderella that we're dealing with here, then what is it?" I felt like a fool as soon as the words were spoken. It was all so *obvious* . . .

Sloane fixed me with a cold stare and said, "I thought you were smarter than this, Henry. If we're not looking for Cindy, then that means we're looking for her Wicked Stepsister. The one who got away."

# # #

We left the cleanup crew to their unenviable task and returned to the office, where we had an unenviable task of our own to undertake: finding a Wicked Stepsister with no active narrative to call her own. Jeff and Andy went for their respective safety nets: the archive for Jeff, and the FBI directory of missing persons for Andy. His logic was good—if the victims of our wayward Wicked Stepsister had never been reported as murdered, he should be able to find them somewhere in the FBI's files. *Someone* had to have realized that they were gone.

Demi sat down at her desk with her hands tightly folded in her lap, looking like she had no idea what she could possibly do in this situation. I would normally have tried to come up with some kind of busy work for her, but at the moment I was preoccupied with a more pressing matter: Sloane.

She hadn't said anything during the ride back from the Marlowe house, and that wasn't like her. What's more, she wasn't going for her computer, either to work or to look at eBay listings. She was just hovering around the edges of the room, expression flickering lightning-fast between rage and despair.

It was worrisome to say the least, and terrifying to say a little more.

I took a breath, trying to calm the too-rapid thudding of my heart. The narrative wants me to be flighty, wants me to be the kind of girl who runs at the first signs of danger. I've been working for my entire life to train myself out of those urges, and for the most part, under most circumstances, I've succeeded. But Wicked Stepsisters are close relatives of Wicked Queens. Under the right circumstances, one can even evolve into the other, shedding the trappings of one story for whatever happens to be available to them. And the Snow White—and the agent—in me knew that we were in danger when there was an active Wicked Stepsister nearby.

Sloane had her own set of narrative impulses to fight with. Going near her when I was showing signs of distress would be like hanging out a big red flag and inviting her to take her shots. She couldn't help it. I didn't need to encourage it.

When I was sure that I wasn't going to have an inconveniently timed panic attack, I walked over to where she was pacing and asked, quietly, "Everything all right with you, Agent Winters?"

"That wasn't my last name when they found me, any more than 'Marchen' was yours," she replied. "You get to be a fairy tale, I get to be a freeze. Somebody in senior management has a real shitty sense of humor, you know that?"

I paused, briefly stymied. Then I tried again, asking, "But is everything all right?"

Sloane's laugh was brief and brittle, like ice breaking in an enchanted forest. "All right? Fuck, Henry, you know me better than that. *I* know me better than that. No, everything is not 'all right.' Everything is never going to be all right. Hey!"

She whirled, stabbing a finger at Andy. "Look for incidents in places where it gets cold. It won't matter if she doesn't have a passport, she's not moving around legally anyway, and she's probably capitalizing on looking young and vulnerable. But she'd want to kill somebody where it was snowing."

"Why?" asked Demi.

Sloane fixed her with a flat stare. "To see if it would feel any different."

"I've got something," said Andy, saving both Demi and me from needing to formulate a response. "There's one in St. Paul *and* one in Chicago. Our Wicked Stepsister has been a busy, busy girl."

"If she's working her way into families that have two teenage daughters already, she must be making contact somehow," I said. "Try looking for new student enrollments at nearby high schools a month or so before those people were reported missing."

"Why are you assuming subterfuge, and not a blitz attack?" asked Andy.

"Because she's a teenager herself, based on the first incident, and it would be difficult for her to force her way inside without being seen," I said. "This way, she gets in, she takes control somehow—"

"She's probably armed; it wouldn't be that difficult for her to get a firearm on the black market, and the pause between the deaths and the reported disappearances means that—" Jeff froze with his mouth still open, his eyes widening behind his glasses. "I am an idiot. I don't deserve to be an archivist. I don't even deserve to be a shoemaker."

I frowned at him. "Care to break that down a little bit?"

"She's using the dead women's *credit cards*," he said. "There's no reason for her not to. Nobody knows that they're dead. There's no one to tell on her, not for several days at least. As long as she abandons the cards before they can give her away— and then she just switches to cash. I'm sure they've all been 'persuaded' to give her their ATM numbers before she killed them."

"The Marlowe family was killed a week ago," I said. "Andy?"

"Already on it," he said, pulling his keyboard toward himself and beginning to type rapidly.

We're not hackers. We're not even computer experts. But it's amazing what access to government systems and official back doors can do. If Elise was using her latest victim's credit cards, we'd find her.

A hand touched my elbow. I turned to find Sloane standing closer than I was entirely comfortable with. The rage had completely faded from her face, replaced by nothing but simple despair. "Can I talk to you while they fuck around with computers and stuff?" she asked. "It's important."

"Sure, Sloane." I looked back over my shoulder. "We're heading for the conference room. If you get anything, call me. My phone is on." I faced forward, offering Sloane a thin smile. "I'm all yours."

"No, you're not, and you should be really happy about that." She turned and stalked away, clearly expecting me to follow her. That broken ice terror that I associated with the Snow White side of myself was back, stronger than before. Snow didn't want me to go anywhere with Sloane, not now, maybe not ever. Snow wanted me to stay right where I was, safe, among friends, where I would be protected.

That, more than anything else, is why I straightened my jacket and followed Sloane Winters down that hall. I've never allowed anything to control me, not my story, not the greater narrative that birthed it, and sure as hell not Sloane. I'd be damned if I was going to start now.

Sloane paused outside the conference room door, waiting for me to catch up with her. "I didn't think you'd actually follow me down this long, dark hall, all by yourself," she said. Her voice was pitched lower than normal, and it seemed to be full of strange shadows, twisting just outside the edges of her words. "That was a brave, stupid thing to do."

"I'm your boss," I said. "Sometimes it's my job to be brave and stupid. What do you need, Sloane? What can I do to help you?"

She laughed again, that same brittle, breaking laugh. "I don't think you can help me, just like I don't think we can help Elise. She's manifested. Whatever she was before this happened to her, whoever she might have grown up to be, that's over now. That girl is dead. She's part of the narrative, and there's no getting away from that. She's been *written*." The horror and venom that infused her final word was practically visible, dripping from her mouth and running down to the floor like so much poisoned water.

I bit my lower lip for a moment, pondering, before I touched her shoulder and asked, "Are you afraid you're going to manifest, Sloane? Is that what this is all about? Because we can step up your counseling, we can see about adjusting your medications—"

"I'm not afraid that I'm *going* to manifest, Henry." She ducked her head, hiding behind the dyed black curtain of her bangs. It struck me, and not for the first time, just how similar we looked. Her coloring was all pancake makeup and Midnight Whisper #9 applied at the salon, but we still came out looking like sisters, or close enough as to make no difference.

Looking like stepsisters.

I froze, my hand still resting on Sloane's shoulder. I wanted to pull away. I somehow knew that doing so would be a huge mistake, and so I stayed where I was and asked, in a voice that had no force behind it, "Then what are you afraid of?"

"I'm afraid I've already manifested," she said. Sloane raised her head. To my great dismay, I realized that she was crying. Her mascara ran down her cheeks, leaving tarry streaks behind. "Remember the three-ten we had last week? The one I yelled at until it went away?"

I nodded mutely.

"I shouldn't have had that kind of power over the narrative. No one who isn't part of the narrative gets to have that kind of power." Sloane started crying harder. "Can't you see? It didn't want a Rapunzel. That's why it let her go so easily. It never wanted *her*. It wanted *me* all along—and I let it in."

"You haven't. You wouldn't." I squeezed her shoulder. "You haven't done anything—"

"Your coffee yesterday." She looked away, focusing on the wall, presenting me with her profile. "I didn't knock it off the desk because I was clumsy, or because I was being a bitch. I knocked it off the desk because I managed to get myself back under control before you drank the poison I'd slipped into your cup."

My blood turned to ice in my veins. And Sloane kept talking.

"The stapler that disappeared. The donuts I threw away and dumped pencil shavings on top of. I've nearly killed you eight times in the last week. I was planning to put a poisoned spindle in your desk when the call came in asking me to join you at the scene. I can't help myself, Henry." She finally turned back to face me. "It's like I'm not even there when it's happening, I'm just watching from a distance, like . . . like . . ."

"Like you're watching a story?" I asked. She nodded mutely. I sighed, and did something I had never believed that I would have a reason to do: I pulled her away from the wall and gathered her into a hug.

Sloane didn't resist me pulling her toward me, but she didn't relax at first either. She endured my embrace like it was part of her punishment, the first step in repaying her crimes. Then, bit by bit she softened, until she was limp in my arms, her face pressed into my shoulder, sobbing. I stroked her back with one hand.

"I won't say it's okay, Sloane. It's not okay. But I will say that you're among . . ." Calling us her friends seemed to be overstating things a bit. "You're among teammates, and we don't give up on our own. We'll find a way to fix this. I promise."

My phone chirped. I dug it out of my pocket one-handed and raised it to my ear, not saying anything. A few seconds later, I nodded, lowered the phone, and patted Sloane awkwardly on the shoulder as I tried to extricate myself from her arms. It was surprisingly difficult.

"Come on," I said. "Andy found proof that Elise Walton bought a gun at a pawnshop downtown last month, and Jeff . . . well, Jeff thinks he's found Elise Walton. We need to roll."

# # #

According to Andy's research, a woman named "Christina Marlowe" had checked into a cheap downtown motel two days previous, and hadn't checked out yet. It made sense. Elise would need time between killings, time to recover and decide where she was headed next. Maybe in the beginning she'd been better about getting out of town fast, but after killing multiple families without a whisper from law enforcement, she'd started to get cocky.

The Bureau had been protecting her all along, even if we didn't know it. That made me angry—and worse, it scared me. How many killers like Elise were out there, protected by the shadows that they cast and by our mandate to preserve the world's ignorance of the narrative that moved beneath reality's skin? How many people had died because we were so good at covering up the tracks that the fairy tales left behind? And was there any possible way for us to change the way that we worked? The ATI Management Bureau is the way it is today because it's had centuries to grow and evolve, going from a loose alliance of storytellers and archivists to a governmentally funded agency with ties to law enforcement and media censorship agencies. We don't change quickly.

We've never needed to.

Sloane took Andy's usual place in the front passenger seat for the drive to Elise's hotel. She buckled her seat belt but only grudgingly, and sat as far forward as it would allow, her fingers tapping against her knees. She looked like a child on Christmas morning. I cast her several uneasy glances before asking, "Are you sure you're up for this?"

"Don't treat me with kid gloves, Henry," she snarled. That was reassuring. If she was snarling at me, she wasn't trying to poison me. "This is exactly the sort of thing I need."

"Yes, violence," muttered Jeff, making no effort to keep himself from being overheard. "That's the best medicine for what ails anyone."

"Sarcasm doesn't help," I said. "We're here."

Elise's hotel was as rundown and nondescript as its website implied: the perfect place for a fugitive Wicked Stepsister to go to ground for a few days while she regrouped and prepared herself for her next attack. A sign out front advertised free Wi-Fi. That would help her figure out where she was heading. Families that fit her extremely specific profile couldn't be all that common.

Of course the narrative would be helping her, in its own implacable way. Failed memetic incursions represented a loss of strength, of self—of substance, in a way that our researchers had never quite been able to pin down or define. By sending Elise around the continent mopping up failed Cinderella stories, the narrative could sow chaos and regain strength in the same gesture. I didn't know how it was directing her movements. I'd never heard of the narrative getting personally involved like that. But that didn't mean it couldn't happen.

We pulled up to the curb in front of the hotel. The local police had beaten us there. They were using unmarked cars to avoid spooking our suspect, but Officer Troy wasn't the kind of man who could just disappear into a crowd, even when he was lurking around in front of a nondescript black Lincoln Town Car. That wasn't going to be a problem; my team was many things, most of them good. We weren't subtle, though. All five of us got out, gathering together on the sidewalk like a flock of black and white birds. Only Sloane's non-uniform attire and my too-red lips broke our color scheme.

"Officer," I said genially, as Troy approached. "I take it dispatch was able to get through to you?"

"What's this I hear about you preparing to make an arrest?" He didn't bother with even the pretense of pleasantries, going straight for the implication that we were somehow trespassing on his jurisdiction.

I looked at him coolly. "I wouldn't call it an arrest, since she's part of the narrative now. It's more of an apprehension. But yes, that's why we're here."

"If this is about your 'narrative,'" I could virtually hear the air quotes around the word, which really wasn't fair, since he had seen its effects up close and personal more than once, "why are we here at all?"

"Because the bitch probably had a gun when she took out the Marlowes, and there's no telling what she'll do when she sees us standing in the hall," said Sloane. She rocked up onto her toes, and then down again to the flats of her feet. "What are we waiting for, the SWAT team? Let's get in there and finish this story."

"I don't think this is a good idea," said Demi.

"I don't think anybody has a better one," said Andy.

"And at this point, I don't think it matters," I said. "We're here. If she's somehow getting cues from the narrative, it's going to tell her to move soon. She'll just get a feeling, and then off she'll go, and we won't find her again until she slips up in another city with a field team. Do you really want to be the ones who let her get away?"

"No," said Andy.

"No," admitted Demi.

Jeff and Sloane didn't say anything. They just looked at me, the one resigned and the other eager, still radiating that kid on Christmas excitement. I turned back to Officer Troy.

"My team takes the lead, and you don't interfere unless you're asked," I said. "If there's an arrest, it's yours."

He frowned. "What do you mean, 'if' there's an arrest? She killed people. Either you're taking her in or I am. There's no way she's walking free."

I didn't say anything. I just looked at him silently until eventually—inevitably—he looked away.

It was time to go in.

# # #

Officer Troy's badge got us past the front desk; my badge got us a key to Elise's room and a promise that no one would be calling up to warn her about our impending arrival. My team and I took the elevator up to the third floor, while Officer Troy and his men took the stairs. It would give us a few minutes where we wouldn't need to worry about anybody deciding to play cowboy, and between us, we had all the exits covered. She wasn't getting away.

When we reached the third floor, I looked to Demi. "You're on."

She nodded and raised her flute to her lips with trembling hands. Andy clapped his hands over his ears, and she began to play.

It was a sweet, eloquent tune, but it lacked the compelling power I'd heard from her before. That was because this song wasn't meant for me. It wasn't meant for any of us, save for perhaps Andy, who wasn't part of any standing story. One by one the doors in the hotel hallway opened, and the occupants of the rooms emerged, blinking and shuffling, into the open. Demi kept playing as she backed into the open elevator. The last I saw of her was the top of her head as she continued to play, luring all the normal people off this floor, away from what was to come.

The other two elevators arrived and were filled, until the four of us were standing alone. Andy removed his hands from his ears. "Remind me not to piss that girl off," he said.

"I'm the one you need to worry about," said Jeff. "I pick all her sheet music."

"Guys, focus. We need to—Sloane?" She was already starting down the hall, moving slowly at first, but gathering speed with every step. As I said her name, she broke into a run. I swore and ran after her, with Andy and Jeff running close behind me.

Most of the doors were standing open or in the process of swinging closed. Sloane made her way straight to the closed door at the end of the hall. There was a piece of white plastic in her hand. I groped for my pocket as I ran, unsurprised to realize that she had stolen the key card to Elise's room.

"Sloane!" I shouted. "This isn't the right way to fix things!"

She didn't stop running. When she reached Elise's door, she swiped the key card, shoving the door open in practically the same motion. I caught a glimpse of a shocked face topped by a spray of carroty red hair. Then the door slammed, and Sloane, and our killer, were blocked from view.

"Shit," I hissed, skidding to a stop just before I would have hit the doorframe. "Sloane!" I pounded on the door. "Let us in! You don't want to do this!"

"What if she does?" asked Jeff. "What do we do then?"

"I don't know," I said, and kept pounding on the door, only to nearly fall forward as it was wrenched abruptly open. Sloane was standing just inside with one hand on the doorknob, and the other wrapped firmly around Elise's throat. The gun was lying on the bed, too far away for either of them to have grabbed it. That was a mercy.

"She's not worth getting my hands bloody," snarled Sloane, and half-shoved, half-threw Elise at Andy. He caught her easily. Elise huddled in his arms, sobbing. Sloane wasn't done with her diatribe, and continued, eyes on Elise, "She turned herself into a Cinderella. You understand? She killed her own mother, turned herself into an orphan, and then went stalking the story. She hoped it would make her better. All it did was make her worthless."

"I don't know what she's talking about," sobbed Elise. "Why does she keep calling me Cinderella? I didn't do anything . . ."

I looked at her, trying to feel something other than pity. "You did enough," I said.

"She's lying," said Sloane. "She knew exactly what she'd done, and what she was trying to become. She wanted to be a perfect little princess. All she did was turn herself into a flawed reflection of an ideal she could never achieve. You hear me? *Never.*"

Elise straightened, her sobs fading as she twisted in Andy's arms to glare at Sloane. She wasn't trying to escape. Maybe she knew that it was pointless. "At least I'm better than you, *sister*," she spat. "You think I don't recognize you? At least I tried. I wormed my way into those families and made them my own. I tried to find another story, one where I didn't have to be the bad guy. You just let our story take you."

Sloane stood frozen for a moment, looking at the girl she might have been. Then: "I'll be in the car," she said, and stalked away toward the elevators.

Jeff watched her go before moving to stand beside me. "Is she okay?"

"No," I said, and we stood there waiting until the police descended.

Fox's Tongue

Memetic incursion in progress: tale type 105 ("The Fox and the Cat")
Status: SUSPENDED

Dr. Reynard—not the name that he was born with, but then, how many people can be truly defined by their original names in both childhood and maturity? A truly sensible culture would grant a person a new name with every decade of their life, until age and perspective allowed them to choose the name that would grace their tombstone—closed his door. The office was cool and dark, filled with the soft, subtle scents of leather and fresh-turned earth. The former was natural; the latter came from a clever atmospheric spray he'd ordered from an online retailer. They made such amazing things these days.

The room was as carefully designed as any home ever featured in a magazine spread. Every piece of paper and bit of memorabilia was positioned just so in front of the leather-bound books that lined the shelves, common enough to suggest eclectic interests, sparse enough not to seem like an unhealthy fixation. The shelves, in turn, lined the walls, creating an illusion of coziness in a space that was actually quite large. It was all very clever, and Dr. Reynard found that to be of the utmost comfort. Better still, the color scheme—all reds and browns and fertile yellows—echoed the soft simplicity of a British autumn. It was a burrow, plain and simple, designed for a thinking man of expensive tastes who also happened to be, through no fault of his own, a treacherous fox as likely to rob a fair maiden as to kiss her hand.

"To thine own self be true" had been Polonius's motto, and the good doctor found that it still served well in this troublesome modern world, where stories were considered to be fiction and those who were afflicted with a trifle too much narrative strength were viewed as outcasts, or worse, as monsters.

One of those monsters was on her way to his office now. Dr. Reynard sat down at his desk, flipping languidly through the folders piled there until he found the one he wanted. "Sloane Winters," he said aloud, feeling out the shape of her name with his mouth. It was a good name. She had almost certainly chosen that surname for herself, after her heart froze over, but the proper name had the flavor of one that had been worn for a lifetime. She had been a Wicked Stepsister-in-waiting from the moment of her first breath. Like so many who attracted the attention of the narrative, she had never been given a chance to be anything more than what she was: a tool, a fulcrum upon which the memetic incursions that sought to devour the world could turn themselves.

"I think I will greatly enjoy getting to know you, Miss Winters," he said, as he picked up a quill. After stealing a glance at the clock above the door—enough time, if only just—he smiled a small and private smile, and began to write.

Truly, they would tell a glorious story together, the sister and the fox. All it needed now was a beginning.

He was so engrossed in the plotting of their story that he didn't hear the back door open, or the thin metallic sound of the knife being drawn from the butcher's block in the kitchen. The carpet in the hallway was thick enough to swallow footsteps whole, gulping them down its padded gullet and replacing them with silence. Unaware of what was coming ever closer to his fine and private space, Dr. Reynard wrote on until, all too soon, his story ended.

# # #

Sloane sat in the passenger seat with her elbows on her knees and her shoulders hunched so that her spine formed one of those eye-bruising angles that always left me with a sympathetic backache. She had left her hair loose for a change, and it was hanging over her face, completely blocking her expression from view. She hadn't bothered to re-dye her roots recently. They showed above the inky black and fire-engine red streaks, dishwater blonde and somehow sad.

"Dr. Reynard used to work for the Pacific Northwest branch of the ATI Management Bureau," I said, feeling like one of us should be filling the silence in the car. The radio wasn't an option: no matter what station we tuned into, it fluxed back and forth between thrash metal covers of nursery rhymes and syrupy sweet acoustic versions of murder ballads. I wasn't sure which one of us was responsible for which parts of the unpleasant musical mash-up, and I didn't want to worry about making her angry right now.

The situation was weird enough as it was. We were both out of uniform—for Sloane, that meant slightly less aggressively overdone eye makeup; for me, it meant gray stonewashed jeans and a dark blue cotton shirt that had been white when I brought it home from the department store. I wasn't entirely sure why the story I had spent my life avoiding felt the need to recolor my wardrobe. It was probably connected to the same memetic leak that occasionally caused wildflowers to sprout on my carpet.

Deputy Director Brewer had been happy to grant my request for time off when I explained that it would be used getting Sloane to a therapist who was slightly more experienced with narrative recursion—a stable freeze starting to narratively thaw—than the stable of counselors, shrinks, and psychologists who were officially employed by the Bureau. Thanks to an outdated rule in our hiring practices, we were not allowed to recruit psychiatric support staff from people who had been directly impacted by a story. In theory, this meant that our psych staff would be able to approach all stories with equal compassion and neutrality. And most of the time, that was how it worked.

But, unfortunately, we sometimes needed something more: people with a degree of empathy that required a more intimate understanding of what it meant to be on the ATI spectrum. The Bureau psychologists had been enough to keep Sloane functional until now. With her story starting to reassert itself, that was no longer the case.

"We're almost there," I added, in case that would somehow prompt Sloane to respond to me. "Dr. Reynard has cleared his entire afternoon to get to know you, and I made sure that our insurance covers him as an out-of-house provider. You won't be paying a penny for your care."

"I have plenty of pennies," said Sloane, without lifting her head. "Almost as many as I have murderous impulses. I'd be happy to trade the one for the other."

"And that's good, that shows you want to break out of your narrative track," I said, turning down a small residential side street. "Luckily, you're not going to have to trade anything. Dr. Reynard specializes in cases like yours. He'll fix this."

Sloane finally sat up, unbending her spine one vertebra at a time, until she was upright and could look me in the face. Her eyes were surprisingly clear and tired, without their usual pigmented armor. "Henry. You're a story, and I'm a story, and there's nothing in the world that can 'fix' us. We're going to be what we are until the day we die. All that matters is whether we can be kept in proper chains until then."

I pressed my lips into a thin line and said, "I don't believe that, and neither should you."

"Do you have any idea how old I am? Of course you don't. I've never let any of you people get close enough to figure that out. But believe me, Henry. You're not the first Snow White I've seen, and you probably won't be the last. You'll do what you can with the resources you have, and you'll *serve your story* by trying to save me." Sloane dropped her head again. "I should be trying to save you. That would subvert the narrative. But instead here we are, you saving me, or dying in the process. Dying is a lot more likely."

"Only if you take things at face value," I said. "I'm not going to eat anything you hand me, drink anything you've touched, borrow your comb, or put on any of your rings. You know what I *will* do?"

"What?" asked Sloane, not sounding as if she believed that the answer could matter in the slightest.

"I'll shoot you in your goddamn head if I really and truly feel that you've become a danger to yourself and others. And then I'll take your body down to the folks in Agricultural and ask them to use you to fertilize an apple tree. And when you've grown to a lovely size and started bearing fruit, I will sit underneath you and not eat a single one of your inevitably poisoned apples."

Sloane glanced at me through her hair, and for a moment I actually saw a wisp of a smile on her face. "You'd do that for me?" she asked.

"Not sure whether you meant the shooting or the burying or the apples, but yes. I would do every bit of that for you." And I meant it.

I pulled up in front of a well-kept Victorian home, its decorative trim painted in shades of red and gold. What looked like a full murder of crows occupied the lawn and perched on the front porch railing. They ruffled their feathers and croaked when they saw us, seeming to object to our presence. I eyed the crows. The crows eyed me.

"Well, you should feel right at home here," I said. "Either this guy is evil, or he has a very unusual set of atmospherics."

Sloane leaned forward, peering past me to the black birds covering the grass. "What story did you say this guy escaped from?"

"I didn't," I said. "I didn't want to prejudice you."

The look she shot me was full of disgust. Given that most of her recent looks had been full of venom and self-loathing, disgust was a step up. "His lawn is covered in crows. Most memetic incursions using crows are negative. I really, *really* don't think that taking me to a fairy-tale villain is the way to neutralize my own negative impulses. Given how much I want to strangle you right now, I'd say that it does exactly the opposite."

"But you *usually* want to strangle me. I don't see the difference," I said. Sloane's glare didn't waver. I sighed. "He's a one-oh-five, okay?"

There was a pause as Sloane flipped through her mental copy of the Aarne-Thompson Index. For a moment, I wasn't sure she'd be able to place the number.

I shouldn't have underestimated her.

"He's a clever fox?" she asked. "Or what, a patient hedgehog or whatever the hell it is that teaches the clever fox to be less clever. Because 'don't be smart, kids, that's what gets you fucked over' is a wonderful moral."

"He was a clever fox, yes, but that means he was never a villain, just an antihero," I said, unbuckling my seat belt. "Now he's a psychologist, and he's the best in the business when it comes to your particular problem."

"Fox, huh? That's why he calls himself 'Reynard,' isn't it?" Sloane rolled her eyes as she retrieved her coffin-shaped purse from the floor. "Why is everyone so on-the-nose all the time?"

"Asks the girl who chose 'Winters' as her surname." I got out of the car. "Come on. Let's go meet your new best friend."

Sloane glowered at me before stomping toward the front door, scattering crows before her like some ancient murder goddess whose story had been thankfully forgotten by the narrative that regularly tried to ruin our lives. I smiled to myself. It was such a *Sloane* thing to do that it actually gave me hope. As long as she was still herself, she'd tell the story that was trying to take her over to fuck off, just to be contrary.

She stopped when she reached the porch, turning and shooting another glare in my direction. "Well?" she demanded. "Are you coming?"

"I'm right behind you," I said, and followed.

# # #

Both of us knew that something was very wrong as soon as we stepped into the front hall. The door being unlocked made sense—this was a place of business as well as a private home—but something about the atmosphere in the room put my back up. Sloane was clearly feeling something similar. She stiffened as the door swung shut behind us, lifting her head and sniffing the air in an almost canine manner.

"Dr. Reynard?" I called. "It's Henrietta Marchen? We spoke on the phone. I'm escorting Sloane Winters for her appointment . . ." I started to take a step forward.

Sloane put out her arm, catching me across the chest. I stopped, frowning at her, until she said, "Something's wrong. Can't you smell it? That shouldn't be here."

"Smell what?" I turned back to the hallway, trying to emulate her position. "All I smell is dust and old books. It smells like library in here, but there's nothing out of place."

"What did he have for lunch?"

The question was rapid enough to seem casual, and I answered without hesitation: "Apple pie." I froze. "Wait. What? There's no way I could smell that from here."

"There's no way you could smell that at all, because he didn't have apple pie for lunch, and that's not what you're really smelling. That's just how your story tells you to filter it." Sloane lowered her arm. "You need to stay here, Henry."

"Sloane, I—"

"*Please.*" There was an urgency in her tone that was entirely unlike her. I frowned at her again. She twisted to look at me, shaking her head. "I won't leave your sight, I promise, but right now, you need to stay here, and you need to trust me. You've been using me as your fairy-tale bloodhound since you joined the Bureau, and people were using me for the same thing while you were still learning your ABCs. Trust me now. Let me do my job. Let me be your hound."

Her eyes were wide and pleading. I bit my lip, trying to come to a decision when it felt like half the data I needed was outside my field of vision. In the end, it was her lack of insults that made me believe her. She hadn't called me a snowy bitch or made any jokes about the smell of phantom apples. She was serious, even if I didn't understand quite why . . . and it scared the hell out of me.

"All right," I said. "But if you need to leave this hall, you call me, and I come with you. Do we have a deal?"

"I won't need to leave the hall," she said, practically jogging in place. She was starting to look pale and drawn, as if standing still took a greater physical toll than anything else I could have asked her to do. "The smell is too close for that. I won't have to go far."

"Then go," I said.

Sloane nodded once, a short, sharp motion, before she whirled and ran down the hall like she was being chased. I'd only ever seen her move that way in the field, when she was trying to close in on a story that we were on the verge of losing contact with. The smell of apples seemed to get stronger in her wake. If we hadn't ridden over in the same car, I would have suspected her of wearing some truly tasteless perfume.

Her flight took her past the first three doors in the hallway. When she reached the fourth door she pulled up short, vibrating like the bloodhound she had compared herself to. Now moving with all the caution and inevitability of one of Bluebeard's wives, she reached for the doorknob. I swallowed the urge to shout at her, to tell her to step away from the door. *This* was her job. I led the team, but it was Sloane who ran into danger, time and again, setting off the traps before the rest of us could trigger them.

The door swung inward at her touch. True to her promise, Sloane stayed in the hall, remaining in full view as she looked at the contents of the room. Her face fell. Then she turned toward me, and with only a shred of her usual bravado, she said, "I don't think this therapist is going to work out for me after all."

"Why not?" I asked.

"Because dead men don't actually help my mental health all that much." She shrugged. "I'm funny that way."

I closed my eyes and groaned.

# # #

Sloane and I sat on the front porch, waiting for the rest of the team to come and join us. The murder of crows had returned two and three at a time, apparently deciding that we weren't a threat. Some of them were even perching on my car, watching us with calculating black eyes. As we didn't seem inclined to feed them, they didn't come any closer. Sloane wasn't even throwing rocks at them. That worried me.

"Why did I smell apples in there?" I asked her. I wasn't sure I actually wanted an answer, but I wanted her talking. Silence was very rarely a good thing where Sloane was concerned.

"Because in your story, blood is the smell of getting away, and death smells like apples," she said, still watching the crows. "I was pretty sure there was a dead guy in there with us. The apples just sealed it."

I frowned, not quite sure I understood what she meant. "So what did you—"

"Don't ask me that, okay? I'm on my best behavior today, just like you asked me to be, and part of keeping me there is you not asking me that question." Sloane didn't look at me.

"Deal," I said quietly. We sat in silence after that, just watching the crows, until a big black van came tearing around the corner. It was moving too fast for this kind of residential neighborhood, and it didn't really slow down as it hurtled down the street, finally dumping all its speed as it screeched to a halt right behind my car.

"Oh, goodie, the clown car's here," deadpanned Sloane.

I shook my head. "Show-offs."

The van doors opened, allowing Andy and Demi to spill out of the back. Jeff—who had apparently been driving—appeared around the hood, drawing quickly ahead of the others. The crows looked at him with disdain, but didn't move even as he made a beeline across the lawn. "Are you all right? Is Dr. Reynard really dead? Did Sloane kill him?"

"Thanks for the vote of confidence," said Sloane, sounding sincerely pleased. "No, I didn't kill the geek. He was already dead when we got here. But I could have totally killed him if I'd needed to."

"Don't think that was meant to be a compliment, Agent Winters," rumbled Andy as he followed Jeff's trail through the grass. The crows *did* scatter in front of him, maybe because of the five of us, he was the only one with no direct connection to the narrative. "Most people would take the implication that they had killed their new therapists . . . poorly."

"I'm not most people, asshole," Sloane replied. There was no trace of rancor in her voice. "We got here, he was dead, we called you. Now here you are, and we can get down to the business of figuring out who ganked the man who was supposed to fix me."

"I'm getting really tired of the dead bodies, you guys," said Demi. "Can I wait outside?"

"Don't worry, Agent Santos; this one is fresh," I said, standing. "He hasn't had time to decay."

"But he will if we don't get in there." Sloane bounced back to her feet, looking more energized than I'd seen her since she stopped herself from killing Elise Walton. Maybe all it took to set her world back on track was an interesting murder.

It couldn't be that easy—nothing ever really is—but it was nice to dream.

"Come on everyone," I said. "Sloane's going to show us to the dead man." With that, I turned and followed her inside. The others trailed along behind me, even Demi, who was looking increasingly unhappy about being here—or rather, unhappier, since she hadn't really seemed happy since she'd joined the team.

That was something to worry about later. Right now, I had a dead man and Sloane to worry about, and the two of them were quite enough.

Sloane took the hallway at a normal pace this time, walking past the three closed doors to what had been Dr. Reynard's private office, where she stopped and beamed, looking as proud as a brand-new mother showing off her specially designed nursery. Since I'd already seen the good doctor, I hung back, allowing Jeff and Andy to go ahead of me into the room. Demi stayed behind me, and I didn't force the issue. She was going to need to get used to dead bodies sooner or later. That didn't mean it had to be today.

Dr. Reynard had been sitting at his desk, a large, ornately carved piece of oak furniture that was probably antique, when he'd been killed. It was unclear whether he'd had any opportunity to react to what was clearly a blitz attack: even without carefully investigating his body, I could see four distinct punctures in the fabric of his waistcoat. Those probably hadn't killed him. The slashed throat was a much better candidate for cause of death.

Andy circled the desk, treading carefully as he avoided the inevitable blood spatter. "The knife's back here on the floor," he called. "Looks like a carving knife."

"There's a kitchen at the end of the hall," said Sloane. "I bet you'll find a bunch more knives just like it, when you get a chance to go and look."

"What's it look like, Andy?" I asked.

"Stainless steel, black handle, good edge," he reported, crouching down to get a better look. "I can't make out the manufacturer. There's too much blood on the blade."

"That's fine," I said. "Agent Santos, go check the kitchen and see if you can find the set this knife came from."

"Alone?" she squeaked.

I turned, frowning at her. "You can go alone, or you can help us examine the crime scene in order to help free up more resources. Which sounds like more fun to you?"

"I'll check the kitchen," she half-whispered, before turning and fleeing down the hall.

"Amateurs," I muttered, turning back to the office. Jeff was watching me, a concerned expression on his face. I frowned. "What?"

"You need to go easier on her," he said. "She's not adjusting as well as we might have hoped, and riding her isn't going to make the process any smoother."

"We've had a few too many dead bodies since she joined us," I said. "Maybe if things had stayed slow, we could have gone easy on her, but as things stand, it's all hands on deck until everything settles down."

Jeff's concerned look actually deepened. "Henry," he said, speaking with the sort of exaggerated carefulness that I normally associated with people trying to talk to Sloane. "Doesn't it seem strange to you that we've had more than a case a week since Demi joined us? I'm not saying that correlation equates to causation—she's a Piper, there's nothing in the Index about Pipers encouraging memetic incursions—but you can't pretend we haven't been encountering more stories recently. We need everyone to be operating at their best, yes. We also need everyone to stay well balanced and stable, or we're going to start falling apart."

I gaped at him for a moment before realizing that the office was far too silent. I turned to find Andy eyeing the two of us thoughtfully. "Mommy and Daddy are fighting," he said, his deep bass voice lending the statement an air of ludicrousness that it really didn't need.

"Think they'll argue over who gets to keep us when they do the custody thing?" asked Sloane.

Andy snorted. "I think they'll bribe each other to take us off their hands."

I groaned. "All right, you two: your point is taken. I will try to be nicer to Demi, and Jeff and I will restrict our discussions of policy to a more private setting. Andy, you find anything else that might shed some light on what happened to our dead man?"

"He didn't struggle," said Andy. "I think his throat was slashed from behind, probably while he was going over Sloane's file."

"How did you reach that conclusion?" Sloane's tone was dangerous.

Andy straightened, holding his hands out to her palms first. It was a placating gesture, and I wasn't sure it was going to work, given the circumstances. "I'm not accusing you of anything, Sloane. Heck, if anything, you're the only one of us who has an alibi, since you were with Henry when this man was killed. But you were his incoming patient, and look at the desk. Something was taken."

Eyeing him suspiciously, Sloane moved forward until she could get a clear view of the bloodstains on Dr. Reynard's desk blotter. "There was something here when he was cut," she said, after a momentary study. "Andy's right. It was the right size to be my personnel file. That doesn't mean it *was* my personnel file, but the timing is suspicious." She raised her head. "Is this my fault?" There was something heartbreaking and small about her voice. It made me want to hug her, even knowing that the gesture would probably result in my having two or three fewer fingers.

"No," I said firmly. "If someone killed him over his work with the Bureau, this is just a case of bad timing. If it was something else, we'll figure it out. We'll fix this."

"We can't fix a bad case of being dead," said Andy.

"Not without consequences, anyway," added Jeff.

I shuddered.

Footsteps from the hall drew everyone's attention. Demi reappeared, pale-faced but steady. "I found the knife block," she said. "The knife was missing, just like you said."

"Thank you, Agent Santos," I said.

She took a deep breath. "There's something else," she said.

# # #

The back door had been left ajar, presumably when Dr. Reynard's killer fled the scene. The now-ubiquitous crows, never content to leave an opportunity unexploited, had taken their chance to invade the kitchen. Most perched on the backs of the chairs pushed in at the small butcher-block table, while one rested atop the fridge, ruffling its inky feathers and watching us with a judgmental avian eye.

"Did this guy feed these things or what?" asked Andy. "Jeff?"

"I'm assuming you're using my name as shorthand for 'is there any mention in the Index of crows associated with type one-oh-five,' and the answer is no, there is no such mention," said Jeff mildly. "If there were, I would have said 'well, that's interesting, this is a rare variant' by now. As it stands, I'm as baffled by the never-ending supply of corvids as you are."

"He must have fed them," said Demi. "Crows are smart. They learn faces, and they know who's nice to them. If Dr. Reynard worked to make friends with them, it only makes sense that they'd hang out at his house."

Exposure to Dr. Reynard was exposure to the narrative, if not in the full-spectrum, blazing way that it would have been if he'd been active, and not in abeyance. Animals exposed to the narrative—especially animals exposed via a memetic incursion with animal echoes of its own—tend to start taking on the qualities we associate with "fairy tale" animals. Dogs get more loyal, sheep get a little less suicidal, and wolves turn into man-eaters. Whereas crows . . .

Crows have always had a reputation for being clever, clever birds.

"Henry?" Jeff touched my elbow. "What are you thinking?"

"I'm thinking that if I'm going to get the side effects of being what I am, I may as well get some of the advantages at the same time." I reached up and pulled the ponytail holder out of my hair, taking advantage of the motion to shoot what I hoped would be a menacing glare at the rest of my team. "This is just a means of gathering information. None of you says a *word* about this, do you understand me?" I snapped the ponytail holder around my wrist.

Demi looked bemused. Andy looked displeased. And Sloane, of all people, looked approving. She nodded as my eyes met hers, and then gestured with her chin toward the nearest of the crows. It felt oddly like she was giving me permission. Somehow, I didn't mind that. I also wasn't sure I liked it.

I turned to the refrigerator, raising my eyes until I was looking at the big black bird perched on top of it. The crow ruffled its feathers and clacked its beak, but didn't squawk or caw at me. I chose to take that as a good sign—that's me, ever the optimist—and I held to it as I reached deep down into myself, finding the place where the snow never melted and where a man's death could smell like apples. I didn't close my eyes, but it still felt like I was opening them when I came back out of the cold, trailing the memory of it with me.

"Hello," I said, to the crow. "You must be a friend of Dr. Reynard's. We're his friends too. We're very upset because something bad has happened to him. You don't know anything that might help us find the person who hurt him, do you?"

The rustle of wings from the kitchen behind me marked the movement of the other crows. From the sound of it, they were making their way closer, drawn in by the inexplicable fascination that all animals seem to have for the seven-oh-nines. I kept my eyes on the crow in front of me. He might not have been their leader before this moment, but he was now. He was being pulled into the story.

The crow clacked his beak, a small, sharp sound, like a maraca being snapped. Then he cawed, a low, rolling sound, something like a kazoo being played into a theremin.

I nodded. "Yes, the red-haired man." I was bluffing—I had no idea what the crow had actually said, if anything—but it was an educated guess.

The crow gave another rolling caw before launching himself from the fridge and flying to land in front of the back door. He pushed it open with his head, looked back at me, and strutted calmly out onto the porch.

"That's a 'come on, stupid' if I've ever seen one," I said, and followed him. My team was close behind me, and the other crows brought up the rear, a moving wall of swirling black feathers and the sound of frantically beating wings. It should have made me nervous. Instead, it made the scene feel more like home.

The big crow continued to walk, hopping down the porch stairs one by one before striking out across the grass. We followed him to a small garden plot, and then past it, to a compost heap. The crow stopped and turned, looking up at me.

"Caw," he said.

"This compost has been disturbed recently," Jeff said.

"Of course it has," said Andy, sounding resigned. "I guess I'll go find a shovel."

"Thank you, Andy," I said. Turning my attention back to the crow, I added, "And thank you. I hope we'll be able to avenge your friend."

The crow cawed again, looking somehow expectant. I blinked.

"Uh . . ." I said.

"Scratch his neck," said Sloane. "Birds like that."

I decided not to ask how she knew that. Hopefully, if she was setting me up for a pecking, the crow would be too annoyed by the attempt to stick around and peck me twice. Bending forward, I hesitantly reached out and scratched the crow on the back of the neck, under the feathers. I was rewarded with a throaty purring noise that barely sounded like it had come out of a bird. Then he launched himself into the air, the tips of his flight feathers brushing my arm as he flew up to land on the roof with what looked like the rest of the murder. They all watched us, dozens of big black birds with judgmental eyes.

". . . that was weird," I said.

"I thought you didn't like being a story," said Demi. "Wasn't that a story sort of thing to do?"

I stopped dead for a moment. Then, carefully, I said, "Yes, it was. But no one who isn't a story can sneak up on a clever fox in his den, which means we're looking for someone inside the Index. Sometimes that means I have to use tools I don't like."

"She's a hypocrite like the rest of us," said Andy, reappearing with a shovel in his hands. I hadn't even seen him go. "Once you come to accept that, everything else will make a lot more sense around here."

Sloane snorted. I glared. And Andy, having moved into position at the edge of the compost heap, started to dig.

It didn't take long. Either our killer hadn't expected us to check the compost pile, or they hadn't cared about anything beyond slowing us down. His third shovelful of dirt exposed a pile of filthy manila folders. Some of them were dirtier than others, probably because they were also bloody, giving the soil something to cling to. Andy stepped back. I started to step forward.

Jeff grabbed my arm. "Stop," he said.

I stopped. "What is it?"

"This was too easy," he said. "It has to be a trap of some kind. Sloane? Can you check for contact poison?"

"Sure thing, shoemaker," she said, recovering some of her usual swagger as she sauntered over to the compost pile and crouched down, assuming a position that only a praying mantis could love. She studied the folders for a moment, frowning, before leaning closer. Her frown deepened.

"Sloane?" I said.

"Gimme a second." She flapped a hand in my direction before leaning closer still, looking utterly perplexed. "Jeff, wasn't there a management discussion like ten years ago about adding—what's it called—urban legends to the Index? Since they're sort of like a new form of memetic incursion that's been getting more codified with every repetition?"

"The choking Doberman and phantom hitchhiker as fairy tales of the modern age, yes," he said. "That didn't go anywhere."

"Well, maybe it should've. These things reek of formaldehyde." Sloane unfolded herself back to a standing position.

"You know, like the story about the girl who buys the super-cheap prom dress, and then it turns out to have come off a corpse? Touch these, you're getting a four-ten if you're lucky, and a shallow grave if you're not."

Andy frowned. "Formaldehyde only kills through ingestion, not brief skin contact. The dead girl prom dress story isn't true. Urban legends aren't *real*."

Sloane gave him a disgusted look. "Fairy tales aren't real either, pretty boy. Crows can't understand English. Rats don't obey musical commands."

"She's right," said Jeff. "If the narrative pushes hard enough, the impossible happens."

"That's a bad sign," I replied. "If the narrative is branching out into urban legends, that means it's getting stronger."

"Most urban legends have some truth to them anyway," said Sloane. "People just don't know the whole story. Poisoned Dresses have been around since the Middle Ages; usually they're deliberate, with needles or skin irritants to get the poison into the bloodstream. They're a Sleeping Beauty variant. They should've been added to the Index years ago."

Jeff frowned. "How do you know so much about it?"

Sloane shrugged. "Poisoning made to look like accident: kind of my thing," she said bitterly.

She stopped talking. Everyone looked to me, like I would somehow have the answers, even when we were dealing with something that no one had ever seen before. I was their team leader. It was my job.

I hate my job sometimes.

"Go to the kitchen and find some plastic bags," I said, to no one in particular. "We'll take these back to the office while I call a cleanup crew to come and secure the scene."

"On it," said Jeff, and turned to head back toward the kitchen. Sloane went with him, presumably to warn him before he grabbed anything else that had been poisoned. The three of us who remained looked at the compost heap, and then at the small, tidy home garden planted next to it.

"Bet he didn't have much of a rabbit problem," said Andy.

"No, but I bet he caused the rabbits a lot of problems," I said.

Demi laughed. It was a small, honest sound, and it seemed somehow more fitting than any words could have been. We had never met the man, after all.

# # #

"I don't know why I bother being surprised that you could go out on your day off and wind up back in the office with a murder case," said Deputy Director Brewer. He sounded annoyed. I had that effect on the man. Since he had a similar effect on me, I decided not to feel overly bad about it. "Do we have reason to believe that Dr. Reynard's death was related to his upcoming appointment with Agent Winters?"

"The evidence is inconclusive at this time, sir," I said. "Agents Davis and Santos are going over the files now." It was a team effort, of a sort: Jeff was organizing them, and Demi was piping the formaldehyde away, thanks to an obscure variation of the Twelve Dancing Princesses—Aarne-Thompson Index type three-oh-six—that treated poison as a living thing, capable of joining in a dance. "We should know more after they get finished."

"And the body?"

"Cleanup brought it back here. It's down in the medical lab, being autopsied. He had no family, and very little contact with anyone apart from his clients, all of whom are on file here at the Bureau. We should have no problem making this disappear." I wanted to feel bad about that, or at least morally conflicted, but Dr. Reynard had been a Clever Fox. Ending his life with a grand mystery would make his spirit happier in whatever afterlife he found than anything else could have possibly done.

Deputy Director Brewer nodded, looking down as he shuffled the pages on his desk. I remained where I was, standing ramrod straight in front of him, my hands folded behind my back where he wouldn't see that they were ever so faintly trembling. Finally, he looked up, and said, "According to Agent Santos, you located the papers hidden in the compost pile by asking one of the local crows to show you where to look."

"Yes, sir." There was no point in denying it. Even if Demi was the only one who'd been stupid enough to put that little fact in her report, everyone else would admit that they'd seen me talking to birds if they were asked directly. We don't lie for each other. We can't afford that.

"Tell me, Agent Marchen: At what point did you decide that this case was important enough for you to risk awakening your memetic potential? It hadn't even officially been assigned to your field team yet."

I straightened a little more, until the small of my back began to ache. "With all due respect, sir, field teams are allowed to operate as their leaders see fit with regards to memetic incursions, both within and without the team itself. The birds were present when Dr. Reynard was killed. It seemed likely that they would have information regarding the reason why. I took a calculated risk. It paid off."

"You took a calculated risk with *your* story." Deputy Director Brewer stood, putting his eyes on a level with mine. "You of all people should know how dangerous that is. You should never have risked opening that door."

"I risk opening that door every time I follow the rules or do my laundry," I said, fighting the urge to snap at him. "Seven-oh-nine is a complicated narrative. It has a lot of pitfalls. Talking to birds may have been *less* risky than picking the wildflowers that grow in my hallway carpet. As for the risk, *sir*, I am well aware of what will happen to me if my narrative ever goes fully live, but given the timing of Dr. Reynard's murder, I couldn't ignore the fact that he may have been killed because he was intending to help Agent Winters with *her* own narrative."

"It was careless."

"It was necessary under the circumstances." I shook my head, feeling my thin veneer of calm beginning to crack and slide away from me. "We've had more manifestations in the last two months than we've experienced in the last two *years*. It's not just my field team that's been hopping—everyone is over-whelmed, even the teams in other regions—but we seem to be getting it the worst. There are more incursions than ever before, and no one knows why. More importantly, no one wants to take any risks in finding out."

"Was Agent Santos one of these 'risks'?"

"Agent Santos was a risk that I took when this was getting started. Talking to a bird was a risk I took today. If this doesn't stop, *sir*, if it doesn't at least slow down, what kinds of risks will we be taking tomorrow?"

Deputy Director Brewer frowned. "Do you really think this man is that important?"

"I think now that we have his files, we can find out."

"I see." He sighed. "Well, then, Agent Marchen, I have no further questions for you. A note will be placed in your file regarding your interaction with your personal narrative."

"Thank you, sir," I said. I turned and fled his office as quickly as I could without actually breaking into a run. All that would have done was inspire more questions that I didn't want to answer, and my team needed me with them, not standing here justifying myself.

Deputy Director Brewer didn't say a word as I fled.

# # #

"What do we have?" I demanded as I walked into the bullpen, trying to sound like I hadn't just been raked over the coals about my interactions with the narrative.

"Demi's cleaned about half the files," said Jeff.

"The other half should be done in an hour or so," said Andy.

"We're fucked," said Sloane.

We all stopped to turn in her direction, varying expressions of bemusement on our faces. Sloane looked up from the paper in front of her. Her lips were pressed into a thin, hard line, all the color blanching out of them at the pressure.

"Does the name 'Alicia Connors' mean anything to you?" she asked.

"She was the four-ten we had earlier this month," said Andy. "The girl we thought was a seven-oh-nine, because her narrative was all confused when she started out."

"She was one of Dr. Reynard's patients," said Sloane. "He was seeing her for a sleep disorder—she had really bad nightmares about not being able to wake up, and she was starting to hurt herself in an effort not to go to sleep. So Dr. Reynard helped her out."

"Uh, guys?" Jeff's normally smooth voice was shaky. "I've found something else that may present a problem."

"What's that?" I asked.

"Jennifer Lockwood was also seeing Dr. Reynard. 'Unspecified anxiety disorder.' She started seeing him six months ago."

Jennifer Lockwood was our one-seven-one, the Goldilocks who had suddenly gone from averted to active, with none of the warning signs that normally fell in the middle. "Scan those files and cross-reference them against active narratives within the past six months," I said. "I want to see how many of our recent cases popped up in the good doctor's office."

"I'll go see if Demi has anything else ready for us," said Andy. He dropped his share of the files on Jeff's desk as he walked out of the bullpen.

Jeff sighed and stood, gathering his double armful of files. "Sloane, give me yours," he said. "I'll get these scanned, so we can cross-reference."

"Doesn't this count as computerizing the narrative?" asked Sloane, even as she willingly handed the remaining files over.

"No, because we're just scanning patient records, not the details of their individual stories," I said. "Although it's interesting that Reynard kept his records only on paper. It's like he was trying to keep the narrative from revising them."

"That's exactly what he was doing," said Jeff, and followed Andy's path out of the room.

I walked to my desk in silence. I could feel Sloane's eyes on me, watching me as I moved. Finally, I turned to her, frowned, and asked, "What?"

"Do you think he had something to do with pushing those stories into active status? Could he have done that to me?"

That pulled me up short. "I don't know." I sat, pushing papers aside to clear a space for me to rest my elbow on the desk. Finally, I shook my head. "I don't think it was Dr. Reynard who was pushing those people active."

Sloane's eyes narrowed. "Why not?"

"Intuition? Wishful thinking?" I waved a hand. "It's just a feeling. But . . . the crows. They were everywhere. Crows are watchers. They like to see what's going on, and they have a good sense for danger. Would they really have stuck around if he'd been doing something dangerous with the narrative in there? I don't think so. I only spoke to him on the phone, but I got the impression that he genuinely cared about the people he worked with, and wanted them to have the best lives possible. In this world, that means *not* becoming the conduit for a homicidal fairy tale."

"His file on Alicia Connors didn't say anything about her manifestation," said Sloane thoughtfully. "Just that she'd cancelled several sessions before contacting him to end their professional relationship."

"So maybe we need to look at this from the opposite direction," I said. "What if Dr. Reynard had nothing to do with either manifestation?"

"What are you—" began Sloane.

She was cut off by Jeff's return, with Andy close behind him. "Demi had four more files ready for us, and I've scanned everything in," said Jeff, sitting down at his desk and beginning to type rapidly. The flat-screen monitor we were supposed to use to project relevant case files came to glowing life. A moment later, names started appearing: some highlighted in red, others highlighted in green. "The red names are patients of Dr. Reynard's who can be connected directly to recent memetic incursions. We've got our Sleeping Beauty and our Goldilocks; we also have a Snow White from the next district over, two of the Three Little Pigs, a Big Bad Wolf, a Goldtree, and a Boy Without Fear."

"How far back did you go?"

"Six months," said Jeff grimly. "The names highlighted in green are people who had been seeing Dr. Reynard up until six weeks ago, only to discontinue their sessions with little or no warning."

"That's not weird," said Sloane. "I've dropped most of my headshrinkers cold."

"Yes, but you didn't drop off the grid immediately afterward." Jeff shook his head. "None of these people have been seen or heard from since they left Dr. Reynard's care."

"So they could have all become active narrative manifestations for all that we know," I said. "Is there any way to track them?"

"I've put Dispatch on it," said Andy. "They're better with this sort of legwork than we are."

"And none of this gets us any closer to knowing who killed Dr. Reynard," said Sloane. "We're wasting our time."

"No, we're not," I corrected, as gently as I could. Under the circumstances, being rude to Sloane was not only unnecessary but also potentially suicidal. "We would never have found these connected stories if he hadn't been killed. He might have been able to help you with *your* story, but we would have learned nothing new about all these other stories."

"So we assume that whoever killed him either didn't want Sloane to get help or that they didn't want her talking to him and maybe learning his secrets," said Jeff. "Who do we have that fits that profile?"

There was a moment of silence before I said, defeated, "No one. We have no one."

"But we have a lot of names," said Andy. "We have a lot of resources. Whoever did this, we'll get them."

"Are you sure?" asked Sloane.

Andy didn't answer.

# # #

Cleanup had done an excellent job on Dr. Reynard's office, removing every sign that someone had been killed there. Even the bloodstains on the blotter were gone, replaced by clean white paper. I stood in the doorway as Sloane paced around the edges of the room, running her fingers over the spines of the elegantly arranged leather books and scowling at nothing. The air still smelled of apples to me, but only faintly, like the distant memory of a dream.

Dishes clattered in the kitchen as Jeff and Andy continued their methodical search of the property. We'd have to call for cleanup again when we were done—otherwise, whoever eventually "discovered" the empty property would assume that there had been a robbery and jump to the conclusion that Dr. Reynard had met with a bad end faster than we wanted them to. Every clatter was punctuated by the croak of the crows, who were still roosting all over the house. They'd come flapping inside as soon as we opened the doors, and none of us had really put much effort into shooing them away. This was their home, in a sense, and with Dr. Reynard gone, we had no authority to make them leave.

"Sloane? Are you sure there's anything to find in here?"

"Yes," she snapped. "He died in here. He was a Clever Fox. There's something to find here."

I frowned. "Not following your logic here, Sloane. Help me out before I order you to go and search the attic."

"Foxes den. This whole house is nice—nicer than yours, that's for damn sure—but this room is the one he set up as his den. Anything that was really important to him would have been kept in here, where he could keep an eye on it."

I decided to ignore her dig at my living situation as I said, "We already found something important that was kept in here. His patient files."

"He worked with people who'd been touched by the narrative. He knew his specialty, and he knew it well enough to get referrals for people like Alicia Connors, who didn't even know that she was on the verge of turning into a story." Sloane kept pacing. "None of the files we found said 'Sloane is about five inches away from going full-wicked,' or 'Henry is destined for a cold glass grave.' There's another set."

". . . oh." It made perfect sense. I was just so accustomed to no one outside the Bureau writing down anything about the Index that I hadn't been able to see it.

"Yeah, 'oh.'" Sloane kept walking.

I stepped away from the doorway and into the room, walking until I was standing just in front of the desk. Sloane's circuit was taking her around the perimeter over and over again, an endless loop. I followed her once around the room with my eyes before letting my gaze drift upward to the top of the bookshelves. They were ornately carved, showing a clever fox going about his daily rounds. Here he was in a garden, gamboling among the pumpkins; here he was chasing a rabbit; here he was giving a rock to a crow in exchange for an interesting stick.

A crow. My eyes widened, and I ran to the door, calling, "Jeff! Bring me a crow!"

Jeff's head appeared around the edge of the kitchen door-frame. "I beg your pardon?"

"We need a crow in Dr. Reynard's office. Get me a crow."

"You're not serious."

I glared at him.

"You *are* serious. Be right there." Jeff withdrew. I did the same.

Sloane was still pacing. She glanced my way and asked, "You have an idea, or do you just want to see Jeff get his eyes pecked out? I'm good with either one, I'd just like to know."

"I have an idea," I said, and walked back to the desk.

"That's probably the better option," said Sloane.

We waited in silence for a minute—her pacing, me standing perfectly still—until Jeff appeared in the doorway with a handful of Wheat Thins, walking backward as he made his way into the office. A glossy black crow walked after him, pausing only to pick up the Wheat Thins that Jeff was dropping. It had somehow managed to stack five of the square crackers in its beak at once, and was going for a sixth when it saw me, and stopped.

"Hello," I said.

The crow bent forward, carefully placing its precious cargo on the carpet and covering it with one claw before croaking a cautious greeting. I didn't understand it, quite, but the meaning was clear, at least to me. Maybe that meant I was skirting up against my story again. I had known that was a risk when I came back here. Demi had been left behind for a reason.

Having an ATI active again would just increase the odds of my beginning a downhill slide.

"We need your help," I said. "Dr. Reynard hid something in this room. We have to find it. I think you know where it is. He was clever. You have wings."

The crow studied me for a moment more, cocking its head to regard me with first one eye and then the other. Then, with a great rush of wings, it launched itself from the office floor and flew to the bookshelf with the carving of the fox and the crow. It landed there, balancing precariously on the edge of a leather-bound book, and pecked at the carven fox. There was a soft grinding noise, and the panel on the opposite side of the room—the one showing the fox safe at home in his den—slid open.

"Henry, there's a whole set of files in there," said Sloane, her statement followed by the sound of a chair being dragged across the carpet. I didn't turn to face her. I was busy watching the crow.

It looked at me and cawed, just once, like a warning. Then it took off, wings flapping wildly, and flew out of the room. It didn't even pause to collect its pile of Wheat Thins.

"What do you have, Sloane?" asked Jeff.

"It's all the files about Dr. Reynard's patients as they connected to the narrative," she said. I finally turned. She was balancing on the back of the desk chair, a file folder crammed up underneath her arm and another held open in her hands. "He kept really scrupulous notes. Everything's here."

"Everything except who wanted him dead," I said.

"So we still don't know," said Jeff.

"There's a letter," said Sloane, a bit smugly.

I stared at her. "You could have led with that, you know. What does it say?"

Sloane took a deep breath, holding up a piece of paper, and read, "'Well done, my poppets. You have found what I have hidden, and for that, I applaud you'—what, like he did that good a job?"

"Just read, Sloane," I said.

She rolled her eyes and continued, "'These are dangerous days. Trust no one. I have erred on the side of trust, and look what it has gotten me. You must not trust the goose-girl, for she will lead you foul. The stories are changing. The danger is growing. Your own house is not safe.'" Sloane scowled. "That's where it ends. He doesn't say who killed him."

"No, but he gave us more information than we had when we started, and that's something." I shook my head. "We have to be careful with this. Very, very careful."

"Why?" demanded Sloane.

"Because someone knew you were coming here—he was killed right before your appointment, and we can't ignore that—and someone knew about his patients. But *we didn't tell people* you were seeking outside help. The only ones who knew were within the Bureau."

Jeff looked at me, horrified. "Are you saying that someone on the inside had him killed?"

"I'm saying that we need to move very, very carefully right now," I said. "If someone from the Bureau had him killed, then someone from the Bureau knew about how many of his patients were going active. Maybe . . ."

"Someone was encouraging it," said Sloane grimly.

I nodded. "We have a mole," I said.

The three of us stood in silence after that, just looking at each other. In that cold, cruel instant, it seemed that there was nothing else to say.

Bread Crumbs

Memetic incursion in progress: estimated tale type 122E ("The Three Billy Goats Gruff")
Status: ACTIVE

Andrew Robinson generally thought of himself as a reasonable man. Sure, he made his living chasing fairy tales through city streets and trying to keep wicked witches from taking over the world, but apart from that, he was pretty much a normal guy. He worked hard all day and then went home to his loving husband, who was surprisingly tolerant given the circumstances.

And none of this could explain why Andy was currently following a goat across a rickety wooden bridge that should have been condemned and torn down years before. None of it even came close.

The goat—a big, shaggy-haired male, or buck, or whatever the hell it was you called a boy goat—stopped in the middle of the bridge and looked back at Andy. Tail swishing tauntingly, it bleated once before trotting briskly to the other side of the creek. It felt like a dare to Andy. He'd never been one to resist a dare. Teeth grinding together, he launched himself across the bridge, hands already outstretched to grab the damn goat by the horns.

The troll that lunged up from beneath the bridge had his hands outstretched too. And he got to Andy before Andy got to the other side.

# # #

"Agent Robinson, report," I snapped, releasing the button on my walkie-talkie as I pulled it away from my mouth. Only silence answered me. No, not quite silence—the Peter Pan that Sloane was trying to talk off the roof of the apartment building was shouting something at her, his weedy, prepubescent voice shredded into wordless tatters by the wind.

The wind found no such purchase with Sloane. "And *I'm* telling *you* that Neverland isn't real!" she shouted. "You can't fucking fly, kid—the laws of physics are for everybody!"

I glanced toward the narrow stretch of lawn between the building and the street. The firemen were trying to position themselves, looking like some kind of silent movie cliché as they moved their portable trampoline from place to place. They all looked terrified, and I couldn't blame them, even if they didn't see this as anything more complicated than a potential jumper. Pans are tricky things. He couldn't fly—probably—but he might prove surprisingly maneuverable once he was in the air, and that could make the difference between hitting a soft, pliable surface and slamming face-first into the pavement.

Not that it would make all that much difference. If he actually jumped, he'd go fully active, sinking deep into the embrace of his own personal story. Some actives could be recruited to the Bureau, like Demi and Jeff had been. Others . . .

No Pan has ever survived past puberty. When their bodies start changing, they start looking for the rope and the razor blades. There are some betrayals of the flesh that they simply aren't designed to endure.

Sloane wasn't my first choice for a hostage negotiation with a high-strung preteen who wanted to throw himself off a roof to prove a point. For the moment, though, she was the best I had.

I raised my walkie-talkie again. "Goddammit, Andy, you're killing me out here. Where *are* you? I need a status report, and I need it five minutes ago!"

Our would-be Pan shouted something else at Sloane.

"Oh *yeah*?! Never grow up *this*!" she shouted back, and something black fluttered down from the rooftop. For a horrified second, I thought the boy had jumped. Then the black thing landed on one of the firemen, and I realized that the answer was slightly more mundane, if no less horrifying: Sloane had thrown her shirt off the roof. Her bra landed on the grass next to a fireman's feet a moment later.

My own story is in a tenuous sort of abeyance, frozen in time and space until I either find a way to avert it completely or unlock the door of my personal hell and let it flood inside. I can't always feel the narrative moving around me like Sloane does. And, that being said, I would have had to be blind, deaf, and locked in a lead-lined container not to feel the memetic incursion that had been feeding our Peter Pan shatter around me. I raised my walkie-talkie for the third time.

"Pan is neutralized," I said. "I repeat, Pan is neutralized. Sloane showed the kid her tits. I don't know how we're going to write this up for the official report. Is there anybody *there*?"

Only silence answered me.

# # #

Memetic incursion in progress: estimated tale type 327A ("Hansel and Gretel")
Status: ACTIVE

According to the maps of the area, the small patch of forest that had been left behind when the new housing development went in was no more than an acre in diameter, bounded on all sides by civilization. A road ran to the east, houses loomed to the south and north, and a small park had been constructed to the west, as a way of tempting families with young children to move into one of the shiny new houses in need of occupants. Demi knew all that. She'd seen the maps with her own two eyes before she'd agreed to go on this little scouting trip by herself, and she *knew* how small the woods really were. There was no way she could be lost. There was just no way.

All that assurance didn't help her figure out where she was, or how she'd been able to walk so far without seeing any lights or hearing any sounds of traffic. But the thought helped a little, as long as she kept it firmly at the front of her mind and refused to let anything come even close to budging it.

Her grip on her flute was almost as firm as her grip on the thought that she was safe; she wasn't lost, she was just . . . turned around somehow, on this domesticated little patch of wilderness. She'd take another step and everything would open up, and she'd be found again.

She took another step. A branch cracked under her foot, and a child laughed somewhere in the darkness up ahead. Demi's head snapped up, her fingers clenching even tighter on the flute.

"Who's there?" she demanded. "Hannah? Gregory? Is that you? My name is Demi Santos. I'm with the police, and I'm here to take you home."

The laughter came again, somehow managing to sound closer and farther away at the same time. Maybe it was a trick of the local acoustics, part of the same twisting terrain that made this forest feel so much bigger than it could possibly be. Or maybe it was a trick of the narrative.

Feeling increasingly like she was in miles over her head, Demi took another step forward, toward the source of the laughter. "Your parents are very worried about you," she called. *Not worried enough to look at the names "Hannah" and "Gregory" and think about a fairy tale about twins dumb enough to get themselves eaten by a witch,* she thought, and promptly reddened with shame. Why should any happy new parents have harbored thoughts like that for even a second? Everyone knew that fairy tales weren't real.

Everyone except for the people who had to fight those fairy tales every day in order to keep the rest of the world happily ignorant, that is.

"I hate my job," Demi muttered, and ran into the dark, chasing the distant and receding sound of laughter.

The forest was smaller than it seemed. She'd come out the other side soon enough.

She had to.

# # #

Sloane retrieved her shirt from the red-faced fireman, pulling it over her head without bothering to put her bra back on. "Pretty quick thinking, huh, Snowy?" she said, walking toward me and pushing her arms through the sleeves at the same time. Apparently mistaking my expression for awe, she said, "I know, I can walk, talk, *and* dress myself without tripping over my own feet. I went through a barfly phase a few decades ago. Disco was fun, but wow did I have to search a lot of parking lots for my pants."

"First, don't call me Snowy," I said, briefly closing my eyes. It didn't help. I opened them again. "Second, I never want to hear about you looking for your pants again. Third, what in the world possessed you to *flash* a Peter Pan? You could have given the kid a heart attack! Or made him jump right off the damn roof!"

"But I didn't, and I didn't, and if he'd jumped, the firemen were all ready and waiting to catch him." She folded her arms and scowled at me. "I thought you'd be pleased. I found a non-violent solution. Not very wicked of me."

"You showed your breasts to an eleven-year-old boy."

"Yeah, but I didn't let him touch them, so it was just PG-13. His parents can sue us later." Sloane gave a one-shouldered shrug and frowned. "This shouldn't be upsetting you this much. What the fuck crawled up your ass and died?"

"I can't raise Andy on the walkie," I said, gesturing with the offending piece of technology. "Demi's not responding either."

Sloane shrugged again. "So they're busy. I wouldn't have picked up if you'd called me two minutes ago. Priorities, remember?"

I glared at her. She grinned.

"You're the one who told me to fight my story by being more upbeat," she said. "It seems to come with the awesome bonus of pissing you off. I'm going to be upbeat forever."

"It's not your story I'm worried about," I muttered, and glanced toward the lawn, where our erstwhile Pan—now wrapped in a blanket, his eyes tracking Sloane's every movement—was being enfolded in his mother's loving arms.

We normally mop up at most one memetic incursion per month per field team. The rest of the time, we're doing paperwork, visiting the range, and recovering from the stress of those few hours spent in the field. The Aarne-Thompson Index is nothing to mess around with, and an agent who isn't at the top of his or her game is an agent looking to become a statistic. With the number of incursions climbing in recent months— shattering all previous records—it was starting to feel like we were on the edge of an epidemic.

And then the clock literally struck midnight one last time, and "on the edge" became smack-dab in the middle.

According to my watch, it was a little after eight o'clock at night, twenty hours since the first report from Dispatch had scrambled the field teams out of the office and onto the hunt. In that time, we'd received reports of no less than seventeen memetic incursions taking place within the same metropolitan area. They ranged from the common outbreak events, like Sleeping Beauties and Beautiful Vassilisas, all the way to the rare—a Donkeyskin at the Westfield Mall. There were even a few that were modern enough to barely belong to our agency, like Sloane's averted Peter Pan. All the field teams had been forced to split up in order to deal with the sheer scope of the problem. Sloane and I were only still together because agents with activated tale types officially categorized as "evil" weren't allowed out in the field alone.

As if there was any such thing as a "good" fairy tale. Even the best and brightest of stories leaves too many victims in its wake to be anything but evil in my book.

The walkie-talkie crackled before Jeff spoke, asking, "Henry? Sloane? Is anyone there?" Our normally calm archivist sounded like he was on the verge of a complete meltdown. I wanted to join him more than anything.

But there would be time for that later. "This is Agent Marchen," I said, as I brought the walkie-talkie to my lips. "Official channels, Agent Davis. Agent Winters is with me."

"Sorry—I forgot." He didn't sound sorry. "Dispatch just called me. They said that the Peter Pan incursion has been officially averted, and that they'll be sending a cleanup team as soon as one comes free."

"What do you mean, 'as soon as one comes free'?" I asked. "We have twice as many cleanup teams as we do field teams. Why can't they send one *now*?"

"Because they've all been dispatched already." Jeff still didn't sound sorry, but he did sound tired—more tired than I had ever heard him. "The good news continues, I'm afraid."

I pinched the bridge of my nose. "Lay it on me."

"Dispatch has just reported a four-ten three blocks from your current location. You need to respond, and stop the subject before he or she can find something sharp to prick a finger on."

"Anything else?" I asked.

"Yes," he said grimly. "Hurry."

# # #

Memetic incursion in progress: estimated tale type 503 ("The Shoemaker and the Elves")
Status: ACTIVE

Jeffrey Davis, agent, archivist, and very, very frightened man, lowered his walkie-talkie and tried to keep focusing his eyes on the screen of the laptop computer that kept him in contact with headquarters. He was the team's only channel to Dispatch, and on a night like tonight—a night that should have been impossible, based on all previous behaviors of the narrative—they needed him more than ever. And he was going to keep on telling himself that until he believed it, just like he was going to keep telling himself that he'd drawn the short straw through pure chance, and not because the narrative wanted to keep him exactly where he was.

Jeff had never been a very good liar, and now, when his sanity might well depend on his ability to spin a decent falsehood, he found the skill deserting him completely.

The sound of tiny nails being hammered into good, solid wood echoed from the van behind him, tickling his nerves and making his hands itch to start doing something *real*, something that mattered more than typing strings of meaningless words into a computer. You couldn't wear words; you couldn't slip them onto your feet and walk a mile in them, knowing that no sharp rocks or unexpected brambles would pierce your tender flesh. There was no *craftsmanship* in words.

"That is not true," he said, through gritted teeth. "I am an archivist. I am a librarian. I collect words because words are the truest and longest-lasting craft in the world. My books will last longer than any pair of shoes."

Even shoes made of lead? The whisper used his own voice, which made it all the harder to ignore. He'd been hearing it since he was a teenager. It hadn't been this loud in years. *Or iron? Seven pairs of iron shoes, that's what a princess needs if she wants to find her husband, the hedgehog, and who will make them for her? No cobbler could make such needful things of such base materials; they need help. They need* your *help . . .*

"I will not be your plaything," Jeff said, shaking his head fiercely, like that could be enough to chase the cruel and ceaseless words away. It never was, and yet he had to try it all the same.

The sound of hammering continued behind him, ceaseless and joyful at the same time. All he had to do was turn around and there would be work enough to fill the rest of his life. He would never have to be idle again; never need to spend an instant wondering what he was supposed to do next, or wishing that he could have been part of some other story, some story where he got a white horse and a princess to save (one specific princess, maybe, with lips as red as fresh-dyed shoe leather, and skin like new-bleached suede . . .) instead of a hammer and an endless aching need for motion.

Jeff Davis closed his eyes, forcing himself to be still, and wished for the tempting agony to stop.

# # #

The four-ten turned out to be a woman with a needle full of tainted heroin that would have plunged her into a sleep deep enough to be classified as a medical coma. I knocked it out of her hand and Sloane restrained her while we waited for the narrative to snap and let her go. As soon as we were sure that she was clear I called the police—no need for a cleanup team on this one, since nothing impossible had actually happened—and stayed with her until a squad car came to haul her off to the hospital. Our old friend, Officer Troy, made the pickup. That was by design. Anyone else might have held us for a statement. He just looked tired, shoved our would-be Sleeping Beauty into his backseat, and peeled off down the street, lights and siren blaring.

"He's going to wind up the target of some hungry Greek monster one day," observed Sloane, leaning against the rough brick wall of the alley. She had produced a nail file from some-where—possibly from our junkie's purse—and was shaping her already-perfect nails. "A name like 'Troy'; he's just begging for it."

"Your opinion is duly noted and dismissed as crap," I said. I raised the walkie-talkie, depressing the button, and asked, "Agent Robinson, are you there? Report. Agent Santos, I'd like to hear from you too. We're sort of thin on the ground out here, and the city's turned into some kind of fucked-up storybook nightmare."

Sloane raised an eyebrow.

"More fucked-up than usual," I amended. "Sloane and I need backup. What's your position?"

I released the button. There was no reply.

"You know, if I believed in having feelings—which I don't—this is about where I would start getting really worried about the assholes we work with," commented Sloane, still filing her nails. "I mean, we've put down, what? Three memetic incursions so far tonight, and they're still off the table? Either they're having pizza somewhere and laughing at us behind their hands, or they're in serious trouble."

"I wish I could think that it was pizza." I raised the walkie-talkie again. "Agent Davis, have you heard from Robinson or Santos? We're starting to worry a little, and we could use the backup if the evening is going to continue in its current vein for much longer."

There was a long silence after I released the button. A sudden chill washed over me.

"Agent Davis, this is Agent Marchen. Please respond."

This time, a whisper came back over the airwaves, so thin and flattened out by the transmission that I had to strain to hear it. "They won't stop . . . Henry, they won't stop banging . . ."

Sloane straightened. "Banging?"

I held up a finger, motioning for her to hold on, and pressed the button to speak. "Jeff, what are you talking about? Are you still in the van?"

His response was instant, if no louder. "They want me to work with them, but I don't want to, Henry. I don't want to, I don't like that story. I don't like the way it ends . . ."

Oh, crap. "Jeff, are you in the van?"

". . . yes."

"Hold on. We'll be right there. Just *hold on.*" Our current position was almost half a mile from where Jeff was parked. I lowered the walkie-talkie, clipping it back to my belt, and slanted a sharp glance at Sloane. "Don't wait for me if I fall behind. We need to get to Jeff, and we need to do it *now.*"

She nodded, pushing herself away from the wall. Before I could say anything else, she broke into a run, racing out of the alley and down the street. I followed her, fighting to catch up even though I knew I couldn't.

Hold on Jeff, I thought. *We're coming . . .*

# # #

Memetic incursion in progress: estimated tale type 440 ("The Frog Prince")
Status: ACTIVE

Getting away from a troll the size of an angry gorilla was easier said than done. Thank God for Tasers—now there was something that needed to go on a T-shirt. Andy collapsed onto the riverbank, panting and glaring at the rapidly dissolving mass of mud that had been the bridge troll—right up until he ran several hundred volts through its ugly face.

"Yeah, that's right," he said. "Suck on that, you ugly-ass bastard." He'd lost his wallet and his walkie-talkie when the troll dropped him in the creek. Hopefully Henry wasn't trying to get hold of him yet. She probably had everything under control and was grumbling about waiting for the rest of the team to reach the extraction point. Night like tonight, with at least three stories going concurrently, she was going to have a lot to grumble about.

Well, she was going to have to wait a little longer if she wanted to extract him. His ass hurt from its impact with the rocks under the water, and every inch of his clothing was soaked through. Groaning, Andy bent forward, pulled off his shoes, and began peeling his sodden socks off his feet. There was only so much a man could take.

Besides, he needed to find those damn goats before he officially declared this memetic incursion dead in the water. The last thing he wanted to do was jump the gun and get yelled at for leaving a narrative unfinished—

A splash from the nearby bank drew his attention, and he turned to see a large, dark green bullfrog with enormous yellow eyes sitting next to him in the mud. "Well hello, Mr. Frog," he said, knowing that exhaustion was powering his lapse into silliness and not caring overly much. At least he was still alive. "I hope that troll wasn't a friend of yours."

"I am not a friend to trolls," the frog replied. It had a very faint British accent, like someone who had been watching old Hugh Grant movies for too long, and had forgotten how their vowels were normally pronounced. "But you, my friend, have lost something in these waters. Something that I could recover for you, if you made it worth my while."

Andy barely managed to swallow the urge to groan. Talking to the frog was a rookie mistake: anyone who had been with the Bureau for more than six months should have known better than to start a conversation with anything that wasn't supposed to answer back. "I'm sorry," he said. "I don't make deals with amphibians. No offense."

"None taken," the frog replied, and this was just plain ridiculous—a frog didn't have the jaw structure for human enunciation, much less the cranial capacity to form a complete sentence. A frog was basically just a squishy sack of muscles and organs, waiting for something bigger to come along and gulp it down. "I just thought you might like to have your wallet returned, that's all. Lots of things in that wallet. Lots of good memories, I'm sure. You even put that plastic sheeting over your pictures to protect them from the elements—I mean, I'm just a frog, and you don't make deals with amphibians, but it seems to me that a man doesn't put plastic over his photos if he doesn't care about them."

Protocol said that he should tell the frog to go away, thus preventing a four-forty scenario from solidifying around him. But suddenly, that wallet felt like it was just about the most important thing in the world. He couldn't imagine going home and trying to explain to Mike that he'd lost all their pictures in the creek, especially since his NDAs meant that he wouldn't be able to tell his husband why he'd been crossing that bridge in the first place.

"What would you want in exchange for getting my wallet back?" The words hung in the air between them, heavy with narrative potential. It was too late to snatch them back. The air seemed suddenly warmer, and it smelled of honeysuckle and brine.

"Oh, not much," said the frog, and hopped a foot or so closer. Frogs can't smile.

In the dim evening light, it looked like this one was trying.

# # #

The van doors were closed and—as I learned to my dismay when I tried to wrench them open—locked. I slapped my pocket and swore. "Sloane, I don't have my keys!" I shouted. "Do you?"

"Like you people let me drive? Fuck, no, I don't have keys to the van." She bent, picking up a large rock from the curb. "On the other hand, I don't really need them, do I?"

"Sloane—" My protest died when I heard Jeff scream inside the van. It was a shrill, agonized sound, and it hurt my heart in ways I hadn't known were possible. "*Throw the fucking rock, Sloane!*"

The words had barely left my lips before Sloane's rock was smashing through the driver's side window and she was hitting the button to unlock all the van's doors. I wrenched the rear door open with a fierceness that would leave my shoulders aching for days. In that moment, I didn't care.

The field van has a fairly basic configuration: front seat, middle seat, open back area that can be used for storage in a pinch—even body storage—or as a makeshift work area when we need someone to stay behind and coordinate. Jeff was huddled in the corner next to the folding desk that he'd been using as a temporary command center. His laptop was still open, the screen casting enough light that I could see how he was shaking. He had one arm looped around his knees and the other holding his head down, like he was afraid that he would float away without something to anchor him.

"Jeff?" My voice sounded small and useless in the thin night air. He didn't respond.

Gravel crunched as Sloane stepped up beside me. Her small gasp was enough to tell me that I wasn't overreacting to his appearance. I motioned for her to stay where she was and climbed into the van, crouching down beside him. There was no point in crowding the man and making the situation even worse than it already was.

"Jeff?" I murmured. "Are you okay? Can you hear me?"

He didn't say anything. He just kept on shaking.

"He's story-struck." Sloane sounded frightened. That wasn't a good sign. I glanced over my shoulder at her, raising my eyebrows in silent indication that she needed to keep talking. She shook her head and said, "Jeff went active with his narrative years ago. It shouldn't be able to tangle him up like this anymore, but it has. Something's feeding it enough power that it managed to throw a rope around him, and now it's trying to reel him in."

"Wait." I put a hand on Jeff's shoulder, trying to ignore the way his body jumped and twitched beneath my fingers, like he was dancing himself to pieces. "Are you telling me he's being drawn *back* into his goddamn *fairy tale*?"

Sloane nodded. "That's exactly what I'm telling you. I don't know how it managed to get its hooks into him again, or what he's hearing right now, but our little shoemaker's elf is falling toward ever after, and he's falling fast and hard."

"So how do we make it stop?"

She hesitated. Finally, voice surprisingly soft, she said, "I have no idea."

# # #

Memetic incursion in progress: estimated tale type 327A ("Hansel and Gretel")
Status: ACTIVE

"Kids? Gregory? Hannah? Are you out there? Your parents are really worried about you. I need to get you home before they worry even more. Answer me and let me know that you're there, okay?" Demi took another step forward into the forest, which seemed deeper and darker and less possible by the second. "Hannah? Gregory?"

The only answer was more of that sweet, childish, mocking laughter. Demi scowled, her fingers clenching convulsively tight around the body of her flute. How dare they laugh at *her*, Demi Santos! Didn't they know who she was? Didn't they know what she could *do*? If they forced her, she could—

She froze with the thought still only half-formed. She could what? Play a come-here-kids song on her flute and lure them out of the woods against their own free will? That might have been a good option, but Jeff hadn't given her any sheet music, and if she called the rest of the team out of the field because she couldn't catch up with a couple of stupid kids, there would be hell to pay. Just the thought of Henry's bloody lips pursed in disapproval—again—made Demi's stomach turn. They kept saying she was one of the most versatile story types in the Agency, but it sure didn't feel that way. Not when Jeff could do three times the paperwork with half the effort, and Sloane could slap the story right out of half the fairy-tale princesses they encountered, and Henry—

Henry was Henry. Demi had always liked *Snow White and the Seven Dwarves* when she was a little girl, but now that she'd met the real thing, she wasn't sure she'd ever be able to watch it again without shuddering.

Whatever she had to do to get the kids and get back without making Henry disappointed in her, she was going to do it. "Hannah! Gregory!" She squared her shoulders, trying to push away the unease that had been threatening to consume her since she stepped off the sidewalk and into the shadow of the trees. "You need to come back here *right now*, or you're going to be in serious trouble!"

Nothing answered her this time, not even laughter. Demi took a furious step forward, and froze as she saw something pale on the forest floor. She stooped, reaching out to gingerly pick up whatever it was with her free hand. The pale thing was soft and spongy and light. She raised it to her face, and the smell of angel food cake hit her, cloyingly sweet and unmistakable.

The kids were leaving themselves a trail of bread crumbs to follow through the wood. Suddenly feeling as if things were much more urgent than they had been a few seconds before, Demi tossed the piece of sponge cake aside and started running again, heading ever deeper into the seemingly endless sea of trees.

# # #

"There has to be something we can do." I looked desperately back at Sloane, my hand still clutching Jeff's shoulder. Part of me felt, however irrationally, like letting go even for an instant would be the same as letting go forever: he would slip away, and I would never find the right combination of words and gestures to bring him back to us.

"I'm not an archivist, okay?" Sloane shook her head. "We could call Dispatch, see if they know anything about snapping somebody out of this sort of fucked-up fugue state—" She took a step forward, reaching for Jeff's discarded walkie-talkie. Why she wasn't going for her own, I didn't know, and I didn't have time to wonder for long.

"No!" I snapped, putting out a hand to keep her from reaching her goal. She stopped, looking at me quizzically, too confused to be annoyed. "Don't call Dispatch. Not yet."

"Why don't you—oh." Understanding washed across her face. "You don't want this going in his file."

"Not until we know what's happening." Jeff had been active but stable for years. If an active narrative flare got entered in his file, he'd be pulled off field duty and trapped in the Archives until someone certified him safe for public duty. It was the exact opposite of the way people with stories like Sloane were treated: the more likely she seemed to flare up, the more likely it was that she'd be shoved into the field at every opportunity. But that was because "evil" stories traditionally had a short shelf life, and Human Resources wanted to suck every drop of useful service out of her that they could before she inevitably self-destructed. Jeff was a solid, hardworking, domestic sort of a story. He could last forever in the Archives. There were people who thought he should have been there all along.

If they took him out of the field "temporarily," it would turn permanent with the application of a single stamp. He'd never see the outside of an office building again. And that would be a shame, in every possible way.

Sloane nodded. "Okay, well, here are our options. We could kill him."

I gaped at her. "That's not an improvement, Sloane."

"I didn't say I was offering options you'd *like*, but fine, we'll take murder off the table for right now. It was just an idea." Sloane shook her head. "We could poison him. A ten-year nap makes most things better."

"I am not poisoning Jeff. Keep trying."

"We could find him a handsome prince and get him kissed. Kisses break all the shit that enchanted naps don't. Hell, they even break enchanted naps."

For a long moment, I didn't say anything. Finally, I asked, "Does it have to be a prince who does the kissing? Because I hate princes."

Sloane blinked. "You're actually considering it? Damn, you are worried. No, it doesn't have to be a prince; it just has to be someone who the narrative has coded as royalty. You know, kings and queens and the occasional duke's eldest son who doesn't know how to feel fear and all that bullshit and—"

Sloane stopped midsentence as I pulled my hand off Jeff's shoulder, grabbed him by the hair, and yanked his head up. His glasses were aslant on his nose, and his eyes were tightly closed.

"Oh, you are *not* gonna—"

"Please, please don't file a sexual harassment suit against me for this, okay?" I muttered, pulled Jeff closer to me, and kissed him.

# # #

Memetic incursion in progress: estimated tale type 440 ("The Frog Prince")
Status: ACTIVE

"I'm a married man," said Andy dubiously, still eyeing the frog, which still seemed to be trying to smile at him. It was a creepy thing to see outside of a cartoon, a frog plastering a pleasant expression across its little froggy face like it wanted to be mistaken for something human. "I can't do anything that would make Mike angry."

"But you see, that's where your conundrum comes into play," said the frog, which sounded more articulate and less . . . well, frog-like . . . with every sentence that it uttered. Andy was reasonably sure that was a bad sign, but he was starting to have trouble remembering precisely why that was. "If you lose the wallet, your precious Mike will be angry. So which is going to offend him more deeply, and be more difficult to repair? One little kiss, or an entire missing wallet?"

"You're a *frog*," said Andy. "I think that kissing random wildlife is sort of inappropriate, Mike or no Mike."

"More or less inappropriate than the time you kissed that sunny-haired boy with the fairy-tale eyes?" The frog hopped closer. Its smile was gone. Somehow that didn't help. "He was trying not to become a Cinderella, and you could have given him bus fare and the address for a safe house, but instead you kissed him behind the bar where he'd been bucking bottles for a dollar an hour, didn't you? You drove him almost a hundred miles and you told your precious Mike that you'd been stuck late at work. You weren't unfaithful with your body—not any more than a kiss, and those haven't been an executable offense in centuries—but you wanted to be, didn't you? You dreamt of it. You're dreaming of it still, when the night is dark and your heart betrays you."

Andy's mouth was dry, and his breath came in short heaves, like his lungs no longer quite knew how to do their job. That had to be what was making him light-headed: he was a big man, he needed his air if he was going to keep going. "You . . . you can't know about that," he stammered. "No one knows about that." Not even Henry. He'd told her that the kid (*Jason his name was Jason*) didn't trust the buses, that he was too afraid of being caught there by his wicked stepfather. And she'd believed it, because Andy was trustworthy, and because she'd never had an impure thought in her lily-colored life.

"I know because you know, and you didn't really think that you were talking to a *frog*, now, did you? Frogs don't talk." The frog winked one enormous golden eye. "I'll just go fetch that wallet for you now, and then we can have a serious conversation about what you're really willing to pay to get it back, all right? You just wait right where you are."

With a single mighty hop the frog was back in the water, disappearing into the black. Andy tried to convince himself to

stand, and found to his dismay—if not to his particular surprise—that his legs would not obey him. He was going to wait,
it seemed, until the frog-that-wasn't came back with his wallet
and the bargaining began in earnest.

Andy Robinson sat alone in the mud and thought that he
had never been so frightened in his life.

# # #

For one terrifying moment, it seemed like my grand gesture
was going to be just that: a grand gesture that changed nothing
and didn't bring Jeff any closer to home. Then the slack lips
pressed against mine shifted, slightly at first, but with increasing intensity, until Jeff was kissing me back with an urgency
that I could never have imagined. He shifted positions, and I
thought he was going to pull away until his hand hesitantly
touched my hair and I realized that he was actually trying to
draw me closer. I scooted forward on my knees, encouraging
the motion. Anything that would keep him with us.

Behind me, Sloane started laughing. "Holy shit, Snowdrop,
you've got the Professor's motor up and running."

I freed a hand, held it up behind me, and flipped her off.
That only made her laugh harder.

I turned my attention back to Jeff, but it was too late; the
damage had been done. As soon as I had become distracted, he
had stopped responding quite so enthusiastically, and now he
was pulling away from me. I leaned back, not forcing the issue.

"You okay?" I asked.

He blinked at me, mouth working silently as he tried to
process the question. His eyes were open now and very wide
behind the wire rims of his glasses. I'd never noticed before

just how brown they were, flecked with little spots of hazel and almost-gold.

Finally, he figured out what he wanted to say: "Henry, you *kissed* me."

"I know, and I'm sorry. You were story-struck, and we needed to get you out of it any way that we could." I tucked a lock of hair behind my ear, grimacing. "I'll understand completely if you want to file a harassment claim or something, but in my defense, we were trying to prevent you getting reported to Dispatch as a victim of the narrative, and—"

Jeff's kiss cut me off before I could get another word out. I squeaked in surprise before allowing myself to sink into it, enjoying the moment while it lasted. It was probably just left over narrative pressure encouraging him to behave like a good prince. And since he hadn't kissed me while I was sleeping in a glass coffin, it wasn't like he could do me any damage, story-wise.

When he pulled away, his cheeks were flushed. "I really appreciate you snapping me out of my story, even though it's going to be hard not to document 'kiss from a beautiful woman' as a means of paying your elves," he said. "But I assure you, I'm not going to be filing any sort of complaint against you for doing something I wanted done so very badly."

"Oh," I said dazedly.

"Yeah, yeah, the dumb bitch is the fairest in the land, we know," said Sloane, sounding bored. It was an affectation; there was an edge of concern under her words that rendered them both softer and more biting than usual. "Now that we've got that out of the way, how about you tell us what happened?"

"The story." Jeff's voice turned hollow. It was like he'd seen a ghost. I shifted positions so that I could sit beside him, letting him see both Sloane and me as he spoke. He caught my hand before I could get too far away, and I stopped moving. If he needed me for comfort right now, he could have me. "It was . . . it was here."

I frowned. "What do you mean?"

"I mean I heard the sound of hammering in the van. Shoes being made, leather being cut . . . it wanted me, Henry." He glanced at me, the streetlight glinting off his glasses. "This isn't happening because of some impossible concordance of events. This is intentional. The narrative is hunting, and I think . . . I think that it's hunting for us."

# # #

Memetic incursion in progress: estimated tale type 327A ("Hansel and Gretel")
Status: ACTIVE

Demi stepped out of the trees and into something out of a dream—or a nightmare. It was impossible to tell the difference, because there was just no way that it was real. No matter how strange her life had become in the past few months, things like this just didn't exist outside of . . . outside . . .

Outside of fairy tales.

The house was the sort of place where you could raise a family or live by yourself, content with your music and your books and maybe a small dog or something, so that the nights wouldn't seem so lonely. It was easily three floors in height, built so that it would have blended easily with the houses in the development outside the wood . . . if not for its building materials. Demi loved it on sight, and feared it, too, because of what it represented.

Every inch of the house, from the base of the foundation to the tip of the roof, was made of sweets. Great slabs of frosted gingerbread formed the walls, decorated with curlicue swirls of frosting and with dozens of pieces of penny candy, candy corn, and jewel-toned hard candies. The windows looked a little too thin and irregular to be glass, but they could be hardened corn syrup and cream of tartar. Sugar glass was easy to make, if you knew how, and she'd learned from her grandmother years ago.

Smoke wafted from the red-velvet brick chimney, and that was the most impossible thing of all. No one could possibly *live* in a house like this, made of sweets and sitting in the middle of nowhere. It wasn't safe. It wasn't sanitary. It wasn't up to building code. It had to be some kind of a trap.

The front door swung open in silent invitation. Demi took a step forward.

"Gregory? Hannah? Are you kids inside the creepy candy house? Because I want you to come out of there *right now.*" Her voice wavered a little at the end, but she felt that it was a good command, overall. It sounded commanding, at least, and that was all she'd really been hoping for.

This time, the giggling came from inside the house. Demi took another step forward.

"Stop messing around!" she shouted. "I have to get you back to your parents!"

The giggles stopped. The candy house didn't change, and yet somehow everything changed, as it went from whimsical and silly to looming threateningly over her, a haunted mansion waiting for its next victim. Demi shuddered as she took another step. The kids were inside. She had to get the kids. She couldn't go back without them. She couldn't possibly—

Her flute felt hot in her hands, like a burning brand plucked from the center of a fire. She would have thrown anything else aside if it had come so close to burning her, but not this, not now. Instead, Demi closed her eyes and raised the burning metal to her lips, fingers already starting to trace a song she didn't need any sheet music to know. This song was part of her story, and since she was part of her story, that meant that the song was a part of *her*. All she had ever needed to do was let go of the things that were stopping her from seeing how important it was.

All she ever had to do was play.

# # #

Sloane twitched. It was a strangely convulsive motion, like she had just been stung by a bee that no one else could see. Jeff and I both turned to look at her. He was sitting on the van's bumper, drinking from a bottle of Gatorade as he tried to steady himself enough to join us in the field. After what had happened with his story, there was no way we were going to leave him alone again.

"Sloane?" I said. "What is it?"

"I don't know," she replied. "The narrative is spiking, and I don't know why." She gave us a serious look. "This is bad."

"We already knew that," I said.

"I can testify on the matter," said Jeff.

"I don't mean this is 'see who can get the snarkiest quip in' bad; I mean this is *bad*," Sloane said. "Jeff, were you recording when the noises started?"

"No, but I talked to Henry on the walkie-talkie while they were going on," he said, reaching up to adjust his glasses. "Why?"

"Henry, did you hear anything out of the ordinary?" Sloane turned to me, a strange, fierce hopefulness in her eyes. "Banging, clanging, anything that would say 'Jeff has opened an illicit elf shoe shop behind his desk'?"

"No," I said. "What's this all about?"

"Before my current issues with the narrative started, I heard this noise for hours. It was just this huge blaring siren that wouldn't slack off and wouldn't stop ringing in my ears. It was enough to make me want to rip the throat out of the world in order to make it stop." Sloane looked grim. "I don't think my parrot could hear it. I don't think *anyone* could hear it, except for me. The narrative started this shit by going after me."

"Why didn't you—" said Jeff.

"You never said—" I said, at the same time.

"Because I didn't want you people to think I was losing my fucking mind, okay?" Sloane snapped. "I start dreaming about poison apples and you start calling for the therapists and reaching for the restraints. I tell you it started with me hearing an alarm that nobody else could hear, and you start looking into rubber rooms. Thanks, but no thanks. As long as I can keep myself from poisoning Blanche over there," she gestured violently toward me, "I can do a lot more to figure out what's going on from out here than I ever could in an Agency institution."

"I wouldn't have let them do that to you," I said.

"You wouldn't have had a choice," Sloane said, shrugging off my loyalty like it was nothing. She focused back on Jeff. "Okay. We have about thirty seconds before Henry does the math and realizes we're down two people, who are probably about to be eaten alive by predatory fairy tales. So tell me before she freaks: What can we do? How can we stop this, how did we start this?"

"I . . ." Jeff stopped for a moment, paling until his skin tone was close to mine. "Oh, God. You and I were both attacked by our stories. Henry's been talking to birds. The narratives are leaking. There's only one thing that could do this." He put his Gatorade aside, sliding quickly to his feet. "We have to find the others."

"You're not the one I expected to go all big damn hero on me," said Sloane, grabbing his arm. "We're not going anywhere until you tell me what your 'one thing' is."

I wanted to intervene, to tell her to let go of him before somebody got hurt. Instead, I stood frozen, thinking about what they were both saying, and thinking about the crow in Dr. Reynard's kitchen. Talking to it had seemed like the most natural thing in the world.

Maybe Deputy Director Brewer was right. Maybe I was being compromised.

"There are tale types that include storytellers," said Jeff. "The whole Scheherazade class of narratives depend on someone who can tell them—and that's just one grouping. We could be dealing with someone, a person, who can control the narrative. And if that's true . . ."

"If that's true, then we're all screwed," I said. "More screwed, I mean. Okay. Let's go."

# # #

Memetic incursion in progress: estimated tale type 440 ("The Frog Prince")
Status: ACTIVE

The frog stayed in the water for at least five minutes. Even a talking amphibian couldn't stop the current from doing its work, and Andy's wallet hadn't been that heavy; it must have traveled some distance down the creek bed before the frog went back in to look for it.

When the frog finally came back out of the water, the wallet clutched smugly in its jaws, Andy was ready for it. He might not have been able to make his legs work, but he was fully capable of moving his arms, and the high weeds around the creek had proved to contain a great many treasures. There were tools there—even makeshift weapons, for a man who knew how to use them.

The frog probably didn't even see the rusty old crowbar coming before Andy smashed it down on the fragile plane of the amphibian's skull. The frog was driven down into the mud, its entire head taking on a distinctly flattened aspect. The wallet shot out of its mouth, coming to rest nearly a foot away.

"This isn't . . . over . . . you fool . . ." wheezed the frog. Its legs started to spasm. "You'll pay. You'll . . ." The spasms stopped.

Andy gave the frog's body an experimental prod with the end of his crowbar. "You dead, or I need to hit you again? You know what, fuck it. I'm just going to hit you again."

He actually hit the frog's body three more times, until it started to feel less like vengeance and more like sadism. Then he climbed to his feet, his legs suddenly working once more, picked up his wallet, and started looking for a way back up to solid ground.

He barely even noticed that he was still holding the crowbar.

# # #

Andy had been assigned to follow a bunch of semi-spectral goats over a creek until he either managed to dispel them or found the troll that was inevitably going to show up and start trying to eat them. The idea was to prevent a troll bridge narrative from establishing itself in the area. There were kids around here.

Jeff, Sloane, and I approached the bridge cautiously. Jeff and I both had our service weapons drawn. Sloane was empty-handed, which made her the most dangerous of us all.

Something was rustling in the scrub grass that grew around the creek. I stopped, motioning for the others to do the same. "Who's that trip-trap-tripping over my bridge?" I called.

"Fuck you," Andy's voice replied. One large brown hand appeared through the grass, followed a moment later by his head and shoulders as he pulled himself up to our level. "Where the fuck have you people been all night? I've been dying out here."

"Nice crowbar," said Sloane.

Andy shot the rusty crowbar in his hand a look, like he'd never seen it before. Then he flung it away into the weeds and climbed to his feet. "You didn't give me all the intel, Henry. I'm pissed."

"I don't know what you're talking about," I said. He was wet and muddy, and there was what looked like blood on the cuff of one sleeve. "Are you all right?"

"I took out the troll, no problem," he said. "But the frog . . ." A bleak look crossed his face. "I think the frog nearly had me."

"You fell into a Frog Prince?" asked Jeff, sounding horrified. "I didn't think you qualified for a four-forty scenario. You're not a prince. I mean, you've never shown any princely tendencies . . ."

"Whoever's driving this thing is trying to take us out," I said. "If they're twisting the narrative to force it to do what they want, it doesn't *matter* if Andy would normally qualify for a four-forty." I turned to the muddy agent. "You okay, Andy?"

"I'm fine," he snarled. "I beat the goddamn thing to death and left it by the water. You think that's far enough from happy ever after to save my ass?"

"I say again, *nice* crowbar," said Sloane approvingly.

"I think you're good, but don't really have time to worry about that right now. There's something more pressing going on, so if you're capable of moving, we need to move," I said.

Andy's eyes skirted over the three of us, drawing an immediate and unwanted conclusion. "Demi?" he asked.

"She dropped off the walkie-talkie the same time you did, and we haven't been able to rouse her," I said.

"Then what the fuck are we standing around here for?" he said. "Let's move."

We moved.

# # #

Demi's assignment had taken her into the little square of wood-land still standing at the heart of the newest neighborhood in the area. It was too small to get lost in, yet somehow two of the local children had managed to do exactly that: Gregory and Hannah, twins, age eight. They were ripe for a three-twenty-seven-A, and when the story came calling, they went after it. Demi should have had no trouble pulling the wayward kids out of the woods and returning them to their homes.

So why the hell wasn't she answering her walkie-talkie?

Sloane was the first one into the trees, with Andy's muddy, rusty crowbar clutched in one hand like a sword. She'd some-how managed to find the thing in the grass, and had refused to leave it behind—probably because she was charmed by the idea of beating someone to death Tarantino-style. As long as she was taking point, I wasn't going to argue with her about it.

Jeff and I moved at the center of the group, while Andy, who wasn't moving as quickly as he normally did, brought up the rear. I kept glancing back to make sure that he was okay, and that another story hadn't swooped out of nowhere to claim him as its own. That wasn't an ordinary fear for me. This wasn't an ordinary night.

It only got worse when Sloane appeared from the trees up ahead of us. "You guys need to see this," she said, sounding subdued. The crowbar was dangling limply in her hand, no longer held like a weapon; she was clinging to it more the way a little girl would hold a teddy bear.

I stopped. "How bad is it?" I asked.

"Bad," she said. "Come on."

This time, when she vanished into the trees, the three of us were right behind her. She only had to lead us a little way, to a small clearing that had probably seen a hundred games of hide-and-seek and tag since the housing development was put in place. Two small bodies were curled at the center of the clearing, their clothes and skin blackened by the fire that had killed them. I had no doubt that when they were examined by someone with the proper tools, they would be identified as Hannah and Gregory. Everything smelled like burnt meat . . . and like sweet vanilla frosting, the kind that children might imagine using as the spackle in a life-size candy cottage.

Jeff moved to circle the bodies, studying them with a practiced archivist's eye. Finally, he knelt and pulled something from the edge of the ashes, holding it up for the rest of us to see. Even in the dim light that filtered through the trees from the street, Demi's badge managed to gleam.

"Is she dead?" asked Andy.

"No," said Jeff. "There are only two bodies here. This is a message."

"We've lost her." My voice sounded hollow. "She failed, and the narrative took her." And I didn't have any idea how we were going to get her back, or if getting her back was even possible. Demi was gone, the narrative was being controlled by a person or persons unknown, and we were screwed.

"The mole," said Sloane.

I nodded. "It's the only explanation."

"We need to go," said Jeff. He walked back to the rest of us, offering me Demi's badge. I took it without thinking. "The narrative may have settled for the night, but we need to get back to headquarters. We need to tell them what's happening."

"Things are about to get ugly," said Andy.

I looked back to the two dead children—the kids Demi was supposed to have saved. "Things already are," I said quietly, and no one had an answer to that. No one said anything at all.

Empty Nest

Memetic incursion in progress: no memetic incursions currently in progress
Status: NO ONGOING THREAT

The four of us made our way back to the van without saying anything. There were things we needed to say—too many things, when you got right down to it—but our voices seemed to have collectively failed us, leaving us as mute as a Little Mermaid who has not yet made contact with her Prince.

The streets outside the little stretch of forest were dark and quiet, giving no indication of the chaos that had been unfolding so nearby only a short time before. The smell of smoke and burnt sugar tainted the air, making it difficult for me to breathe in through my nose. Jeff was still unsteady on his feet; I looped an arm around his waist, keeping him stable as we walked up the grassy knoll at the edge of the park. Our van was waiting for us there, representing the closest thing to safety we were going to find.

Andy stopped a few feet from the van and pulled out his phone. I looked at him, raising an eyebrow in silent question. He nodded: yes, he was calling for cleanup, and yes, he trusted me to keep Jeff and Sloane safe until he was finished. I echoed his nod, and guided Jeff the rest of the way to the vehicle.

"Sloane, get the door," I said. My voice seemed too small for what we had just seen, lacking the strength it needed to make any impact on the scene.

For once in her life, Sloane didn't argue. She just opened the already unlocked rear doors, disappearing into the depths of the van. I stopped, pulling Jeff to a halt along with me. He blinked.

"We don't know if it's safe," I said, trying to project a level of calm I wasn't actually feeling. I might never be that calm again. I shook my head to clear the thought away and said, "The narrative has just stopped trying to kill us. There's a chance it left us a little surprise in the van."

Jeff frowned, glaring at the open van door even as he leaned against my shoulder, trying to keep himself upright. "Sometimes I truly hate fairy tales, Henry," he said.

"Yeah." I sighed. "Me too."

"Here's something else to hate," said Andy, moving up on my other side. "The cleanup crews are all stretched as thin as the field teams, thanks to the number of incursions we've had to deal with tonight. It'll be about an hour before anyone can get here."

I stared at him. "An *hour*? Did you tell Dispatch that we have civilian casualties? And that Demi's gone missing?"

"Yes. That's why the cleanup crews are getting here as fast as they are." Andy looked grim. "We're to remain where we are until we can formally hand off the scene. We have not been instructed to maintain a perimeter, but we are to intervene if we see anyone trying to enter the woods."

Sloane's head popped out of the van door. "Are they high, or just stupid?"

"Maybe both," I said. "How's the van?"

"Clear. Nothing here that isn't ours."

"Good. Move." Miracles happen, because Sloane didn't argue this time, either: she just hopped out of the van, allowing me to help Jeff over to the rear bumper, where he sat down heavily. If she went along with my orders one more time, the Vatican might have to seriously consider her for sainthood. "Is there a convenience store or something near here?"

"There's a 7-Eleven a few blocks over, at the edge of the commercial district," said Andy. "Why?"

"Because Jeff looks like he's been run over by a bus, and you don't look much better. Sloane, stay here and keep an eye on them."

Sloane frowned at me. "What, you're making a munchies run?"

I shrugged. "Yes."

"Cool. I want some of those little ice-cream bites and a Slurpee. And I won't let anybody hurt the boys, since they're too wussy to defend themselves." Sloane produced a file from inside her shirt, and began addressing her nails. She didn't offer to give me any money.

I hadn't expected that she would. "Call me if you need anything," I said. "Andy, which way was the 7-Eleven?"

He pointed wordlessly. I turned, and started walking.

# # #

The 7-Eleven was virtually deserted: just me, the night clerk, and a homeless man who blanched when he saw me. From the way he was twitching, he was probably high enough that my dead-white complexion made me look like the Angel of Death, coming to punish him for his past transgressions. Thankfully, punishing people isn't usually a part of my job description. I stood aside and let him rush out of the store, leaving me with open aisles and the freedom to browse at my leisure.

The clerk barely even glanced in my direction. Her attention was fixed on the TV mounted above the register. She had twisted her torso at an angle that even Sloane would have been impressed by, and she stayed that way the whole time I was shopping, not even untwisting when I approached the counter with my armload of drinks and salty snacks.

"Hell of a thing, isn't it?" she asked.

That was the first sign she'd given of knowing that I was in the store. I nodded, putting my things down on a stretch of counter where she hopefully wouldn't knock them over as soon as she moved. "Not sure what you mean in specific, but I find that 'hell of a thing' is usually a good description of the world."

"This night." She finally unwound herself, sliding easy as you please onto her stool before beginning to ring up my purchases. "It's all over the news. Five fires, three murders, some missing kids . . ."

Three murders was better than I'd been expecting, given the number of incursions the Bureau had been trying to handle. "You're right," I said. "That's definitely a hell of a thing. Does anyone have any idea why all this is happening?"

"Something in the air, I guess," she said. "It's probably not terrorists."

"I guess that's a good thing." I swiped my credit card before she could give me the total. "The last thing this city needs is a terrorist attack right now." It was interesting that the clerk would use that word, since terrorism was one of the few things we'd never used to cover up an incursion. The scars that sort of lie would leave on the city would be impossible to heal.

"Amen," said the clerk. She bagged my purchases—all but Sloane's Slurpee, which she simply passed back to me—with a quick efficiency that didn't seem possible, given how laconic she'd been otherwise. Thrusting the bag in my direction, she flashed me a smile. "Have a nice night. Try to stay safe out there."

"I'll do my best," I said.

Exiting the store with Sloane's Slurpee in one hand and the bag in the other, I was struck by just how quiet the city had become. Most of my night had been spent racing from one emergency to another. Suddenly, with the stories no longer trying to force their way back into the human world, it was like everything could rest. Moments like this were part of why we kept on fighting. Sure, we all had our own reasons to hate the narrative, but that didn't necessarily mean we had an over-whelming love for humanity. So we loved the quiet instead. The spaces where there were no stories, where anything could happen.

The walk back to the van was quick and peaceful: something else I needed, and wasn't going to get much more of, if the shouting I heard when I came around the corner was any indication. I broke into a jog, careful not to spill Sloane's Slurpee. If I was running into danger, I didn't need to get it from two directions at the same time.

The van came into sight. Andy was standing near the bumper, one hand clenched in a fist at his side, the other shaking a finger in the face of a familiar figure in a slim-fitting charcoal suit. Sloane was crouching behind him in the open van door. Jeff was nowhere to be seen.

Deputy Director Brewer was focused on Andy, who was the most immediate potential threat in the area. I slowed when I was about ten feet away, taking a quick glance around the area as I looked for the rest of the deputy director's team. There: a plain white van parked illegally near the corner, with a man in mirror shades in the driver's seat. It was a surveillance vehicle. That was probably all that we'd had remaining in the pool, with all the field and cleanup teams scrambled and out trying to stop stories from destroying us all.

"—and I'm telling you that you're not going to remove *any* of us," said Andy, shaking his fist again.

"Something the matter here, gentlemen?" I strolled up as casually as I could, holding Sloane's Slurpee out for her to snatch from my hand as I focused my attention on the deputy director. "Deputy Director Brewer. I didn't expect to see you out tonight. Don't things need supervision back at headquarters?"

"Headquarters is a ghost town. Dispatch is relaying anything that comes in directly to me." He tapped the Bluetooth headset clamped onto his left ear. "Right now, we have a window. Maybe it's a short one; maybe it's a sign that this was the last burst of the storm, but it's a window."

"That's great," I said. "That takes us back to my first question: is something the matter here, gentlemen? We're not in the best of shape right now, but I can't imagine that the rest of the field teams are doing any better."

"No, you're right on the money: twenty percent casualties seem to be the order of the night." His voice was Arctic cold, with no room for movement. I felt myself starting to freeze under his regard. He continued, "Now if you'd just release Agent Davis to me, I'll be able to let you continue whatever monitoring work you've been doing here."

I blinked at him. Moving slowly and deliberately, I set my bag of snacks down on the van's rear bumper before turning back and asking, "Agent Davis? And why would I be releasing Agent Davis to you?"

"He's somehow under the impression that Jeff's gone rogue," said Andy, shooting a poisonous glare at Deputy Director Brewer. "He wants him for 'observation.'"

"Radio signals were intercepted, and Dispatch reported a spike in narrative activity from this location," said the deputy director. "Agent Davis is not in any trouble, but we do need to observe him for the next few days."

"With all due respect, sir," I said, despite feeling zero respect for the bureaucrat now standing in front of me, "no. Agent Davis is not experiencing a spike. We've all been through a lot tonight, and some of those stories are more than capable of creating a smoke screen when they feel like they're about to be detected. Whatever Dispatch intercepted wasn't real."

"Well, then, it's time that he was reassigned," said Deputy Director Brewer. "This isn't the normal way of doing this, but field teams are maintained at four for a reason. You can't—"

"There are only four of us left."

Sloane sounded utterly calm when she said that. The rest of us turned to face her. She was sitting in the van's open rear doorway, her Slurpee in one hand and an open bag of chips in the other. Looking unconcerned, she took a long sip of frozen sugar water before she said, "Demi's gone. Went into the woods chasing a three-twenty-seven-A, and when we arrived to extract her, she wasn't there anymore. I don't know how you don't know this already, but you can check the logs. We called Dispatch to report her disappearance and request cleanup for the civilian casualties a good twenty minutes ago. So if you pull Jeff off our team, you're not rebalancing us, you're crippling us—and you're breaking up one of the most effective field units you have. I don't know the whole picture, but I don't think you can afford that right now."

"Gone?" Deputy Director Brewer rounded on me. "What does she mean, Agent Santos is gone? Where did she go? Why didn't you tell me this before?"

"I don't know, sir. Agent Winters described the scene accurately: we got to the woods, and Agent Santos was not there. Her badge was, however, which leads me to believe she was either abducted or went willingly, but was not killed. There were no signs of a struggle. As for why we didn't tell you . . ." I shrugged. "Maybe we got a little defensive when you started talking about running off with our archivist. Sloane hits things, Andy does public relations, and I keep them from killing each other. Without Jeff, we'd never know where we were supposed to be standing. So we don't like having people threaten to take him away from us."

"We had reports of a narrative spike from your team's location."

The change in tactics threw me for a second. I opened my mouth, preparing to lie, but stopped as Andy stepped forward and rumbled, "That was me, sir."

Deputy Director Brewer stared at him. I did much the same. "Excuse me?" said the deputy director.

"The spike was me, sir. Your readings probably indicated that it was a solo team member who was potentially compromised, which explains why you thought it might be Agent

Davis. It was an easy mistake." Andy shook his head. He was still imposing, even in his muddy, water-damaged clothes. "I would have thought the same in your place. Honestly, I wish it had been him. I never wanted to encounter the narrative face-to-face, as it were."

Deputy Director Brewer's eyebrows were climbing so high that it seemed like they were going to meet his hairline. "*You*, Agent Robinson? But you're not connected to any ongoing story."

"I think that's why the narrative came after me, sir. I'm a blank page; you could write anything on me, if you tried hard enough." Andy somehow managed not to look disturbed by the words that were coming out of his mouth. That was all right; I was looking disturbed for him. "I separated from the rest of the team in order to pursue a Billy Goats Gruff scenario that was playing out near the local creek. It terminated easily, and was immediately replaced by a Frog Prince. It took up a temptation approach, trying to convince me to agree to let the narrative perform a service for me."

"A service?" said Deputy Director Brewer. He sounded appropriately horrified.

"Yes, sir. I had dropped my wallet when I fell into the creek. The, ah, talking frog offered to retrieve it for me, in exchange for a favor to be named later." Andy shook his head. "I did my best not to listen, but I'll be honest with you, sir—that little fucker was smooth as hell. I knew that going along with him was the worst thing I could possibly do. I wanted to do it anyway."

"And did you?" asked the deputy director.

"No, sir. I beat it to death with a crowbar instead." Andy's mouth twitched upward in a smile. "Violence may not be the healthiest response, but it seems to work for Agent Winters."

Deputy Director Brewer only hesitated for a moment before finding a new approach. "If this is true, and you experienced the narrative spike, then where is Agent Davis?" he demanded.

"Right here," said Jeff mildly. Deputy Director Brewer whirled in time to see Jeff stepping off the sidewalk next to our van. He must have gone out the van's front door and then crept around the side, concealed by the bulk of the vehicle, while he listened to our argument. "I thought it best to stay out of the way until you had decided not to haul me back to headquarters for monitoring."

"What makes you so sure I've decided that?" asked the deputy director.

"The fact that you're a smart man," said Jeff. He walked over to stand beside me. "If Agent Robinson is dealing with a potential narrative compromise, and Agents Marchen and Winters are already narratively compromised, there's no reason to pull me out of the field. You said that all field teams had suffered an average twenty percent loss tonight. That means we're strained, resource-wise. You need me here, with my people, more than you need me being handed off to Research for further examination." He removed his glasses, polishing them against the tail of his shirt as he delivered the killing blow: "My story is nonviolent and not very useful. We have better things to focus on right now."

"Like the missing Piper," I said grimly. "Sir, if Demi has been taken by someone who intends to use her against us—and we have to assume that anyone connected to the narrative would have that as a goal—we may be in serious trouble. You need us at full operating strength."

"You brought her into this agency, Marchen," said the deputy director. His voice was suddenly low and menacing, and I realized that we had somehow strolled right into his trap. He'd threatened to take Jeff because it made enough sense to keep us talking—keep us defending our own long enough to incriminate ourselves. He took a step toward me, eyes burning. "You decided that she needed to become active, rather than leaving her alone. This is on your head, and if you fail to bring her back—alive or dead, it's all the same to me—I will see to it that you spend the rest of your snowy-white life being poked and prodded by people who want to understand the cause of your fatal apple allergies. Do I make myself perfectly clear?"

No, I thought, almost dizzily. *This shouldn't be happening on a street corner, in front of my team; this should be happening behind a closed door, in a space that we control.* But that wouldn't have the right gravitas, would it? The narrative wouldn't like that.

Someone was playing with us.

I schooled my face into as composed an expression as I could manage, nodding. "Yes, sir," I said. "I understand completely."

"Good," he said. "Now bring her home." He turned on his heel and stomped away before any of us could say anything further. He was getting the last word. We let him, standing in frozen silence until he climbed back into his unmarked van. Its engine rumbled to life, and it drove off quickly down the street.

"Well, we're fucked," said Sloane, and took a slurp of her drink.

Not one of us tried to argue.

# # #

The office was still essentially deserted when we made our way into the bullpen. Empty desks and screen savers spoke volumes about the night that the entire department was having. Normally, there would have been at least a skeleton crew of field and cleanup agents loitering around, ready to respond to an emergency call. If anyone had an emergency tonight, they were going to be waiting a long time for a response.

Jeff looked uneasily around at the empty desks. "Maybe we should tell Dispatch that we're available to be sent back out if necessary—"

"No." I said the word as calmly as I could, running him up against the wall of my refusal. "The main thrust has passed, and we have work to do here. We need to figure out who's manipulating the narrative, and we need to find Demi before she's irrevocably damaged."

"It may already be too late," said Sloane, pushing past me to her desk. She knelt, opening the bottom drawer as she continued, "Narrative's got her now, and she's an active. There's no telling how far it can twist her if she says the magic words."

"Demi's smarter than that," I said. My words were hollow even to my own ears.

Sloane raised her head and looked at me. "Really? Because from where I'm standing, she disappeared in the middle of an active narrative and she left her badge behind, which means she has *nothing* that was created by the Bureau. We can't track her, we can't follow her, and we can't save her if she went willingly. That sure sounds dumb enough to say 'once upon a'—"

"That's enough," said Jeff sharply. "We're going to locate Agent Santos, and we're going to bring her home intact and ready to explain what happened. Any other outcome is not to be considered. Do I make myself clear?"

"As glass," I said, a bit taken aback by the vehemence from our normally quiet archivist. "What do you need us to do?"

Jeff smiled wearily. "Research."

"My favorite waste of time." Sloane pulled something out of her desk drawer, holding it up for the rest of us to see. It was a book, wrapped in brown paper, about as thick as a dictionary. "The 1936 ATI index," she said. "I'll start here."

"The Aarne-Thompson Index index?" asked Andy blankly. "Isn't that a little repetitive?"

"The Index is several volumes long, with a master index at the end," explained Jeff. "What are you hoping to find?"

"Stories about stories," said Sloane. She sat down, opening the book.

I looked to Andy and Jeff. "You both know what you're doing?" They nodded. "Good. I'll be right back."

"Where are you going?" asked Jeff.

I flashed him a tight-lipped smile. "To see Dispatch."

# # #

Dispatch was responsible for all field assignments: if there had been any Piper sightings, or any other sightings in the three-twenty-seven range, they would have them on file, and would be in the process of transcribing them for the permanent record. I made my way along the halls faster than was strictly safe, but I knew the office was virtually empty. More importantly, I could feel the weight of the potential narrative looming over me like an uninvited guest. The thought of Demi alone out there with the stories was enough to motivate me to go even faster, and I was opening the door to Dispatch in what felt like only seconds after leaving the bullpen.

The room was chaos personified. Every desk was filled, some with Dispatchers holding fountain pens and frantically scribbling out notes about the night's narrative incursions, others typing frantically, their fingers flashing over their keyboards as they directed their teams around the city on cleanup and recovery assignments. Not one of them looked up at my entrance, not even when the door swung closed behind me with a sepulchral boom.

I started walking across the room, unable to shake a feeling of growing unease, and froze as I realized that my initial assessment had been incorrect on one point: not *every* desk was filled. Birdie's chair was empty, and her computer monitor was dark. I stayed frozen for a few seconds, trying to make sense of what I was seeing, before I walked to the next dispatcher down the line. He kept typing, ignoring me. I cleared my throat. He still kept typing.

"Excuse me," I said.

No reply.

"Where is Birdie Hubbard?"

No reply.

"I need to request some records."

No reply.

I rapped my knuckles against the edge of his desk. "Excuse me? This is Agent Henrietta Marchen, ATI Management Bureau field agent, about to go Big Bad Wolf on your ass if you don't start answering me."

That got a response. His head slowly swiveled around to face me, revealing eyes as round and yellow as an owl's. "That threat is unprofessional and should be reported to Human

Resources," he said. His voice had a fluting quality to it that matched his eyes, and I found myself wondering what his tale type was.

"You know what else is unprofessional?" I asked. "Ignoring a field agent who needs access to records. You don't tell on me and I won't tell on you."

The dispatcher's eyes narrowed for a moment as he considered my offer. Then he nodded, and said in that same fluting tone, "Agreed. What do you want? You're not on any of my field teams."

"No, my team is normally dispatched by Birdie Hubbard. Any idea where she is?"

He shook his head, a flicker of irritation crossing his face. "She called in sick. The rest of us have been picking up her slack, and we don't have the resources to be down even one body. You people think you've got it hard out there tonight? We're directing you to all those stories without time to put together full dossiers. It's a miracle that there haven't been *more* casualties."

Hearing this owlish little man who had probably never seen the narrative in action since his own story activated dismissing the deaths of my friends and coworkers made me furious. I tamped down my rage, allowing my expression to harden. "There have been enough," I said flatly. "One of my team members is missing. We think the narrative took her. We need your records on tonight's dispatches."

He blinked again. "You want records on all the dispatches your team was involved with?"

"No," I said, and smiled coldly. "I want all the records from all the field teams that were scrambled tonight. I need to see the shape of this story."

The owl-eyed dispatcher stared at me for a moment before swallowing heavily and pushing his chair back from his desk. "I'll just get those for you," he said.

"Good," I said. "I'll wait here."

# # #

Not all the records were available yet: our scribes and non-field archivists were working their fingers bloody—in some cases literally—as they tried to transcribe everything that had happened since the sun went down and the narrative started working in earnest. The records I *could* get extended from six to eight in the evening. That would have to be enough for the moment. I hefted the stack of folders, gave the owl-eyed dispatcher one last stern reminder to have any additional records sent to my desk, and turned to leave Dispatch.

Birdie's desk caught my eye on the way out. I paused, not quite sure what was bothering me, apart from her absence. My frustration was just that: frustration. I didn't like the fact that someone I regarded as a satellite member of my team was unavailable when one of my actual agents was MIA. I shook my head and resumed walking.

This time I made it out of Dispatch and all the way down the hall to the bullpen, where uncharacteristic silence greeted my return. I frowned as I wove my way between the desks to my team's quadrant. Sloane was sitting cross-legged atop her desk, hunched over a large clothbound book. Jeff was standing nearby, an equally large book propped open in his arms. Only Andy wasn't reading; he was at his computer instead, skimming local news sites as he tried to assemble a timeline of the Bureau's viciously unpleasant evening.

The slap of my file folders hitting my desk rang through the room like an alarm. Everyone looked up. Sloane scowled.

"What the fuck are you trying to do, scare me out of a year's growth?" she demanded.

"No," I said shortly. "What are you working on?"

"Storyteller archetypes," she said.

"Looking up Piper variants," Jeff said.

"Local damage reports," Andy said.

I sighed. "All of which are good and vital things to be doing. Shit." I sat down, reaching for the first folder. "If anyone needs me, I'll be up to my ass in action reports."

"We'll pray for you," said Jeff, his nose already firmly back in his own book.

The silence lasted for some time after that. Reading and research may not be the most interesting parts of our job—they're definitely not the parts that are most interesting to *me*, which is why I chose fieldwork when I graduated from training, instead of something more staid and less likely to get me turned to stone or seduced by some wannabe Prince Charming—but they're absolutely vital if we want to keep the world turning the way that centuries of rational thought have established. The narrative is an old, dark force that keeps trying to worm its way back out into the light, and sometimes the only thing that keeps it locked away is knowledge.

Our weapons are strange and some people don't recognize them as weapons at all, but they've worked for us for a very long time. Don't change what works.

Sloane made a small, irritated sound as she turned a page. "Why does everyone assume that all storytellers are magically good and wonderful and have your best interests at heart no matter what? Don't they realize that someone had to tell these fucking stories in the first place?"

"Ah, but you see, the stories were told by storytellers," said Jeff, looking up. "When a man tells a story of heroism and glory, he's going to cast himself, or someone like himself, in the lead role. All men were storytellers before television supplanted the need to create entertainment in the home, and so a great many stories—"

"Lecture heard and received and oh sweet Grimm will you shut the fuck up if I get Henry to show you her tits?" Sloane turned another page. She didn't raise her head, which meant she didn't see the truly impressive blush that spread across Jeff's nose and cheeks. "Everybody wants to be the hero, and so they make the people they don't like—like their sisters—the villains. I get that. What I don't get is why no one ever said 'this narrative thing screws with us every chance it gets, and people who tell stories are sort of working for it, so maybe they suck too.' It seems like a logical extension of the archetypes."

"Sometimes I forget that you're smarter than you act," said Andy from his desk.

"Really? Because sometimes I forget that you're not asking me to break your nose," said Sloane.

"Hang on, everybody," I said, raising my hand for silence. They all stopped and looked at me. Grimm bless my team: they might squabble like children when things got tense, but they always doubled down when I needed them. "Something's bothering me. Sloane, what were you saying about storytellers?"

"That they're all evil fuckers," she said helpfully.

"Okay. Jeff? What have you found about Pipers?"

He shook his head, lips pressed into a thin line. "There's a lot of unity in the narrative since it's a relatively recent story, as such things go. The Piper comes to town, is hired to pipe away the local vermin, is cheated by his employers—"

"That. Right there." I stabbed a finger at Jeff for punctuation. "The Piper turns on the town when someone convinces him that he's been cheated out of what was rightfully his. So what happens if someone convinces Demi that she's been played by the Bureau? That we've somehow cheated her out of something that she was supposed to receive?"

"Like what?" asked Andy. "Vacation benefits? Fat lot of good those'll do her. She'll never get the chance to use them."

I frowned. "What are you talking about? Sloane uses vacation days all the time."

"Yeah, but I've been with the Bureau for more than fifty years," Sloane said. "I have like, infinity vacation time banked up. They only let me take any of it because the shrinks say it's good for my mental health and probably keeps me from stabbing people, and even then I have to cancel half my vacation days because we come up in the rotation."

A chill washed over me, like snow falling in a forest I'd never seen, but that knew my story intimately. "What do you mean?"

"Shit, you've never taken vacation, have you?" Sloane wrinkled her nose. "Days off can be canceled for any reason, at any time, and we have enough vans and magic carpets and flying horses and crap like that that if you're wanted back at the office, you'll *be* back at the office. No slacking allowed. How did you never pick up on this?"

"All I've ever wanted was to do my job and do it well," I said. "As long as I can do that, what would I need vacation time for?"

Andy looked at me gravely. "Henry, that is about the damn saddest thing I have ever heard in my life. You need a vacation."

"How about we worry about me having a social life *after* we get Demi back and avert whatever the hell is going on in this city, huh?" I glared at Andy for a moment before turning back to Sloane and saying, "I need you to really consider your answer. If you had taken a vacation day or called in sick today, tonight, would you be here now?"

"What, *tonight*?" Sloane snorted. "I would have been dragged kicking and screaming out of the pleasure domes of Xanadu. This is an all-hands-on-deck situation, and you know it. Why?"

I stood, dropping the folder that I'd been reading from and yanking open my desk drawer in almost the same motion. I pulled out a fresh clip of ammunition, sliding it into my pocket. "Because our dispatcher didn't show up for work today. Demi may not be the only member of our team in trouble."

"Birdie?" asked Jeff.

"Yeah," I said tightly. "Now let's roll."

# # #

There were a few other field teams outside in the parking lot, clustering around their vehicles like trauma victims—which they technically were—as they eyed the building. Once they went inside, they would need to start their paperwork. I knew from experience just how exhausting that could be. I avoided eye contact as I hurried toward our van, the rest of my team trailing along behind me. It said something about how anxious we all were to find out if Birdie was safe that Sloane didn't say anything nasty to any of the people we passed.

To my surprise, Jeff crammed himself into the front passenger seat. I gave him a startled look. He held up one of the file folders from my desk. I hadn't even seen him pick them up. "I'm going to see if I can find anything in here that suggests a pattern," he said. "Not to demean your research skills—"

"But they're not as good as yours," I said. "I know that. Everybody buckle up, we're going to break a few speed laws."

I hit the gas.

Birdie's home address was programmed into the van's GPS, along with everyone else on the team. It made the vehicle a liability if it was ever stolen, but the risk was counterbalanced by situations like this one, where trying to contact Personnel to find out where someone lived could mean the difference between a timely rescue and a corpse. I pulled up her name even as we roared out of the parking lot, following the route appearing on the tiny display screen.

"Thirty minutes out, people," I said.

"Where the fuck does she live, Jupiter?" asked Sloane.

"Close," I said. "She's in a housing development out near the edge of the wildlife preserve. I guess she likes being close to nature."

"Or she's cuckoo-bats," said Sloane. "That's a horrible commute. I'd be road-raging weekly."

"That's why we don't let you drive," said Andy. "Henry, you going to light it up?"

"No," I said. "No lights, no sirens. We do this quiet."

"Because we're so subtle," said Sloane.

I rolled my eyes and focused on the road. The local police would let us go without so much as a warning if we got pulled over, but that wouldn't give us back the time we'd lose flashing our badges and explaining that the lights were off because we were trying to run quietly through the dangerous hours of the night. I didn't know exactly why I was so against turning on the notifications of our official presence, but something about the idea felt wrong to me. Call it a hunch; I have them rarely enough that I try to listen to them when they show up, if only for the novelty. We needed to do this without attracting attention.

"Henry." Jeff's voice was soft enough that I would have missed it had the siren been running. As it was, it was almost drowned out by the sound of the wind rushing through the broken driver's side window. I glanced to him. He wasn't looking at me. His eyes were fixed on the file in his lap, and the small block of text illuminated by his handheld flashlight. "I think we may have a problem."

"I think we have about thirty, so cutting it down to one would be a real treat," I said. "What've you got?"

"All of the stories that went live tonight were under observation at some point, although several of them had been marked as too minor to ever be at risk of activation," said Jeff, moving his flashlight's beam down the page slightly. "We knew about all of them, at one point or another. It looks like less than half were ever routed to a field team for examination. The rest were just filed and forgotten."

"Okay," I said. "That sucks, but it happens."

"In every case, the Dispatch officer who decided that the story would never activate—meaning it could be dismissed without further action, and didn't have to be investigated by a field team—was Birdie Hubbard," said Jeff. "She signed off on every one of these."

"Our dispatcher is evil?" Sloane stuck her head up between the seats. "Okay, well, that's new. Does that mean I can smash her skull in with Andy's crowbar as punishment for making me flash a preteen?"

"No," said Jeff.

"You did what?" asked Andy.

"We don't *know* that Birdie was involved," I said. "Dr. Reynard was killed for his files. Maybe Birdie is in trouble because the same person wanted to have access to *her* files." The excuse sounded weak and mealymouthed even as I was making it. Dispatchers all put their files in the same repository. That was how we'd been able to access them. What would have been the point of attacking Birdie?

Unless she was taking work home with her, that was. If she had files that hadn't been stored at headquarters, that might have been sufficient to put her at risk. For one sickening moment, I found myself hoping for exactly that. Better an endangered dispatcher than one who was doing the endangering.

"How much farther?" asked Jeff in a tight tone. I glanced in his direction. From the look on his face, his thoughts had been mirroring mine.

"Not far," I said.

"I am reluctant to give you driving advice, but Henry . . ." He paused for a moment before shaking his head, the light seeping in from outside the van casting glints off his glasses. "Floor it."

I did exactly that.

# # #

Birdie Hubbard lived in exactly the sort of house that you would expect a woman named Birdie Hubbard to live in, especially if that woman existed in a world where fairy tales were real and had teeth. It was small, burdened with an excessive amount of decorative gingerbread carving, and painted a lovely shade of eggshell white accented with a variety of pastel colors. There was a white picket fence around her perfectly manicured lawn, and beds of wildflowers nestled close to the house like baby birds cuddling up against their mother.

The four of us stood on the sidewalk outside the fence, briefly frozen by the sheer storybook perfection of the scene in front of us. As usual, it was Sloane who recovered her wits enough to speak first.

"She has *garden gnomes*," she said, tone somewhere midway between horrified and impressed. "Those are contraband. She could be seriously disciplined for allowing a representation of the Fair Folk this close to her home."

"I think we have a bigger problem," said Jeff. I turned. He was pointing to her mailbox where, I saw, someone had painted a line of cursive script on the side. "This says the house belongs to 'M. Hubbard.'"

"Is Birdie married?" I asked.

Jeff shook his head. "No; she's single, no family, no close friends outside the Bureau. All dispatchers are like that. You can't work in Dispatch if there are people in the outside world who might wonder where you go all day."

"Hell, you can barely work in the field," said Andy.

I decided not to comment on that particular sore spot. "We can't stand out here forever," I said. "Birdie may need our help. What are you getting at, Jeff?"

"I think that 'M.' refers to Birdie—that it's her first initial, or at least the one she uses with the world," said Jeff. "But I don't think it's a name. I think it may be short for 'Mother.' Does that ring any bells?"

"'Old Mother Hubbard went to her cupboard to fetch her poor dog a bone,'" said Andy. "It's a nursery rhyme."

"A woman who calls herself 'Birdie' and uses a nursery rhyme as a mask between her and the world." Jeff shook his head, expression grim. "We need to be careful here, Henry."

"We will be," I said, and opened the gate. "Sloane, you're on point. I want to know if you pick up anything strange. Andy, take the rear."

"I have no fucking clue what you people are talking about," said Sloane, slinking nimbly around me and beginning to stroll down Birdie's front walk. She made it look utterly casual, like there was no potential for bloody mayhem in our immediate future. "Is Birdie a bad guy or not?"

"There are a lot of characters in nursery rhymes named 'Mother,'" I said, following Sloane but directing my words at Jeff, who was staying close behind me. "She could have just chosen the name to be ironic. Or that could be the narrative she's tied to. Maybe she has trouble keeping food on the table."

"Or maybe she was hiding in plain sight," said Jeff. "All anyone ever had to do was stop and go 'Hubbard, isn't that from the rhyme about . . .' and the rest of it would fall into place."

"Still no clue what you're talking about, getting sort of pissed off about it," said Sloane, in a singsong drawl. She stopped as she reached the door, twisting around to look back at me. "Now what?"

"Knock. If she doesn't answer in thirty seconds, you can break it down." I didn't like sanctioning property damage, but Birdie could bill the Bureau if she was just taking a nap.

Sloane grinned. "That's the sort of instruction I like to hear." Turning back to the door, she hammered her hand against it, pounding loud enough to wake the neighbors—if Birdie had

had any. I reached out and grabbed Sloane's wrist before I could think better of it, stopping her arm in midhammer.

Andy made a small, dismayed sound. Jeff went still. And slowly, deliberately, Sloane turned around to stare at me. I didn't need light to know how dangerous her expression was. Malice was practically rolling off her in waves.

"Now I know you're not stupid enough to touch me without a damn good reason, so how about you tell me what that reason is, and I'll decide whether I'm getting written up for breaking your nose or your neck." Sloane's tone was perfectly reasonable, like she was asking me how I took my coffee.

"Does Birdie have neighbors?" I asked.

Sloane blinked. "Snow bitch says what?"

"Does Birdie have neighbors?" I repeated. "When we drove up, when we came up the street, were there any other houses? *Don't look.*" My hiss caught her in the process of turning her head to the right. She stilled, attention flicking back to me. "Just answer the question. Are there any other houses here?"

"No, it's just forest," said Sloane. Then she froze, her eyes widening. "But that's impossible. You can't have a suburb with just one house. We would have noticed. Someone would have said something about Birdie living too far from civilization, you need to keep people around you as a stabilizing influence . . ."

"Turn now," I said, letting go of her wrist.

Sloane turned. So did the rest of us, and as a group we stared into the tangled wood that encroached on Birdie's perfectly manicured property, slinking up on all sides until it was stopped by the delicate barrier of the white picket fence.

"It's like something out of a fairy tale," said Andy in a choked voice. "The little house in the middle of the forest, with the flowers and the . . . and the garden gnomes. This isn't right. This isn't right at all."

"Knock again, Sloane," I said tightly.

She looked at me thoughtfully before swiveling and resuming her pounding on the door. There was no motion from within. "Guess we're breaking it down," she said, and started to raise one foot to kick the wood.

"Try the knob," said Jeff suddenly.

"What?" Sloane shot him a dirty look. "You spoil all my fun." But she reached for the doorknob, only hesitating for a moment before she closed her hand around it and twisted.

The sound of the latch opening seemed very loud in the stillness of the nighttime air.

"Huh," said Sloane, and pushed the door open, releasing it rather than stepping over the threshold. It bumped to a stop against the wall of a small, spotlessly clean hallway, with woven rag rugs on the floor and knickknacks lining the walls. The smell of baby powder, chocolate chip cookies, and apples drifted out to greet us.

"Does anyone else smell apples?" I asked faintly, swallowing the sudden urge to be sick.

"No," said Sloane, her posture shifting into something predatory. She looked more like a fox or a wolf in human form than an actual human as she stepped over the threshold into the hall. She froze there, chin up, nostrils flexing as she scented the air. "I get baby powder, cookies, and arsenic. Don't ask me how I know what arsenic smells like."

"I wouldn't dream of it," said Jeff. "For reference, I can smell the powder and the cookies, but apart from that I smell leather. Fresh-tanned and supple."

"All I smell's cookies," said Andy.

"That fits," said Jeff. "The narrative may want you, but you aren't naturally one of its possessions. It can't control you the way that it can the rest of its toys."

"Fuck that; I want to be a dentist," said Sloane, and stalked down the hall, leaving the rest of us to follow. Which we did, without hesitation: Sloane might be unpleasant and bad-tempered, but in the years that she had been working with my team, she had never once put any of us intentionally in danger. The fact that she had entered the house meant that it was safe, and I clung to that thought as hard as I could as I moved to cover her.

Andy was the last one inside. The door slammed shut behind him. We all stopped and turned to watch as he tried the knob, first calmly, and then with increasing urgency.

"The damn thing's stuck," he finally reported.

"Somehow, that isn't a surprise," I said. I turned back to Sloane. "Find Birdie, and then find us a way out of here. I don't feel like becoming a statistic tonight."

"Didn't you get the memo? You already are." She started walking again, moving more cautiously now that she didn't have an escape route waiting for her. At the end of the hall she paused, sniffing the air, and finally pushed open a swinging door, sticking her head inside. She leaned back to inform the rest of us, "Kitchen," before stepping forward and vanishing.

"Dammit, Sloane," I said, and followed her.

Sloane already had the light on by the time the rest of us joined her. Birdie's kitchen was as homey and pleasant as the rest of the house. Given the circumstances, I would have felt more comfortable with stained Formica, or maybe something in an Addams Family "cobwebs and cleavers" motif. Instead, we got cookie jars shaped like strawberries and decorative salt-and-pepper shakers that looked like they spanned a period of about eighty years. There was a large freestanding butcher's block in the center of the room. I paused, frowning, as I tried to remember where I'd seen that layout before.

Jeff got there first. "This is like a mirror image of Dr. Reynard's kitchen," he said. "Move the cupboards, change the décor a bit, and you'd be standing in the same room."

"Yeah, except his kitchen had a back door," said Sloane, prowling in a circle around the butcher's block. "This one has a solid wall. Nowhere near as useful, unless one of you has been holding out on the fact that you're actually a ghost."

"Ghosts aren't real," said Jeff, moving to examine the wall in question. "They're just echoes of the narrative. They have no free will, and they certainly can't be employed by the Bureau, much less 'hold out' on the living."

"You're like a walking Index sometimes," said Sloane, and didn't mean it as a compliment. She shot me a look. "See what you're signing up for?"

"Shut it, Sloane," I snapped. "If there's no back door, how are we getting out of here? And where's Birdie?"

"The smells were strongest in here," said Sloane. "If she was anywhere in the house, it should have been this room."

"So what do we do now?" asked Andy. "Split up and search?"

"No," I said firmly. "Splitting up is how you die in situations like this one. But we should move on—Jeff? Did you find something?" He had started picking at the wallpaper, and was peeling it away from the wall in a long strip.

"Property damage always make me feel better, too," said Sloane amiably.

"Henry, maybe you'd better come and have a look at this," said Jeff, continuing to pull the wallpaper away. We all moved to cluster around him. The smell of apples grew stronger, and I saw the writing on the wall.

Hello, my pets:

You certainly took your sweet time getting here, didn't you? You should have moved faster. You should have guessed my name long ago, and handcuffed me to a rowan tree to keep me from troubling you. But you didn't, and you didn't, and you brought me such a wonderful toy that I simply could not resist any longer. Thank you for that. I promise to use her well in the story that's to come.

As your reward, your deaths will be as quick and painless as I can make them.

I loved you best of all,
Mother Goose

"Our dispatcher thinks she's Mother Goose?" said Sloane, sounding baffled.

"Our dispatcher *is* Mother Goose," corrected Jeff. Sloane turned to stare at him. He took a step back. "I am an elf, and you are a cruel sister, and Henry is Snow White. Why shouldn't Birdie be Mother Goose?"

"Uh, because even I know that Mother Goose isn't in the Index," said Andy. "She can't be something that doesn't exist."

"The Index was written by humans," I said. "There can be holes."

"Okay, normally, I love the 'we work everything through by talking about it and then we all go out for lattes' chick-flick vibe that you guys have going, but does anybody else feel like they're standing in a trap arguing about whether or not the crazy bitch who put us here is delusional?" Sloane shook her head. "I, for one, vote for getting the fuck out of here and arguing about this shit later."

"I agree," I said. "Sloane, find us a way out."

She grinned disturbingly and picked up the strawberry-shaped cookie jar. "I was waiting for permission."

# # #

Whatever the narrative had allowed Birdie to do to the house might have locked the front door and removed the back door, but it couldn't Sloane-proof the windows, especially not when Sloane was armed with a stolen cookie jar and a lot of free-floating aggression. She slammed the cookie jar against the picture window in the front room three times. On the third slam, the cookie jar shattered, and so did the window, sending shards of glass flying everywhere.

"Let's get the fuck out of here," said Sloane, and boosted herself onto the windowsill. The wind drifting in through the broken window smelled of green grass, and carried the distant sound of piping.

I barely grabbed the tail of Sloane's shirt before she could jump down to the lawn.

Sloane froze. She didn't turn to face me as she said, in a dangerous tone, "This 'grabbing me' bullshit is becoming a habit, Henry. It's a bad one."

"Don't you hear that?"

Sloane stepped back down from the windowsill. I let go of her shirt. "No," she said. "But I'm willing to listen."

I pressed a finger to my lips, motioning for everyone to be silent, and indicated the broken window. We all went still, listening.

We didn't have to listen for long. The sound of Demi's pipes grew rapidly, until it seemed to fill the entire world with its sound. Sloane made an incoherent snarling noise, leaping for the windowsill again. This time, it was Andy who grabbed her, wrapping his arms around her chest and bodily restraining her as she snarled at the empty lawn.

"Jeff, what's the song?" I asked.

"I don't know," he said.

Then Demi herself appeared. Her uniform was gone, replaced by a pied harlequin's outfit that wouldn't have looked out of place at a Renaissance Faire. She was too far away for me to see her face, but she was turned toward us, and I was suddenly, horribly sure that she had known we were there all along.

"Let me *go*," snarled Sloane.

"Demi!" I stepped closer to the window. "Put down the flute and come home, honey. We're not mad at you. We're here to rescue you."

"I don't think she wants rescuing," said Andy, sounding horrified. Sloane stopped her struggles and just gaped. Jeff reached for my hand, and I let him take it, standing frozen as I watched an army of vermin pour out of the forest, taking up a position between us and the van. Raccoons, opossums, coyotes, owls and pigeons and songbirds and endless, endless rats seethed on the lawn, blocking it from view.

We were trapped.

Whiteout

Memetic incursion in progress: tale type 280 ("Pied Piper")
Status: IN PROGRESS

The four of us stood frozen in the frame of the broken window as Demi's army of wildlife filled the yard. Their bodies packed the sidewalk and the street beyond as well, turning everything into a teeming mass of animal flesh and eyes that glittered in the starlight. The sound of Demi's flute echoed over it all, shaping and directing the scene. The part of me that was still capable of analytical thought noted that she *did* have limitations: she couldn't play to compel both us and the animals at the same time. Another, even smaller part of my mind reminded me that I didn't know that for sure. Maybe Demi was leaving us alone because she wanted whatever was going to happen next to hurt as much as possible.

"Sloane?" I murmured. "You're the closest thing we have to a brute squad. Think you can take on the entire cast of *Bambi* and get us to the van alive?"

"Alive, except for the ticks, fleas, and probably rabies?" Sloane hesitated as her gaze flicked back and forth across the crowd, assessing the odds. I started to hope we might have a chance. But then Sloane shook her head, expression briefly flickering into honest regret. "No. Best I can come up with is maybe Andy could throw one of us onto the roof of the van if the rest of us were willing to die to get him out onto the lawn to make the throw. Too many teeth, too many claws. We're fucked."

"In more ways than one," said Jeff, sounding horrified. I spared a glance in his direction. He wasn't looking at the yard anymore. His attention was reserved for the grandfather clock on the other side of the room, which he was regarding with open horror. The hands were set at five minutes to midnight. "Henry, we need to get out of here."

"Well, if you have any ideas about how we can accomplish that, I'm all ears," I said.

"You don't understand. We *have* to get out of here." He turned to me, pointing at the grandfather clock with one trembling hand. "That thing just started ticking."

"Clocks do that," said Sloane.

"So do bombs," said Jeff.

That stopped the rest of us for a few precious seconds, and I nearly barked the order for Andy to go and check it out. Swallowing the words that would probably have seen us all blown straight to ever after, I asked, "Are you sure?"

"Positive," Jeff said. "It's not ticking at one beat per second. It's a countdown that doesn't tie exactly to the clock. Birdie set a trap for us."

My chest tightened, and it felt suddenly difficult to breathe. I turned slowly back to the broken window and the animals clogging the yard, suddenly seeing them in a new light: they weren't the sword. They were the shield. They were supposed to keep us inside long enough for the bomb in the clock to take care of everything. All we had to do was keep arguing, keep analyzing—keep doing all the things a field team was supposed to do when the story wasn't actually swinging for their heads.

There was a way out of this. I could see it, if I stopped and allowed myself to be honest about my circumstances and what I was willing to pay to get us out of here alive. "In the kitchen," I said, as much to myself as to the group, and then, louder: "Sloane."

"Yeah?"

"Were there apples in the kitchen?" I had never eaten an apple. Not once in my life. It was too dangerous. No matter who gave me the forbidden fruit, there was always the chance that it would be somehow poisoned, and that this would be the thing that triggered my story.

Sloane paused, looking at me in surprise. Her amazement faded quickly into understanding, and she nodded. "I'll be right back." She turned and bolted for the hall, running as fast as her legs could carry her.

"Henry?" said Jeff. "What are you going to do?"

"Something I should probably have done a long time ago. I mean, what's the worst thing that can happen?" I turned my gaze back to the crowded lawn. Demi was still playing, but her music had lost the manic air it had initially possessed: she was just keeping the animals where they were, not ordering them to do anything else. All she needed to do was wait until the bomb inside the grandfather clock went off and did the wet work for her.

Andy stepped closer. I saw his frown out of the corner of my eye. "Are you planning to tell the rest of us exactly what you're doing?"

"Not unless it works," I said.

Footsteps behind me marked Sloane's return, and her hand fell on my shoulder with the finality of a headsman's axe. "Henry," she said, and thrust her stolen apple under my nose. "Here."

It was perfect. It couldn't have been more perfect. I knew the varietal instantly: Lady Alice, whose pale pink flesh and rosy skin were prized among apple aficionados. "Know thy enemy," that had always been my motto, and there wasn't an apple in the world that I hadn't tasted in my dreams.

I took it from her hand. "Did you poison this?" I asked, surprised to find that I felt only academic interest. Whether she had poisoned it or not, my next steps were finally clear. I wasn't going to hold back.

"Maybe," said Sloane. "There's only one way to find out."

"Isn't that always the way," I said, raising the apple to my mouth.

I think Jeff realized then what I was about to do. I heard him shout something. I heard Sloane snapping a response. Their words were too far away and too blurred by the sudden sound of crows crying against a winter sky for me to make them out. All that mattered was the rosy skin of the apple in my hand, and the crisp snapping sound my teeth made when they broke through it to the flesh beyond. My mouth filled with the taste of sweetness, and the world broke open around me, exposing the face of once upon a time.

# # #

The first bite of apple tasted like autumn incarnate, perfect and indescribable and somehow more nourishing than anything else I had tasted in my life. It was the first frost and the hint of snow, and it was what I had been waiting for my whole life, revealing every other meal I had ever eaten as dust and ashes. I closed my eyes as I chewed, swallowed, and took another bite, the possibility that Sloane had poisoned our salvation dismissed in the ecstasy of eating the apple.

The second bite tasted like blood on snow, like rose thorns and needles pricking the finger of a queen-to-be (and *that* was the answer to why Sleeping Beauties were so often the mothers of Snow Whites; it was so clear, it had always been so clear, I just needed to sink a little deeper into the story if I wanted to see it properly; both our stories began in needles and ended in slumber), like black crow wings spread wide to catch the winter winds. I chewed again, swallowed again, bringing the story a little closer to the heart of me.

I had no stepmother. I had no palace to flee from. That didn't matter, that had never mattered, because this was the truth at the heart of the story: the girl, and the apple, and the broken glass around her.

Jeff was still shouting. I held up my free hand, signaling for him to be quiet, and miraculously, he obeyed. Maybe it was the fact that I reacted at all. Maybe it was relief at the fact that I was still enough myself to give orders. Maybe he was just confused. I raised the apple one last time. A final bite to buy myself the final act.

The third bite tasted like exotic poisons, like a glass coffin sitting lonely in the snow, and like a prince who never came. I choked a little as I forced it down, but in the end, down it went, and I opened my eyes on a world that was no longer quite the world that it had been only a few moments before.

The lawn was still clogged with the bodies of the local wildlife, but they didn't look like vermin to me now. Every one of them was a distinct individual, and I knew instantly that I would be able to recognize them all on sight for the rest of my life. Every squirrel, every songbird—they were all their own beasts. And if they were their own beasts, that meant that they didn't have to belong to Demi.

They could belong to me instead.

I stepped up onto the windowsill, causing the nearest row of animals to fidget and snarl nervously. The remains of the apple slipped from my hand, forgotten, as I stepped down and onto the grass. I raised my head enough to catch a glimpse of Demi, still playing her flute at the rear of the crowd. She looked nervous. That was good. She *should* be looking nervous. Turning my attention back to the animals, I smiled as beneficently as I knew how, and I began to sing.

The song didn't have words, exactly; it was more the equivalent of Demi's piping, all sound and feeling, going on forever if that was what it had to do. I've never been able to carry a tune in a bucket, and that didn't seem to matter. Maybe animals hear music differently than humans do. The ones nearest to me stopped fidgeting. Then they began inching closer, eyes going wide and glossy with what could only be described as adoration. Still singing, I motioned for the other agents to follow me.

"What the hell is going on?" demanded Andy.

"She's gone active," said Jeff. He sounded utterly broken, and I wished I could stop singing long enough to explain my choice to him, to make him understand that this didn't have to be the end of anything, not even my career with the Bureau. Field team leaders weren't supposed to be actives, but it had happened before. Deputy Director Brewer would understand,

provided I could bring the rest of my team home alive and relatively unharmed.

"Why the hell did she do that?" Now Andy just sounded
confused.

"To save us," said Sloane. She pushed past me, walking
forward until the animals began getting restless again. Then
she stopped, looking back, and offered me her hand. "Come
on, Henry. Don't fight it, but don't let it take you either. You're
stronger than this. You've been putting up with my shit for
years. That's more backbone than most Snows will ever show."

I glared at her as I kept singing, moving forward one cautious step at a time. The taste of apple was strong in my mouth,
and half of me wanted to run away from the girl with the red
and black hair, recognizing her as an enemy. The rest of me recognized that impulse as belonging to the sort of Snow White
I'd always feared becoming, and shoved it fiercely to the back
of my brain. My story might have started with a spoiled little
princess who was scared of her own shadow, but it wasn't going
to end that way.

A hand touched my shoulder. I turned to see Jeff standing
there, expression grave.

"We need to go faster," he said. "The clock is about to strike
midnight."

I nodded my understanding and picked up my pace. As I
did, I started to sing a new song, asking my animal friends to
do me a great service, one that would never be forgotten—one
for which they would be mourned and memorialized always.

Demi was still playing, and maybe that was good enough
for the animals who were close to her and her flute, but I
was newly activated and in my element, here in front of a little house on the edge of the forest. Birdie had planned for a

great many contingencies when she put this trap together. She clearly hadn't figured on my breaking the one rule I'd held sacred since I was a little girl: never activate your story. Never let the narrative take you.

But it was the narrative that had changed things. If it was going to target us actively, I was going to fight back. And if you're supposed to fight fire with fire, then it made sense to fight narrative with narrative.

The animals began pouring past us, leaping and hopping and crawling through the broken window, moving slowly at first, and then with increasing urgency as I pushed onward toward the street. Sloane walked in front of me, the animals flowing past her and joining their fellows in the house. They were packing their bodies in so tight that some of them had already probably been crushed, and still they kept on doing as I asked, forcing their way inside.

We were almost to the sidewalk when the bomb went off, filling the air with a concussive bang. If not for the animals muffling it, the blast would have killed us. As it was, it came with a burst of hot air that flung us all forward onto the grass. Almost all—Sloane somehow turned the push she got from the blast into momentum, running straight toward the stunned-looking Demi. I pressed my face down into the lawn as the second blast hit from inside the house—*Didn't spot the second bomb, Jeff, you silly boy*—and so I didn't see Sloane make impact. I just heard Demi scream. Then everything was raining fire, and I found that I had more pressing concerns to worry about, like losing consciousness.

# # #

Everything was white, and cold, and frozen.

I was standing in the middle of a vast forest, the bare black limbs of the twisted trees that surrounded me reaching up toward the frigid winter sky. I turned, one hand going to my gun, and was relieved beyond measure when I found it strapped in its accustomed place; I was still armed. More, I was still dressed like myself, in a plain black suit and sensible shoes, not magically stuffed into some ornate ball gown that would never have survived a minute in any natural forest.

"Hello?" I said. I didn't raise my voice, but the wind caught and amplified it, hurtling it into the trees until it echoed back at me from all directions, like the ringing of a cloister bell. "Is anyone there?"

"We're always here," said a voice from behind me.

I swallowed a frustrated groan. "Is this one of those idiotic clichés where I turn around and see myself in the mirror of my own story, and the narrative tries to tell me that this was my destiny all along? Because I have shit to do, and if I'm not dead, I'd really like to skip the DVD extras and get back to my team before Sloane strangles Demi or something."

"It's not all about you, Henrietta Marchen, and it's not all about the narrative, either," said another voice. While I'd been able to mistake the first voice for my own, this one was deeper and sweeter, with a Nova Scotia accent that I couldn't have mimicked on my best day. "Now turn around, and don't make us come over there."

I was standing in a frozen forest, lost in the grip of what must have been a fever dream invoked by my own awakening story. I didn't really have that many options.

I turned around, and gasped.

The trees had seemed unusually widely spaced when I first looked at them, and now I saw the reason why: the spaces between the matte black trunks could be interpreted as doorways, each of them opening into a forest that was almost, but not exactly, like the one where I was stranded. And now that I was looking properly, those doors were full—each and every one of them—occupied by girls with skin as white as snow, lips as red as blood, and hair as black as (*black as coal, as tar, as obsidian, as the bottom of a well, as black, as black as a raven's wing*) the space between the stars that glittered overhead.

They should have seemed identical, those white-red-black girls, but they weren't anything alike, not now that I was really *looking* at them. They came from every ethnicity on the planet, skin bleached into alien pallor by the story that had shaped them, but features remaining as unique and individual as fingerprints. Some wore their glossy black hair at shoulder length; others wore it long, or in cascades of curls, or buzzed so close to their skulls that it seemed more like gray ash than anything else. They had blue eyes, brown eyes, green eyes—even red eyes, in the few cases where the narrative had used the genes for a kind of albinism to reach its desired effect.

"Hello, Snow," said the nearest of the whiteout women, the one with the Nova Scotia accent. She was taller than I was, and curvier, with a round jaw and a swelling bosom that strained against the buttons of her red flannel shirt. "We wondered if you were ever going to join us."

"Where am I?" I asked.

"Inside the story," said another woman, this one of Japanese descent, wearing jeans and a silver-foil T-shirt covered in kanji that I didn't know how to read. "Inside the story, which is inside you, just like a heart inside a duck's egg."

"Don't mess with her," scolded a teenage girl with six piercings in each ear and a flat Midwestern accent. Pure dairy princess from the farmlands, if you ignored her coloring. "She's new and she's confused. We were all new and confused once. It comes with the territory."

A tall, thin woman with ash-gray freckles spattered across the bridge of her nose moved her hands in a series of sharp but fluid gestures, her brown eyes burning into me. I recognized ASL, even if I didn't speak it. The woman from Nova Scotia translated, saying, "'We were all new and confused, but we got over that long before we came here.' You have the advantage over us, Snow-my-girl: you're still Henrietta, because you're still alive."

I looked at her, and I didn't say anything. I didn't need to. The taste of apples was hot and sour in my mouth, and I knew where I was: in a forest full of ghosts, surrounded by the specters of all the Snow Whites who had come before me.

"Nice way to drop the 'everyone around you is dead' concept into the conversation," said the farm girl, almost apologetically.

"It had to come up eventually, and we don't have that much time," said the Japanese woman. "She's new and she's old all at once. That isn't usual."

"Regardless," said the Nova Scotia woman. "Henrietta, look at me."

I looked. I couldn't resist: not when she spoke to me like that, not when her voice carried all the weight of our mother—our mutual mother who had never existed, the queen with the pricked finger who sat in the windowsill and first dreamed all of us into being.

The whiteout woman smiled sympathetically when I turned back to face her. "This is hard, I know, but you need to listen. Yes: We are dead. We are the ones whose glass coffins broke before we could be rescued, or who never found our way to the coffin at all. We died in motel beds and in alleyways, in hospitals and in hovels."

"I died on a parade float," said the farm girl. "It was Homecoming. My dress was white as snow, and my lip gloss tasted like apples and cyanide."

"I died on a plane above the Atlantic Ocean," said the Japanese girl. "It glimmered like a mirror in the sun. There wasn't a doctor on the flight."

"An amusement park, during the Princess Parade," shouted a wiry teenager.

"A cruise ship."

"A Starbucks."

The woman with the ashy freckles waved her hands, telling a story I didn't have the language to understand. But I knew the coldness in her eyes, the downturned corners of her mouth, and I knew her ending. Whatever the details, she was a seven-oh-nine, a whiteout girl, daughter of the apple and the thorn. She was my sister. She was me.

"We had names then."

"We had lives."

"But we shared a story, and in the end, the story wanted to be told." The Nova Scotia woman stepped out of her doorway and into the white snow of my clearing. It felt like a violation and a reunion all at the same time. The feeling intensified when she reached forward and put a hand on my shoulder. "We've been waiting for you for a very long time."

"I didn't have a choice," I said.

She smiled. "You had more of a choice than most of us. You had people around you to hold you out of the narrative flow, to keep your feet on solid ground while the story pooled around you. Most of us weren't born this way. Most of us didn't look exactly like this when we were alive—we were pale, or we dyed our hair, but we still looked more like individuals than ideas. You've had your whole life to live inside this skin, to learn the shape of what you are. You can use that."

"To do what?" I asked.

"To stop the story." The Japanese girl didn't step out of her own doorway, but she glared so hard that I knew something had to be stopping her: there was no other reason for her to be so restrained. "We're tired of frozen girls in boxes made of ice. We're tired of new faces in the forest."

"I've been trying to stop this story for my entire life," I said.

The woman from Nova Scotia shook her head. "You've been standing outside of it and fighting against it. You've been wasting energy fighting *yourself*. Now you can finally start using what you are to win this war."

"And you *have* to win," said the farm girl. "For all of us."

"For all the ones who aren't here yet," said another whiteout woman.

The woman with the freckles slashed her hands through the air, angry and pleading all at once.

I looked back to the woman from Nova Scotia. "So that's all? Just fight? There's no magical fairy-tale wisdom waiting for me here?"

"Just us," she said. "We'll always be waiting for you here. We're your sisters. We're your future. This is the only thing we will ever ask of you, and we already know it's too much, because the story has gone on for centuries."

"Every story has to end eventually," I said.

"Yes," she said. "So end this one."

Snow began to fall around us as I stood and looked at her—only her, that one whiteout woman who had come into what I was struggling not to think of as my space. This was my piece of the forest: I knew that, deep down, just like I knew that the ice here would never freeze me, but that the sun would never rise. It would never be summer for the Snows.

"How?" I asked. "I don't know how to leave."

"Oh, that's easy," she said. "For us, everything begins with an apple, and ends with a glass coffin and a kiss. Hold on tight now. This isn't easy." She raised her hand, and she was holding an apple: the Lady Alice I'd eaten to start my story. The bites I'd taken were still gone, the apple flesh showing pale and tempting through the rosy cloak of the skin. She took a dainty bite from the untouched side of the apple, her teeth crunching loudly through the fruit. My mouth watered and my stomach churned at the same time, a dissonance that was somehow only natural.

She handed me the apple. I took it. It was easier, this time, to raise it to my mouth and eat. The forbidden fruit was no longer quite so forbidden, now that I had eaten it and lived.

"Remember us," she said softly, taking the apple from my hand. "We'll be waiting for you, when your own glass coffin comes." Then she leaned forward and pressed her lips against my forehead. This close, she smelled like warm flannel and apple blossoms, and part of me—the part that wanted to think of this as home—wanted to wrap my arms around her and never, ever let her go.

The snow began to fall harder. She pulled back, and was instantly lost in the tumbling sheets of white. Even the trees disappeared, and then the ground beneath my feet was gone, and I was falling, falling into endless whiteness—

—only to slam, hard, into the blackened ground of a blasted plain. There was no snow here, not on the ground or in the air, and the trees were burnt-out husks, their branches less like fingers and more like claws as they grasped toward the sky. It wasn't night anymore, either; I pushed myself upright and looked into a poisonous sunset that seemed somehow vilely familiar. I stared at it for a moment before I realized that I knew every shade of red, pink, orange, and snakebite yellow in that sky. I had seen them all appearing on apple skins.

"Well, hello, new girl," said a voice from behind me.

I shoved myself back to my feet, all pretense of caution abandoned as I whirled to face the speaker. I'd been fighting the narrative long enough to know danger when I heard it.

If the whiteout women in the snowy wood had looked like my sisters, this woman could almost have been my twin. She was a perfect manifestation of the story we shared, and some-how made her orange prison jumpsuit look like the robes of a princess. She smirked as she looked at me, her perpetually bloody mouth twisting into a cruel line.

"You're alive," she said. "That's a change. I can fix it for you, if you like."

And just like that I knew her. Knew why she looked so familiar. Knew why she was here in this barren wasteland instead of stranded in the comforting snow with all the others. I straightened, my hand going to the gun at my belt. "You're Adrianna," I said. "You're the one who went bad."

She snorted. "Good, bad, what's the difference? As long as we keep our hands filled with poisoned apples, no one's going to care who's eating them."

"People cared."

"Did you, new girl? From the looks of you, you didn't even exist when I walked among the living and made them remember why they should fear the name Snow White. And I'm not Adrianna. Not anymore. Adrianna died. We're all Snow White here, and we're all a part of the same story."

I could see it when she spoke: the vast shape of our story in all its tangles and permutations, and here, this small patch of land, where a fully manifested part of the narrative had turned so sour as to twist and taint everything around it. Adrianna might not have been the first Snow White to go wrong—but then again, maybe she was. Either way, as soon as one of us learned how to fall, the rest of us knew exactly what to do to follow her.

She made it look so easy, like eating an apple, said the voice of my inner Snow, and for once, I didn't try to make her go away.

"I'm not Snow White," I said. "My name is Henrietta Marchen, and I am a field agent with the ATI Management Bureau."

Adrianna's eyes widened. "Oh, really? You're a member of the fairy-tale police? Isn't that quaint. How much do you think they're going to trust you now that you've fallen into storybook hell? You'll be just like the rest of us in no time. It doesn't matter whether they lock you away in a nice padded room or shoot you in the back of the head. Glass coffins can take many forms. Our story always ends in death—and looking at you now, I'd be willing to bet that you'll wind up here with me and not in that stupid forest with all those mewling princesses. You're going to fall like a blizzard, Snowflake, and I'm going to cheer you every step of the way."

"You're wrong." Why was I even here? Adrianna rep-resented a part of the story that I hadn't encountered in the snowy wood, but the woman from Nova Scotia had seemed so *sure* that she was sending me home. She'd given me an apple. She'd given me a kiss.

She hadn't given me a glass coffin.

"Am I?" asked Adrianna. She pulled her hand from behind her back, and I was somehow unsurprised to see the long glass sliver she was holding, its edges stained red with her own blood. It was the third piece in the puzzle. It was out of order, but that didn't change what it represented. This was a storybook night-mare: symbolism was all that mattered here. "I guess we're going to see, aren't we?"

"Yeah, I guess we are," I said, and forced my hands down to my sides, forced myself to remain calm and unflinching as she walked calmly toward me across the blasted ground, forced myself not to close my eyes or look away as she raised the glass shard and aimed it at my heart.

This is part of the story too, I thought. *I can't die here. The narrative wouldn't throw me away like that.*

But I couldn't entirely believe it, and that belief grew even thinner when she slammed the glass home, slicing through fabric, flesh, and bone without any perceptible resistance. I think I screamed, but Adrianna was gone; there was no one in front of me. So I screamed again, and there was no one there to hear me, and then I was gone, and there was no one there at all.

# # #

"Don't kiss her, you idiot—are you trying to kill her?" Sloane's voice was very near, as angry and acidic as always. As I heard it, I became aware of the ground pressed against my cheek, and the smell of crushed grass and smoke filling the air.

"She needs to wake up!" Jeff. There was an undercurrent of panic to his tone, running dangerously close to the surface, like a razor blade concealed in a Halloween apple. If he bit down on his own fear, he would cut himself so deeply that the bleeding would never stop.

Am I going to be thinking in apple metaphors for the rest of my life? I wondered.

Yes, the part of me that was Snow answered.

I groaned.

The sound must have been louder than I thought, because the shouting around me stopped. A hand touched my shoulder, and Jeff said, "Henry? Are you okay?"

"She's not on your side anymore!" shouted another voice that I recognized—Demi. Sloane must not have murdered her after all. That was a relief. I had *not* been looking forward to the paperwork. "She's with us now!"

"Can we gag her?" demanded Andy.

"Absolutely," said Sloane.

"Can someone get me some mouthwash?" I pushed myself upright, not shrugging Jeff's hand away but not reaching for it either. My eyes were still closed. I didn't want to open them. I understood explosives well enough to know what must have happened to my borrowed army of woodland creatures when they charged into Birdie's house, and I didn't want to see their bodies just yet. "Everything tastes like apples, and I'm not too happy about that."

Sloane laughed. "She's still Henry."

"Was that in question?" I asked, finally cracking one eye open.

Jeff was right there next to me, not holding me up, but hovering in a way that made it clear he would do so if I needed him to. At that moment, I wouldn't have minded being held. Andy was a short distance away. His jacket was gone, and red stains on his shirt and trousers marked the places where the blast had flung broken squirrels and shattered pigeons against him. Sloane loomed suddenly into view, dropping into a crouch as she peered quizzically into my eyes. Unlike Jeff, who was relatively untouched, and Andy, with his few small splotches of red, Sloane was *covered* in blood. Even the red streaks in her hair had taken on a deeper color, almost blending with the black.

I blinked. She grinned.

"Don't worry—most of it's Demi's," she said. "You still feeling bossy and cantankerous in there, Snow-bitch, or are you thinking about digging little graves for all your little animal friends?"

"Don't make me report you to Human Resources," I snapped. "Now somebody help me up before something else explodes."

"Ladies and gentlemen, the boss is back," said Andy, a wide smile splitting his face. "You scared the crap out of us, Henry."

"We're not out of the woods yet, people," I said, and grimaced, my eyes cheating toward the trees growing on all sides. "No pun intended. Sloane, were you being serious when you said that most of that was Demi's blood? Because I'm not quite ready to condone beating her to death."

"She got a nosebleed," said Sloane, reaching forward and taking my hand in hers. Her fingers left red stains on my skin. "Sure, I had to punch her four or five times to make that happen, but nosebleeds are a normal part of being a traitorous bitch who goes over to the dark side at the first sign of trouble."

I thought of the forest while Sloane pulled me to my feet. "She may not have had a choice, if the narrative shook her hard enough when she was already standing on unsteady ground," I said. My knees wobbled as I tried to stand on my own, and Jeff was there, putting his arm around my shoulders without waiting for permission. I leaned gratefully into him. I wasn't sure whether this was a good idea, but this whole night had been built on a foundation of potentially bad decisions, and at least I knew that Jeff would never blossom into a Prince Charming. That was one roller coaster I could still avoid.

Andy frowned. "You all right there?"

"Not even a little bit, but thanks." I wiped the mud from my cheek. For the first time in my life, I was genuinely glad to be a second-generation story. First-generation Snow Whites usually had *some* of the signature coloring, but it intensified after they became active. I couldn't have coped with suddenly losing my melanin after everything else that had happened since the sun went down. "What's Demi's condition? Apart from the nosebleed."

"See for yourself." Sloane pointed at something behind me. I turned.

Demi was sitting on the street with her back propped against the side of the van. Her arms and legs had been taped together with black electrical tape, and there was a ball of wadded-up fabric in her mouth, held in place with another strip of tape. Blood covered the lower half of her face, and one of her eyes was starting to swell nicely from what I judged to be a rather solid punch. She glared daggers at me as I looked at her.

"Please tell me that's not a sock," I said.

"It should have been a sock; she deserves a sock," said Andy. "But no. It's my tie."

"Good. That's a little more sanitary. Where's her flute?"

"We saved all the pieces," said Jeff.

Under the circumstances, I couldn't argue with their decision to take Demi's weapon away. In fact . . . "We need to secure her feet better," I said. "She's a Piper. If she can hammer out a rhythm, she can use it against us."

Demi's eyes widened in sudden realization.

"I didn't think of that," said Jeff.

"Apparently, neither did she," said Sloane. "Good job, Henry."

"Stuff it," I suggested mildly.

"Play nicely, please," said Andy, as he moved to wrap more tape around Demi's feet. She glared at him. He ignored it. "What next, boss?"

I needed a shower, and something to take the taste of apples out of my mouth. Sometimes I hate being in charge. "We head back to base," I said. "The deputy director needs to know what happened out here, and we can dispatch someone to get us all clean clothes." There are advantages to being located in an old biological research facility. An on-site shower room is one of them.

"I keep a change of clothes in my desk," said Sloane. We all turned to blink at her. She shrugged. "What, you think I have all those packages shipped to the office for my health? It's always 'Sloane, go into the sewer after the gremlin,' or 'Sloane, wade into the abattoir to save the baby.' I throw out six pairs of tights a month."

"I am not having this conversation right now," grumbled Andy. "It's too weird, even for me."

"None of us are having any more conversations right now," I said. "Jeff, get some plastic sheeting over the seats in the van. Andy, you and Sloane get Demi into the back. We're going home."

It was time to face the music, in more ways than one.

# # #

Of the five of us, only Jeff and I were completely unwounded: Andy had some shrapnel in his left shoulder—bits of wood and bone flung outward by the explosion—and Sloane had skinned her knuckles on Demi's teeth. Jeff had been shielded from the blast by Andy, and I had been in the front, sending the animals back inside to die. All I really needed to be presentable was a wet wipe from the glove compartment.

Demi, of course, had had the crap beaten out of her.

The wet wipe's plastic packaging smelled faintly of the barbecue joint that it had originally come from, some forgotten fast-food-run ago. I resisted the urge to lick it as I wiped the mud from my cheek and chin. Anything to get the taste of apple out of my mouth. Jeff, who was driving, kept stealing glances in my direction, almost like he couldn't believe that I was really there. I wasn't sure that I believed it myself.

When we pulled up in front of Bureau headquarters I dropped the wet wipe on the van floor—it already needed a thorough cleanup after the events of the night; one more piece of garbage wasn't going to make a difference—and said, "Does everybody know where they're going?"

"Holding cells and then the infirmary," said Andy.

"Infirmary and then the holding cells," said Sloane.

"Archives," said Jeff.

"Good. I will be updating our beloved deputy director. If anything explodes or catches fire, call me. And for the love of Grimm, somebody order a goddamn pizza or something. If I don't get this taste out of my mouth, I'm going to scream."

I hopped out and slammed the van door behind me, stalking toward the darkened building. It was strangely satisfying, like a denial of the placid little fairy-tale princess that the narrative wanted me to be. It wanted a Snow White? I'd give it a Snow White, and make it sorry.

My key card still worked when I swiped it across the reader. I hadn't realized I was worried about that until the light turned green and the door clicked open. Birdie had been in Dispatch for years, so there was no telling how deep her control of our systems might go. If she knew that I'd gone active, she could have called security and reported me as a threat before her own clearance was revoked by our report.

The thought that I might be walking into a trap was still trying to form when I opened the door and found Piotr waiting for me. His whipcord-thin frame was draped in a black suit that was the virtual twin of my own, but on him it seemed funereal, like he was perpetually on the way to someone's graveside. The two largest members of his field team flanked him, one a former linebacker, the other a half-activated three-one-three, with the characteristic strength and stature of the giant's daughter she had been born to represent.

I looked at the three of them, one by one, before settling on Piotr. "You're being manipulated," I said.

"Your breath smells like apples," he replied. "Give me your hands, Agent Marchen."

"This is a mistake," I said, and presented my hands, wrists together, for him to cuff.

"I hope you're right," he said. He fastened the handcuffs loosely enough that they didn't cut off my circulation. I was grateful for that.

My team would be catching up with me any second. I didn't want them to see this. "All right," I said. "Let's go."

Piotr and his team closed in around me, and together the four of us walked off down the white-walled hall, toward the room that would decide my future.

# # #

Demi was probably in a room a lot like this one by now: small, with gunmetal-gray walls broken only by the large rectangular block of a mirror, as if anyone in the world still believed that they were looking only at their own reflections and not at the ghosts of the people hidden behind the glass. My hands were cuffed to the table in front of me; they'd taken my badge, jacket, and gun, leaving me feeling naked and defenseless. Worst of all, they hadn't given me any mouthwash, and the taste of apples was still thick in my mouth.

"You know, while you hold me here, Birdie is getting farther and farther away," I said to the mirror. "I've broken no laws, and my team supports my story. So while I understand that psychological torture is a big part of what we do in these rooms, I'd really appreciate it if you'd get on with things before we completely lose control of the situation."

"I'd say you lost control of the situation when you picked up that apple, Agent Marchen," said Deputy Director Brewer as he entered through the door to my left. He had a file in his hands, with my name written on the tab. "What the hell made you do that, Henry?"

"There was a bomb, sir. Escaping required me to think outside the box."

He fixed me with a stern eye, walking across the room and sitting down on the other side of the table before he said, "The narrative has been pushing you to think outside that particular box since infancy, Agent Marchen. Why should I see this as a selfless choice, and not as the final excuse you needed to do what you had always wanted to do?"

"You know, Deputy Director, I've always sort of wished you were on the spectrum. It would make this easier for you to understand, which would make things easier on all of us." I leaned as far back in my chair as the handcuffs would allow, looking at him. "I never wanted this. *Nobody* wants their narrative, not if they're aware of what it means. We had no other way out of that house."

"You keep saying that," he said, opening my file. "Care to explain yourself?"

"That depends. Are you going to listen, or are you just letting me talk myself dry before you have me locked up as a dangerous memetic incursion?"

He hesitated, and for the first time since he had entered the room, I felt like he was honestly looking at *me*, and not the story that I represented. "I don't know," he said.

"That's something, I guess," I said, and began my explanation.

It took a while to tell him everything that had happened at Birdie's house, from our arrival—when we thought we were on a rescue mission, not walking into a trap—to the moment that I bit into the apple and everything changed. He paled slightly when I told him what I'd done to the animals, less I think because that sort of behavior was unusual, and more because people tended to forget that the seven-oh-nines were just as dangerous as any other tale type. Everyone thinks of them in terms of poisoned apples and glass coffins, and forgets that they represent girls who walked into dark forests and remade them into their own reflections.

Worse, they forget that we're still remaking those reflections. The whole "woodland creatures" thing is a relatively recent addition to the tale, borrowed from Disney and internalized by so many children that it has actually modified the narrative itself. Even as the narrative drives us, so do we drive it.

I wish I could find that thought more comforting.

I didn't tell him about the whiteout wood filled with girls who could have been me in another lifetime; I just told him that the strain of activating my story had knocked me unconscious, and that when I'd woken up, Demi had already been taken into custody, and we had agreed to return to the Bureau. I stopped talking then, waiting for his response.

Minutes slithered by like snakes moving through tall grass while Deputy Director Brewer and I stared at each other. It was like he was daring me to blink first.

Do it, urged the small voice of Snow. *Let him think he's won. Kings like to think they've won.*

But he wasn't a king, and this wasn't a fairy tale, and I was not a princess in hiding. I was Henrietta Marchen, field agent, and fuck the narrative if it wanted me to be anything else. I kept my eyes on his, daring him to look away.

In the end, he did. "This is your formal report?" he asked, looking down at the file. He hadn't been taking notes. He didn't need to; we both knew that we were being recorded.

"Yes, sir." The only parts I had omitted were the parts that no one could give to him but me. My secrets, such as they were, would be safe until I chose to share them.

"This is what your team will tell me as well?"

"Yes, sir. Although they were awake when Demi was captured, so they may have additional details."

"I never expected this from you."

"Are you relieving me of duty?" It seemed like a silly question, given the situation, but it encompassed every other question I could possibly have asked. Was I under arrest? Was I going to disappear into that private warren of safe houses and sealed rooms where we kept the narratives that couldn't be averted but couldn't be trusted among the general population either? Sloane had always been afraid of vanishing into that maze. Until this moment, until this night, I had never really considered that as something that could happen to me.

Glass coffins take many forms, whispered a new voice, almost Snow, but not quite. Adrianna. I should have known that she'd be back to haunt me.

"I should," said Deputy Director Brewer. "I refuse to believe that you truly had no other choice but to activate your story. Considering the training and experience represented by your team, you should have been able to find another way."

He'd called them *my* team. "But?" I prompted.

"Birdie Hubbard is missing, as are many of the files she worked on," he said. "The archivists are reviewing the last several years now. We have no real idea of the scope of the damage she's done—or the damage she could still do, depending on what she's managed to take with her. No one knows her better than your team . . . and your team is refusing to return to the field without you."

Gratitude and satisfaction warred for dominance over my mood. In the end, they reached a peaceful compromise, and washed over me in equal measure as I fought the urge to smile. "I suppose that means your hands are tied. You need to return me to the field if you want Birdie apprehended."

"Don't think this is some sort of victory, Marchen," he snapped. "You're going to be watched more closely than you have ever been. The director has already requested regular updates on your activities, and that scrutiny is going to extend to the rest of your team. Do you understand? By agreeing to go back into the field and lead them, you are committing them to constant monitoring." Deputy Director Brewer's expression was oddly sympathetic. For the first time, I wondered if he might not be on our side after all.

That made me think of Jeff, and his brush with the narrative, and Sloane, who was just barely keeping herself from pouring bleach into everyone's coffee. Casting an additional spotlight on them couldn't do anything good.

Leaving them wouldn't do anything good, either. "I understand the risks, Deputy Director, and I am willing to accept them. I believe my team shares my willingness. Anyone who doesn't can request a transfer to another field team as soon as the issue with Birdie Hubbard has been resolved."

Deputy Director Brewer nodded. "I thought that would be your answer. Agent Marchen, do you have a plan for what you're going to do next?"

"I thought I'd start with asking you to take off these cuffs." I raised my hands and offered him a thin smile. "Come on, Deputy Director. Let me go back to my team. Let me figure out how we're going to stop her."

"Don't make me regret this," he said, reaching into his pocket.

"Believe me, that's *not* my plan," I said. Then I shut my mouth, watching silently as he unlocked the handcuffs holding me to the table. There was nothing else I could safely say, and I didn't want to risk changing his mind at this juncture. I had too much left to do.

It was time to get this story started.

# # #

Jeff, Andy, and Sloane were already in the bullpen by the time I finished taking a quick shower, rinsing my mouth with three different kinds of industrial-strength mouthwash, and changing into a clean uniform from the locker room. It was a purely psychological choice: I would feel better if I was appropriately attired for the situation ahead of us. It would also help my team if they saw me looking like myself. At least that was how I justified things, and after the night I'd had, I felt entitled to a little justification.

I paused in the doorway, watching the three of them cluster around Sloane's computer, staring at something that I couldn't see. They were all I had left of the strange little family I'd built within the ATI Management Bureau. Demi was compromised, and Birdie . . . Birdie was the enemy, and had apparently been the enemy for a long time. These people and my brother were all I had to defend, and I was going to get them to happily ever after if it killed me.

True to form, it was Sloane who sensed my presence first. She'd always been sensitive to the stories around her, one more gift she hadn't requested from the narrative. As I watched, she stiffened, pushed her chair back, and swiveled to face me. Jeff and Andy turned a few seconds later. Andy looked wary; Jeff looked hopeful. Sloane looked like Sloane: suspicious, bored, and annoyed.

"So they decided to let you go?" she demanded, not rising.

"Looks that way," I said, finally walking toward them. "Show a little respect. I'm your field team leader."

"Really?" asked Andy, the wariness not fading. "They're going to let you stay in charge?"

"For now, yes. Once the Birdie issue has been resolved, well. I guess we'll see." I looked from face to face, trying to distance myself from the scene enough to be objective. I couldn't do it. "Having me in charge is going to mean extra scrutiny. If any of you wants out, Deputy Director Brewer has indicated that he would be willing to approve a transfer."

"Fuck Deputy Director Brewer in the ear," said Sloane. "You may be a Snow-bitch, but you're *our* Snow-bitch."

"We're staying," said Andy.

"*I'm* staying, and don't think you can change my mind," said Jeff.

I flashed him a quick smile. "I wouldn't dream of it. Now: Where's Demi?"

# # #

I had been correct: Demi was being held in a small inter-rogation room very much like the one where I'd been kept, with one major difference: the walls were draped in sheets of sound-dampening foam, and her wrists and ankles were bound with plastic cord instead of the normal cuffs, with very little "play" left to enable her to keep her circulation going. Her health mattered less than the prevention of music. She wouldn't be able to get a good percussive beat out of the things she had available to her.

I walked into the room, feeling the eyes of my team through the mirror to my back, and moved to take the seat across from Demi. The scene felt faintly unreal, like something out of a story, and I made a note to ask Jeff whether the narrative could be making use of modern television tropes as well as urban legends and the like. I didn't particularly want to find myself in the kind of crime drama where someone always gets shot right before the commercial break.

"Hello, Demi," I said. "I'm sorry about the restraints. You understand that they're necessary, don't you?"

"Yes," she said dully. Her head was hanging until her chin almost brushed against her chest. All the fight seemed to have gone out of her. I hoped that was a good thing. "You're going to lock me up forever, aren't you? I'm never going to see my family again."

"That's sort of up to you at this point," I said. "We need to understand what happened tonight. We need to understand why you decided to start working with Birdie."

"But I *didn't* decide to start working with Birdie." She raised her head, anger and bewilderment dancing in her eyes. "I was in the forest and then I was in a different forest, and I was so *angry* that when she said to start playing, I did. I don't even know what I was mad about. I was just mad, and following orders seemed like the right thing to do. I didn't even realize it was you until Sloane was punching me in the face . . ."

I frowned. If Demi had been controlled by the narrative, she had a reasonable chance of getting out of this cell without permanent damage. We just had to prove it. "Do you remember anything about what Birdie said to you?"

"Not much. It's all sort of blurry, like I'm looking at it through glass." Demi suddenly stiffened. "No, wait—there was one thing. She said that you might take me back. That I hadn't been hers long enough. She wanted me to give you a message."

"What message?" Demi could be lying, but I couldn't stop myself from hoping she wasn't. She was part of my team. I wanted her back.

Demi worried her lip between her teeth before she said, "Birdie wanted me to tell you to concede or die. And then she laughed and walked away and left me in the woods." Tears were starting to pool in her eyes. "She *left* me."

"I'm sorry." I stood. "We're going to get the Bureau's best psychologists and archivists, and we're going to figure out what she did to your story."

"You mean you're going to figure out whether you can trust me."

"Yes," I said. "I hope we can."

"Yeah," said Demi, letting her head drop forward again. "So do I."

I stood there for a moment, looking at her. And then I turned and left the room. Demi might have more information for us; we'd get it out of her. But right now, there was something I needed to do.

# # #

Sleepy crows roosted in their patched-together nests in the aviary on the roof. Jeff stayed outside as I walked into the small structure, clucking and croaking with an ease that I wouldn't have possessed just a few hours before. Finally, a large crow stood and stretched its wings before cawing a cursory greeting.

I held up the letter in my hand. "Take this to Mother Goose and I'll feed your entire flock for a week."

In a twinkling, the crow was in the air, snatching the letter as it flew past me. I followed it out of the aviary, watching as it soared away into the dawn. Jeff stepped up to stand beside me. His hand found mine, and I tangled my fingers through his, holding tight.

"Are you sure the crow will find her?"

"It would work if this were a fairy tale," I said quietly.

"What does the letter say?"

The sunrise was pink and gold and red, and it didn't look like apple skins at all. I smiled, stepping a little closer to Jeff, and answered, "That she's going to lose."

Not Sincere

Memetic incursion in progress: tale type 138.1 ("The Little Mermaid")
Status: IN PROGRESS

Michael stood frozen in front of the mirror, one hand pressed to the hollow of his throat, like that would somehow magically give him back the voice he'd so casually allowed to be taken away. He wanted to scream. He wanted to throw back his head and howl to the skies until some fairy godmother from a kinder story turned and took notice of him, waving her magic wand and making it all better. Making wishes had gotten him into this situation, hadn't it? Was it being so greedy to ask for just one more?

Nothing made sense anymore and nothing was ever going to make sense again.

When he'd decided on plastic surgery as the solution to his troubles, he hadn't been expecting miracles—just an improvement, maybe, to the face that he'd been left with after the automobile accident that had killed his parents and left his little sister a wheelchair-bound mermaid of a girl. Linda would never walk again, and was free to move on her own only when she was in the swimming pool in their backyard. Michael still had his legs, but he'd wanted . . . God, he didn't even know what he'd wanted. Normalcy, maybe. A face that didn't make the boys down at the club turn away and gag when he worked up the courage to ask them to dance. Lips that someone might want to kiss someday, once they'd managed to get past those first few all-important steps, like saying hello and learning each other's names.

He hadn't been expecting miracles, but he'd received them all the same. The face the plastic surgeons crafted from the ruins of his own could have belonged to an angel. His eyes were large and liquid, his lips were soft and kissable, and everything about him was unscarred and symmetrical. He had never even dreamed he could see a face like that in his mirror.

But there had been complications: an infection in the tissue of his throat, growing with silent, malicious hunger until the day the bandages came off and one of the nurses noticed the swelling in his lymph nodes. They'd done everything they could to save his voice. It had been far too late. His vocal cords were utterly destroyed; he would never speak again, and would need to monitor his diet for the rest of his life, since his already-narrow esophagus wasn't equipped to handle acid reflux or vomiting, let alone swallowing food that wasn't mashed or chopped into tiny pieces.

Such a little thing. It had seemed like a reasonable price to pay when he was learning ASL and teaching it to his sister, who had laughed and laughed at the straightforward bluntness of his new language's phrasing. It had seemed like something he could live with when he'd first gone to the club and met Kyle—beautiful, capricious Kyle—who was dance-floor royalty if such a thing had ever existed. It had seemed like it was going to be okay.

And then Kyle had told him that he couldn't be with someone who couldn't speak. "If you can't talk, how are we supposed to be a thing?" he'd asked, somehow making the question sound completely reasonable, even though it was the most unreasonable thing in the world. "You're a cripple. Maybe that's a shitty way to put it, I don't know, but it's not going to work. You understand."

Michael understood. He understood that he'd given up everything about the man he'd been to become a man that someone like Kyle could love, and it hadn't been enough. Nothing was ever going to be enough.

Linda had been keeping a knife under her pillow since the accident. "I have to be able to defend myself," is what she'd always said. She hadn't heard Michael creep into her room and take it. He was very good at being quiet.

Michael dropped his left hand from the hollow of his throat and raised his right hand, looking thoughtfully at his sister's knife. He didn't have to say anything.

The knife already knew.

# # #

Snow fell all around us in an icy curtain, guided by gentle winds to create a small island of perfect calm in the middle of the clearing. The woman from Nova Scotia—whose name was Tanya, when she wasn't embracing her fairy-tale fate—sat on a tree stump, looking at me gravely. I struggled not to squirm. The rock I was using as a chair was uncomfortable; my ass was freezing; and since I always landed in the whiteout wood in whatever I'd been wearing when I went to sleep, I was wearing nothing but socks and a flannel nightgown. Not the best winter gear the world has ever seen, but I couldn't fall asleep if I went to bed in a thermal jacket and snow pants.

This had been happening every night for the two weeks since my story had fully activated. I was starting to get used to it, even if I missed being able to dream like a normal person.

"What are the means of putting us under?" Tanya asked, for the third time.

"Poisoned apple, poisoned comb, poisoned ring, too-tight girdle," I said, with the prompt, irritated precision of an honor student forced into the remedial class. "The girdle has fallen out of favor in the past few decades, but had a resurgence in the Goth community in the early nineties, and still shows up from time to time in certain fannish settings, like the steampunk community. Or fetish groups, of course."

"What form does the comb take?" asked Tanya, her tone relaying no pleasure at my accurate answer.

I frowned. "It's a comb. It's the least common of the variants anymore. I don't know—it could be a hair clip, I guess? Maybe bobby pins. That would make sense." The poison on the comb was usually a variant of the type used on the apple. It was weaker nine times out of ten, since the Snow White needed to recover long enough to foolishly eat the forbidden fruit. Maybe that was why the combs got dropped from the narrative: people realized that they were being redundant, or maybe they collectively decided that their fairy-tale icons shouldn't be stupid enough to let themselves get poisoned twice.

Tanya frowned at me. "You're not taking this seriously."

"You're appearing in my dreams to teach me how to be a better Snow White," I pointed out. "I'm not sure how seriously I can take this without losing my grip on reality completely."

"There are dangers in the world. Dangers that prey specifically on our kind."

"I've been an ATI Management Bureau agent for my entire adult life," I said. "I think I know about the dangers."

"Henrietta . . ."

"Henry," I corrected firmly. "My name is Henry."

"Henry, then, if you insist. You've been fighting those dangers from the outside. You're *inside* the story now. Some things can no longer touch you. Others . . ." Tanya shook her head, looking mournful. "Others will be a hundred times more dangerous."

I saw my opening and I took it. "Is that what happened to you?" I asked, trying not to show my eagerness.

Everyone who existed in the whiteout wood was a Snow White. Most of them—like Tanya—were dead, their bodies having been lost forever in the waking world. Some were just sleeping, living out their comas on life support and in forgotten hospices all around the world. Most of the girls I'd been introduced to so far were among the dead. They dealt better with strangers, since they no longer hoped for rescue.

I'd been looking up the other Snows since my first trip to the wood, trying to ferret out the details of their lives and deaths based on the few facts that I'd been able to glean. What I was finding so far was deeply unnerving. At least two-thirds of the women in the wood didn't seem to be in the records. Either Birdie's meddling had gone deeper than any of us had guessed, or we'd been missing incursions for years, letting the narrative slip things under the radar. Of Tanya, whoever she'd been in life, I had thus far found no trace. That didn't mean that I was going to stop looking.

Tanya sighed, and for a moment I thought she might actually answer me this time. The moment passed. "No," she said finally. "I was done in by a piece of fruit, because I was a traditionalist. Can you please try to focus? We don't have long."

The snow was falling harder now, starting to actually drift into our little island of calm. I stiffened. "Why not? Is it Adrianna?"

"She doesn't like us teaching you," Tanya said. "She'll stop us if she can. That's why you have to focus."

"Why? What's the worst she could do?"

"*Focus*, Henry," said Tanya, and the snow was coming down hard now, blocking out her coal black hair and blood red lips, until everything was white, and the snow was falling, and *I* was falling—

—and I opened my eyes on the pleasant dimness of my bedroom, and the distant, too-familiar sound of bluebirds beating themselves to death against my window. My phone was ringing. I sat up, reaching for the sound on autopilot. One: grab phone. Two: press button. Three: bring phone to ear. "Hello?"

"Henry, it's Jeff."

I blinked, looking around my room for some clue as to the time. With the blackout curtains drawn, it could have been any time between dawn and noon. "What's going on? Did I sleep through a call?"

"No, no, you didn't miss anything. It's a little after five in the morning."

That explained why I'd still been asleep: my alarm didn't go off until six. I fell backward into the pillows, closing my eyes as

I asked wearily, "Is there a *reason* you're calling me this early? Better yet, is it a *good* reason?"

"We have a case."

"That's annoying and regrettable, and unless I hear it from Dispatch, I'm not seeing where this is our team's problem. Did you sleep at the office again?"

Jeff sounded faintly defensive as he said, "I had things to do. You should be getting the call from Dispatch in about five minutes."

"Why five minutes?"

"Piotr is calling Sloane first."

That was enough to make me open my eyes again. Waking Sloane was something best done from a distance, and always done at your own risk. The rest of us tended to wake up grumpy. She had the potential to wake up homicidal. "So it's ours?"

"It's ours."

"Got it. I'll see you in the office." I hung up and sat up again, pushing the covers back. This was the first call my team had received in the two weeks since my story had gone active. This was our chance to prove that we could still do our jobs, even though I was technically compromised. Which meant that above all, we couldn't fuck this one up.

Swamp mallow had sprouted in the corners of my room, treating the carpet like a preternaturally good growth medium. I wrinkled my nose when I saw it. Then I picked up my phone, snapping a few quick pictures. Jeff would want to know what I'd found growing out of my floor *this* time. He could cross-reference it against whatever story we were about to get involved with, and that would give us one more way of predicting what was coming.

I don't know what swamp mallows normally smell like, but these smelled like apples, making my mouth water and my stomach clench at the same time. I was starting to think that most Snow Whites were thin not because the narrative liked skinny girls, but because they couldn't force themselves to eat once the smell of apples had started permeating everything.

I was standing in front of my closet, selecting the appropriate black suit to wear to work, when my phone rang. I clicked it on. "Henry," I said, sounding considerably more awake than I had only ten minutes before.

"Agent Marchen, this is Agent Remus with Dispatch, we have reported incursion in your region, what's your status?"

"Available, preparing for the field," I said, grabbing a jacket from its hanger. "I just spoke with my archivist, and he's also preparing to be dispatched. Do we know what kind of incursion we're dealing with here?"

"Confirmed one-three-eight dash-one."

I made a disgusted sound. "A Little Mermaid."

"Directions will be sent to your phone," said Piotr. "You now know everything that we do. Try not to get yourself killed this time."

"Don't worry, Piotr," I said, balancing the phone between my cheek and shoulder as I closed the closet with my free hand. "Once a month is my limit."

Now it was his turn to make a disgusted sound before he hung up. I chuckled to myself, and then turned to the business of getting ready to go.

# # #

The address Piotr provided took me to one of the smaller suburbs that clustered around our fair city like shelf fungus ringing a tree stump. Our van was already parked in front of a low-slung colonial home when I pulled up. The front door was open, and Andy was standing on the lawn, consoling a yellow-haired girl in a manual wheelchair. I turned off the car and opened the door, sliding my keys into my pocket as I stood.

"You took your time getting here," said Sloane's voice from directly behind me.

I jumped, yelping in surprise as I whirled to face her.

She watched me struggle to catch my breath with apparent disinterest. Finally, when I was sure that I wasn't about to have a heart attack, she said in a flat deadpan, "Boo."

"I will report you to Human Resources so fast you'll still be standing here when they show up with your formal reprimand," I said. It was pure reflex, and we both knew it—she had startled me, and now I was threatening her. We'd been doing this dance for a long damn time. "What did you do to your hair?"

"Are you really going to stand outside an active incursion and grill me about my hair? I guess you really *are* a fairy-tale princess now." Sloane reached up to pat one of her bleach-white ponytails in an exaggerated preening gesture. Streaks of bloody red and poison-apple green wormed through the bleached strands, somehow looking less like Christmas and more like a crisis getting ready to happen. "I figured it was time for a change. Between you and Demi, all the 'black-haired girl' slots are taken."

I arched an eyebrow. "So sorry."

"You should be. My field team leader before you was a Snow Queen. She's why I started dyeing my hair black in the first place. Blondes may have more fun, but I hate getting shown up by people whose hair is naturally blue."

I lowered my eyebrow, my dubiousness fading into a frown. "Why are you stalling?"

Now it was Sloane's turn to jump, a guilty look flashing across her face. "I'm not stalling."

"You met me outside an active incursion because you wanted to talk about your hair. Don't try telling me I brought it up—you only put it in ponytails when you want us to ask if you've had a haircut recently. Why are you stalling?"

Sloane hesitated. That put my back up further. Sloane *never* hesitated. Finally she said, "The girl in the wheelchair isn't our target."

I blinked. Until Sloane said it, I hadn't even realized I was making that assumption. It was a natural one, though. Fully half of the Little Mermaids we encountered were people who had been injured in an accident of some kind, and who wanted to walk again almost as much as they wanted to find true love. "She's not?"

"He came home to drown," said Sloane bleakly. She met my eyes for only a moment before looking back toward the little suburban house with its sheltering ring of unmarked black cars. There were more vehicles here than would have been needed for simple team transport. That alone should have tipped me off about our target being dead: cleanup was already on the scene. "He took the knife into the water with him. I guess he figured the chlorine would wash the blood away."

That caught my attention. "Blood?"

Sloane nodded. "His clothes were covered in it. And here's the upsetting part: none of it's his."

"Oh," I said faintly.

As if the rest of it weren't upsetting enough already.

# # #

Little Mermaids are a relatively recent addition to the Index: technically, they're not listed in the ATI, since the version used by mundane scholars only looks at true folktales and motifs, not stories whose authors have been identified and listed in the public record. Maybe we shouldn't list the voiceless girls and boys either, but our job is hard enough without splitting our best defense into multiple rulebooks. Everything goes into our official Index—the Thumbelinas and the Peter Pans, the Match Girls and the Captain Hooks. And the Little Mermaids. Always the damn Little Mermaids.

Like so many stories, the Little Mermaid narrative requires multiple players: the Mermaid, the Prince, the Sea Witch, and the sibling or siblings who can provide a murder weapon. I walked past Andy and the crying girl in the wheelchair, keeping my eyes fixed firmly on the front door to prevent her getting too good a look at me. She was already upset. Seeing someone who looked like a modern-day interpretation of Death walking into her house wasn't going to help.

Jeff was in the living room directing a group of cleanup staffers when Sloane and I came through the door. He turned toward the sound of our footsteps, and offered a genial nod. "Agent Marchen, Agent Winters."

Professionalism: right. He probably suspected at least one of the cleanup crew's members to be reporting our activities back to headquarters, and he wasn't likely to be wrong about that. "What's the situation?"

"Michael Christian, age twenty-four, deceased," said Jeff. "He was found floating face down in the pool by his younger sister, Linda, who called the police. Dispatch had been monitoring a narrative spike from this area. We were able to intercept the call, and have taken possession of the scene."

Including the little sister, who probably had no idea what was going on, and who had just lost her brother. Shit. "Any sign that someone else was involved with getting him into the water?"

Jeff shook his head. "He's still in the pool—I assumed you'd want to see the body before we moved it—but there are no signs of foul play. Everything is consistent with a single person drowning."

"Except for the blood."

"Except for the blood," Jeff grimly agreed.

"Okay, this is portentous and spooky and all, but can we go see the dead guy now? Because you people are seriously boring me." Sloane rocked back onto her heels, giving the living room a seemingly disinterested once-over before adding, "And they're orphans. Parents have been dead five, six years. Probably explains why he was such a good target—if they had any fairy-tale potential at all, losing their parents was like a flare to the narrative."

"Somebody check the records on this family, find out what happened to the parents and when," I snapped to the cleanup crew, neither arguing with Sloane nor asking her to explain her reasoning further. "Agent Davis, take me to the body."

"Right this way," said Jeff, and started toward the back of the house, plainly expecting us to follow him.

As we walked I scanned the rooms around us, first the front room, and then the hall that led into the dining room adjoining the backyard. Sloane was right. The décor was elegant, obviously chosen with exquisite care—and at least five years out of date. Something had caused the people who lived here to stop caring about whether or not their pictures reflected reality. And in all the full-length shots, Linda was standing on her own two feet, not confined to the chair I'd seen in front of the house.

The backyard was as large and well-designed as the rest of the house, and here at least they'd been keeping things up, maybe because hiring a landscaper was easier to deal with than the local homeowners association. A brown-haired man floated in the middle of the pool, the back of his shirt soaked through with blood. It was still leaking into the water, sending out little crimson tendrils that dissolved as the tireless action of the pool cleaner sucked the blood away.

I walked to the edge of the pool and stopped, crouching down. "How sure are we about drowning as the cause of death?"

"Fairly sure," said Jeff. "We'll need to do an autopsy and toxicology screen to make sure that he didn't drug or poison himself before going into the water, but one of the cleanup staffers got in and swam beneath him to check for a cut throat." He caught my look and put his hands up, adding, "We tested the water for biohazards before anyone went in."

"How?"

"I dropped in a unicorn's horn. It didn't glow. There's nothing in the water that can hurt you."

"Cheap but effective," I said. Michael's pants were so tight that they could have been painted on, and his shirt looked like silk. I frowned. "What's that on his wrist?"

"Looks like a club ID band," said Jeff. "You know, the ones that mark you as over twenty-one, so you can drink?"

"I don't know, actually. I've never been to a bar when it wasn't on official business." I leaned over, checking the depth listing on the side of the pool. Three feet. Fair enough. Bracing my hand on the concrete, I slid my legs down into the water, until I was standing on the bottom of the pool. It was a warm morning. Good thing, too; the pool was unheated. I splashed toward Michael's body, calling back, "Once this is done, tell cleanup we're going to need his body removed from the pool, you got me? We don't want him to start falling apart."

"You're wading with a corpse, Henry," said Sloane with malevolent glee. "There's dead man juice in that water."

"I know," I said. I reached the body and paused, murmuring a quiet, "I'm sorry," before I turned him over. Michael was gone; he wouldn't hear me. The gesture still made me feel a little better as I looked at his dead eyes staring up at the pre-dawn sky.

The diver had been correct: there was no mark on the body. I unbuttoned his waterlogged silk shirt, revealing an undamaged chest. He was uninjured—but not unmarred. The entire right side of his chest was covered in scars, thick ridges of white tissue that looked painful even now. I frowned as I reached up to touch his face, feeling behind his ear until I found the thin telltale scars left behind by plastic surgery.

"Jeff, go talk to the sister," I said, taking a closer look at the line of Michael's neck, the way his muscles fit together. The signs were subtle. They were still there. "Find out when he had reconstructive surgery, how extensive it was, and whether there was any damage to his vocal cords in the process."

"I'm on it," he said.

Sloane sat down on the diving board, leaning forward to look down into the water. "Knife's here," she said. "You going to swim down and get it now that you're a mermaid, too?"

"Cleanup can do that," I said. "We're going to confirm that it belonged to his sister. That's how this story goes. There's just one factor that we're missing."

"What's that?" she asked, giving me a speculative look.

"The Prince." I started wading toward the pool ladder. I was going to need a towel before I got back into the car. "In the story, the mermaid receives the knife to enable them to kill their Prince before he can marry someone else. It doesn't happen in the traditional narrative. The mermaid can't bring herself to kill her true love, and goes back to the sea instead. But this time, we've got a man with no wounds and an awful lot of blood. So where's the Prince?"

For once, Sloane didn't have a smart-ass comment.

# # #

We beat Michael Christian's body back to the Bureau, since we didn't have to deal with wrestling him out of the pool—or with subduing his sister, who had become hysterical when two members of the cleanup crew walked past her with the stretcher. I guess she'd been holding out hope until that moment that he was somehow alive. My team and I had bailed as the police were finally rolling up the street. Let cleanup deal with the interface and paperwork. That was part of their job after all, and we had a potentially wounded Prince to find before he went and triggered someone else's story.

Most Princes are like skeleton keys: they can open many doors. Left to roam, a fully active Prince could do more damage than any single furious fairy-tale princess could have dreamed.

"I've got Dispatch monitoring the police bands and going through the admissions records from the local hospitals, looking for stabbing victims," said Jeff, walking back into the bullpen with a pile of folders in his hands. "If our Prince is well enough to have sought medical care, we'll find him."

"If he's a corpse, he won't be calling his doctor," said Sloane. "I've emailed my contacts at the local morgue, and on the body bits black market."

"You make 'I know people who can get you a human kidney for the right price' sound so casual," said Andy, looking away from his computer. "It's not right."

"Go fuck yourself," said Sloane genially. She brought up a new browser window, the eBay logo splashed bright across the top of the page. Turning her back on the rest of us, she began surfing shoe listings.

That was actually comforting: if Sloane was shopping on company time again, at least *something* was normal. Unlike the story we were trying to unsnarl. "This isn't right," I said. "Mermaids either kill their Princes or themselves. They don't do the murder-suicide thing. It would be a waste of narrative resources."

"This one appears to have missed the memo," said Jeff. He put his folders down on the edge of the nearest desk—which happened to be Sloane's—and flipped open the top one. "I've pulled the files on every nascent Little Mermaid or compatible Prince that we've documented in the last two years. There will be holes, of course."

"Of course," I said grimly. Our monitoring systems have never been perfect—stories slip through the net all the time, camouflaged by their surroundings or just manifesting in unexpected ways. The difference between a four-ten and a seven-oh-nine is sometimes as small as the availability of spindles in the local environment. Tracking them sometimes bordered on impossible, and that was *before* Birdie screwed us all over by punching holes in all the recording systems.

Yet none of that explained why our latest Little Mermaid had elected to go murder-suicide on us—or whether he'd succeeded in killing his Prince.

"Hey Henry, listen to this," said Andy, tapping his computer screen for emphasis before he read, "'Local college student Michael Christian is seeking plastic surgery for his extensive scarring, following a gift from an unknown benefactor. Michael, who is the primary caregiver for his younger sister, Linda, was overcome by the generosity of this mysterious stranger'—it goes on to talk about the car crash they were in. There's pictures, too. He looked pretty bad before things got patched up for him."

"How long ago was that?" I asked.

"Looks like he went in for the first surgery a year ago." Andy started typing again. "I'll see if I can find anything on his post-surgical follow up."

Sloane abruptly stood and crossed to my desk, yanking open the bottom left-hand drawer without saying a word to the rest of us. I blinked.

"Can I help you with something, Sloane?" I asked. "That's the wrong desk. I don't have your makeup kit."

"You have Dr. Reynard's files," she said. Producing them, she dropped them on my keyboard and began sorting roughly through the thick manila folders, finally holding one up and triumphantly announcing, "Linda Christian. And look, he's doodled little fish scales all over her name tag."

"So you think he was tracking *her* as the potential Little Mermaid?" I stuck my hand out, motioning for her to give me the folder.

"We would have been, if we'd known about her," said Sloane, slapping it into my palm. "With the narrative circling the house, she would have seemed like the logical target. As fucked-up as his face was, I'd have cued him as a Beast."

I paused, understanding washing over me. "That's how it got to him."

Sloane frowned. "What?"

"That's how the narrative got to him. Beasts and Mermaids are both defined by how much they long to be human." I flipped open the file, scanning Dr. Reynard's notes on Linda. "According to this, Linda was pretty well-adjusted. She liked to swim, she liked the freedom of movement she had in the water, but she was happy to be alive, and didn't waste time wishing for things that she was never going to have. Based on her medical records, it would have taken a miracle for her to ever walk again."

"So the narrative circled her as a potential Mermaid, couldn't get through to her, and switched focus to her brother?" Jeff frowned. "Male Mermaids are common enough, but it still reads more as a Beauty and the Beast, or even a Frog Prince—"

"And yet we have the sister, the knife, the pool—all that's missing is the stolen voice."

"Actually, that's not missing," said Andy. He had pulled up another news article. This one showed the angelic face of the boy we'd found floating in the pool. "According to this,

Michael's plastic surgery was an incredible success, only there were complications. His throat got infected, and before anyone knew what was happening, the bacteria had eaten out his vocal cords. He was never going to speak again. Couldn't make a sound."

I winced, thinking of the freckled woman with the fast-moving hands who existed in the whiteout wood. She hadn't been a Mermaid, but maybe she could have been, if the narrative's aim had been just slightly different. "So the surgery that made him beautiful made him mute?"

Andy nodded. "Yeah. And if he thought of getting a new face as 'becoming human,' that would have fulfilled the narrative's needs."

"You don't have to be attractive to be human," said Jeff.

"Don't worry, cobbler, Henry still thinks you're pretty," said Sloane, in an almost singsong way.

I resisted the urge to throw a stapler at her head. "It's what he thought that matters here. He thought he was becoming human. He lost his voice as part of the deal. Even if the narrative didn't want him before all that happened, it wanted him afterward."

"No," said Sloane. We all turned to look at her. She shook her head, meeting my eyes as she repeated, "No. You'd be right if not for the whole 'anonymous benefactor' angle. Somebody paid for this. Somebody looked at this dude, who was fucked up sure, but lots of dudes are fucked up, and said 'Gosh, wouldn't it be nice if he could fall into a story.'"

"You think Birdie was his benefactor," I said.

Sloane nodded. "I do. She's been here a long time, and Dispatch makes good money. Building this guy a new face was probably pretty expensive, but she's a storytelling bitch who knows how to work the narrative."

"That could explain the deviations," said Jeff. "If he was meant to be a Beast, which is a very active role, but became a Mermaid, which is more reactive, he could have unconsciously combined aspects of the two stories."

"Do stories normally mix like this?" asked Andy.

"No," I said. "Birdie has managed to turn everything into a special case."

"Gee, lucky us," said Andy.

I made a small frustrated noise, trying to think. A lot of Beauties wound up on slabs in the Bureau morgue when their super-strong, super-abusive boyfriends hit them just a little too hard. That was another relatively recent development: the original Beast had been a monster on the outside and a gentleman on the inside. It was only in the last few decades that they'd turned violent. "The situation is weird, but it's still what we're dealing with, and none of this gets us any closer to our missing Prince."

"Sure it does," said Sloane. She stood. "The band on Michael's wrist was for a club downtown called La Maison Verte. Beauty and the Beast is a French story, and 'verte' means green, which also hits the 'could have been a Frog Prince' angle. I refuse to believe he went to a club that references the two stories he didn't manifest and didn't murder anybody while he was there."

I blinked at her. "You recognized the club from the wristband? Why didn't you say anything?"

"Because we didn't need to go there yet, and because it's closed at this time of day, so it's not like there's going to be a line," she said mildly. "Maybe you should put on some pants."

I was wearing black sweatpants with the Bureau logo on one hip, since my original pants were soaked with pool water and stuffed into a plastic bag in the trunk of my car. I reddened. "We'll stop by my house before we go to the club," I said. "It'll give Jeff a chance to see the swamp mallow growing from my carpet before I yank it all out."

"I love field trips," said Andy.

This time, I threw the stapler.

# # #

The van seemed too conspicuous for where we were going, and so we were split into two cars: Jeff and me in mine, Andy and Sloane in Andy's. Jeff sat with his hands folded in his lap, not touching anything during the drive. I gave him a sidelong look. His eyes were fixed firmly on the windshield. I thought about showing him the swamp mallows I'd photographed earlier, but this didn't seem like the sort of problem that could be solved with flora. I sighed.

"Is there something on your mind, Jeff?" He hadn't really spoken to me, or spent any time alone with me, since we'd gone up to the roof to send the message to Birdie. I should probably have noticed that sooner. In my defense, I'd been busy.

"Not that I'm prepared to discuss, but thank you for asking," he said.

I blinked. "Wow. Did you mean for that to sound like 'fuck off,' or was that just a lucky side effect of timing?"

"What?" Jeff twisted in his seat, finally looking at me. "I would never tell you to fuck off. If I've seemed unprofessional—"

"Are you really going to play the 'keeping it professional' card? You've been looking at me differently for the last two weeks."

"Maybe that's because you *are* different, Henry," he said, a note of self-loathing in his voice that was as blatant as it was surprising. "You activated your story. You didn't even ask us if we were willing to look for another way first. You just . . . you just did it."

"Ignoring the part where it's my life and no one gets to say that I couldn't activate my story if I wanted to, what other options did we have? You saw how quickly that bomb went off. We all would have died."

"At least you would have died while you were still you."

I stared at him—dangerous, since I was still driving, but I couldn't stop myself. "Are you seriously implying that I am no longer myself because my story has gone active? Because if you are, please feel free to ask the Deputy Director for a new assignment. I'd hate to have to break in an archivist at this point in time, but it would be better than dealing with one who can't trust my judgment."

Jeff groaned. "That's not . . . that came out wrong. I didn't mean to imply that you weren't yourself anymore. I'm sorry."

"Then what *did* you mean to imply?"

"I hated shoes when I was a kid." The statement was abrupt enough that I just blinked at him. Jeff continued, "I was barefoot whenever I could be. During the summer I only put shoes on when I was going into the library—they didn't let you go barefoot there. I know *why* I hated them. We couldn't afford to buy me new shoes every time I grew, and so they always pinched and squeezed my feet. That didn't change the hatred."

"Why are you telling me this?"

"Because when my story awoke, I blew my entire savings account on shoes. Men's shoes, women's shoes, vintage shoes, new shoes, it didn't matter. I needed to own them all. I needed to fill my apartment. I was a hoarder with a very specific addiction, and it came on like a wave. The story had me. Do you understand? *It changes you.* You may feel like it doesn't, but it does, and it's never going to stop."

I scowled at him before turning back to the road. "And here you were just saying that you didn't think my story going active would turn me into someone else."

"I'm still me. I was always a bookish, nerdy guy who liked to look things up for fun. But there are aspects of me that came in with the narrative, and they're never going to go away."

We had reached my house. I pulled up in front and killed the engine. "Wait here," I said. "I'm going to get some pants I can wear in public, and then we're going to deal with this story once and for all."

"Henry—"

"Don't, Jeff." I got out of the door, slamming the door behind myself. I didn't look back to see whether he was watching me walk away. I didn't really want to know.

# # #

Sloane and Jeff had exchanged places while I was inside putting on dry clothes, and she spent the ride to La Maison Verte spinning the dial on my radio like she was going to win some unnamed musical jackpot. More distractingly, she would stop on each station long enough to identify the song and sing along for a few bars before changing it again. By the time we reached the darkened facade of La Maison, I was starting to wonder whether there were any Snow White variants that included killing the Wicked Queen for being too annoying to be allowed to live.

I turned off the engine. "You been here before?" I asked.

"A few times," Sloane said. "The owner sleeps in an apartment above the bar. He's not supposed to, since this area isn't zoned residential, but he does it anyway. I'm sure he'll be *thrilled* to see us." She kicked her door open, pausing only long enough to say, "Jeff's not wrong, you know. He's just shit at explaining himself." Then she was out of the car and heading for the club doors at a clip she shouldn't have been able to maintain in her platform heels.

I groaned. "Great," I muttered, undoing my seat belt and following after her. "Now they're ganging up on me."

Sloane beat all the rest of us to the door. She was leaning on the doorbell when we trooped up to meet her, a smirk on her face. "You know, this asshole had me kicked out once because he decided that my ID had to be a fake. He was all 'we can't afford to have underage drinking in this establishment,' and out onto the street I went."

"Be fair, Sloane," said Andy. "Your ID *is* fake. I mean, you're one hell of a lot older than anything that has your picture on it will admit."

"Only because people are small-minded about the capabilities of Botox," said Sloane, still leaning on the doorbell. "I figure the noise will start driving him out of his tree any second now, and then we can come in for a little chat."

"Annoyance as an interrogation tactic is so very you," I commented, and glanced at Jeff. He looked away, refusing to meet my eyes. I sighed. "Did anybody get any hits on a body while we were driving?"

"Three John Does came into the morgue last night, but none with stab wounds," said Andy. "The only stabbing victims we have all came with confirmed attackers who weren't our Mermaid."

Someone started shouting unintelligibly from behind the club door. Sloane kept her finger on the doorbell, leaning even harder into the malicious act of driving everyone inside La Maison Verte out of their minds.

Then the door swung open, revealing a tall, skinny man in dirty jeans and nothing else, which gave us an impressive view of the colorful tattoos that covered his chest. He snarled at Sloane in a language I didn't understand, making a grab for her arm.

I don't think he saw her move. One second, he was trying to make her stop ringing the doorbell, and the next, she was holding his wrist firmly in one hand, while the other hand kept up the racket. "Didn't anyone ever tell you that it's not polite to hit a lady?" she asked, in a voice so sugary-sweet that it was terrifying.

Time for me to step in, before she actually started breaking bones. "Hello. We're from the ATF," I said, stepping forward and flashing my badge too quickly for him to read the writing. He went pale and stopped struggling against Sloane's hand. "We had a report of a stabbing here last night?"

"How did you—"

"You shouldn't answer questions with questions," said Sloane, doing something complicated with her fingers. The man groaned, sagging in her grip. "It's rude."

"Yes, okay, yes!" the man half said, half gasped. "One of our regulars. He didn't want to go to the hospital. Said it wasn't that bad. I let his friends take him home."

I leaned close, looking at him coldly. "We're gonna need a name."

# # #

Jeff worked his magic on the local DMV database, and we quickly determined that our stabbing victim, Kyle Johnston, lived in a suburb less than five miles from the Christian house. We piled back into our cars and took off, ignoring traffic and safety regulations in favor of getting to the wounded Prince as quickly as possible. As callous as it sounded, things might still be okay if he died. If he fell into a coma . . .

The narrative *loves* comas. It can use them in all sorts of interesting, horrible ways that will do nothing good for anyone who comes into range. "Sloane, call the Bureau, ask them to put Demi on the phone," I said, turning onto the freeway. "I need to ask her something."

"Is it how to play 'Mary Had A Little Lamb' on the recorder? Because I can teach you that." And yet she was already dialing—Sloane might be snarky and unpleasant when she had the chance, but she knew her job.

I focused on the road while Sloane talked, snapped, and shouted her way through the various levels of bureaucracy between us and our imprisoned team member. Finally, she said, "Demi, it's Sloane. Henry needs to ask you something. I'm putting you on speaker."

"Henry?" Demi's voice was rendered thin and tinny by its passage through the phone.

"Here," I said. "Demi, do you remember the other day when we were talking about Birdie's plan and what you'd managed to ascertain while you were undercover?" That was the word we were using now, at least when there was a chance that we could have been bugged by the Bureau. Not "enthralled," but "under-cover." It seemed so much more, well, on our side.

"Yes," said Demi. "I told you I don't know much—"

"But you know more than the rest of us. You said that Birdie was planting stories like bombs. What did you mean by that?"

"Just that she'd be triggering unstable narratives when she could, to see if the blowback could make other stories go active. Chain reactions. Why?"

"Because we have a Little Mermaid who should have been a Beast, and who tried for murder-suicide instead of picking one," I said grimly. "Sound unstable to you?"

"I don't know the Index as well as you do," Demi said hesitantly. "Maybe?"

"Demi, did she say *anything else* about what she was planning to do with the unstable stories? Anything at all?"

"Just that there were a lot of them."

Every time Demi started a sentence with the word "just" I felt like there were a dozen things she wasn't telling me—things she might not even know she knew, because they were buried under a hundred inconsequential things, and she hadn't been with us long enough to learn to *listen*. Demi had barely received enough field training to keep her from getting killed before we were shoving her into the path of the narrative.

I should probably have felt guilty about that. Maybe I would have, except that I knew I would activate her again if I had to. I would do it again in a heartbeat. "Okay, Demi. Thanks for that. I'll let you know how this turns out when we get back to the Bureau." I gestured for Sloane to hang up before Demi could say anything else. She'd already contributed as much as she could, and I didn't want to upset her when there was nothing she could do to help. "Sloane, thoughts?"

"You mean do I think Birdie set our Mermaid up as a narrative hand grenade? Yeah, I do." Sloane tucked her phone back into her pocket. "Let's hope the Prince is dead," she added, echoing my earlier sentiment. "I don't want to think about what's going to happen if he's still breathing."

"Me neither," I said, and hit the gas.

# # #

"Kyle Johnston, this is the police." Andy hammered on the door, shouting in his most booming voice at the same time. It would definitely have been intimidating if I hadn't known him. The fact that Kyle wasn't answering spoke poorly for his continued survival. "Please open your door, or we're coming in."

"He's here," said Sloane, pacing back and forth behind Andy like a chained dog. She had the half-starved look she sometimes got when we were close to an active story, nostrils flaring and eyes taking on a feral gleam. "He's inside that door."

"Is he alive?" I asked.

She shot me a glare. "Story wouldn't still be here if he wasn't."

"Got it," I said. "Andy?"

"Step away from the door!" he shouted, just in case Kyle was close enough to hear.

The sound of Andy kicking in the door was viscerally satisfying in a way that was difficult to describe. I drew my gun, holding it low as I motioned for Andy and Sloane to lead the way, and we entered Kyle Johnston's home.

If Michael and Linda's house looked like it had been decorated several years ago and then allowed to slip slowly,
inexorably out of style, Kyle's condo was the polar opposite.
Every article of furniture and piece of artwork on the wall was
perfectly hip, perfectly new, perfectly *now*, like there was a
chance that a lifestyle magazine could arrive and start grading
at any moment. The only thing out of place was the trail of
blood that started halfway down the hall and extended toward
the back of the condo.

I pointed to the blood trail and then to Andy, indicating
that he should go that way. Looking to Jeff and Sloane, I pointed
in the opposite direction. We needed to cover the whole place,
and we needed to do it as quickly and quietly as possible.

Sloane scowled, pointing in the direction of the blood. I
shook my head and pointed again at the door on the other
side of the room. Still glaring at me, she grabbed Jeff's arm and
dragged him with her as she finally deigned to follow orders.

Andy had waited for me—less out of respect than out of a
healthy desire not to go wandering off into a narrative-infected
house all by himself. He raised an eyebrow as I turned to face
him. I rolled my eyes and started following the blood, my gun
braced against my wrist and Andy a looming, familiar presence at my back. We had done this routine before. That didn't
make it any easier.

The blood trail ended at the bathroom, where wads of gauze
and bloody towels carpeted the floor. There was no sign of Kyle
Johnston. Andy and I still searched the cupboards, closet, and
bedroom before turning and retracing our steps, looking for
the rest of our team.

We didn't have to go far. Sloane and Jeff were in the kitchen,
where a slim, good-looking man with bandages wrapped

around his otherwise bare chest had collapsed on the linoleum. He wasn't dead. He was breathing, and what's more, there was a certain strange vitality about him that caught and held my eye, almost like it was daring me to come close, to smell the lingering traces of his cologne and read the birdwing traceries of his collarbones—

Sloane's hand caught my elbow as I started to step past her. "Maybe you shouldn't," she said, and for once, her voice was almost kind. "A woman in your condition and a narrative running this close to the surface, there's no telling what could happen."

I reddened. "I wouldn't," I said, my protest sounding hollow even to my own ears.

"You're a fairy-tale princess, Henry. You get too close to a sleeping prince and you're not going to have a choice." She let me go and pushed me back a step in the same motion, somehow making it seem like it had been my decision to retreat. "We've got this. Go wait by the car."

"Dammit," I muttered, rubbing my eyes hard with the heels of my hands. "All right. Call if you need anything." I'd always known that there would be downsides if my story ever went live. I had never considered that an inability to stand near an active Prince might be among them.

Footsteps followed me out of the condo and down the walkway to my car. I didn't stop or look behind me until my hand was resting on the hood. Then I turned, looking at Jeff, and asked wearily, "Is this where you say 'I told you so' and tell me all about how I was inevitably going to wind up enthralled by the first sleeping prince I saw? Because I'm not in the mood."

"No, this is where I ask if you're okay," he said. He took a breath before ducking his head and adding, "I also wanted to

say that I was sorry, if you're in the mood for an apology. I was
stupid before."

"You've been being stupid for a couple of weeks now, and
we're on a case," I said, folding my arms. "What makes this the
right time to come and apologize to me?"

"Well, there's the fact that you may need to be distracted
to keep you from going and flinging yourself on our currently
comatose guest—not that you'd want to, you understand, just
that there's a chance the narrative would try to manipulate
things so as to leave you no choice." Jeff reached up and nervously adjusted his glasses. "There's also the fact that our fight
earlier this morning was about princes, and now we're dealing
with one. That seems unlikely to be a coincidence."

"If you think the narrative wants you to apologize—"

"I think that if the narrative wants *anything* where the two
of us are concerned, it's exactly what it's getting right now: a
fight. It wants us to be alienated from one another. It wants me
to be so . . . insecure about what your story means that I with-
draw and stop trying to build on what we may have. It wants
you to be alone. Lonely people are easier prey for the idea of
true love in a single kiss and a partner who's too busy sleeping
their life away to protest."

I frowned slowly. "You think the narrative made you pick a
fight with me?"

"No. I think my own insecurity and inexperience with
dating since my own story started and my desire not to mess
up our friendship made me pick a fight with you. I think the
narrative wants me not to apologize." Jeff shrugged, his mouth
thinning to a firm line. "I have waited a very long time to be
able to have inappropriately timed discussions about the status

of our relationship with you. I don't intend to let my own stupidity take this opportunity away from me."

"I'm not an opportunity, Jeff," I said. "I'm a person. I lead your field team. We're always going to be peers before we can be anything else."

He shrugged. "I know all that. I also know you're the one who brought me back when my story was trying to take me away—and we've all seen Demi, we know what would have happened to me if it had succeeded. I don't know how my story could have been turned offensive, and I don't particularly want to. The kiss didn't work because kisses break spells, Henry. The kiss worked because it was *you*. I really want to give us a try. I'll do my best not to freak out on you like I did today."

"I hate princes," I said, without thinking about it. I just spoke, letting the words flow through me and out into the air. "They don't even get *names* half the time, they just get passed around like little narrative explosions, and all you can do is hope you won't get caught in the blast. I've never thought much about what I'd want in a significant other, but I've always known that it wouldn't be a prince. Being active isn't going to change that."

"So what do you want?"

I thought about it for a moment before I smiled and said, "You."

We were both professionals and we were technically at work, even if I wasn't allowed to go anywhere near the crime scene until Kyle Johnston was safely stowed in the backseat of Andy's car. So we just stood there, smiling awkwardly at one another, until Sloane came out and gave us the all clear. She was smirking when she did it, like she could tell what we'd been discussing just from the way that we stood.

Let her smirk. I was too happy to care.

# # #

We were done in the field and back in at the Bureau by four o'clock—plenty of time for me to walk up to Deputy Director Brewer's office and tell his secretary that I needed to see him. He let me in five minutes later. It was an impressive response time, especially considering the number of active stories we'd had recently. I guess when you're at the center of the storm, you stop putting things on hold.

"Can I help you, Agent Marchen?" he asked, walking back around his desk and retaking his seat.

"Yes, sir," I said. "We have reason to believe that the next stage in Birdie's plan involves modifying borderline stories to guarantee a dangerous and potentially violent resolution."

He looked at me like I was speaking Latin.

I tried again: "She's weaponizing fairy tales, sir."

"As if they weren't dangerous enough already?" He leaned back in his seat, still staring at me. "What do you suggest we do about this?"

"Sir, I am down a body and dealing with things that have been twisted out of true. I think you know what I want to do about this."

His gaze hardened. "You're making a request that could end your career."

"With all due respect, everything I've done in the last month could end my career. What's one more?"

"Are you sure you can manage her?"

"I think she wants to prove herself. The archivists have confirmed her claims: her story was vulnerable to Birdie's targeting. We can prevent that from happening again."

"Are you sure enough that you're willing to risk your entire team on it?"

That was the real question, wasn't it? I nodded. "Yes, sir."

He sighed. "Then I'll sign the papers. But I hope to God you know what you're doing, Marchen."

"I do, Deputy Director. I really do."

Kyle Johnston was in the Archives, sleeping and receiving medical care. Jeff and I were going out for coffee after work. And I was getting Demi back.

I knew exactly what I was doing.

I just hoped that I was doing the right things.

Scarlet Flowers

Memetic incursion in progress: tale type 426 ("The Two Girls and the Bear")
Status: IN PROGRESS

Gerald March, high school English teacher and purposefully ordinary guy, had not started his Tuesday expecting to end up running for his life.

He'd been having a reasonably good day, as school days went: his students had been about as well behaved as high school students are capable of being, and some of them had even read the material before first period, which verged on the miraculous. The weather was good, the cute barista at the Starbucks had given him extra whipped cream on his morning mocha, and he'd even managed to snag one of the faculty parking spaces in the front row. Everything had been going just fine until fourth period.

Fourth period was when the herd of deer had appeared on the quad.

Thanks to the modern wonder of smartphones and data plans, the entire school had known about their visitors in a matter of minutes. He'd lost control of the class before he'd fully grasped what was going on. They'd rushed to press their noses to the windows, and he'd followed them, trying to figure out what all the excitement was about.

As soon as he'd appeared behind the glass, the deer had turned, every one of them, their heads swiveling toward him with a predatory intensity that was rare in herbivores. He'd paled, taking a large step backward, and then—to his shame—he'd turned around and run. He hadn't even stopped by the office on his way off campus. That would mean the end of this teaching job for sure. No matter how good a teacher you are, you can't just run off and leave a class of high school sophomores on their own. He was dimly aware that he should call the school and tell them he was sick, or that he'd suffered a family emergency, or *something*, but he didn't have time for that. If he stopped running, they would catch up with him, and if they caught up with him . . .

Gerald March had spent his entire life working to become the man he wanted to be. He wasn't going to let some stupid story pull him back into its clutches now. So he ran, and he hoped that his sister—who had never had the sense to step away from her own doorway into the narrative—would be there to break him loose.

# # #

It had been a long damn day. There are workdays that fly by, and others that seem to last forever. This one fell into the latter category. Birdie was off somewhere licking her wounds, and things had returned at least temporarily to something approaching normal. The only narrative incursion reported in the area had been a Cheshire Cat, presumably looking for an Alice to latch onto, and it had been handled by another field team, leaving my team to finish the paperwork we'd been slacking on for weeks. I lifted a sheet of paper and scowled at it, like that would somehow fill in the rest of the blanks in my after-action report. It didn't.

"Anyone care to finish this for me so that I can go home and commit to a long evening of drinking hard lemonade and not doing paperwork?" I asked.

Sloane didn't even raise her head as she flipped me off. Andy scowled. Jeff, who was the only one of us who didn't have a pile of paperwork to get through, laughed at me. I silently pledged to hate him.

"It wouldn't be so bad if you did it every night like you're supposed to," he said.

"I do the important parts every night," I protested. "The parts that can actually impact the narrative are filed with the Archives before I leave the office."

"Yes, and that's why you haven't been reprimanded or otherwise disciplined for setting a bad example for a field team, but that's only a small amount of the job's required documentation." Jeff somehow managed to make the bureaucratic nonsense sound less like a lecture and more like normal human conversation. I wasn't sure whether that came from his connection to the narrative, or whether it was something that was inherently *him*. "And before you ask, no, I won't do your paperwork for you. I will, however, go and get more coffee."

I amended my previous pledge from hatred to adoration. "Coffee would be wonderful. Thank you."

"It's the least I can do to keep you all from murdering me," he said, and left the bullpen.

"Think he'll remember cream and sugar?" asked Andy.

"It's Jeff, and he's fetching coffee for Henry," said Sloane. "He'll probably remember cream, sugar, biscotti, and a portable Starbucks."

Demi, who had been sitting silently at her desk during this entire exchange, lifted her head and asked cautiously, "Is that a thing his story can actually do?"

"No, but he could probably build a Starbucks overnight if we hooked him up with a barista who was on the verge of starving due to a lack of available franchise coffee shops to work in," I said. I tried to keep my tone light, despite my general irritation with the world.

"Mouthful much?" asked Sloane. "I thought Snow Whites needed to breathe."

"Bite me," I suggested genially. Demi had only officially been back with us for two days, and she was still jumpier than I liked. I was fairly sure we'd missed the Cheshire Cat call because it would have meant taking Demi into the field, and while I was grateful to have a little more time for her to get reacclimated, I also knew that we couldn't put off her full return to active duty forever. The narrative doesn't work that way. If we tried to keep her behind a desk, the narrative would see her as a weak spot and go out of its way to force her back into the field. We needed to beat it to the punch.

"I think that's something that's better left to our archivist," said Sloane. Her voice took on that singsong quality that meant she was preparing to taunt me as she continued, "He's a useful boy, you know. Have you come up with any new uses for him recently?"

I reddened, aware that my blush would look like clown makeup on my snowy complexion. "Back off, Sloane."

"Make me, snow-bitch," she said.

"Please don't make her," said Andy. "We'll just wind up with two more hours of paperwork if Henry assaults a teammate."

I sighed. "What's really sad is that's a legitimate reason not to hit her. Sweet Grimm, what I wouldn't give for a distraction right now." I dropped the paper I was holding, following it a split second later with my head. My forehead made a pleasant bonking sound when it hit the desk.

"Ask and ye shall receive," said Andy, sounding faintly amazed. "Look what the cat dragged in."

That was enough to make me lift my head again. Andy was staring wide-eyed at the space behind me. Sloane, who had finally looked away from her own pile of paperwork, was doing the same thing. I closed my eyes for a moment, sending up a silent prayer that whatever was behind me was *not* some horrible, dangerous beast, and opened them again as I turned.

Jeff was standing in the aisle of the bullpen, next to a redheaded, blue-eyed man in chino slacks and a white button-down shirt. He looked haunted and slightly rumpled, like he had just taken a long road trip with little preparation and less sleep. I found myself on my feet without fully realizing that I was going to stand. Old anger and fresh confusion warred for control of my actions, finally fighting each other to a draw.

"Gerry?" I whispered.

The smile that tugged at the corners of his mouth didn't quite make it to his eyes. He looked so much older. He'd always looked older than me, but now . . . he could have been five years my senior. "Hey, Henry," he said. "Long time no see."

A third contender for control of my actions rose: relief. "Oh my God, Gerry!" I cried, and started to throw myself at him, trusting him to catch me the way he always had, ever since we were little kids. Anger could come later.

Sloane caught me instead. I didn't know how she'd managed to move so fast, but she was suddenly there, her fingers an iron band around my wrist, holding me in place. "Not so fast, *Princess*," she hissed. "Make sure our prodigal son knows the score before you go doing anything you're going to regret later."

I froze. "Oh my God," I repeated. This time there was no relief in the words. Gerry started to step forward, looking puzzled. I shied back against Sloane, shouting, "Stay away from me!"

"Uh, Henry?" Gerry stopped moving. That was something at least. "What's going on? Because I'll be honest, I thought you might not be happy to see me, but I sort of expected a warmer welcome than 'don't touch me.' I've had a really rough day."

"Oh, because you've given so many fucks about the sort of days *we've* been having," snapped Sloane, keeping her protective grasp on my wrist. "How long has it been, Gerald? Eight years, and not even a Christmas card? We've had some pretty rough days ourselves."

"Could I get an introduction if we're going to fight?" asked Jeff. He adjusted his glasses with one hand before looking Gerry slowly up and down, clearly taking his measure, or trying to. "I found him in the lobby with a visitor's pass, asking for an escort to the bullpen. I thought it was best to bring him here, but I'd still like to know who he is."

Sloane started to laugh, although her iron grip on my wrist loosened not one bit. "Oh man, is the cobbler *jealous*? All right, Gerry, welcome home, and Snowy, I take it back. This is the best day we've had in months. Let's see if he suggests a duel at dawn."

"It's good to see that some things around here haven't changed," said Gerry wearily.

"Some things never will," said Sloane. "What are you doing here?"

"Why are you restraining Henry?" Gerry countered.

"She's holding me back because there's something I haven't told you yet." I straightened. "Sloane, you can let go now. I'm not going to fling myself at him."

"That's not what you would have said a minute ago," said Sloane.

"I hadn't had a chance to think things through a minute ago. It's okay."

"If you blow us all up with fairy-tale stupidity, I'm going to kill you," she cautioned, releasing my wrist. Her fingers had left livid red marks on my skin. I rubbed it, feeling the beginnings of a bruise. Just what I needed.

I took a deep breath, turned to the rest of the team, and said, "Everyone, this is my brother, Gerald Marchen."

"It's 'March,' actually," said Gerry. "I changed it when I went into teaching."

Jeff blinked at him, looking utterly baffled. "I'm sorry, I don't understand. I've read Henry's file, and—" He stopped midword, the reality of what he was about to say hitting him. Both Gerry and I watched him curiously, briefly united in the synchronicity of our twinship as we waited to see what he was going to do. Jeff swallowed, obviously making adjustments to the files in his mind, before sticking his hand out and saying, "Agent Jeffrey Davis. I'm a member of your sister's field team, and a fully activated five-oh-three."

Gerry cast me a half-panicked sidelong look. I smiled. This, too, was totally familiar: the unprepared twin looking to the prepared one for the answers to an unexpected quiz. "He's connected to the Elves and the Shoemaker."

"Oh. Nice to meet you, Agent Davis." Gerry finally took the offered hand, apparently adding Jeff to his list of safe people. My heart broke a little as I watched.

I wasn't on that list anymore.

And I wasn't sure whether I wanted to be.

"A pleasure," said Jeff, shaking Gerry's hand before pulling away.

Gerry turned to look at me again, expression turning quizzical. "Now do you want to tell me why Sloane—hi, Sloane—"

"Hi, Gerry," said Sloane, with a little wave. "Go fuck yourself."

"—decided to go all human chain on you when you tried to give me a hug?"

"About that." I kept rubbing my wrist. It gave me something to focus on beyond the betrayal I knew I was about to see in his eyes. "She didn't want me to touch you because . . . well, because you were almost Rose Red."

"Tell me something I don't know." From him, the statement wasn't sarcastic: it was an honest request for me to tell him what was wrong, what he was missing about the scene. "I've lived with that story for my entire life."

"I know. But I . . ." I hadn't even been thinking of my brother when I ate the apple. I hadn't hesitated to sink my teeth into the forbidden fruit and change both our lives forever. To be fair, it had been eight years since I'd seen him. Not thinking about my brother was practically a daily activity. "I'm a Snow White now. For real. My story's gone active."

Gerry blinked at me. The betrayal I'd been expecting didn't appear. Instead, a quiet, resigned understanding flooded his face and he shook his head, stepping forward to wrap his arms around me. I stiffened. We were almost the same height, and I could see Jeff over my brother's shoulder, staring at me with a bemusement that echoed my own.

"Don't worry, Henry," said Gerry, still embracing me. "You can't activate my story. It's taken care of that all on its own."

I tried to pull away. "What?"

"A bunch of deer showed up on my campus this morning. They were looking for me. Don't ask me how I know that. I just do." Gerry tightened his arms, refusing to let me go.

"I don't have to ask," I said. I stopped trying to get away. If he needed something to hold on to, I could play that role, at least for now. If he was falling into his story, he had just become my responsibility. "When they come for you, they're impossible to ignore."

"Yeah, well. I've been ignoring them for weeks. Birds in the bushes outside my apartment, a runaway horse that someone had been transporting to a vet until it somehow got out of the trailer and wound up standing in front of my car—standing." Gerry laughed unsteadily. There was an edge of madness to the sound that I didn't like one bit. "That thing wasn't standing. It was *posing*, like it thought I was going to swoon and jump onto its back and let it carry me off into the sunset."

"Gerry . . ."

"I thought I got away from all of this." He finally let go, taking a step back and running one hand down the side of his face. He needed a shave. Glaring at me now, he asked, "Is this really your fault? Did you wake up my story by waking up yours?"

"I don't know," I said. "I didn't have a choice. It was activate or die."

"The solo Snow White narrative doesn't line up precisely with the Snow White and Rose Red narrative," said Jeff, stepping up on my other side and looking coolly at my brother.

"Four-two-six versus seven-oh-nine. If anything, Henry activating in solo mode should have made it impossible for you to go active, unless you were somehow suited to a different story. Once she ate the apple, the Rose Red door should have been closed to you."

Gerry eyed him, the same mistrustful look he'd worn since we were children, identical in all but coloration. Me, black and white and red all over, like a kindergarten joke; him, rosy cheeked and red haired and somehow just as subtly *wrong* in his pinkness as I was in my pallor. "Well, it's pretty obvious that didn't happen. So can you tell me why it didn't?"

"No," said Jeff. "But I can start pulling files, and together, we can probably figure it out. If you're willing to trust us."

"Like I have a choice?" Gerry raked a hand through his hair, leaving the short red strands sticking up in all directions. "Shit, Henry. I never wanted to be a fairy tale."

"You know what, asshole?" Sloane was suddenly in front of me, sliding her legs over my desk as she eeled her way into the conversation. She planted her hands on her hips, the back of her head virtually blocking my view of Gerry. "*None* of us signed up for this. You got that, right? Everyone in this room has had their life fucked up by a fairy tale at one point or another. Some of us are being fucked right now, while you watch. At least you got out for a little while."

"That was unnecessarily graphic," murmured Jeff.

"Shush," I said.

Sloane didn't appear to have noticed our interjections. She took a step forward, revealing Gerry's startled expression as she poked her finger at the center of his chest. She was taller than he was, her five eleven virtually towering over his five seven even without the platform boots she was so fond of. Even if

INDEXING

she'd been shorter, her tone would have been enough to make a brave man shrink where he stood. "We didn't ask for this. We didn't do anything to deserve it. We didn't volunteer, and we're not being punished for things we did in a previous life. We got *screwed*, and now you're getting screwed too. Boo-fucking-hoo. It's not Henry's fault, so back the fuck off, lover boy, or I'll give you something to be upset about."

Gerry blinked at her. The collapse began at his chin, which dropped down until it almost met his chest. His shoulders sagged, and then his knees began to buckle. I started to step forward, but Sloane was already there, slinging her arms around his waist and holding him up against her. Gerry didn't fight her. Instead, he twisted, burying his face against her shirt and beginning to cry silently. He'd always cried like that—silently—ever since we were kids.

"We'll be in the break room if you need us," said Sloane, with uncharacteristic gentleness. Still holding my brother up, she turned and led him away, first out of the bullpen and finally out of view. I stayed frozen where I was, feeling colder than any time since I had eaten the apple, and wondered what the hell we were going to do next.

Demi, of all people, broke the silence, saying hesitantly, "I thought Snow White and Rose Red was about two sisters." We all turned to look at her. She reddened, and said, "I read a bunch of fairy tales right after I joined the Bureau. I thought it would help me understand what we do here."

"Did it?" asked Jeff.

"It just confused me more," admitted Demi. "Fairy tales are *weird*."

"Did you read the one about the bird, the mouse, and the sausage?" asked Andy. "Because I have to say, that's when I decided I was leaving the research to the archivists and sticking to my fieldwork. I can only convince people that fairy tales aren't real if I'm not gibbering in a corner somewhere."

"Fairy tales rarely cause actual madness," said Jeff. "Demi's right, however: the Snow White and Rose Red narrative normally fixates on twin sisters. If you were connected to the story, Henry, you shouldn't have been able to wind up connected to seven-oh-nine. The only thing they have in common is the name and coloration of one of the two sisters. I don't . . ."

I was suddenly glad Gerry was out of the room. It didn't make the explanation easier, but it did mean he wouldn't be glaring at me if I said the wrong thing. "Gerry's my brother," I said. "We don't know which of us is older, because our mother died when we were born, but we were found together in her hospital room. We were identical, except for the coloring. That's part of why the ATI Management Bureau took custody of us immediately. You find two babies, one a redhead, one with black hair, both with the same blonde mother and brunet father—"

"What?" asked Demi.

"It doesn't take a genius to know that they're fairy tale–bound," I said.

"But you can't have been identical," said Demi. "Identical twins are always . . . you know."

Jeff, who had already figured out the situation, winced and looked at me, waiting to see how I would react.

Luckily for both of us, this was a conversation I'd had before. It didn't make me angry anymore. It just made me tired. Gerry was my brother. Anyone who met him could see that. So why did the world keep requiring me to explain the situation? "Identical twins will always have the same assigned birth gender, and that's what the story keyed off of," I said. "I guess even the narrative isn't smart enough to look into the mind of a newborn infant and know whether it's dealing with a boy or a girl."

Those first years had been rough on both of us. Geraldine and Henrietta Marchen, the darlings of the fairy-tale foster-care system. We'd been placed with a pair of agents who had the space and relative career stability to take care of us— Andrew and Maya Briggs, who had been with the Bureau for twenty years, and who had chosen not to have kids of their own because they still had lives to save. It seemed like providence to everyone involved. A couple who had always wanted children would finally get to have them, and two little girls who needed a home would grow up safe and loved. It was perfect.

Perfect, except for the part where Andrew Briggs was a dyed-in-the-wool conservative who hated ATI incursions not because they were dangerous or because they got people killed, but because they were unnatural. Maya didn't fight him. Maya never fought him, not even when he slapped Geraldine for telling him that she wanted to wear jeans to school instead of dresses, not even when he told us that we'd go to bed without supper for a week if either one of us said word one about wanting to cut our hair. He had his perfect home, his perfect wife, and his two perfect little girls. He wasn't going to let either one of them be flawed.

I'll never forget the look on his face when he came into the bathroom and found Gerry and me with our hair cropped off in uneven hanks, none of them more than two inches long. I was better with the scissors than Gerry was, and had actually managed to craft something that looked almost like a decent haircut. My hair looked like it belonged on a doll from the thrift sale dollar bin. But it was worth it to see the way my brother smiled—and he had always been my brother, even if most people refused to understand that. Both of us had always known exactly who we were.

We'd entered the Bureau's odd excuse for foster care not long after that incident, being shuttled from family to family until we turned fourteen and could be enrolled in boarding school. Gerry had bound his breasts, cut his hair, and lived as a male from the day we walked onto campus. Neither of us had been sure it would work . . . but halfway through the first semester I woke up and it was snowing in my room. Actual snow, falling out of the air and landing on my bed. Gerry's share of the narrative had snapped and was rebounding on me, now its only target, because Rose Red is a girl, and Geraldine Marchen wasn't.

It took almost fifteen minutes to explain the situation. By the time I finished, my throat was dry and Demi's eyes were so wide that it seemed like they might fall out of her head. I glanced at Jeff, afraid of finding judgment or disapproval in his eyes. Not because it would change the way I felt about my brother, but because I liked Jeff, and it would be a shame to have to find a place to hide his body.

My earlier fondness only grew deeper as Jeff said, "As a way to avert a narrative, that smacks of genius, although it would only work if the subject was genuinely gender dysphoric—otherwise you'd be inviting a 'hidden princess' scenario, and that could force you into a Sleeping Beauty or worse."

"What's worse than a Sleeping Beauty?" asked Andy, sounding half horrified and half curious.

"Have you ever read the Oz books by L. Frank Baum?"

"Okay, we're going to stop right there," I said hurriedly, so we didn't get even further off track. "So here's the situation: I became a potential seven-oh-nine when Gerry averted our mutual four-two-six. Only now I'm a full seven-oh-nine, and somehow this has caused Gerry to activate as part of a story he shouldn't even be eligible for. How can that happen? More importantly, how can we make it *stop*?"

"Are you sure you're a seven-oh-nine?" asked Andy. "Maybe you activated as part of the other story, and that's what's dragging him back in."

I hesitated. I hadn't told anyone about the forest full of whiteout women. It seemed private somehow, like it wasn't meant to be shared with people outside of our story. "I'm sure," I said finally. "Four-two-six doesn't say anything about snow or apples, although it's pretty heavy on the woodland creatures. I'm definitely an apple girl."

"Many people have forgotten that the two stories are meant to be separate," said Jeff, with the particular slowness that always accompanied his thinking hard. "It's obvious in the original German—it's like assuming that girls named 'Mary' and 'Marti' are the same—but once you translate the stories into English, they become easier and easier to conflate. The narrative has been evolving. Maybe it's found a way to combine the two tales into a coherent whole."

"I don't want to marry a bear," I said. It was the first thing that popped into my mind. There was a moment of silence while we all considered it and then, by mutual unspoken agreement, ignored it.

"So Gerry's a Rose Red now, even though Henry's part of a different story," said Andy. "Is it going to try to force him to be a girl?"

"That's a risk, and the narrative has done stranger things," said Jeff.

"Great, we're going to get to see my brother punch out the narrative," I said. "That'll make our jobs a lot easier."

Demi blinked. "Is that possible?"

"Probably not," I said, and looked toward the door that Sloane and my brother had vanished through. "I should go and check on them."

"Do you want me to come with you?" asked Andy.

"No," I said. "I bet he's waiting for me to come. I'll be right back." I started across the bullpen, trying not to focus on worst-case scenarios. This was my brother. I was going to help him.

Whatever it took, I was going to help him.

# # #

Memetic incursion in progress: tale type 426 ("The Two Girls and the Bear")
Status: IN PROGRESS

It had been a long damn day, and while it wasn't getting any shorter, Gerry March was no longer quite so pissed off about it. He sat on the edge of the break-room table, Sloane leaning in between his knees and kissing him like she thought that the act of physical affection was on the verge of being outlawed. One of his hands braced her hip, holding her against him, while the other explored the lines of her back, which were so familiar and so forbidden. He found the clasp of her bra and slipped two fingers underneath it, making it clear that he could strip it away at any moment.

Her anger had melted into kisses with no warning. He was fully aware that it could turn back, and he was going to take advantage of every second that he got.

Finally, after what seemed like forever and nowhere near long enough at the same time, Sloane pulled back just far enough to offer him a languid smile and say, "See, this is why you should never have left. You miss me too much when you go away."

"You're too old for me," Gerry countered. "Isn't that what you said the last time you dumped me? That you were too old for me and I should find a nice girl my own age who could grow old by my side?"

"That sounds like the sort of bullshit I spout when I get maudlin, sure," said Sloane, leaning in to kiss him again. This time she was quick, in and out in a matter of seconds, leaving his lips still smarting from the rasp of her teeth. "Besides, cougars are in now, right? I could be your Mrs. Robinson."

"I'm not sure that the way to celebrate turning into a fairy tale is by fucking one," said Gerry. He immediately winced. "Sloane, I'm sorry, I didn't mean—"

But she was already pulling away, the familiar walls sliding back into place across her expression, until the cold, heartless mask she showed to the world was gazing at him with impassive eyes. "No, no, it's good. It's useful to hear what you really think of me. It helps keep me from doing things I'll regret later. Who knows? I might get called to play the bad guy in your story, and then where would we be?" She turned, stomping toward the door. "I'll tell your sister you're in here."

"Sloane, please."

She kept walking.

Gerry took a deep breath, and said, "Rose Red's supposed to be a girl, you know."

Sloane stopped.

"Ten years of hormones and surgery and more therapy than I like to think about just to be the man I was always supposed to be, and now this story comes along and all that keeps running through my head is 'well, it was fun while it lasted. At least you got to be yourself for a little while.'" Gerry looked down at his hands, lying limp and useless between his legs. "I grew up knowing magic was real, and the one thing it could never do was fix me. I just wanted to recognize the person in my mirror. I just wanted to know what it was like to be normal."

"None of us are normal," said Sloane. He raised his head. She was standing in front of him again, her red- and green-streaked hair tumbling to almost cover her eyes. "We never got to be normal."

"No, but you got to live in a world that didn't judge you for the ways you were strange," Gerry said. "Henry can put on foundation or go to Goth clubs. You're happy in your skin. I've had to work my ass off for every inch of normal I've ever had, and now I'm going to lose it all."

"You don't know that." Sloane sat down on the edge of the table, resting her weight on her hands. "We did cleanup for a male Little Mermaid just last week, and Demi—that's the new girl, the Latina chick with the scared rabbit face—is a Pied Piper. Sometimes the narrative flips the gender of a story to throw us off the scent."

"Yeah, but Henry's a girl." Gerry shrugged. "I don't think the narrative can handle that kind of complexity. It's going to want us both to be women in order for the story to hang together. Something's going to go wrong with my hormone treatments, or there's going to be an accident and the hospital will give me the wrong medication, or *something*. Everything I've worked for is going to go away because of the goddamn narrative."

"I guess you're right," said Sloane sadly. "You're doomed."

Gerry raised his head and blinked at her. "What?"

"I mean, why did you even bother trying? You always knew that the narrative would come for you one day. It would have been better to just put on a pretty dress and live a lie. That way you wouldn't have had anything to lose. That would have really shown the narrative, right? Making yourself miserable for your entire life, pretending to be something you weren't—that would have been a much better choice."

"Sloane, what the fuck is—" Gerry stopped midsentence, his mouth shutting with a snap. He eyed her for a moment before he asked, "Are you messing with me?"

"Yes," said Sloane blithely. "You're being stupid, and so I'm messing with you. It's one of the simple joys of my life. Besides, I'm still pissed at you for running off and leaving me with your sad sack of a sister."

"That's not very nice, you know."

"Since when has 'nice' been a part of my job description?" countered Sloane. "I'm a Wicked Stepsister, remember? I'm not active, but I'm a lot closer to it than I used to be, thanks to the narrative and our old dispatcher." Gerry looked at her blankly. She frowned. "Didn't Henry tell you about that?"

"Henry and I . . . we don't really talk," said Gerry slowly. "Not for the last few years."

Sloane's frown deepened. "I knew you weren't talking to the rest of us, but I thought you were still in touch with Henry. How long is 'the last few years'?"

"I changed my last name to March eight years ago," he said. "So . . . about eight years, I guess."

"You haven't spoken to your sister in *eight years*?" Sloane stared at him, looking genuinely stunned. All her masks had fallen away, revealing a woman who was older than she looked and younger than she should have been. "How can you *do* that to her? How can you do that to yourself?"

"You never called me," Gerry said.

"Uh, one, I didn't have your number. Two, you were pretty clear when you left here that you didn't want to have any contact with the freaky fairy-tale people. And three, I'm not your sister. Henry's your sister. I'm just the girl who took your virginity in a supply closet. Totally different relationship." Sloane stood. "Come on. We need to talk to the team. We're going to find a way to freeze your story so that it won't mess with you, and you're going to make things right with your sister."

Gerry frowned as he stood, watching her carefully. "Why are you so upset about this?"

"Gerald . . ." Sloane took a deep breath, visibly calming herself down. Then she took his hands in hers and said, "My family died a long time ago. All of them. If I have blood relatives left in this world, I'm not allowed to know about them, because my story means that I might hurt them. But I had a family once, and I'd give anything—*anything*—for the chance to have them back for just a day. Just an hour. Your family is back in the other room, and she's probably been worried about you this whole time. You're going to make things right with her, or you're going to regret it for the rest of your life. I'll make sure of that."

Gerry took a deep breath. "Okay," he said, and kept hold of her hand as she led him out of the room, back into the future.

# # #

I was heading down the hall toward the break room when Sloane came around the corner up ahead, hauling a frazzled-looking Gerry by one hand. I stopped, blinking, and let them come to me. Sloane yanked Gerry to a stop before releasing his hand, grabbing his shoulders, and shoving him in my direction. If we hadn't been essentially the same size, he would have knocked me over. As it was, he caught himself against my shoulders as I caught his upper arms. Both of us blinked at Sloane.

"You two, talk, now," she snapped, and stormed toward the bullpen, where she would doubtless improve everyone's day with her sunshine-bright demeanor.

"What did you do to Sloane?" I demanded, pushing Gerry away from me. "She looks like she's going to start microwaving baby bunnies to take the edge off."

"Uh, nothing," he said, a blush creeping into his cheeks.

It wasn't as good as one of my blushes—the lucky bastard actually inherited some melanin from our mother, even if it wasn't enough to make him more than Irish pale—but it confirmed one of my suspicions. I stepped back and folded my arms, glowering at him. "Did you go off to make out with Sloane?"

"No," he mumbled. "I went off because I needed to get my head together, and Sloane was willing to help me do it. The making out was sort of an unexpected bonus."

"Oh my God you are such a *boy*," I groaned. "I thought you were freaking out or something."

"To be fair, I sort of was. I just found my focus."

I paused. I was still mad at him—maybe I was always going to be mad at him—but he needed me, and I couldn't let anger be the only thing that was left between us. Even if I wanted to do that to him, I couldn't do that to myself. So I cleared my throat and said the first thing that popped into my head: "Does your focus look like Sloane's ass?"

Gerry grinned unrepentantly. I groaned again, but my heart wasn't in it. If Gerry was grinning at me like that, he wasn't too depressed to cope with the world.

"You're a pig," I informed him. "Not in a literal, house of straw sense, but still."

"It's good to see you too, sis," he said, and hugged me. "I'm sorry I was all weird before. This situation is sort of messing me up."

"I picked up on that," I said, hugging him back. "We're not going to let this thing hurt you, okay? We're going to figure out what's going on and why your story has activated—it shouldn't have been able to, not with me squarely invested in being the wrong kind of Snow White—and then we're going to stop it."

"Can you do that?" he asked dubiously.

"Sure," I said. It wasn't entirely a lie: stories can be averted. I just had no idea how we were going to manage it with this one. "In the meanwhile, I'm not letting you out of my sight. I hope you like couches, because you're staying with me for the next few days."

"Do you still have bluebird issues?"

I laughed. I couldn't help it. "Oh, dude, you have *no* idea."

# # #

Gerry emerged from the bathroom, a toothbrush in his hand and a perplexed expression on his face. "There's a frog in your toilet," he informed me. He was wearing sweatpants and a shirt with the Bureau logo on it, having forgotten to pack pajamas in his hurry to find me and make me fix whatever was going wrong with his life.

"I know," I said. "Just ignore it. Try not to pee on it. It gets pissed off when that happens, no pun intended." Since I had access to my entire wardrobe, I was in one of my normal flannel pajama sets. This one had been a gag gift from Andy the previous Christmas: red, printed all over with happy moose. I looked like something out of a bad holiday special. I was okay with that. They made me happy, and they didn't seem princessy at all.

Gerry looked at me flatly for a moment before shaking his head and walking back into the bathroom, which was apparently less perturbing—frog and all—than trying to deal with me. I laughed and went back to tucking sheets into the couch. If a little frog was enough to freak him out, this was going to be a fun sleepover.

Having Gerry in my house was probably a terrible idea, but we didn't have any better options. If he was on the verge of going full princess, sending him to Sloane's could get one or both of them killed, since Sloane was still fighting her natural tendency to murder any princesses in her immediate vicinity. Andy's place was reasonably safe, excepting his husband, who was tolerant of him bringing work home, but not quite *that* tolerant. Jeff didn't offer. Demi couldn't, since she still lived with her parents. That left me, and my living-room couch, and my carpet with the marigolds and cinquefoil growing around the edges. I paused to pull out my phone and take a few quick pictures of the little yellow flowers. Jeff would probably be able to figure out something about our current situation by studying the patterns of their growth.

And if he couldn't, well, at least they were pretty.

Gerry emerged from the bathroom a second time, announcing, "All done. And I didn't pee on your frog."

"I thank you, the frog thanks you, and your own butt thanks you," I said, tossing him a pillow. "Like I said, the frog gets pissy when pissed on, and angry frogs jump around a lot."

"Do I want to know why you have a frog living in your toilet?"

It was a reasonable question. It probably deserved a reasonable answer. It was really too bad for both of us that I didn't have one. "Having a frog in my toilet was the best out of a list of lousy options," I said, sinking down onto the freshly made couch and resting my elbows on my knees as I looked up at him. "Get rid of the frog and you get talking goldfish sometimes, or garter snakes."

"Garter snakes?" he asked, sounding horrified.

I nodded. "I had to call Jeff in the middle of the night to come and get them out. It was that or pee in the sink."

"Jeff, huh?" Gerry walked over and sat down on the couch next to me, his shoulder almost brushing mine. "Looks like you're getting pretty cozy with that guy. How come I haven't met him before?"

"How about because we haven't spoken for eight years as a starter?" I asked.

Gerry grimaced and looked away. "I guess that would be part of it," he admitted.

I sighed and took mercy. "Jeff has been with the Bureau since about a year before I got assigned to my current field team," I said. "He was on track to go into a permanent position in the Archives, but he managed to argue his way into something more active. His story doesn't lend itself well to sitting still. I get the feeling that he was never much for idleness before he found out that he was part of the narrative."

"And is he your boyfriend?"

Yes. "No. Maybe. I don't know. It's . . . complicated." I shook my head. "We've been having trouble with the narrative lately. It's getting more aggressive, and it's been changing the way that it attacks. He nearly got swallowed by his story. I kissed him to snap him out of it. I guess he's had a crush on me for a while now."

"Uh-huh. What about you? Do you have a crush on him, or is this some sort of fairy-tale compulsion?" Gerry's lips twisted into a grimace. "I don't like how much power this thing has over us. I really don't want to think about it making you do things that you wouldn't—"

"It's not like that," I interrupted, before he could take himself any further along that unpleasant line of thought. "I've liked Jeff for a while too. He's kind. He's funny. He doesn't look at me like I'm a freak. Those are pretty rare qualities to find in a man, and they're rarer when you consider that I could never be involved with someone who doesn't know my line of work. I don't know what we are to each other yet—things have been hectic, what with my story going active and everything—but I'm happy to find out. Don't go all protective brother on him. He doesn't deserve that."

"As long as you're happy." Gerry leaned back into the couch, closing his eyes with a groan. "God, Henry. I thought I got clear of all this fairy-tale crap, and then the damn deer show up at my school . . ."

"Not just the deer," I said.

He opened one eye. "What?"

"I said, 'not just the deer.'" I shook my head. "I know you, remember? There's no way you would have freaked out and run for the Bureau just because you saw some out-of-place deer. You might get spooked, but you hate the narrative too much to be that easy. There has to have been something else."

"Yeah." He closed his eye again. "There was something else."

"So? What is it?"

"I've been having these weird dreams lately. The kind that you remember the next day, and that seem so *real* . . ." Gerry frowned, eyes still closed. "I'm in this big field full of roses. Red roses, naturally. Anything else wouldn't be symbolic enough, you know? And I can see another field nearby, full of white roses, and I know—in the dream—that if I can just get there, this can all be set right. Because that's the other thing. In the dream, something is terribly wrong. I just don't know what it is. So I wade through red roses, trying to get to the white ones, and I never quite make it, and eventually, I wake up."

"How long?"

"How long does the dream last, or how long have I been having it?" Gerry didn't wait for me to answer. "The dream seems to last for days, which is part of how I can remember that it's a dream, even when it's happening. I'd starve if I spent that much time alone in a field of roses. I've been having it for about a month. Only once a week at first, and then every other night. It's been every night for a couple of weeks now."

That explained why he looked so tired. "You should have called me," I said gently.

"I was hoping I'd never have to. But you asked why the deer were enough to make me come here—why the deer meant my story was going live and not, I don't know, that we needed to call Animal Control." He finally opened his eyes, turning toward me as he held up his left wrist. I gasped before I could stop myself.

There, on the inside of his wrist, was a row of livid red scratches. They had scabbed over, but were clearly still fresh.

"When did this happen?" I asked.

"Last night. I almost made it to the white roses. I thought, 'this is great, I'm going to reach the finish line and then I won't have this stupid dream anymore.' I reached out too fast, and I cut my wrist on the thorns." He wrapped his hand around his wrist, hiding the scratches from view. "I woke up with blood on my pillow. That's when I knew that this was serious."

"I *really* wish you'd called me sooner."

Gerry grimaced. "So do I. But I'm here now. That has to count for something, right?"

"I sure hope so." I leaned over and hugged him before standing. "I'm going to get some sleep. You should do the same. Tomorrow's going to be a long day of tests, questions, and research, and while that may sound boring, you're going to want to be awake for it."

"I can do boring," he said, with a small smile. "Boring has sort of been my life's goal."

"Then let's see if we can get your life back on track. Good-night, Gerald."

"Good-night, Henrietta."

He was still sitting up, holding his wrist, when I turned off the living room light and walked into my bedroom, leaving him alone in the dark.

That night I dreamt of the wood, but all the whiteout women were missing, and the air carried the distant scent of roses.

# # #

As always, my alarm went off too early, yanking me back into a world I wasn't quite prepared to deal with. I looked automatically toward the window as I sat up. Only three bloody crescents marked the spots where bluebirds had managed to slam themselves to death against the glass. My new bird netting was working. More cinquefoil had sprouted from the carpet near the bed, now joined by a riotous spray of snowdrops and crocuses. All of this was normal.

The scent of coffee and bacon hanging in the early morning air . . . now that was a bit more unusual. I rolled out of bed, rubbing my eyes with the back of my hand as I shambled toward the bedroom door, pausing only long enough to snag my phone. I didn't want to miss a summons by being too interested in what smelled very much like breakfast.

The front room was empty. Gerry had even stripped the sheets off the couch, folding them in a neat pile on one cushion. His pillow rested on top. I touched it lightly as I passed. The fabric was cool. He'd been awake for a while.

Then I stepped into the kitchen and stopped, blinking at the edifying sight of Sloane operating a waffle maker that I was more than reasonably certain I didn't own. Jeff was sitting at my small dining table, sipping from a glass of orange juice, while Gerry flipped bacon at the stove. I gawked at them for a moment before asking the only question I could think of: "Where are Andy and Demi?"

"Good morning to you, too, snow-shine," said Sloane, almost kindly, as she looked over her shoulder at me. "I thought we should come over and make sure you two survived the night. Andy didn't feel like getting up early, and no one wanted to prod Demi. She's still too fragile to fuck with much."

"You have no idea how strange it is to hear you say that," commented Gerry, leaning away from his bacon long enough to press a kiss to Sloane's cheek. "Morning, sis. Jeff told me your alarm would be going off soon, so it seemed better to just let you sleep until then. You looked like you needed the rest."

"And you didn't?" I folded my arms and leaned against the door frame, eyeing the bustling kitchen. My apartment hadn't contained this many people since the movers dropped off the last of my things seven years ago. It was unnerving. "You're the one who hasn't been sleeping."

"I know." Gerry started sliding bacon onto a plate. "Unfortunately, my brain didn't really care that I needed sleep. As soon as I appeared in that damn field, I was awake."

"Shared dreamscapes are a function of some stories," Jeff said. I turned toward him, suddenly interested. "Sleeping Beauties tend to find themselves in endless castles, for example, and Cinderellas share a maze of kitchens and graveyards."

"Oh, that's charming." I unfolded my arms, starting toward the coffeemaker. "What purpose do they serve?"

"For the stories that are connected to them, they act as a unifying factor of sorts—a way for the narrative to track everyone who is currently living out that set of tales. We don't know much about them. It's hard to document something that requires an active connection to a very narrow slice of the narrative." Jeff gave me a thoughtful look, and I tensed, waiting for the inevitable question. To my relief, he said only, "We have a few books on the phenomenon back at the Bureau. I was planning to start my research there, since Gerald has confessed to accessing one such dreamscape. It may come to nothing."

"Any port in a storm." I sat down at the table next to him, watching Gerry and Sloane going through the surprisingly domestic motions of producing breakfast. "I really appreciate you helping out with this."

"Yes, well." Jeff smiled, reaching up to adjust his glasses with one hand. "You can thank me after we've found an answer to your brother's situation. Perhaps with dinner?"

I blinked at him before slanting a glance back at my brother and Sloane. Both of them were steadfastly ignoring us. I looked back to Jeff and smiled, more shyly than I had intended. "Dinner would be lovely," I said.

"Breakfast is better," pronounced Sloane, and dropped a platter of waffles on the table between us. "Eat up. I'm sure something's going to fuck up the rest of the day to the point where we miss lunch." She turned and walked back to the counter.

The waffles were golden brown and perfect, filling the air with the scent of doughy sweetness. I blinked. "Wow. I didn't know you cooked."

"I live alone. It's cook or live on takeout Chinese, and I'm not that fond of dealing with delivery men." Sloane returned with a stack of plates and forks in one hand and a large plate laden with butter, syrup, and sliced, sugared strawberries in the other. She set these down with more care than she'd shown the waffles, which I appreciated. Cleaning syrup off my kitchen floor wasn't my idea of a good way to start the morning.

"Eat," commanded Gerry, joining us at the table with his own large plate, this one covered in bacon. "I hate wasting food."

"That's not likely," I said, and snagged a waffle.

For a while, everything was quiet except for the sound of cutlery scraping against IKEA plates and the occasional smack of lips or crunch of bacon. It was surprisingly homey, and comfortable in a way that things all too rarely were. I found myself wishing that Demi and Andy had been able to join us, even though they wouldn't have fit around my tiny table; we were squashed in as it was. Their absence was still the only flaw in what could otherwise have been a perfect morning.

Gerry still looked tired, but he looked more relaxed than he had the night before: maybe sleeping on things had allowed him to come to terms with his current circumstances. Having Sloane around probably didn't hurt. His brief flirtations with her before we'd gone off to college had been seen as a rebellion by our foster parents and a terrible idea by me—what potential Snow White wants to see her brother getting involved with a poison-apple girl? Not this one, that was for sure. And yet . . .

She was smiling as she ate her waffles, and Gerry was smiling back, stealing glances at her when he thought that no one else was looking. I wouldn't say that they were in love, but they were definitely in like, and I cared enough about both of them to want them to be happy. Weird as that was, considering Sloane.

"These waffles are amazing," I said.

"Old family recipe," said Sloane. This time the smile was for me. I blinked, and smiled back at her.

We were definitely going to have to make breakfast a regular team thing.

Before we left for the office, Gerry wrapped up the last of the bacon in foil. "For later," he explained.

"Never leave me again," I said, and kissed his cheek.

He grinned. "Yes, ma'am," he said, and the four of us made our way out of my apartment. It was time to get to work.

# # #

Andy munched leftover bacon as he frowned at the piles of paper on his desk. "They're definitely two different stories," he said. "You can't be both kinds of Snow White at the same time, and if you're the kind who has apple issues, you're not the kind who has a sister."

"We may be thinking about this all wrong," said Jeff, wandering back into the bullpen with a large book open on his arms. He was frowning at the text, not looking at any of us directly.

"How's that?" I asked.

"We're all assuming Henry is *Gerry's* Snow White," said Jeff. "But what if she isn't?"

"She's my *sister*," said Gerry. Sloane didn't say anything. She just sat up a little straighter and frowned, nostrils flaring.

"Yes, but 'sister' can be interpreted a great many ways by the narrative. Close female friends can be sisters. Coworkers. Even other children who were in foster care at the same time that you were. If one of *them* is a four-two-six . . ."

"Then we're not looking for her, because we're all too focused on me," I said slowly, beginning to understand what Jeff was getting at. "Do we have a tracked list of potential four-two-sixes in this region? Or hell, in the region where Gerry's been living? You may have run *away* from the other half of your story, Gerry, instead of running toward it."

"This is all very confusing," said Demi. "I didn't even know that there *were* two kinds of Snow White before I joined the Bureau."

"We have a problem," said Sloane.

"Most people don't know, sadly," said Jeff, looking at Demi. "It's a translation error. Like having two men named 'John,' one with an 'h' and one without, and no one knowing who's being talked about."

I yawned. "Can we stop the story if we don't find the Snow White in question?"

"It'll be harder," said Jeff, hiding a yawn behind his hand. "We can try, but we should really locate her and make sure we're not just averting half of the story."

Someone was shouting in the hall. I turned toward it, frowning even as I yawned again. "What the hell's going on over there?"

"I *said*, we have a *problem*," snarled Sloane, sliding out of her chair and running for the bullpen door. "There's someone here that shouldn't be."

"I don't know what you're talking about." I wanted to follow her—I should follow her, lead her even, as her superior—but I was so tired all of a sudden. I just couldn't get my legs to obey me. "We're all here." Demi's head was down on her desk, and she was snoring gently. Poor kid must have had a long night.

Sloane didn't slow down long enough to answer me. She just kept running, which meant that she was in the right spot to catch the woman who stumbled through the bullpen door.

The stranger was tall and dark-skinned, with long black hair in a braid down her back. She was wearing a lab coat over jeans and a plain button-down shirt, and I had never seen her before. She collapsed into Sloane's arms, reaching up with one hand like she was pleading. Then she went limp, all the tension going out of her body in an instant. Sloane staggered under her weight. I tried again to stand. My legs again refused to obey me.

There was a thump. I turned to see Andy collapsed on his desk, already snoring. Jeff was wobbling, eyes gone wide and terrified behind the frames of his glasses. Then he fell.

"Gerry . . ." I forced my eyes to stay open as I turned toward my brother, struggling for consciousness. He was slumped backward in his borrowed chair, mouth hanging open. I could see him breathing. Thank Grimm for that.

"Sleeping . . . she's a Sleeping . . ." My eyelids were so heavy. They slid closed against my protests. Everything was slipping away.

Sloane was shouting at me from somewhere far away, in the dark, but I couldn't answer her. I couldn't do anything but fall, and fall further, and the world went away.

# # #

Memetic incursion in progress: tale type 410 ("Sleeping Beauty")
Status: ACTIVE

Priya Patel slept peacefully in the arms of the woman with the red- and green-streaked hair, and didn't think about the future, or the past, or anything at all.

Around the foundation of the building she'd been deposited in front of—the strange, unmarked building in the almost-deserted business park—the thorny vines began to worm their way up out of the earth.

Everyone except for the woman with the red and green hair slept, and really, what did one woman matter?

What did one woman matter at all?

Bad Apple

Memetic incursion in progress: tale type 410 ("Sleeping Beauty")
Status: ACTIVE

"Oh, shit."

It wasn't the most intelligent thing that Sloane had ever said, but considering the circumstances, she thought she was doing pretty well. The pretty Indian woman in the lab coat who had collapsed into her arms didn't react to the profanity. Sloane gave her an experimental shake. She didn't react to that either, and so Sloane shook her harder, hoping that maybe *that* would do something. All it did was cause the strange woman's arms and head to flop around until Sloane started to worry about accidentally breaking her neck. The paperwork for that would be, well, murder. Not to be crass or anything.

Lifting with her knees and not her back—since the last thing she needed to do was incapacitate herself at this point—Sloane hoisted the stranger up and moved her carefully to the nearest desk, sweeping its contents to the floor with one elbow. When the space was clear she stretched the stranger out, checking to be sure her limbs were straight and her breathing wasn't obstructed. Once this was done, Sloane began the much more important process of patting the stranger down for ID. Luck was with her: the stranger—who she should probably start thinking of as "the Sleeping Beauty," since that was *obviously* what was going on here—was carrying a plastic badge connecting her to a biotech firm downtown. Which meant she couldn't have walked to the Bureau. Considering how quickly she'd passed out, she probably hadn't been in any condition to drive for several hours.

"All right, Ms. Patel, do you have a bus transfer?" muttered Sloane, as she resumed combing through the strange woman's pockets.

Ms. Patel did not have a bus transfer. Since the local bus line used them as proof of payment, that meant she hadn't come on the bus. And if she hadn't come on the bus and she hadn't walked, someone had to have brought her. Someone had to have guided her past security and into the building just in time for her to fall asleep.

"Shit," said Sloane again, and transferred her focus to the woman's hands. There was a needle mark on Priya's right index finger. Wincing a little, Sloane squeezed the wound, trying to force out any splinters or shards that had been stuck inside. That wasn't the most common variant anymore, but it would be the easiest to deal with.

Nothing emerged from Priya's finger. "So much for that idea," muttered Sloane. She started to push herself to her feet, and stopped as something pricked her ankle. Heart sinking, she twisted and looked behind herself.

There, growing from the carpet like it was the most natural thing in the world, was a thorny rose briar. It had twisted partially around Sloane's calf, the trailing end of it hovering just above her leg. Any question about what sort of narrative incursion she was dealing with died when she saw that briar. Lots of princess archetypes could make your carpet sprout flowers. Only one of them would go for full-on roses, and only one would do it this *fast*.

"Technically this is assault and Henry would tell me to verbally request that you not file a sexual harassment claim against me," she said, turning back to Priya. "Honestly, I don't give a shit. I just want you to wake up. Although you know, you're pretty hot and all." This, too, was part of the story. Sleeping Beauties liked declarations of love, or attraction, or just "damn, girl, look at that body" before they were kissed awake. Something about their story made it work better that way.

Sloane bent forward and pressed her lips against Priya's. The unconscious woman was wearing menthol-flavored lip gloss, and when Sloane pulled back, Priya didn't open her eyes. Sloane swore and checked the woman's pulse. It was still slow and steady, showing no signs that her kiss had even registered.

"True love, lacking," she muttered. "Fucking variations." Not every Sleeping Beauty required true love, thank God, or the world would have been ass-deep in sleeping princesses. Unfortunately, it didn't change the fact that *Sloane* was still ass-deep in sleeping princesses.

Moving carefully now, Sloane reached back to untwine the briar from her ankle before she stood and started back across the bullpen to her team. More rose briars had sprouted from the carpet between them, making her footing treacherous. None of them were blooming yet. She couldn't remember whether that was a good sign or a bad one. This would have been so much easier if Jeff had been the one who'd stayed awake.

But Jeff definitely wasn't awake. He had fallen on the floor between two of the desks, knocking his glasses askew and trapping an arm under his body at an angle that would probably cause him a lot of pain when he woke up if she didn't do something about it. The skinny bastard was easy enough to hoist into a chair. Sloane only hesitated for a second before wheeling it over to park next to Henry, propping Jeff's head on the pale woman's shoulder. "There—you're finally sleeping together," she said, a gallows grin on her face.

Henry's story hadn't saved her from falling under the Sleeping Beauty's spell either. That was an interesting narrative collision that would probably delight the geeks in the Archives, once they were all awake again. There had been potential Snow Whites caught in a Sleeping Beauty's event horizon before, but never a fully active one.

Sloane looked at the pair for a few more seconds before she moved on to check on Andy, Demi, and Gerry. All three of them were sleeping peacefully, and since they had passed out while seated, she was saved from scooping anyone else off the floor. She paused to remove the gun from Andy's belt, pulling back the slide to check that it was loaded. She wasn't supposed to carry a weapon while at the Bureau—something about her semi-Wicked Stepsister status making her a safety hazard—but under the circumstances, she didn't think she could be blamed. She started to turn away, hesitated, then put down the gun and bent to remove her shoes. Platform heels were great for cutting an imposing figure and stomping your way through life, but they weren't exactly conducive to stealth, or to traversing an actively growing briar patch.

Gun clutched in her hand, Sloane padded on stocking-clad feet toward the hall.

# # #

The snow was falling more heavily than I'd ever seen, coating my face and body before I could push myself upright and wipe it out of my eyes. A frantic look around confirmed what the snowfall had already tried to tell me: I was in the whiteout wood, surrounded by the black skeleton trees. The other Snow Whites stood in the spaces between them, their hands folded and their expressions filled with a strange sorrow that I almost understood.

"What's going on?" I demanded, spinning around. Tanya was behind me, that same sadness hanging heavy in her eyes. "Why am I here? I'm not sleeping!"

"Maybe not on purpose, but you're asleep all right," said the dairy princess, shaking her head. "Didn't you feel the curse take you down?"

"Glass coffin time," confirmed the Japanese girl. "You should have watched what you put in your mouth."

"I didn't eat anything," I insisted. "I was at my desk, prepping for the day, when this woman walked in—" I stopped, eyes widening. "Oh, hell. We have a four-ten."

The Snow Whites looked at me blankly. I resisted the urge to groan.

"A Sleeping Beauty came into my office and collapsed," I explained. "That's why I'm asleep. I didn't eat any apples or use any poisoned combs. I'm not supposed to be here."

"Then why are you here?" asked Tanya. "If you weren't meant to be here, you wouldn't be. That's not how the forest works."

The silent woman with the gray freckles on her nose looked suddenly alarmed, her hands flashing in a question I couldn't understand. The Japanese girl frowned, a flicker of concern sliding across her own face as she turned to Tanya and said, "Adrianna."

That one word—that one name—had a galvanizing effect on my guide. She swore in French as she lunged forward and grabbed me, yanking me out of my patch of snow and into hers. "Everyone, check the boundaries; make sure that nothing's melting," she snapped. "Close any lines you find." The Snow Whites nodded and scattered, so many black and white birds flying into the whiteout wood like magpies in search of something to scavenge.

In a matter of seconds, only I, Tanya, the Japanese girl, and the silent woman remained.

"Uh, does someone want to tell me what's going on here?" I asked, trying to pull my arm out of Tanya's grip. It didn't work. For a dead woman, she had incredibly strong hands. "What does Adrianna have to do with anything?"

"She'll steal you if we don't stop her," said the Japanese girl. I looked at her blankly. She shot an accusing glance at Tanya. "I thought you were mentoring the new girl?"

"I am, but she doesn't sleep much," said Tanya wearily. "We've barely managed to get through the causes of coma."

"Not helpful," said the Japanese girl, while the silent woman's hands flashed and dove in what I could only assume was an angry screed against Tanya's priorities. Turning on me, the Japanese girl said, "Hi. My name was Ayane before it got changed to Snow White. My friend here," she indicated the silent woman, "was Judi. She didn't die when she fell into her coma, but she got trapped here because one of our restless sisters used the wood to take her body over."

My eyes widened. "That can happen?"

"What, you think every Snow White wants to go back into her story? Some of us choose to stay here. Some of us don't. Judi didn't." Ayane shrugged. "She's still a little angry about that."

Judi chose that moment to use an angry sign that I didn't need to know any ASL to understand.

"Don't frighten the girl," said Tanya. "Henry, it's going to be fine. Adrianna can't take your body if she can't get to you."

"But she's gotten to me a bunch of times," I said. "She stabbed me in the chest the first time we met!"

"You weren't in an enchanted sleep then," said Ayane. "As long as you wake up before she finds you, you'll be fine."

"And what are the odds of that?" I demanded.

None of them would answer me.

I stood in the whiteout wood, snow falling around us like a curtain, and wondered whether I was ever going to make it home.

# # #

Memetic incursion in progress: tale type 410 ("Sleeping Beauty")
Status: ACTIVE

The hallway was choked with bodies. One of the other field teams had apparently been returning to the office when Priya collapsed; they were strewn about like broken toys. An open cat carrier was lying on the ground next to their driver. Sloane gave it a wide berth. The trouble with Cheshire Cats was the way they could lurk in shadows, and she wasn't in the mood to be scratched with psychotropic claws just at the moment.

Dispatch was just as bad as the bullpen and the hall. Everyone was asleep, ignoring the strident beeping from their phones and computers. Sloane stalked silently through, grateful for the noise. Anything that could give her a little bit more cover was welcome, considering the circumstances.

She was reaching for the door that would lead her out of Dispatch to the lobby when she heard the voices. Immediately, she stiffened, backed up, and started looking for a place to hide. There wasn't one. This was Dispatch, the cleanest, most open space in the building. She was trapped.

When the door swung open less than half a minute later, Sloane was facedown on the floor, her feet mostly concealed beneath the nearest desk. She wasn't sure it looked like a natural fall, but it was the best she could do under the circumstances. *Please don't stop to check my pulse*, she thought. *Please just keep walking.*

A familiar peal of laughter struck her like a dagger in her chest, followed by an even more familiar voice saying smugly, "That's one down—mark it off. Now we just need to find the others, and we'll be safely in business."

Sloane remained where she was as she listened to the footsteps cross Dispatch and fade into silence. Even when they were gone she kept still, counting silently down from one hundred before she lifted her head and looked around the motionless room.

Birdie was back.

"Fuck this," said Sloane, and bounced to her feet, stalking onward to the lobby.

# # #

Stillness had fallen across the whiteout wood once again as the four of us waited for Adrianna's attack. I shifted my weight from one foot to the other before blurting, "What makes you so sure she's going to come for me? Maybe she'll leave me alone."

"You're in a coma, and that makes you a doorway," said Tanya. "Doorways have gotten rarer as the story has adjusted to a world with less magic and more consequences; we have to seize them when we can. Dreamers aren't doorways. Neither are the dead. She wants out of here. She doesn't like the way we run things, and you're the best chance she's had at an escape in a very long time."

"Besides, taking you over would make her an ATI agent," said Ayane. "Do you have any idea how much damage she could do if she had one of those badges?"

Judi's hands flashed and danced. No one translated for her. I had to wonder how frustrating that was, to be trapped forever in a forest full of people who should have been your sisters, but who didn't make any effort to give you a voice.

"If I get out of here, I'm signing up for an after-work ASL class," I muttered. Louder, I said, "I'm assuming a lot. She'd have access to our files, to our records . . . to everything." And how long would it take for the others to realize that something was wrong? I'd always held myself mostly apart from everyone who wasn't directly on my team. She probably wouldn't be able to fool Jeff or Sloane for very long, but Andy? Demi? She could play them like fiddles, as long as she moved quickly and didn't look behind herself.

"So we keep you safe," said Tanya firmly. "Our story is not going to be the one that brings down the monomyth."

"What?" I asked.

"Haven't you heard the word before? The monomyth? Basic pattern at the heart of all the other stories? Some people say it's the hero's journey, but that's too simplistic."

"It's too complicated, too," interrupted Ayane. "The monomyth is the story that's managed to win. The one that beat up all the other stories and sent them crying home to Mommy without their schoolbooks and lunch money."

Unpleasant realization dawned. "You're talking about reality."

"Of course we are, dummy," said Ayane, giving me a sidelong look. "What, you thought that one story was somehow more real than all the others, just because it's the one that has the most people living in it? Shit, if it worked that way, all the narratives would focus on quantity over quality, and we'd be buried under something featuring rabbits. What we think of as reality is just the tale type that took over longest ago. The others keep fighting back."

I stared at her as the snow fell all around us. I couldn't think of anything else to do.

# # #

Memetic incursion in progress: tale type 410 ("Sleeping Beauty")
Status: ACTIVE

A pathway had been hacked through the briars choking the lobby. Peering into the tangle of thorns and branches, Sloane could see the security guards who had been on duty when Priya was smuggled inside. They were sleeping soundly—or at least she hoped that they were sleeping. One of the guards had blood on his collar, and from what she could see, those thorns weren't being too careful about where they grew. If his jugular had been pierced . . .

If the thorns had grown into a major artery, he was already a dead man, and there was nothing she could do for him. Sloane crept along the makeshift path until she could see out the door, wincing as wayward thorns dug into the soles of her feet. Birdie had left two men guarding the sidewalk, their sleekly tailored black suits making them look like they belonged at the Bureau. Sloane didn't recognize either one of them though . . . and that was a good thing. She didn't want to think about Birdie having too many people on the inside.

"What are you doing there?"

The voice from behind her wasn't familiar, but it was male, and it was angry. Sloane stayed where she was, sinking a little deeper into her stance as she braced herself.

"Did you not hear me, or are you stupid?" A heavy hand landed on her shoulder.

Sloane moved.

Someone who had never seen her in the field couldn't have been blamed for thinking that a woman of her height and generally curvaceous build would be slow, even ineffective in hand-to-hand combat. Anyone who thought Sloane couldn't fight would have been quickly disillusioned by watching her in the lobby as she twisted, uncurled, and sprang.

Her fingers found her assailant's wrist before she even started to turn, pulling him forward as she rolled her weight onto one hip and pivoted on her left foot, effectively flipping him over her shoulder into the thorns. As soon as he fell, she was driving the heel of her right foot down on his instep—not as effective a move as it would have been had she been wearing shoes, but the combination of her weight driving down onto his boot and her grip on his fingers left him briefly incapacitated from the pain. That was good enough.

Sloane pushed back one more time before she drove her elbow up into his jaw, snapping his head back into the thorns. This time he tried to scream, only to find her right hand smashing his mouth shut while her left hand gripped his nose and yanked his head hard to the side. There was a small, almost inconsequential snapping sound, and the man stopped fighting.

"Asshole," Sloane muttered, straightening up. Birdie would realize that she was down a man soon; if they were patrolling the building looking for people who hadn't been caught by their Sleeping Beauty, they'd probably be doing it in pairs. She needed to move.

He had a gun clipped to his waist. He'd been so sure that he couldn't possibly be overwhelmed by a lone woman that he hadn't even bothered to open his holster.

"Amateur asshole," Sloane amended, and took the gun, retreating with it back into the building. She needed backup, and she needed it now.

# # #

"When's the last time Adrianna got out of the wood?" I asked suddenly.

Tanya stiffened. Ayane frowned. And Judi burst into a gale of silent laughter, her hands moving in patterns I didn't need interpreted for me. I crossed my arms.

"You weren't planning to tell me that she'd managed to escape before, were you?" I demanded. "You were just going to let me think that this was business as usual when you had a potentially open doorway. What's her deal?"

"Adrianna wants to replace the monomyth," said Ayane finally, earning herself a bitter glare from Tanya. She shrugged. "What? New girl knows that something's up, and it's not like we can hide Princess Crazy-pants and her world revision brigade forever."

I frowned. "Wait—brigade? That implies that she has help."

Judi's hands flashed as she directed a pointed look at Tanya. I turned. The other whiteout woman was red cheeked and looked ashamed.

"What aren't you telling me?" I asked softly, and my words fell between us like snowflakes, one more layer of accusation and betrayal lain at the foot of this damned, impossible forest. I couldn't stay here much longer. I wasn't safe. I never had been.

"Most of the ones who go bad are sealed away for our own protection," said Tanya, choosing her words with care. "We lock them in the mirrors. Sometimes they figure out a way to communicate despite their situations, and they whisper in the ears of anyone who will listen. They reach out. They . . . influence."

I blinked at her, a piece of the endless puzzle of my existence snapping into sudden clarity. "That's where the magic mirror entered the story, isn't it? It was all simple poisons and jealousy once, until suddenly there was real magic, and everything changed."

"We didn't mean to shift the narrative," said Tanya.

"We never do," I replied. "So every magic mirror is a Snow White gone wrong. All of them, all the way back to the beginning?"

Tanya didn't answer me, but Judi nodded, tugging Ayane's sleeve before her hands flashed and flew like milk-white birds.

Ayane signed something back, a frown on her face. Judi nodded. Ayane turned to me.

"Some of the mirrors are other stories, but most are ours," she said. "That was part of the codification process for our narrative."

"And the Bureau doesn't know." I glanced desperately around. The snow was still falling heavily, and between that and the black trunks of the trees surrounding us, there was no way I'd be able to pick Adrianna out of the wood. If she was coming, she was coming. "There's something this major about one of the most common narratives, and the Bureau doesn't know."

"There's something major about *every* narrative that the Bureau doesn't know," said Ayane. "That's the nature of stories. No one ever gets to know the entire thing. We just get to know the parts we have to deal with right here, right now. Before they rip our throats out."

The snow was falling even harder. I was starting to be afraid—really afraid—that I was going to die here. I was starting to be even more afraid that I wasn't going to die at all.

# # #

Memetic incursion in progress: tale type 410 ("Sleeping Beauty")
Status: ACTIVE

Sloane left bloody footprints through Dispatch, a clear sign to Birdie and her minions that someone in the building was up and about. It couldn't be helped. She'd make too much noise if she put her boots back on, and the first-aid kit in the break room wasn't extensive enough to stop the bleeding. She kept her head down and moved quickly, her stolen gun held out in front of her the way she'd seen a hundred action heroes hold their weapons. That wasn't her narrative. It was still pretty damn powerful in this modern world, and maybe that would work for her. Maybe some kid was already dreaming up a Cinderella remix with guerrilla fighters in place of stepsisters, and she could tap into that sweet vein of potential story.

It was funny, in a twisted sort of way. Sloane Winters—not her original name, not by a long shot—had been with the Bureau longer than anyone really knew, held in a permanent teenage dream by the story that didn't want to let her go. As long as she didn't pour the poisoned cup for anyone, time couldn't touch her. That meant she'd had longer to practice her arts than anyone ever wanted to give her credit for, and longer to learn how to feel the edges of the narrative, what it was doing, what it was growing into. The war fantasies of her childhood had matured into the spy dreams of her second adolescence, and now the male power games of the modern day. They were all part of the narrative, if she dug down deep enough, and if she was willing to let them finally have her.

Sloane liked being her own woman. She liked being alive even more. So she crept through the building and thought of ninjas, of barbarians, of anything that might give her just that little extra added edge.

One of Birdie's men was in the hall between Dispatch and the bullpen. Sloane didn't hesitate before whipping her stolen gun hard against the side of his head and then, when he crumpled into an insensate heap, pulling the knife from inside one of her striped stockings and opening his throat in a gleaming ear-to-ear smile.

Something giggled behind her. She turned to see the tabby-striped cat slink out of the shadows, tail held down low and an all-too-human grin distorting otherwise perfectly animal features. The cat—or Cat, as was more appropriate—couldn't take its eyes off Sloane's latest kill.

"Hello, kitty," she said softly, crouching down. "I was hoping I'd run into you. Do you want to make a deal with me?"

The Cat giggled again, slinking closer still.

Sloane struck like a snake, her hand grasping the back of the Cat's neck and pulling it close to her before it could respond. She held it in front of her face, forcing it to look at her, and said, "I'll kill them for you, if you'll loan me your stripes for just a little while. Think about it. These men are just like the ones who brought you here. They don't care about the tea parties or the topiary. They don't care about Alice. Poor little Alice, all alone with no one to take care of her. You don't want that, do you?"

The Cheshire Cat blinked, smile fading as the thought percolated through its simple feline mind. If it was here, and Alice was not here, then Alice was unprotected. An unprotected Alice was an Alice in danger, because Alices were foolish things that never knew how fragile they really were. An unprotected Alice might get *hurt*. The Cat's ears flattened against its skull, and it made a small, querulous sound.

"Give me your stripes, and we can save her," said Sloane. "All you need to do is trust me."

The Cat meowed. Sloane sighed, looking put-upon.

"Yes, I swear by the red *and* the white that I'll give them back to you. I don't need to be a Cheshire Wicked Stepsister, I just need to be a Cheshire girl who isn't dead." She tucked her gun into her waistband and lifted the hand that wasn't holding the Cat, turning her palm outward. "You can trust me, or you can leave Alice to the jabberwocks and borogroves. It's up to you."

The Cat lashed its tail. The Cat growled, deep and low and dangerous in its throat. And the Cat slashed its claws across Sloane's palm, cutting deep into the flesh. She hissed and dropped the Cat, falling from her crouch onto her ass. She hissed again when her butt hit the floor, somehow managing to swallow the urge to yell. Blood welled up in the scratches the Cat had left across her palm—and then shadow-gray stripes began to slither up her arm like snakes, spreading until they covered her entire body.

Sloane watched the march of stripes with wide, solemn eyes, looking momentarily like an Alice herself: younger than she should have been, older than any child should ever need to be. Then she shook off her surprise and bowed her head to the Cat, which was grinning again as it licked her blood from its claws.

"Thank you," she said. "Now hide yourself. These aren't people that you want to have interfering with you."

The Cat yawned, displaying a full array of razor-sharp teeth. Then it vanished, leaving nothing behind it but the smile.

"I'll probably regret losing sight of you later, you little creep," murmured Sloane. She stood, watching her own shadow-striped arm as it began to blur into the background.

Once she was on her feet she froze, holding perfectly still while the Cat's borrowed camouflage worked its magic. Less than a minute later she turned, and a Sloane-shaped shadow slunk toward the bullpen, leaving only the dead man on the floor to mark her passing.

# # #

Someone tugged on my arm. I turned to find Judi standing too close for comfort, a pleading expression in her overly blue eyes. She moved her hands in a quick, almost perfunctory motion. I shook my head.

"I'm sorry," I said. "I don't speak ASL."

Judi frowned and moved her hands again.

"Neither did most of the girls when they first came here," said Ayane. "I was a translator—amusement parks, concerts. Judi beat me to the wood by almost twenty years, and before I arrived, she was lucky if anyone realized she was talking."

Judi flipped her off. I laughed.

"Okay, *that* sign I know," I said.

"It's pretty universal," Ayane agreed. She signed something back to Judi, who nodded. Ayane frowned. This time, it took longer for her to sign her message—whatever that message was. "I'm sort of stuck here. As a translator, it was my job to relay what my clients were saying, regardless of how I felt about it. As a Snow White, I'm supposed to listen to the wood before I listen to the other girls."

I froze. "What?"

Judi signed something frantically. Ayane sighed.

"The wood talks. Haven't you heard it whispering? It tells you to let the Snow White side of yourself get stronger, because she's older and wiser than you are, she's been here before, she'll keep you from making mistakes that you'll regret later." Ayane shook her head. "Judi can't hear it. It's not . . . smart the way a person is smart, you know?"

"Be quiet," hissed Tanya.

Ayane ignored her. "It doesn't adjust the way it approaches people just because its usual tactics don't work on them. So it whispers to Judi constantly, and she can't hear it, and she spends a lot of time frustrated with the rest of us over the things that we can't say."

"Oh," I said, slow realization dawning. "And there are things that you can't say, is that it?"

Ayane nodded silently.

"Well, it seems to me that if you're translating for Judi, you're not *saying* them. You're just doing your job as a translator—and your duty as a part of the same story. We're here because we're supposed to learn from each other, right? Well, what does it say about us as a narrative if we shut Judi out just because she can't hear us? That's not fair. We have to let all our Snow White sisters participate." I felt like a snake-oil salesman, peddling a bill of goods that wasn't actually good for anyone.

It seemed to work, at least. Ayane smiled, a relieved expression peeking through her frown as she turned back to Judi and signed something, hands flying too fast for me to follow. Judi signed back, and for a moment the world narrowed down to the two of them: Judi explaining what she wanted Ayane to say; Ayane making sure she understood.

A hand caught my arm. This time when I turned, it was Tanya who was looking at me with concern. Snowflakes were caught in her bangs, unmelting. Had we really all become so cold? "She's not going to say anything you should want to hear," said Tanya earnestly. "All she's going to do is make it harder for you to accept what you are, and to accept that you belong here."

"I thought you were supposed to be teaching me," I said, pulling my arm out of her grasp. "Wasn't that what you promised me that you were going to do?"

"I *have* been teaching you," she protested. "I haven't told you any lies, and I haven't withheld any information that you genuinely needed to have."

"You didn't tell me the forest talked to us!"

"I thought you knew," she said, with a shrug. "All the rest of us figured it out eventually, although some of us had to do it more on our own than others. The oldest Snows don't come out of their clearings anymore. They stand and talk to the forest, and the forest talks back to them, and that's all they really need out of the world. I think—no, I *know*—that there were white-skinned, black-haired girls before those Snow Whites came to the wood, and that they *are* the wood now, and someday we'll all be the wood, and we'll talk to the girls who come here after us. We'll tell them not to be afraid."

I stared at her. "But you told me to break the narrative. To end the story."

"Yes, and we meant it. We're tired of being a parasite on the monomyth. But there will always be girls who find their way here, even if they don't know the name Snow White. Places like this don't die. They just get repurposed to serve a different storyteller."

"Henry?" Ayane sounded more hesitant than she ever had before. I turned toward her. Judi was standing with one hand on the shorter woman's shoulder, like she was afraid that if she let go, Ayane would turn and run into the trees, rather than delivering her message. "Judi has something she wants to tell you."

"I'd really love to hear what Judi has to say," I said.

Ayane took a deep breath and said, "'The forest speaks to the girls who find their way here. It tells them not to be afraid, because this is the place that comes after fear, and that's good; some of us were afraid for far too long in our lives before. But it also tells them to be good and to be patient and to wait for their Prince to come. It makes them weak if they listen for too long.

Do you understand what I'm trying to tell you? It's talking to you now.'"

"How?" I asked, directing my word to Judi. Ayane echoed it with a gesture.

Judi nodded and signed back, saying something that must have been fairly complicated, since it involved both arms and most of her upper body. It was beautiful, like watching someone dance their way through a paragraph.

"'It talks through the snow,'" said Ayane. "'The snowflakes are words, the blizzard is its voice. You can hear it if you listen closely, but you shouldn't listen, and you shouldn't stand still when the snow is falling, or it will tell you things you shouldn't hear. It makes you soft. It makes you scared. Why are you still standing here? You aren't the kind of woman who stands and waits to be protected, but that's what you're doing, because the forest wants you to do it. It wants Adrianna to take you. It doesn't like having her here—she's a disruption, she makes things dark and frightening, and so it wants her to go away, even if it has to sacrifice you to accomplish that.'"

I stared at her for a moment before I turned back to Judi and asked, "What should I do?"

She made a small, declarative gesture with her hands. I barely needed Ayane's translation: "'Run.'"

# # #

Memetic incursion in progress: tale type 410 ("Sleeping Beauty")
Status: ACTIVE

Sloane slipped into the room the way a knife slips into a wound: silently, and with the potential to do a lot of damage to anything that happened to get in her way. Birdie and her people were standing next to Henry's desk, digging through an open file drawer and piling its contents carelessly atop the nearest desk. Sloane gritted her teeth and forced herself to hold her ground.

Birdie was down to two men inside, both of them larger and stronger-looking than Sloane herself. That was fine: that just meant they'd put up a decent fight before she put them down. Most of her attention was reserved for Birdie herself. The ex-dispatcher was still short, plump, and crowned with a corona of fluffy blonde hair, but there was an air of menace about her that Sloane had never noticed before. Birdie was playing the villain, finally, and she was loving every second of it.

Sloane hadn't been sure up until that moment that she would be able to kill someone who she used to work with. Looking at Birdie gloating over Henry's motionless body, she stopped worrying about whether she'd be able to get the job done.

Killing her would be easy.

"How long is this spell supposed to last?" asked one of the men, looking anxiously toward the briar-wrapped body of Priya Patel.

"A better question would be 'how long is our protection from the spell supposed to last,'" said Birdie. "Now that she's out, our Sleeping Beauty will slumber for a hundred years, or until she's awakened by true love's kiss. She's actually manifesting brambles. That's not common anymore; I blame the narrative concentration in this building, since it warps the laws of reality in some very exciting ways. Anyway, no one expects a thorn hedge to have a chewy princess center anymore. I doubt anyone's going to fight their way to her rescue. She'll sleep the full century, and die of old age five minutes after she finally wakes up."

The man frowned at Birdie. "You mean you're not kidding about this fairy-tale mumbo jumbo?"

"You're asking me that *now*, after everything that we had to go through to reach this point? Oh, my dear hired goon." Birdie actually reached up and patted the much taller man on the cheek, murmuring, "The ability that humans have to block out what's actually happening around them will never fail to astonish me," in a tone that implied she was speaking to no one in particular. Then she sharpened, and continued, "Yes, dearie, all that 'fairy tale mumbo jumbo' is real, and we're going to help it become even *more* real, because once the rules of the world are rewritten into something more . . . pliant . . . people like me and our benefactor will be as gods."

"What about us?" asked the other man.

Birdie looked at him coolly. "As long as you continue following orders, you'll be the ones that the gods look upon with favor. Now pick up those files. Some of what we came here to get is missing. We need to check the deputy director's office."

"So what about *them*?" asked the first man, indicating Henry and the others with the back of his hand.

Sloane tensed. She didn't want to blow her camouflage yet, but if she had to, then she had to. She was capable of a lot of things. Under the right circumstances, she was even capable of murder. What she wasn't capable of was standing idly by while a demented Mother Goose archetype told her hired goons to wipe out the only family that Sloane had left. If anyone was going to kill Sloane's team, it was going to be *Sloane*.

Birdie sniffed dismissively. "It smells like apples in here, didn't you notice?" she said. "The little tart decided to go full-on fairy tale in order to fight me, and she failed. I know where she is now. Killing her would be a mercy, and I'm not feeling very merciful."

"So we leave them?" asked the man.

"We leave them," Birdie confirmed. "Come on."

Sloane tensed again as the trio turned to go. If they took the hall that connected to Dispatch, they'd see her handiwork soon enough; not even a Cheshire Cat could hide that much evidence that someone was awake and fighting back. Luckily, Birdie started instead for the door at the back of the bullpen that would lead her to Deputy Director Brewer's office. Sloane didn't know what he would have there that was so important, and she didn't care. She just cared about getting back to her people and waking them the fuck up before she ran out of tricks.

Birdie and her two goons vanished through the door. Sloane held her position, counting slowly backward from thirty before she dared to move. Safety was better than sorrow, or so the saying went.

Her feet left little red marks on the floor, bloodstains that looked more like paw prints than footprints. She stopped when she reached Henry, leaning in close and inhaling. She *could* smell apples when she got in close enough.

"Wait a second . . ." Sloane straightened, eyes going wide.

There were only two confirmed ways of waking a Sleeping Beauty—true love's kiss or childbirth, neither of which was on the table, since Priya was a stranger and not visibly pregnant. Sloane would have needed a turkey baster and nine months to put childbirth on the table, and while the situation was dire, it wasn't quite that bad—not yet, anyway. She couldn't speak for how she'd feel if the Bureau was still wrapped in an enchanted sleep at the end of the week.

There were other offices, of course, other field teams and directors who could be counted on to make logical decisions about illogical situations, but none of them were *her* team. None of them understood her, or gave one good goddamn about what happened to a would-be Wicked Stepsister whose story had somehow managed to shoehorn her into the villain's role such that the Beauty's spell had missed her. And that, possibly, was the solution.

"I'm not your true love and I'm not going to kiss you," said Sloane, delivering a kick to Henry's ankle. "I want you to remember this if you wake up and think I have hands in bad places." Then she knelt, and began undoing Henry's belt.

# # #

Tanya shouted something behind me, her voice washed out and muffled by the snow. Now that I was aware that it was speaking, the whiteout wood seemed to have lost all desire to keep quiet: I could hear the voices whispering with every flake that fell, telling me to be good, to be meek, to be merciful and dutiful and all the other qualities that the kings of frozen kingdoms must work to imbue in their princesses. I wanted to listen, deep down, in the place where I was more fiction than flesh. And still I ran.

Where did it begin? If Snow White was just the latest face of this eternal winter, what was my story before the modern narrative got to work on it? I was direly afraid that I knew, and that I even understood why the latter-day whiteout women would be content with what they had. There are names, after all, for stories that involve running into the wood with a huntsman chasing after you, his knife naked to the wind. There are stories about the meaning of blood on the snow. The snow whispered for me to be still, and the wood whispered for me to be calm, and I thought of temporary kings and divine figures killed to bring the springtime back around again.

The snow fell so fast behind me that it filled my footprints, covering them up in the veil of endless winter. That would make me harder to track. That was a good thing; I just hoped that it would be good enough.

My socks were soaking through with snowmelt, and my shoes offered little protection against the cold. I normally didn't feel it that much—but I normally stayed safe with Tanya and the others, didn't I? I did what the wood wanted.

For the first time, I started to think that maybe that so-noble command to break the narrative, end the story, was something other than altruistic. None of the harvest tales started out as parasites. They were the most powerful pieces of the narrative, once upon a time. We fought back, turned them tame, gave them names and labels that pinned them like butterflies in the textbooks of religious studies professors and folklore teachers all around the world.

It didn't have to be like that, murmured a voice in my head, and I couldn't tell whether it was the wood speaking or my own inner Snow White. *It doesn't have to be like that.*

I didn't answer her. I just ran.

I was so focused on running that I stopped paying attention to what was in front of me, so it was a shock when Adrianna's arm caught me across the throat, knocking me off my feet and onto my ass. The snow promptly soaked through my pants. I made a choking sound, reaching up to hold my bruised throat.

Adrianna stepped forward, looking imperiously down at me. "You were smart enough to run, huh, new girl? Well, I suppose that makes sense. They must have given you *some* training to go with that badge you're wearing. But there's no training in the world that could get you ready for me." She lunged before I could react, filling her fingers with my hair and yanking me back to my feet. "Any last words, little doorway?"

I coughed and tried to speak. My words came out as a broken rasp.

"Aw, did you lose your voice? That's a different story, you know." Adrianna leaned closer, a smile twisting her features into something terrible. "I'm going to wear your skin like a coat, and I'm going to break every heart you've ever given a damn about, and who knows? Maybe when they're all cursing your name, I'll come back through the door and let you go home."

I rasped again, finally managing to find my voice enough to whisper, ". . . wrong about . . . my training."

"What's that?"

I struggled to look pathetic, gesturing for Adrianna to lean even closer as I whispered, "I said . . . wrong about . . . my training."

She narrowed her eyes. "I have no idea what you're trying to say."

Her fingers were still knotted in my hair. She seemed to think that was enough to immobilize me. I straightened abruptly, removing all the slack from her grip as I slammed my forehead into hers. There was an audible crack, and bright stars of pain burst into existence inside my skull, going supernova before fading away. Adrianna howled as she dropped my hair and staggered backward, one hand flying to her injured head.

The trouble with forehead smashes is that they hurt you as much as they hurt the other person. Unlike Adrianna, though, I'd been braced for the pain. While she was still reeling, I closed in and punched her twice, once in the stomach, once in the left breast. She howled again. I kicked her in the knee, and she fell, a red and black splotch against the white, white snow.

"I said, you're wrong about my training," I snarled, aiming a kick at her head. "I was trained to survive sharing an office with *Sloane*. You're just a Snow White reject who couldn't hold on to her own goddamn body, and I am not afraid of you." I followed the kick with two more. "Do you hear me? I. Am not. Afraid. Of you."

Adrianna wasn't howling anymore. I kicked her a few more times anyway.

Just to be sure.

# # #

Memetic incursion in progress: tale type 410 ("Sleeping Beauty")
Status: ACTIVE

Henry's belt had come off easily, and removing it didn't make any difference in her condition. She wasn't wearing a girdle. Sloane hesitated for only a moment before unhooking the other woman's bra. That didn't do anything either.

"Worth a shot," she muttered, and pulled the elastic out of Henry's hair. That didn't do anything either. Sloane leaned back and frowned, studying her field team leader.

Snow Whites went into comas when they ate poisoned apples, put on cursed girdles, did up their hair with cursed combs, or . . .

"Poisoned rings." Sloane grabbed Henry's hands, looking for anything that could be charitably called a ring. Her fingers were bare, and so were her wrists. "Dammit, Henry, don't you wear *any* jewelry?" Unpierced ears. No necklaces. The only thing that could even remotely be considered decorative was her badge.

Sloane didn't stop to think. She just grabbed the badge and flung it as hard as she could across the office, not bothering to watch as it vanished into the briars. Henry stayed limp and unmoving, sunk as deep into her enchanted slumber as the rest. Sloane grabbed her by the shoulders and shook her fiercely back and forth, saying, "Come on, wake up, I can't do this by myself, all I'm good for is killing them, I can't *stop* them, so wake up, Henry, wake up, please," as loudly as she dared. "*Please.*

"Just wake up already."

# # #

Adrianna grabbed my foot as I was pulling it back for one more kick to the side of her head. I probably deserved that for kicking her while she was down, but I still fell back onto my ass, sending snow flying everywhere. She let go of my foot with a snarl, grabbing me around the waist and clawing her way back toward my face. I managed to get a knee up and into her stomach. She gasped as the air was knocked out of her, and still she kept on coming.

"You need to calm the fuck down," I snarled, grabbing a fistful of her hair and yanking hard. "This is not how a princess behaves!"

That was the wrong thing to say. Adrianna found her second wind and shoved herself the rest of the way into position, grabbing me by the shoulders and beginning to shake me like a rag doll. The snow fell all around us, blurring and distorting the landscape. Her fingers dug into my arms, painful and anchoring.

"Let me go," I snarled.

"You're no better than me," she responded. "If anything, you're worse. You're—" Her words blurred and became inaudible, drowned out by a screech like a radio being tuned.

There were words in the noise. Just for an instant, but that instant was long enough: "—up, I can't do this by myself—"

Then Adrianna was back, shouting, "—weak! Do you hear me? You're *weak*!" She shook me again, harder. The snow was almost blocking out her face.

Every time I left the wood, the snow was falling, and my eyes were closed. As I watched the snow obscuring Adrianna, I realized what I had to do. It was dangerous, but I couldn't think of any other way. I closed my eyes, going limp while she shook me harder and harder, and the radio static was back, wiping out the sound of her voice, wiping out the feeling of snow on my face, until it was just Sloane's voice, alone in the world, saying the words I needed to hear more than anything else: "Just wake up already."

And I opened my eyes.

# # #

The figure above me was blurry, like a woman carved out of living shadow, with stripes of darker gray moving across her skin in a way that made my eyeballs itch. I didn't think: I just reacted, punching upward as fast and as hard as I could. She hadn't been expecting that. She yelped, lurching back, and I recognized Sloane's voice even as the impact registered with my suddenly aching knuckles.

"God*dammit*, Henry, you can't just go around punching people!" The figure clapped a hand over its face, continuing to use Sloane's voice as it muttered, "I think my nose is bleeding. You have a mean right hook, snow-bitch."

"Sloane?" I straightened in my chair before struggling to my feet. Taking my eyes off Sloane's disorientingly blurry form, I looked around the bullpen, which was choked with rapidly growing rose briars springing from the walls and floor. That meant—right. I frowned as I spotted the stranger lying motionless at the heart of the overgrowth. "Sleeping Beauty?"

"Got it in one," said Sloane. "She staggered in here and passed out. No bus transfer, too far gone to have driven herself. Birdie imported her to fuck with us."

"So how are you awake? And why can't I see you?"

"Neat trick, huh? I sweet-talked the Cheshire Cat that was brought in just before shit got ugly, and he loaned me his stripes. They should fade before too much longer, so it would be good if we got moving." I heard Sloane shift her weight behind me. "As for why I didn't fall asleep, I think I got the villain loophole. The evil fairy never passes out when Sleeping Beauty goes down for the count, and that's the only role I fit in this story. We should be safe as long as we don't wander into a christening or anything idiotic like that."

"Wasn't on my list." I tried to check my belt, only to discover that it was missing, and my gun along with it. Weirder still, my bra was unhooked. "What the—Sloane? Did you try the girdle approach?"

"Yeah," said Sloane's voice. "It didn't work."

"Right." I scanned the floor, finding my belt a few feet away with my gun still clipped securely into place. I picked it up and put it back on, feeling some of the tension leave my shoulders. "Well, if that didn't work, why am I awake?"

"True love's kiss, of course," purred Sloane from behind me. I jumped.

Her laughter had a distinctly feline twang to it. She'd clearly borrowed more than just a set of stripes from the Cheshire Cat. "Relax, Princess, I didn't do anything we'll have to report to HR. I took your badge off."

"What?" I reached around behind myself to rehook my bra.

"We both know that I'm not your true love, which means kissing you wouldn't have done a damn thing. But a Snow White who's fallen into an enchanted sleep is just waiting for someone to find a way to wake her up. The girdle approach didn't work, and you aren't wearing a hair comb or a ring. Sometimes the poison is in a brooch. So I went for the closest thing you had."

"That is ingenious, and you have to tell Jeff about it when he wakes up. He'll probably give you a medal. Just don't mention messing with my bra." Speaking of Jeff, someone—presumably Sloane, as the only person who'd been actually *awake*—had moved his chair so that it was sitting right next to mine. He was facedown on the desk, and looked like he was sleeping peacefully. I hoped that that was true. "You said Birdie was in the building?"

"Yeah." Sloane's tone turned grim, borrowed levity leeching away. "She's heading for Deputy Director Brewer's office."

"Okay." I unsnapped my holster, drawing my gun. "Let's go stop whatever it is she's hoping to accomplish."

Sloane's smile suddenly appeared in the air in front of me, all the more disturbing because it didn't have the rest of Sloane visibly attached. "Oh, Snowy. I thought you'd never ask."

# # #

Sloane had clearly been hard at work while I was sleeping: there was a dead man in the hall, his body already halfway overgrown with briars. There was no sign of the Cheshire Cat. Even without its stripes, the creature was designed to hide. It just wouldn't be able to teleport away until it got them back.

"I told you they went the other way," grumbled Sloane.

"That's why we're going this way," I said. "Birdie isn't expecting anyone to still be moving around the building, but she's more likely to watch the door she came through. Humans are funny that way."

"If you say so."

Passage was slower than it should have been, thanks to all the thorns. They'd left wide-open trails in some places, narrowing the hall to nothing but a sliver in others. I gritted my teeth and kicked the briars aside, snagging my trousers and trying not to cut my skin too much. Sloane made a soft, pained sound behind me. I glanced back, seeing the expected nothing.

"Sloane? Are you all right?"

"It's nothing. I just had to take my shoes off for stealth, and my feet are getting a little sore." There were small red drops on the floor, marking out our passage like signposts.

I stiffened, torn between yelling at her for leaving bloody bread crumbs behind us and yelling at her for hurting herself. Yelling at all was a terrible idea. I swallowed the bulk of my anger before asking, "Can you keep going?"

"Oh, yeah. I can keep going. She came into our home. She hurt us *in our home*. I could walk on burning coals right now."

"Let's hope you won't have to." I started moving again—but I took more care to shove the briars aside now, trading a little bit of speed for a clearer trail. If Sloane couldn't stand by the time we caught up with Birdie, I would be facing the first fully active Mother Goose on record by myself. We didn't know what she was capable of, except that it included manipulating the narrative and somehow staying awake despite the Sleeping Beauty in the other room. I didn't want to learn what else she could do. Not without backup.

I was moving as quietly as I could. Sloane might as well not have been there at all. Birdie and her men were being nowhere near as careful. I could hear their voices when we were still several offices down from Deputy Director Brewer's open door.

"—a book? We did all this for a book?"

"Not just any book, Samson. *The* book. The book that will make all our troubles go away forever." Birdie's voice was reverent. "They should have given this to me years ago. I could have made everything so much easier for them, if they'd just learned to let me work."

There was only one book she could be talking about. I signaled for Sloane to follow as I broke into a run.

Birdie had the Index.

# # #

Every field team had a copy of the Aarne-Thompson Index, entrusted to their archivist and used to track and identify narrative incursions within their sector. They were mass-market printings, culled from the print run supplied to schools and libraries around the world. They weren't safe by any means, but they were essentially magically inert.

And then there was the true Index. The first copy of any revision, containing all the carefully written adjustments and notes that would go into the *next* revision, shaping our understanding of the narrative's powers—and thanks to the force of the human subconscious, shaping the narrative for the next twenty years. The rest of us were virtually forbidden to write anything down too close to the record books. Whoever held the Index was *required*.

Had Deputy Director Brewer been holding the master Index this whole time? That would explain why Birdie had come out of our field office, and not one that was more central, like New York or Huntsville. We were targeted because we had something worth stealing.

I drew my gun as I swung myself into the door frame, shouting, "Freeze!"

Birdie looked up from the massive book in her hands, eyebrows rising in mild surprise. "Oh," she said. "You're awake. That's interesting. Hans?"

A massive hand reached down from my right and plucked the gun from my hands. "Done," growled a deep voice.

"Excellent. Shoot her." Birdie looked back to the book. "I have no time for failed experiments."

"Yes, ma'am," said Hans. He leveled my own gun on me, only to scream and stumble backward as his throat suddenly opened in a wet red gash that sprayed blood everywhere. A shadow clung to his back. Sloane.

Birdie looked around, expression betraying her surprise, even as I grabbed my gun back and aimed it at her again.

"Birdie Hubbard, you are under arrest," I said, as levelly as I could. "Put the Index down and come with me."

"No, I don't think that's going to happen." She ran her finger down the column. "Snow White, Snow White . . . where are you? Oh, yes, here you are. 'Meek, pliant, nonviolent.' Put the gun down, Henrietta. Such things are not for you."

"You can't—" I began . . . but I was already bending to set the gun gingerly on the floor, unable to stop my hands from shaking. I had been holding a *weapon*. Weapons could *hurt* people. Why, if I'd hurt someone, I would . . .

I would . . .

I raised my head and glared at Birdie. "Get the fuck away from my story, you bitch."

"Uh-uh, language," she chided gently. "It's not befitting a princess. Samson, restrain her. She won't fight you."

Hans, who only had so much blood in him, finally gave up the fight against gravity and collapsed with a thud. Birdie watched with disinterest.

"I know you're there, Sloane," she said. "You're a villain. You should be on my side."

"Yeah, but HR would have my head if I touched hers," said Sloane's voice, punctuated with giggles, from somewhere at the back of the room.

Birdie's only remaining goon—the aforementioned Samson—looked nervous. "I don't want to touch the dead girl," he said. "What happened to Hans—"

"Henry didn't do it," Birdie said. "Take her."

I tried to force myself to run, but found that my feet were more interested in obeying the story than they were in obeying me. I watched, terrified, as Samson closed in on me.

A shadow detached itself from the wall behind Birdie as Sloane took advantage of the confusion to go after her own prey. It slunk closer and closer—only to stop dead and bleed away, revealing Sloane pinned against the air like a moth pinned to a lepidopterist's table. Her stripes were gone. Birdie turned and smiled at her.

"You're a villain, darling, and villains never win when they go up against the forces of good. You really should have chosen your alliances better."

Samson seized me by the shoulders. I struggled against his grasp, but it was no use: he was stronger than I was, and Birdie's reminder of my story's essential nature had sapped my will to fight. I was just a whiteout girl after all, and I was going to die the way the whiteout girls always died: badly.

The smell of snow swirled through the air around us. I froze, inwardly as well as outwardly. There was still something I could do.

It was going to hurt like hell.

"Hey, Mother Goose," I called, no longer fighting against Samson's hold. "You forgot one thing."

"What's that, princess?" she asked.

"Blood on the snow," I replied, and whipped my head around, and sunk my teeth deep into Samson's hand.

He howled, jerking me backward so hard that I felt my shoulder dislocate. It didn't matter, because the smell of snow was getting stronger, and the blood from his hand was falling to the floor, where the briars grew up to meet it.

Birdie was the reason my story had gone active. Birdie was the one who'd been twisting the narrative away from what was normally true. But what she hadn't considered was that a thing that is twisted too far can snap back—and Snow White began as its own monomyth, with dead girls in a whiteout wood, and with blood to stain the snow.

She shouted something as, behind her, Sloane peeled herself off the invisible dome of the storyteller's sphere and began to prowl around the office, looking for a weapon. I didn't hear exactly what Birdie said. The wind that blew through the wood on the other side of my story was howling, blurring her words and whipping them away.

Samson yanked on my shoulder again. I closed my eyes and fell backward, knocking him to the floor, where the briars wrapped themselves around him and pulled tight. The sound was horrible, crushing and squishing and tearing sounds. Not a single briar touched me. I stood, meeting Birdie's shocked stare, and smiled.

"You can't be the good guy and stand against me," I said, bending to wrest a rope of briar from the floor. The thorns sank deep into the flesh of my hands, and I let them; what I bled on belonged to me. That, too, was a part of my story. "You can't be a bad guy and stand against Sloane. You screwed up, Birdie. You manipulated us because you thought we'd kill each other, didn't you? Well, all you did was set up a rock and a hard place for you to catch yourself between."

Sloane was still pacing. She was even more unnerving without her borrowed stripes to hide her. Blood covered her virtually from head to toe, and her face was distorted in a constant snarl that I was glad was directed at Birdie, not me.

"You can't do this," said Birdie. "You *can't*. You won't come out the other side."

No, I wouldn't, would I? Henrietta Marchen was a pretty story that I had enjoyed telling to myself, but she didn't have the narrative weight of Snow White, princess of a kingdom with no name, born in the sacrificial purity of a slit throat and a frozen wasteland. *It always takes blood on the snow when you want to bring the summer home*, I thought, and it wasn't my thought, and it wasn't anyone else's. "Once upon a time," I said, tightening my hand around the rope of thorns.

Birdie's mouth moved. Again, the wind took her words away, while I took a step forward, dimly aware that it was beginning to snow inside the office. *Monomyth, eat your heart out*, I thought. Another, slightly more coherent part of my mind screamed that Birdie was right and I needed to stop: if I went too far into the story, I wouldn't come out. Not as Henry, anyway.

But that didn't matter. If Birdie walked away with the Index, none of us were going to be who we thought we were ever again. We would be rewritten into her perfect little stories, and we'd lose. We'd lose ourselves, we'd lose the fight, and we'd lose each other.

Sloane stopped pacing and closed her eyes, pointing at Birdie. For some reason, I *could* hear her when she spoke, each word like a stone dropped into still water: "I am a Wicked Stepsister. Whomever I stand with must thus be an Evil Queen. Evil Queens are always defeated." She opened her eyes, looked at me, and smiled sadly. "I cast my alliance with Mother Goose, who shapes the story. I set myself against you, daughter of the winter wood."

"If you're my ally, then *help* me!" shouted Birdie.

"I am helping you," said Sloane, and didn't move. "I'm helping you fulfill your place in the narrative."

Tears sprang to my eyes, instantly freezing on my eyelashes as I looked at Sloane, and then looked away. The wind was blowing too hard now; I couldn't hear what Birdie was saying.

The snow fell harder as I walked across the room toward her. Birdie backed away. The bubble around her offered me no resistance. Calm now—too calm—I reached out with my rope of briars and wrapped it around her neck, drawing her close. I didn't want to kill her. The story had other ideas. I fought it, forcing the briars to stay loose enough to let her breathe.

Please, I thought. *Please.* Not every monomyth could win. Not every princess could become a queen. Not every little girl who bled in the whiteout wood had to die there.

There were so many things I could have said. Any one of them would have ended the scene, and would have determined who I was going to be hereafter. I swallowed them all, seeking the one that meant Henry Marchen, the one that meant early mornings and late nights and fights with Human Resources and a brother I never saw and a Shoemaker's Elf who might eventually be able to kiss me out of a coma. It wasn't easy. She didn't have as much of a story behind her.

"Birdie Hubbard," I finally managed, ripping every word out of the blackness behind my eyes, "you are under arrest."

Then I lost consciousness again. I didn't feel myself hit the ground. Given the number of thorn briars growing there, that was probably a mercy.

# # #

I woke up in the back of the van, parked six blocks from headquarters. Sloane was crouching over me like a particularly vicious gargoyle, her spine bent at one of her favorite improbable angles.

"What the—"

"What's your name?" she interrupted.

"Henry," I replied. "How did we get here?"

"I carried you out of the building," she said, with a shrug. "After I carried Birdie out of the building, that is. She's handcuffed in the back of the deputy director's car."

"Did you also carry him out of the building?" I asked, bemused.

"He wasn't in the building. I called him at home. He's pretty pissed off, although not at us, which is a nice change." Sloane straightened, apparently having decided that I wasn't the victim of a fairy-tale body snatching. I pushed myself into a sitting position as she continued, "Our Sleeping Beauty has been moved to one of the secure cells, and everyone inside has managed to wake up. Well, most everyone. Half of Dispatch is still asleep, but I think they're just tired."

"What's going to happen to—"

"Miss Hubbard is being moved to a secure facility," said Deputy Director Brewer, coming around the side of the van and looking at me coldly. "Agent Marchen."

"Deputy Director." I nodded, but didn't attempt to stand. I know my limits. "Sorry about the mess, sir."

"We're going to need new carpets," said Sloane.

"Be that as it may . . . I will expect a full report on my desk by Friday." Deputy Director Brewer looked from me to Sloane, slowly, before he said, "The Bureau thanks you for what you accomplished today. If Miss Hubbard had been able to leave the building with the Index, there's no telling what she could have done."

"Bad shit," I said. "Is my team okay?" *Was my team still mine?* I wanted to ask the question, but I wasn't brave enough. I had summoned snow out of the air. I was in deeper than I had ever been before.

Deputy Director Brewer turned back to me. For a moment—just a moment—I thought I saw a glimmer of amusement in his eye. "Yes. They've been waiting for you to wake up." He turned away. "She's ready for you now."

Jeff and Andy rushed around the side of the van, with Demi and Gerry close behind. Gerry was carrying Sloane's boots. Jeff's glasses were askew, and he knocked them further askew as he locked his arms around me and kissed me like he thought tomorrow had been cancelled pending further review. I thought about pushing him away—too many fairy tales end with a kiss—and then melted into his embrace. I could worry about everything else later. And there *were* things we still needed to worry about. And yet . . .

We were alive, we were ourselves rather than subsumed into our stories, and Birdie was going to prison, where she would never get her hands on a book of fairy tales ever again.

No matter what might be coming down the road ahead of us, this looked a hell of a lot like happily ever after.

Acknowledgments

Indexing has had a wild journey from concept to competition. It began life as a short story, grew to become a full-fledged story setting, and finally, through the grace of the Amazon Kindle Serials program, became my very first serial novel. I am so grateful to everyone who has participated in every stage of this book's creation, from my faithful Machete Squad to the editorial staff at 47North. Big thanks to my editor, David Pomerico; my agent, Diana Fox; and my loyal sanity check, Michelle "Vixy" Dockrey, who has learned more than any innocent soul should have to learn about fairy tales in the process of my writing this.

The Aarne-Thompson Index to Motifs in Folk Literature is a real thing, and is used by folklore and fairy-tale scholars the world over. My copy weighs about twenty pounds, and can be used to squash spiders of any size. If you're interested in learning more, I highly recommend checking the folklore section of your local library. There's so much to learn about the stories that we have created, and which have created us in turn.

Now rest my dear, and be at ease; there's a fire in the hearth and a wind in the eaves, and the night is so dark, and the dark is so deep, and it's time that all good little stars were asleep.

About the Author

Seanan McGuire was born and raised in Northern California, where she has lived for the majority of her life. She spends most of her time writing or watching television, but also draws a semi-autobiographical comic strip and has released several albums of filk music (science fiction and fantasy themed folk music). To relax, Seanan enjoys travel, and frequents haunted corn mazes, aquariums with good octopus habitats, and Disney Parks. Seanan is remarkably good at finding reptiles and amphibians wherever she goes, sometimes to the dismay of the people she happens to be traveling with.

Kindle Serials

This book was originally released in Episodes as a Kindle Serial. Kindle Serials launched in 2012 as a new way to experience serialized books. Kindle Serials allow readers to enjoy the story as the author creates it, purchasing once and receiving all existing Episodes immediately, followed by future Episodes as they are published. To find out more about Kindle Serials and to see the current selection of Serials titles, visit www.amazon.com/kindleserials.